WINGS
of
STEEL

WINGS *of* STEEL

BY
DONNA NOBLICK

XULON PRESS

Xulon Press
555 Winderley Pl, Suite 225
Maitland, FL 32751
407.339.4217
www.xulonpress.com

© 2024 by Donna Noblick

All rights reserved solely by the author. The author guarantees all contents are original and do not infringe upon the legal rights of any other person or work. No part of this book may be reproduced in any form without the permission of the author.

Due to the changing nature of the Internet, if there are any web addresses, links, or URLs included in this manuscript, these may have been altered and may no longer be accessible. The views and opinions shared in this book belong solely to the author and do not necessarily reflect those of the publisher. The publisher therefore disclaims responsibility for the views or opinions expressed within the work.

Unless otherwise indicated, Scripture quotations taken from the New American Standard Bible (NASB). Copyright © 1960, 1962, 1963, 1968, 1971, 1972, 1973, 1975, 1977, 1995 by The Lockman Foundation. Used by permission. All rights reserved.

Paperback ISBN-13: 979-8-86850-558-4
Ebook ISBN-13: 979-8-86850-559-1

Acknowledgements

A special thank you to my husband, Bruce, this work would never have been completed without your support and encouragement. Thank you for your interest in the characters and for your brain storming and "weird" ideas that often materialized into plot twists or development of characters.

Thanks also to Christopher Shingleton, and all the professionals at Xulon Press for the opportunity to present a professionally finished work for my readers.

My heavenly Father gave me the inspiration and determination to write this story. He provided little "prompts" along the journey from many different sources.

2 Timothy. 2:13

If we are faithless, He remains faithful, for He cannot deny Himself.

One

Rand Gray pinched his lips into a thin line as he paused before stepping off the ship. He examined the immediate area with fixed concentration and keen observation. It was payday and he was approached several times recently by longshoremen who were less than happy with their wages. A few even accused him of miscalculating their hours. Tempers were especially short this week because of longer hours and a larger workload.

A briny ocean mist moistened his sun-tanned skin while he glanced at the cloudless azure sky. He licked his lips and longed for an ice-cold soda. A gust of wind pulled at his black T-shirt and faded Wranglers as he took long strides down the gangway. His steel toed shoes resounded with a clomp-clomp, clomp-clomp on the boards while waves slapped against the wooden dock. He stopped to wait for a forklift to cross his path.

The bellow of a ship's horn, the call of seagulls, the shouts of men, and machines that hummed, knocked, and roared, mingled to accost his ears. The dock was busy with men as they moved cargo, checked equipment for safety, and unloaded another ship. The odor of oil, diesel, and hydraulic fluid filled the air while insects buzzed around his head.

As stevedore he supervised and coordinated the activities of the workers and calculated the number of hours and personnel required to load and unload the ships and various barges moored along the docks. Today they had transferred a large cargo of machinery from a ship to the dock for storage before it was transported locally by semi-truck. He took a deep breath and exhaled. His final responsibility on paydays was to distribute checks to the longshoremen under his supervision.

He strode quickly toward the office and left the ship's inventory on the superintendent's desk before he signed out for the day. He stifled a deserved rebuttal as he sidestepped a forklift that swerved into his path.

"Sorry, boss." The driver called with an insolent grin.

Rand acknowledged the man with a quick bob of his head but his intense gaze followed the man until he was out of sight. After Rand left the superintendent's office, he stepped out of the building, strode toward the parking lot, and tried to ignore the tightness in his chest.

He reached his light blue Ford pickup, removed his hard hat, and flung it behind the driver's seat. He snatched his boots, took off his shoes, and slid his feet into cowboy boots, which were his preferred footwear. After he tossed the work shoes and hard hat into the truck, he rolled his shoulders to relieve their tension, which escalated as he passed out checks to his crew. A few of the men flashed a glare at him as they received their pay.

Rand's teeth clenched when two longshoremen suddenly appeared from behind a semi parked next to his pickup. His stomached hardened.

Buz Sloan and Kane Hollis approached Rand. Sloan was sweating profusely and crossed his beefy arms in front of him. His nostrils flared over his thick unruly moustache. He elbowed Hollis who stood an arm's length from his side. "Since when did they allow stinking cowpokes to boss us around? Maybe we should show the pony rider who the real men are around here." Sloan snickered.

Hollis was a small built man, agile, and quick on his feet. He skimmed the entire area with beady eyes. "The big boss can't hear you yell for help way out here, boy!" He scoffed.

"But I can." Gage Fuller, another longshoreman, shouted as he ran to join the three men.

Rand focused on his opponents and stood tall and wide with his hands on his hips. His heartrate increased, but he refused to acknowledge their taunts. "Stay out of this, Gage. That's an order." Rand was three inches taller than Sloan and at least as quick as Hollis. "What can I do for you boys?" His eyes were cold, hard as he addressed Sloan, who outweighed Rand by at least thirty pounds.

"You docked us four hours last week. We want paid for it, now!" Hollis glared at Gage and doubled his fists at his sides before throwing a piercing gaze at Rand.

He mentally prepared for any sudden move from either one. "You don't work, you don't get paid." His jaw clenched, but his voice remained calm and controlled.

"We were guaranteed forty hours." A corner of Sloan's lip rose in a vicious snarl as he stretched his bulging shoulders.

Rand emanated a cool composure. "Zeke warned you'd be docked for fighting on the job." His flinty gaze focused on both men. "You ignored his warning. End of discussion. Go on home."

Sloan eyed Gage as he swung at Rand.

He blocked the punch with his forearm.

Hollis threw a punch at Rand's head and clipped his lip.

Rand countered with a right hook to Hollis's chin, knocking him off his feet.

Sloan grasped Rand's neck from behind.

Rand struggled to pry Sloan's hands loose.

Sloan hung onto Rand, ripping his shirt as he clawed at his neck.

Rand pivoted his body just as Hollis slashed with a knife he'd pulled from a sheath in his belt.

The blade sliced Sloan's side and he dropped to the ground, clutching himself as blood oozed through his fingers.

Hollis hurled the knife at Rand, who dodged it.

In his peripheral vision, Rand spied it as it spun on the ground.

Hollis leaped to retrieve the knife.

Rand shoved him away from it.

Hollis sprawled on his belly and grasped the knife.

Rand stomped on Hollis's hand.

He cursed as he cradled his injured hand against his chest. "You'll pay for this, Gray!"

Rand kicked the knife under a nearby semi and stood with feet spread and fists held in readiness for another attack. He breathed heavily as a fine sheen of sweat beaded on his forehead. "You're both fired."

Hollis speared Rand with a hate-filled glare as the two men stumbled toward their car.

Rand raked a hand through his hair and observed the men until they were gone.

Gage tossed Rand a towel he'd taken out of his truck, which was parked adjacent to Rand's. His boyish face broke into a grin. "I was willing to jump in but you had it under control."

Rand winced as he pressed the cloth against his mouth and gave the younger man a dismissive shrug.

Zeke Finn, the superintendent and a six-foot medium built man, joined them as he ran a hand over his salt and pepper beard. "You alright, Rand?"

He folded his arms across his chest, flexed his fingers, and stared at his damaged knuckles. "Yeah."

"Gage told me he saw those two follow you. Since they've made trouble before, I called the police." Zeke told them. "They should be here by the time we get back to my office. They'll want to talk to both of you and I'll report the incident of their previous fight."

With a heavy sigh, Rand climbed in his faded blue pickup. The seats were gray and white checked cloth, worn nearly threadbare in places. He bought it with the wages he received while he worked on Frank Sim's ranch in Arizona. It was his pride and joy.

Returning to Fire River, he parked in front of Candlewood, a mansion with three stories that was built in 1880. It was full of exquisite furniture, artifacts and antiques from that period. Rand's half-brother, Rod, named it Candlewood. Nearly every room held at least one glass chandelier, now lit with electric candles, which hung gracefully from the ceiling. The mansion was decorated with intricate wooden doors, arches, staircases and mantles.

Rand sat in his truck, stared at the edifice, and dreaded to go inside. The old place reminded him more of a mausoleum than the residence it became for him alone after Rod married and moved his family to their new home a few miles north of the village.

Once inside Rand's footsteps on the tiled floors echoed through the large halls, and expansive rooms. The hollow reverberations magnified his longing for the presence of his brother and family. He hurried to his bedroom located at the rear of the ground floor. Giving the door a shove, he stripped off his dirty, sweat drenched clothes and headed for a small bathroom in the connected alcove.

Half an hour later, he emerged, wearing clean Levi's, a T-shirt, jean jacket, and scuffed cowboy boots. He jogged down the steps, across the terrace to his truck, and retrieved his helmet from behind the driver's seat. He then secured it to the seat on his road-worthy trail bike, cruised around the village square and onto the highway.

Wings of Steel

After a stressful day at work, Rand often chose to ride and leave the village behind for the freedom of less traveled roads and trails. He wore his helmet when practicing for a race, but otherwise preferred to let the wind sweep through his hair. The drone of the engine filled his ears and he inhaled the tang of dust and scrub along the side of the road. Riding was one of his preferred pastimes and he constantly challenged himself to improve his skills, especially when preparing for a race.

He shut his mouth against the dirt and grit stirred up from the road. Upon reaching a favored spot, he cut his engine, pulled to the side of the road, parked, and dismounted. He climbed a steep embankment careful where he placed his feet because of the scree scattered over the surface of the rock. Pebbles shifted beneath his feet as he climbed. The scream of a condor high above compelled him to pause and observe its flight.

A waterfall cascaded gently down a rock face not far from where he stood and a western fence lizard scuttled across the rough path at his feet. The air was crisp and scented with juniper pine, oak and various flowering plants. It was a pleasant relief after the stench he breathed while working on the docks. Rocky boulders and craggy cliffs dominated the landscape in the distance.

Rand sat on a large rock, closed his eyes and stilled his mind. He imagined himself in harmony with the brown, gray, and distant black rock that surrounded him. Peace filled his soul, and he thanked God for the beauty and harmony of creation. He was comfortable here away from the noise and bustle of people and machinery.

He sighed as he recalled the day's events. Zeke released him to go home after the police took their report. He was not one to initiate a fight unless compelled to protect himself or someone else. His mouth pinched at the memory. *Did that once, pal.* He shook his head, scowling at the vividness of the past event.

Staring at the shadows that grew more pronounced among the crags on either side of him, he stood and began to cautiously descend the rocky slope. When he reached his bike, he swung his leg over it and rode around in a circle on the back wheel. His muscles relaxed. It was a thrill to be in control of the bike and he was reassured of his skill when it responded to his practiced maneuvers.

His good friend, Jess Ferris, who lived in the small town in Arizona where Rand was born, gave the bike to him. It was also special because he'd learned to ride on it. Jess taught Rand everything he knew about trick riding and safety. After practicing a few other complicated operations, he headed back to Fire River.

Netty DuBois, the red-haired barber, peered out the window of her shop when Rand's motorcycle roared to a stop across the street. Hurriedly she locked her door and scurried over before he went inside. She stepped up behind him, while he was placing his helmet inside his truck, and touched his shoulder. "Hey, cowboy, would—"

Swiftly pivoting his body toward her, he threw up his hands with palms turned outward. "Good way to get yourself hurt." He growled.

Choosing to ignore his surly attitude, she inspected the cut on his lip and scratches on his neck. She leaned toward him and her eyebrows arched. "What happened to you?"

His hand went self-consciously to his injured lip. "Run in at work."

"Hope the other guy got worse than you." She tilted her head and stared at him with a smirk. "I could come in and give you some TLC."

Briefly, he closed his eyes.

She wrapped one arm around his waist, pulled him close and gazed into his unusual eyes. The left was blackberry-blue and the right coffee bean-brown. Both were so dark they were almost black, making their difference barely noticeable even in close proximity. She eyed his delectable five o'clock shadow and her fingers tingled as she recalled the texture of his luscious espresso-brown hair when she'd last trimmed it. "I bet you haven't eaten yet. I could fix some—"

"Not tonight." He kicked at a tire on his truck while he contemplated her offer. His lips hitched and he rubbed the back of his neck. "Rain check?"

She put her hands on her hips as her cheeks heated. "Your knuckles are a mess. Did you put anything on them?"

He frowned. "They'll be okay."

She huffed. "You know where I live if you change your mind."

"Yeah, thanks."

She heard him mumble to himself while he ascended the steps. He half raised a hand to wave at her before he disappeared inside.

She stood with her hands on her hips. Even though he was one of the handsomest men she'd ever met, he infuriated her at times with his aloof and variable moods. She knew he struggled with things and on occasion, as happened moments earlier, he reacted in self-defense, but never before with her. Maybe there was more to the run in at work than he admitted.

The next day, Netty turned the Open sign to Closed on her shop door. Her deceased father left her the shop in his will. He opened it the year he deserted her and left her with his sister in New Orleans. He named it after himself and since he acquired a solid business, she didn't change the name. She held no particular fondness for him but the shop provided the means to escape the life she once lived. A gal needed all the help she could get in this life and who it came from made no difference to her. She was a licensed beautician and masseuse, but kept that part of her business low key in order to keep her mostly male clientele.

She stood at the door and peered across the street through the window. Rand's pickup was parked in the usual spot in front of Candlewood with his motorcycle beside it. It was a perfect day and with or without him, although she hoped for the former, she was determined to enjoy it.

She stopped to check her hair and makeup in the mirror over her single customer station. She applied lipstick, walked through her supply room and left through the back door. She drove her red Mustang convertible around her shop, parked beside Rand's truck, and hurried up the steps. She knocked, but only waited a few seconds before she opened the door to enter. "Hey, cowboy, where are you?"

He appeared in the doorway of his workshop on the left side of the hall. "You close your shop already, Red?" He cocked an eyebrow at her.

"I'm going shopping for a friend. Thought you might like to tag along." She blurted out, eyeing him from head to boots.

He scrunched his nose as he tugged a varnish-stained rag from his carpenter's tool belt and wiped his hands. "Why would I want to do that?"

"Dare you to come with me." She figured he wouldn't resist a dare, no matter what it was.

His lips hitched as he placed a screwdriver in the belt. "Dare me, huh?" He removed the belt, laid it on a side table, strutted toward her, and snatched his cowboy hat off a peg by the door.

"I know you can't resist a dare." She tilted her head to scrutinize his unusual eyes, which twinkled with mischief.

He rested his hands on his hips. "Is that right?"

Her lips curved upward while she scanned the black T-shirt that stretched across broad shoulders and exposed corded biceps. His Levi's hugged his narrow waist, hips and long legs perfectly. Her perusal continued down to his faded tawny-brown cowboy boots and then back up to his unruly hair, poking from under the enchanting black hat, which he just seated on his head. Her gaze skated across his high cheekbones and chiseled jaw to focus on his slightly upturned lips. Her fingers tingled with the urge to touch them. His scrumptious appearance coupled with his aversion to talk about his apparently troubled past made him even more of an enigma to her.

He waggled an eyebrow as he studied her with obvious interest. "Like what you see?"

She winked at him. "You bet, cowboy!"

He chuckled. "Ditto."

She scurried to the steps. "Last one in the car is a chicken!"

"Not me!" He strode past her and leaped down the wide steps, landed at the bottom, ambled to her car, and climbed inside. He greeted her with a cheeky grin when she slid into her seat. "What took you so long?"

She stuck her tongue out at him and started the car.

They arrived in Montecito in less than half an hour and Rand began to question why he'd allowed her to cajole him into such an excursion.

She glanced at him as she parked. "You ready for this, cowboy?"

He tugged the brim of his hat a little lower. "Ready as a cowboy waiting for the shoot to open." He chewed on the inside of his cheek while nerves quivered in the pit of his stomach. *You have no idea what to expect, pal.*

"Ha! Bet you'll enjoy this more than riding a bucking horse!" She teased. They made their way to the first dress shop. "Hi, we're looking for something for a future bride." Netty told the shop owner.

"You may want to start with the lingerie. It's in the back."

Rand's eyes narrowed and heat rushed to his cheeks. He crossed his arms. "I'll wait here." He delivered his response in a steady low-pitched tone and pivoted to stare out the shop windows at nothing in particular. He spent the remainder of the shopping experience following Netty from one dress shop to another, each time going no further than the entrance.

Finally, they left the last shop and walked back to where she parked her car. "Why are you so glum? I didn't ask you to come back to the dressing room with me."

"Would you have let me in?" He asked with one eyebrow arched.

She grinned. "There's always hope. After that first shop, I didn't think you'd set foot in another one."

He shrugged and let her remark slide without commenting. *Think of something she'd hesitate to do, pal.* "So, what do I win?"

"A steak dinner at the Lighthouse, my treat. They have a bar so they'll be open late." She winked at him.

"Is that right." He considered her as he crossed his arms. *At least she's paying, but couldn't she just say she wanted to go out for dinner.*

She withdrew one hand from the steering wheel and clutched his upper arm. "We have a reservation for seven o'clock."

"Good to know." His response was carefully subdued.

Later that night at the restaurant after they ordered their drinks, Rand sat staring out the window at the ocean view as the sun set on the horizon. The water reflected orange, red and deep blue hues as the sun disappeared. *She chose the most romantic place in the village, maybe in the entire area. Beware, pal.*

Netty caressed the back of his hand. "What's on your mind, cowboy?"

He tilted his head. "What sounds good to you?"

"I'll have the shrimp scampi." She licked her lips.

He lowered his gaze to the menu to avoid staring at her inviting mouth.

The waiter appeared with his iced tea and her glass of wine. "Are you ready to order, sir?"

Rand placed their order and the waiter left. He gazed at Netty who appeared to be appraising him. The color of her blue-green eyes reminded him of the Eastern white pines back in Arizona.

"I would have totally understood if you refused to go into any of those shops after the first one."

He shrugged. "I chose to accept your dare." *All is forgiven, but not forgotten.*

She took a sip of her wine. "I never thought you'd be embarrassed."

He engaged her challenging stare with his steady one. "How about you going horseback riding with me?" His lip curled in a smirk.

Her eyelashes fluttered. "You'll never make a rodeo queen out of this gal, cowboy. That's where I draw the line!"

"You're afraid of horses?" He gave her a toothy grin.

She punched his shoulder. "Of course not, but I'm a city gal through and through."

He crossed his arms and leaned across the table, so close to her face that his breath fluttered her hair. "Can't blame me for trying?" He waggled his eyebrows.

Leaning against the table she met him in the middle and her mouth touched his.

He jerked his head back, but not before he tasted the wine on her lips. He forced a smile and focused on his empty plate. His heart raced, but to avoid telegraphing how much her brief kiss affected him, he stood and offered her his hand. "Let's dance." He took a deep breath and held it in as he led her to the dancefloor.

Once they began swaying to the song the band was playing, he sang along to occupy his mind with something besides her body moving in sync with his.

"You should go up there, cowboy." She whispered in his ear. "You're way better than him!" She indicated the band's singer with her head. "Have you ever sung, professionally?"

A shiver ran the length of his spine at the puff of her breath on his neck. "Played in a few bars." They danced several slow songs in silence, while he enjoyed the way she fit in his arms. Her perfume tantalized him as he fought off wayward thoughts. He liked Netty, but the volatile emotions she stirred within him? One moment he wanted to draw her close and the next he needed to push her away. Only one other woman ever affected him that way.

The next song was a fast one and he quietly expelled a relieved breath. When the song ended, he ushered her toward the exit. "It's getting late, are you ready to go?"

"Can I finish my drink first?" She grasped his hand and tugged him back to their table and sat down.

He was aware of the response the little hairs on the back of his neck made while she stared at him with acute interest over the top of her glass. He tugged at his collar, which was suddenly too tight. He was not inclined to take relationships lightly but neither was he ready for anything serious. There were too many obstacles he needed to overcome before he could even think about romance. He couldn't even decide what type of work he wanted to pursue, except it wasn't being a stevedore.

The shiny black-dress she was wearing fit every curve to perfection, but the neckline nearly drove him to distraction so that he tried to focus on her face. That didn't work either and a wry smirk played on his lips. He stared at the table before picking up his glass of water-logged iced tea and drank it in one gulp.

Finally, she set her glass down a little too hard. "I'm ready if you want to leave."

He pulled out her chair, ushered her out of the restaurant and to his truck. Once there he opened her door and quickly stepped around the hood to avoid another opportunity for a kiss.

In no time, he parked in front of Candlewood. Before getting out, he spied a man, heading toward the alley, in his rear-view mirror. "I'll walk you to your apartment." The fire escape leading to her door was located in the direction the man disappeared.

She hooked her arm over his. "It's only across the street, cowboy, but if you insist."

"A gentleman always walks his lady to her door." He interrupted, intending to use the mysterious man to avoid her invitation if offered. They crossed the street, strolled around to the alley and climbed the fire escape. As he waited for her to open the door, he scrutinized the immediate area.

When her door opened, he started back down the steps. "Goodnight, Netty."

"Rand." She grasped his arm. "Thanks for a wonderful evening, would you—"

"A man is wandering around the alley. I'd better check it out." He removed her hand and gave it a gentle squeeze. "See you later."

She stared at him with her mouth open.

He sent her a backhanded wave as he quickly and quietly as possible made his way down the steps.

After scouting the immediate area behind her apartment and finding nothing threatening, he made his way back to the mansion, stepped inside and leaned against a wall. He paid for dinner even though it was supposed to be his reward. His head pounded from the cigarette smoke in the restaurant, the stuffiness of the atmosphere and Netty's perfume. None of those things alone bothered him, but her unexpected kiss combined with the strong attraction between them almost made him forget he was a different man now. The way her penetrating gaze did funny things to his insides raised a red flag in his mind. Even now as he stood behind Candlewood's closed doors, his heartrate increased just thinking about her hot gazes. *Careful, pal, she's not a forever kind of woman.* He scrubbed his hand over the stubble on his chin. *Are you any different?* He shook his head. *Thought you were, once.* The phone rang and he strolled into the library to answer it. "Yeah?"

Netty's panicky voice nearly deafened him. "There's a man on my steps!"

Rand's brow puckered. "Take it easy. I'll be right there."

He crossed the street and made his way around to the alley. The man was half sitting and half laying at the bottom of Netty's steps. Rand approached him cautiously.

His shirt was torn and he appeared to be falling asleep or drunk.

Rand stopped next to him, but didn't smell alcohol. "Are you okay, pal?"

He took an awkward swing at Rand and fell off the steps. "I told you, I ain't got the money." He swung his fist again and connected with Rand's shin.

He pulled the man to his feet. "Easy, I'm not your enemy. Did someone attack you?"

The man shook his head and grabbed Rand's arm to steady himself.

"Are you hurt or just dizzy?" Rand asked. "Would you like me to call a doctor or the sheriff?"

"No!" He squinted up at Rand. "But I'd appreciate a ride home if you got time."

Rand frowned. The man appeared to have suffered some rough treatment, but wasn't willing to involve the law. "Can you make it around the corner and across the street?"

"Guess so. What's over there?"

"My truck. I'd leave you here and go get it, but if the neighbors spot you, they might call the sheriff."

"Then what're we waiting for?"

Rand helped the man into his truck and as he began to drive around the square, he glanced at his disheveled passenger. He was several inches shorter than Rand and appeared to have been muscular at one time, but now his skin hung in wrinkles on his bare arms. "What's your name, pal?"

"Chester Yarrow. Yours?"

"Rand Gray. Guess you better tell me where you live Mr. Yarrow."

"Six fourteen East Twelfth Street." He muttered with a downcast expression.

A few minutes later, Rand parked in front of a house whose steps, what was left of them, crumbled to the ground on one side while the roof sagged on the other. "Hold on, let me help you." He jogged around his pickup just in time to catch Chester before he slumped to the ground. Rand steadied him and managed to get him up the steps.

The door flew open and a woman with hair sticking out in all directions stood with her hands fisted on her hips. "Ain't you a fine mess!" She yelled so loud the neighbors could have heard her a block away.

"Shut up, Sally! If you'd stay sober once in a while maybe I'd stick around!"

"Dad!" A boy, having a lighter version of Chester's russet-brown hair, came running into the living room.

Rand managed to get the man inside, during the screaming match between him and the woman along with the boy's sudden appearance.

"Dad, are you okay?" The boy put his arm around the man's waist.

"He's stinkin' drunk! Smells like a skunk like always." Sally spat at the boy. "Throw 'im in his stinkin' bed!" She stumbled, fell and then crawled out of the room.

Rand shook his head, thinking the man seemed in better shape than her, but not by much. "I'll stay and help with your dad." He offered.

"Now that's right kind of you, mister." Chester pulled away from Rand. "My boy can handle things from here."

Rand studied the youth, who appeared to be a teenager. "I don't mind staying." He directed to the boy.

He shook his head. "I can help my dad to bed."

Rand frowned. "What about the wom—?"

"She'll sleep on the floor like she always does!" Chester snarled.

"It's okay, mister. Thanks for bringing my dad home."

Rand was hesitant to leave the boy alone with his parents in such a state. "What's your name, pal?"

"Cory."

Rand frowned. "Do you have a pencil and paper? I'd feel better leaving my phone number in case you need anything."

Cory rushed across the room and rummaged in the drawer of an end table. He came up with a scrap of paper and a pencil stub and gave them to Rand.

He wrote his name and phone number on the paper gave it and the pencil back to Cory. "I live alone so, call me any time."

The boy peered at the paper and then gazed at Rand with a shy smile. "Thanks Mister Rand."

He winked at him. "Sure thing. Let me know if you ever need anything." He opened the door and stepped out, shaking his head while he strode to his truck.

When he got back to the mansion, there were no lights on in Netty's apartment. He was thankful he wouldn't have to try telling her about the strange little family with the teen who affected him in ways he couldn't begin to explain.

Three

The following Monday night, a hulk of a man with a serpent tattooed on his arm from his shoulder to the back of his left hand, where its head was drawn, swung his black Honda 750 onto the road leading into Cove Creek cemetery. He rode around the paved driveway winding between the graves and passed carved headstones of various shapes and sizes. He stopped at the older gravesites located in the back of the cemetery. It was nearly ninety degrees, and his long jet-black ponytail made a soggy streak down the middle of his back. He wiped sweat from his brow with his sleeve as he climbed off his bike. The stench of his own body mingled with a fresh pile which a dog recently left on the side of the pavement.

He glanced to the right and left with quick jerks of his head and sighed. Except for a few birds chirping and a couple of squirrels scolding him for disturbing their chase, he was all alone. A bouquet lay wilting in the baking sun. He shook his head, muttering to himself. "Stupid waste of money. He grumbled. Many of the stones and other markers in this part of the cemetery showed signs of neglect. People buried here were long ago forgotten by those still among the living. He made his way over and around dead trees, patchy grass and crumbling, discolored headstones.

He stopped at the base of one newly vandalized large stone. A flat stone lay beside it, and he dropped to his knees in front of the larger one. Tears began to roll from his eyes, down the sides of his face and fell unnoticed onto the ground. "I miss you, little brother." He traced the name on the stone with his thumb. Alfonso, born January 30, 1945, died March 17, 1960.

He gazed at the flat stone next to him. His dad, Maxwell, born July 6, 1901, died May 11, 1962. "I found mom and asked if I could move in with her. She told me to get off the property, or she'd shoot me." He fell on his face between the two graves and wept until he fell into an exhausted sleep.

The next day, he entered the Cove Creek, Arizona post office and swaggered up to the counter and rang the bell.

A scrawny young woman with an unsuccessful dye job on her beet-red and brown streaked hair approached the counter from the opposite side. "Hey, Virg," she greeted him as her left eye twitched. "I got something for you." She slid a piece of scrap paper across the counter.

He snatched it, glanced at the name and address, and gave the woman a snide grin. "You did good, scarecrow."

"Don't tell where you got it. I could get in trouble for even showing it to you."

His hand streaked across the counter to grab her neck. "If you know what's good for you, I never ever came here."

"I, I, I ain't seen you, honest. I ain't seen nothin'!"

He winked at her. "You'll live longer that way."

Four

Rand arrived at Candlewood after six-thirty on Friday evening, and parked at the curb. He sat staring at the mansion for several minutes. *Maybe if you'd left a light on, pal, it would at least look like someone lived here.* He expelled a heavy sigh. Finally, he left the solace of his truck, climbed the steps to the double front doors and trudged to his bedroom.

After a shower, he changed into a clean T-shirt and Levi's and strode into the library to stand, staring at the cold hearth. After only ten months on the docks, he was promoted to stevedore even though he was the newest member of the crew. His position was constantly challenged by those who felt they were better qualified.

He rolled his shoulders and meandered to the front doors to peer through the windows at the barbershop across the street. All was dark there and also at Netty's upstairs apartment. He rubbed the back of his neck, retraced his steps along the hall, entered the drawing room and sat at the piano. He played a series of cords and then hit several keys at once, hard.

The phone rang and he nearly toppled the piano bench in his haste to answer it.

"Hey, Rand."

"Hey." He returned Cab Martel's cheerful greeting. Cab was a newly-acquired friend, who was also a long-time friend of Rand's brother, Rod.

"Sorry, man. The parents of a boy from my youth group called and asked me to visit them. I doubt I'll be able to jam with you tonight."

Rand leaned against the wall and forced cheerfulness into his response. "Another time then." He expelled a heavy sigh as he hung up the phone and trudged into the library. Absently he rubbed a hand over his chest to dispel the familiar ache as he stared at the bare hearth. He carefully placed kindling there, lit it, added logs on the grate and lingered while staring at the bright tongues of fire.

With slumped shoulders he stepped out the library door. A slight breeze danced along his arms and pulled at his hair, sending a shiver along his spine. The sky was clear and stars twinkled as he followed the garden path, bordered by various kinds of shrubs and trees. The sweet vanilla scent of Jeffrey pines evoked a memory, which he refused to entertain. His throat constricted and he crossed his arms as if to protect his heart from the uninvited thoughts.

He meandered along the path to the fountain, stopped to stare at the dark ripples, and listened to the gurgling of the water as it cascaded into the pond. He raised a foot to rest on the stone wall, which surrounded it, and leaned on his knee. A breeze stirred, chilling him to the bone and he rubbed his bare arms. The peacefulness of the garden failed to relieve the heaviness in his chest. In the past he'd have found a game of pool or a woman to ease his longing, but those diversions no longer held any appeal. He left his wayward thoughts along with the pond and slogged back to the library.

Netty watched Rand glance toward the hearth as he stepped inside. She frowned at his glum features and was tempted to run to him, throw her arms around his neck and plant a kiss on his downturned lips.

His mouth dropped open when his gaze collided with hers.

"Surprise!" She laughed, springing up from an armchair. She caught the appreciative twinkle in his deeply expressive eyes as he stood momentarily frozen in the doorway. She was glad she stopped at a restaurant on her way home. "I didn't think you'd be gone long. The fire was just getting a good start when I got here. I brought dinner. It's in the kitchen."

He hesitated before crossing the room and gathering her in his arms. "I thought I smelled coffee. This is a nice surprise. I'm really hungry." He caught her hand, and they skipped into the kitchen, laughing like teenagers.

The counter held a fresh pot of coffee along with their meal. Plates filled with steak, baked potatoes, and rolls were keeping warm in a shallow pan on the stove.

He drew her into his arms for a quick hug and then twirled her in a circle, singing "This Magic Moment." He swayed with her in the small space between the stove and a table for four.

When he stopped singing, she laughed, pleased that his mood was greatly improved. His voice was smooth and seductive. "Jay and the Americans, right?" She found this man to be dangerous to her heart.

"You win the prize." He announced, making a swooping gesture with one arm.

At times he took her breath away. With a cheeky grin, she placed an index finger on her chin. "Dare I ask what the prize is?"

He placed a hand on his chest and donned a pained expression. "The pleasure of spending the evening with me, of course!" He winked at her.

She snatched a dish towel and tossed it at his head. "Set the table, cowboy." She'd never met a man who could be comical and charming all at once.

He draped the towel over his arm and bowed towards her. "As you wish, my lady." He chuckled.

She appraised him for several moments. His T-shirt and jeans were both dark blue and his cowboy boots were chocolate brown. His black cowboy hat was the only item missing of his usual attire. His appearance reminded her of the bad boys in movies, but his personality was the mysterious part of him that she found most irresistible. His woodsy aftershave wafted around her when they danced and she waited for an opportunity to kiss him until he was breathless.

He studied her with one eyebrow raised. "Whose birthday?" He pointed at the cake on the counter.

"Mine." She laughed because he'd caught her staring at him, "and I chose to spend it with you!"

"You should've told me. I'd have taken you somewhere special." He enfolded her in his arms and kissed her cheek. "Happy birthday, Netty. My birthday's on the twentieth. Let's celebrate and go someplace out of the ordinary."

She smiled. "I'll hold you to that, cowboy." She knew there'd be nothing ordinary about spending an evening with him. After their leisurely meal at the table in the old-fashioned kitchen, they lingered in the library over after dinner coffee and then she coaxed him into the drawing room.

She paused in the doorway of the spacious room as the wooden floor beckoned her to dance the night away. She brought her record collection to ensure there was not a fast song among them. In his arms and in close proximity to him was where she planned to spend the entire evening.

He grew tired of dancing before she did and they retired to a sofa in the library, which he pulled toward the hearth after adding more wood to the fire.

This was her favorite room with its ceiling to floor bookcases, large comfy armchairs, sofas and love seats. The fireplace and hearth were massive and made from black oak, which she recalled Rand's brother told her once. She frowned. Any reminder of Rod's stuffy religious attitude and obvious disapproval of her and Rand being together irritated her.

When they were seated, she gave Rand a sideways hug. "I've never known anyone quite like you, cowboy."

His lips hitched as he waggled his eyebrows at her. "Is that a good thing?"

"A very good thing." She peered at him as her heartrate accelerated. "There's something I've been trying to figure out."

He rested his arm across the back of the sofa and gave her his full attention. "Anything I can help with?"

"Maybe." She appraised him before she raised her hand to trace the delicious stubble on his chin. "Why do you stay at a job you obviously hate?"

His brow furrowed as he removed his arm from behind her. "After Rod went to work for Coolidge, work was hard to find. Zeke offered to give me a chance even though I'd never worked on a dock."

She crossed her arms. "Why couldn't Rod pay you to keep working here?"

He expelled a short breath. "He isn't the one who wanted this place restored that was Dad."

She uttered a snort. "Why do you always defend him? What's he done for you?"

His jaw clenched as his gaze locked on the hearth. "I showed up here for work uninvited and Rod gave me a job without question. He trusted me when no one else did." Rand paused to raise an eyebrow at her. "When I was forced to disclose my birth name to him, by a certain unnamed redhead," he eyed her pointedly, "he welcomed me without hesitation." He drew his fingers through his hair.

She stared at his hands, which he'd lowered onto his knees. "I'm sorry, let me try again. You're a remarkable man, cowboy, but I can't figure you out."

He raised an eyebrow. "I'm just a simple man."

"You're different than Rod or the rest of them at least when you first came to Fire River. What made you change?"

He raised one foot onto his other leg and leaned back. "I studied Rod as he was harassed by the citizens of this community," his brow wrinkled, "especially my mother. No matter how insulting or suspicious of him they were, he never gave up trying to discover who was sucking the life out of the businesses here. I witnessed his devastation after he was trapped in the fire in his bungalow and then while he had difficulty getting the authorities to believe it was arson.

"I observed his determination to trust people when it would've been easier to wash his hands of the whole thing, leave and let someone else figure it out. He stayed even though they threatened to run him out of here. He loves this village, Netty, and the people who live here. He proved it by staying and chipping away at the problem until he found enough information to prove to the authorities what was happening and who was behind it.

"I couldn't help myself. I wanted what he had. Now I know who was behind Rod's loyalty to the people here and His name is Jesus Christ. He's the One who changed me, not Rod. Jesus can change you too, if you let Him."

Netty batted her eyelashes at him. His response baffled her. "I guess we have different views of Rod. Are you going to find another job?"

His lips formed a straight line as he tilted his head to the side. "Thinking about it."

Netty sat contemplating all he'd said about Rod, but she didn't appreciate the influence he had over Rand, in spite of what he'd claimed about God. She pondered how a non-existent person could have that much influence over anyone?

A past image of Smokey Roe, Rand's alias, crossed her mind. She'd sat across a table from him at the time and enjoyed the way he laughed at danger and that aspect of his character appealed to her. She also recalled how his expression often appeared hard as steel. Just the thought of the cold, calculating sensation she'd sometimes seen in his eyes made her shiver.

Smokey was a careless and dangerous man, but Rand was neither. The only people in danger from him were the ones who threatened those he cared about. Gazing at him she found mostly kindness and sensitivity, but hoped she could discover the mysteries he kept to himself. She recalled how he accepted her, a not-so-distant woman of the street, without asking or expecting anything of her in return.

Even though only half listening, especially when he sang his half-brother's praises, she was content to scrutinize him as they talked. The corners of his mouth were usually tilted slightly upward even when he wasn't smiling as if one waited to adorn his features. He had a perpetual five o'clock shadow

Wings of Steel

over his upper lip. She continued to admire him, as his eyes took on a smoky intensity and crinkled at the corners.

"You're staring." His voice dipped to a husky whisper.

Her eyelashes fluttered, and she licked her lips. "Just enjoying the scenery, cowboy." She traced his angular jawline with her index finger and then drew it across his sensuous lips. When he closed his eyes, she leaned into him and kissed him deeply.

He pulled away from her all too soon for her liking, drew her to his side and began telling her about a World War II pilot story he was reading.

She sighed and was more than a little offended that he'd thwarted her intentions. "It's getting late." She stretched, got up, and ran her hands up and down her arms as she stood near the hearth.

He stood beside her and grasped her hand. "I care about you, Netty, but there's a lot I still don't understand about walking with God."

She pulled her hand from his. "It's a lot to take in."

He eyed her steadily. "I understand, but I'm always willing to answer your questions if I can."

She forced a smile. "Now that I've brought it up, you'll never let me forget it." She started walking toward the door with him following her.

"I promise you'll always be the one to bring it up."

Alone in the chilled and darkened library after Netty left, he allowed the events of the evening to replay in his mind. Netty was fun to be with and in many ways, they were a lot alike. He sensed she was interested in being more than a friend, but for now, he wasn't. He rested his elbows on his knees, lowered his head into his hands and forked his fingers through his hair. *Eight years ago, today Claire left you and never looked back, pal.*

Five

Rand parked his pickup in front of Candlewood. Quitting time was early at the shipyards, unlike Monday and Tuesday when he worked late. He went inside showered, put on a clean pair of Levi's, a green and white chambray shirt, his boots and snatched his cowboy hat off his dresser. As he went out the door, he set the hat on his head and went down the steps two at a time.

He crossed the street, planning to ask Netty to have lunch with him. When he strolled into her shop, she was sweeping up quite a mess. Hair products and broken glass were strewn all over the floor. His brow wrinkled as he spotted patches of missing paint and holes in the wall. He wrinkled his nose as strong scents of mint, floral and citrus wafted around him. "Need some help?"

"Darn shelf fell!" She growled, pointing at the wall. The phone on the desk rang and she scrambled to answer it. "Sam's barber shop and salon." She paused to listen to the person on the other end of the line. "Two o'clock is fine. Thanks, Tom."

Rand's back was toward her as he inspected the wall while she was on the phone. "It won't take much to fix—"

She slammed the receiver on the desk.

He threw a puzzled glance at her. "I'll get my tools."

"Thanks."

He caught her grumbled response as he went out the door. A few minutes later, he returned and was careful to avoid stepping on the debris. Using a stud finder, he drilled two more holes a few inches from the others.

"What are you doing?" She demanded sharply as she paused from sweeping up the remainder of the fragments.

He glanced at the ceiling and suppressed a sigh. "Putting your shelf back up, anchoring it in the studs."

"I don't want it there." She snarled. "I want it where it was!" She pointed to the first set of holes.

He pushed his hat back off his forehead with a grimace. "It's too heavy to stay up there without studs."

She stood glaring at him with hands on her hips, "that's not—." She interrupted herself and then continued sweeping, mumbling to herself.

He cocked an eyebrow at her, filled in the old holes and plastered over them. "After work tomorrow, I'll sand and repaint the wall. It'll be good as new. I'll make you another shelf to set on the floor." He paused, hoping his offer would take the edge off her irritation. When she didn't respond, he cleaned up his mess, collected his tools and started for the door.

She stopped him with a hand on his arm. "I'm sorry. It's been a bad day and I took it out on you. I'm making jambalaya for dinner. Want to join me?"

He avoided eye contact. "What time?" They often coordinated their evening meal since neither of them enjoyed eating alone.

"How about seven?"

"Want me to bring anything?" *Maybe she'll be in a better mood by then, pal.*

"Just yourself." Her smile quickly faded.

He waited for her to say more, but when she didn't, he shrugged and left, closing the door behind him.

He quickly strode across the street, sprinted up the steps, and inside Candlewood, grabbed a quick bite to eat and then snatched his jean jacket from a kitchen chair as he left. He slipped into his jacket, tied the bandana around his neck, which he kept inside his helmet, mounted his bike and left the Village.

As he rode along the coast, he snatched glimpses of dirty strands of seaweed scattered along the beach and rolling in the surf. The crash of waves as they swept ashore wafted briny air in his face while sea gulls darted up and down at the water's edge. Once away from the ocean, he headed eastward toward the mountains.

Turning off the highway, he chose a less-traveled road and slowed to enjoy glimpses of scrub oak and gray pine. He pulled over to the side of the road and unfastened his helmet from the seat. While he fastened the strap under his chin, he peered up at the cloudless azure-blue sky. He took a deep breath and his cheeks puffed outward as he rolled his shoulders and let the problems at work and Netty's surly mood fade into the recesses of his mind. The corners of his lips lifted. He was in his element, one with the mountains, trees and creatures who lived there.

He often enjoyed hiking and riding and won several trophies racing in the past. The challenge of the trails helped him gain clarity of mind and also relief from the pressures of life. He'd been riding for several hours when he stopped and tilted his head to listen to birds of prey as they called or hooted while flying overhead.

The scent of rotting trees and vegetation filled his nostrils and he caught an occasional whiff of the fragrant gray and Coulter pines. A forceful breeze whistled among the crags as it pulled at his clothes while a white-eared pocket mouse scampered through the sage scrub in front of him. He followed the trail around the base of a huge rock as it curved upward and stopped to stare at a pile of dirt and small rocks that obstructed the path.

Some twigs snapped and small rocks clattered down the mountainside from above, pelting his helmet and making the hairs on his arms and neck tingle. With no desire to encounter a mountain lion or a black bear while unarmed, he quickly turned his bike around and sped toward the main road. The trail suddenly dipped and he attempted to jump at the crest of the hill, planning to land near the bottom. When he hit the ground, the front wheel skidded in loose dirt and the bike slid sideways.

He tucked his head. Stunned, the next thing he knew, he was on his back, trying to breathe normally. It was several moments before the reality of what happened registered. He tilted his head slowly from side to side and checked his hands and arms. A couple of cuts on his arm would need attention. Carefully he moved his legs and finally sat up slowly. One leg of his jeans was ripped, and there was a gash in his skin that was bleeding, but didn't appear overly serious. Last of all, he removed his helmet and checked it inside and out for damage, but the exterior only contained a few new scrapes. He rested, giving time for his adrenaline rush to subside. *Fear causes carelessness, pal.*

The sun was sinking below the distant horizon when he finally stood, dusted himself off and limped over to where his Harley lay on its side. He bandaged his leg with the bandana he wore around his neck. He'd twisted an ankle, making walking uncomfortable, but not impossible. The front wheel of his bike was bent. At first, he thought he could ride slow once he reached the paved road. He began walking the bike over the rough terrain, keeping alert to his surroundings for predators. It took considerable time and effort to get down to the road and by then it was apparent he would not be riding back to the village. Not wanting to leave the bike beside the road, he chose to walk it back to the Village.

Once he arrived at the Square, he left the bike at W. T.'s garage along with a note asking if he could fix the wheel. After crossing Cambria Avenue, he tramped wearily through Riverdale Park in the center of the square to the back entrance of Candlewood's Garden. He entered the mansion and shuffled through the dining room to the sound of pounding on the front door.

He groaned when he spied Netty through the glass in the double doors. Until that moment, her dinner invitation was the last thing on his mind. He tried not to limp as he plodded down the hall and opened the door. "Hi." He greeted her, crossing his arms and avoiding her intense gaze.

She entered without speaking.

His mind replayed her earlier mood as the door closed behind her.

"I was wor—what happened to you?" Her brow wrinkled as she gave him the once-over.

He shrugged. "A few scratches. Nothing to worry about."

"You left hours ago!" Her voice rose in pitch. "Have you been in another fight?"

His cheeks heated and he rubbed the back of his neck. "I just—" He focused on the floor instead of her face. "Sorry about dinner."

"I can reheat it." She grasped his arm.

His shirt pressed against raw flesh inside his jacket, making him flinch. He managed a wry grin at her repeated invitation and checked his watch: 9:45. He was exhausted from the ordeal and in dire need of a shower. "Thanks, but it's late and we both have to work tomorrow. Are we still on for Saturday night?"

"I hope so." She reached for his hands, which hung at his sides and her gaze perused him from head to toe. "Are you sure you're alright?" She pointed to the torn leg of his jeans with her chin.

The sultry tone in her voice made him determined to discourage her scrutiny. His face heated so he stared at the floor. "I'm good."

"Goodnight, Rand." Her voice no longer held any hint of compassion as she spun on one heel and stormed out, leaving the door open. "See you later." She called over her shoulder.

"Later." He responded. His lips pinched together while he stared at her retreating form. *Should have gone, pal.* Hesitantly, he closed the door. A low whistle startled him from behind. Inhaling sharply, he turned to face Cab Martel.

"What happened?" Cab crossed his arms as he peered at Rand from where he stood in the hall. Cab also had a key to the mansion as well as Rod.

Rand crossed his arms. "How long have you been here?"

"About an hour. Netty's been here a couple of time so I stayed when she said she was worried about you." Cab shook his head as his silver-blue eyes scrutinized Rand. "She really likes you, man."

Rand's face flushed. "Yeah." He stuffed his hands in the front pockets of his jeans. "Guess I can't blame her for being upset." He mumbled to himself.

Cab's brow wrinkled as he eyed Rand's dirty and torn clothes. "Are you okay, man?"

He shrugged. "Bent a wheel, but I'm good."

Cab studied him as if considering Rand's assessment of his bent wheel. "I dropped by to ask if you'd like to double date with me and Katie Saturday night." He grinned.

Rand rubbed the back of his neck. "Thanks, but I already have plans."

"Sorry I didn't ask sooner. It's late so I'll see you later." Cab headed for the library and glanced back at Rand. "I almost forgot. Rod wants you to call him."

When Cab left, Rand stood gazing through a window at Netty's upstairs apartment. He imagined the taste of her jambalaya, which made his mouth water. She'd almost convinced him to accept her offer, but he was tired and in serious need of a shower, but he'd call Rod before it got any later.

After work the next day, Rand drove to W. T.'s gas station and garage. He passed the dull orange gas pumps, parked next to the building and climbed out of his pickup.

"Wal, lookey who's come to visit!" W. T. greeted him as he left the station's small building. "Betcha stopped to ask 'bout your ride." A straw hat with a floppy brim hid much of the man's grizzly salt and pepper hair.

"Yeah, about that." Rand pushed his cowboy hat back off his forehead.

W. T. was much shorter than Rand and twice his age. "Kin read yer face like a newspaper. Cain't fix it fer ya. What'd ya hit anyhow? I ain't never saw a wheel bent like that."

He grinned. "Thought you could fix anything, old friend."

"Hump! Ain't gonna tell me, are ya? Best you learn how to monopolate that thang, boy, afore ya hurt yourself." W. T. crossed his arms.

Too late, pal. He stopped in his tracks and frowned. *Monopolate? Operate or manipulate?* He shrugged. "Where is it?"

"Out back, best thang you kin do is git a new one." He headed for the pumps to serve a customer who pulled into the station.

"You're sure perceptive for an old man." Rand called after him.

"An you're a wisenheimer if I ever knowed one." W. T. countered as he put gas in an old Plymouth.

Rand snorted as he headed around the garage to retrieve his bike. Returning, he responded. "Thanks for the wise, but you can keep the hammer."

"Dang, young whipper snapper." He spoke louder.

He caught W. T.'s remark and grinned as he walked the bike toward his pickup while the customer drove away. A whiff of gasoline and motor oil assaulted his nose. "Next time, I'll take it to a real mechanic." He snickered.

W. T. rubbed his whiskered chin. "Boy, you best git that thang in yer truck and hit the road afore I show you who's who 'round here!"

Rand chuckled. "Come on, old friend, can't you take a joke?"

He grinned. "Git on outta here afore I fix your haid, boy!"

Rand swung the tail gate to the side and hoisted the ramp from his pickup. "I'll leave soon as you give me a hand."

The two of them loaded his bike, Rand secured it, put the ramp back in place, and closed the tailgate.

"That's mighty handy." W. T. indicated the ramp. "Ain't never saw the likes of it."

Rand laughed. "Had it made special right after I got the bike, otherwise I'd have to fly it up there."

"Thinks he's one a them dang comedy fellers." W. T. complained to himself before moseying up to the truck's door as Rand was about to climb inside. W. T. put a hand on his shoulder. "Heard ya had a bit a trouble on the docks."

Rand frowned and tugged on his hat. "Nothing I couldn't handle." He swung into the driver's seat and drove away. In his rearview mirror, he spied W. T. shaking his head as he shuffled toward the station.

Saturday night Netty opened the door to her apartment and stared at Rand. He was wearing a light blue button-down shirt with a navy suit coat, dark blue Levi's and black cowboy boots. His thick wavy hair was windblown and swept across his forehead. In his hand was a bouquet of red poppies. She continued to stare, as a slow grin lifted the corners of his mouth when he placed the flowers in her hands.

"Happy belated birthday, beautiful!"

She took the flowers from him as he stepped into her living room. "Thank you, darlin' they're lovely!" She kissed his cheek and inhaled a subtle mixture of leather and cedar. "I'll put them in a vase and then we can go."

"Take your time." He remained in her living room.

Her cheeks heated uncomfortably when the springs in her old tan couch squeaked as he sat on it. She was thankful for the partial wall between her kitchen and living room and was glad Rand wasn't in a hurry. Slowly she took a vase from the cupboard because she needed a brief moment to give her heartrate time to calm down. The only other occasion she'd ever seen him in a suit coat was for Rod and Saun's wedding.

Rand was an attractive man, but tonight she found him more than gorgeous and just gazing at him made her insides flutter. She arranged the flowers studiously. No man ever affected her so intensely and she didn't want to be distracted until after they enjoyed their celebration. She planned to invite him in when they got back and give him attention he wouldn't soon forget.

She chose to wear a form-fitting emerald-green silk dress with spaghetti straps and a flirty skirt surrounding her legs just above her knees. Dark-green satin high heels completed her attire and a diamond-teardrop necklace with matching earrings complimented her dress. Her skirt swished around her legs as she hurried to place the bouquet in the center of the table.

She paused to set the vase down and focused on the way his suit coat stretched across his broad shoulders. She drew a deep calming breath.

He stood next to the bookshelf beneath the living room window and stared at a picture he held.

She sashayed over behind him, put her chin on his shoulder and peered over it as her arms enclosed his waist and her hands rested on his chest. "That's my dad and me just before he left New Orleans."

Rand set the picture back on the shelf and turned to face her. "Were you and your dad close?"

She watched his Adam's apple bob as he concentrated on her face and she enjoyed, getting lost in the smoky depths of his gaze. Something lingered there. Was it desire? She blinked as he raised an eyebrow and she quickly placed a kiss on a corner of his mouth. "Your eyes are captivating." She whispered.

He tilted her chin upward with his thumb. "That gives me an excuse to enjoy yours. They remind me of the blue-green pines in Arizona."

She blinked, and hoped he would kiss her as she focused on his mouth. Could she kiss away his resistance?

He paused to give her a thorough once over. "Green is my favorite color. You look beautiful, Netty." His lips hitched. "It's going to be a cool night. Do you want jacket or something?"

She winked at him and hoped to hide her disappointment when he didn't kiss her. "Your arms will be warmer than any jacket. Shall we go?"

He ushered her out the door and they descended the fire escape together. "Mind if we take your car? My truck isn't fit for a lady who's all dressed up."

She appreciated his consideration and placed her keys in his hand.

He opened the passenger door, waited until she settled inside and then closed it before going around the Mustang's hood.

He was ever the gentleman. She watched enthralled as he adjusted the seat as far back as it would go to accommodate his superbly long legs.

At the restaurant, the headwaiter seated them in an alcove within view of the stage. A lighted candle was in the center of their table and all the others as well. Rand surveyed their surroundings, taking note that the tables were painted bright red and the walls were dark chocolate along with the stage. The only other lighting was small unadorned bulbs, which were scattered around the interior, hanging from the high ceiling and giving the room a soft glow.

He pulled out her chair and sat across from her. She ordered a glass of wine with her meal and he chose iced tea. Their dinner of lobster tail with grilled vegetables and baked potato satisfied his pallet and by the smile on her face, he could tell she was also pleased.

They lingered over after dinner coffee while waiting for the music to start. He appreciated the way the candlelight brought out golden highlights in her ginger-red hair and made her eyes sparkle.

She winked at him. "Is this the band of the guy you work with?"

He flashed a cheeky grin at her. She'd caught him staring. His head bobbed in response. "Gage Fuller's the lead guitarist. I think you'll enjoy this. I've heard them before, they're fantastic musicians!"

The band started with a slow song so Rand stood, offered her his hand, and led her to the dance floor. The high heels she wore allowed him to easily rest his head against hers. He inhaled her fragrant perfume, which reminded him of flowers and spice with more emphasis on the latter.

Netty exuded a poignancy that both attracted and perplexed him, often at the same time. He found nothing ordinary or insignificant about her and he was intrigued by the challenge to discover who she was beneath the externals she presented to the public.

After they danced to several songs, he led her back to their table. "Have you talked to Saun lately?" Saun was his brother's wife and she and Netty were friends.

"Yesterday. She was excited about adding new stock to her shop, but she isn't open enough to really develop a solid clientele. It seems more of a hobby than a business. I think it's a shame she doesn't spend more time there. She was so excited about it before her and Rod were married."

Rand almost objected to her brusque remark, but ignored it instead. To his knowledge, his brother did nothing to deserve her cryptic remark. "Would you like another drink?"

"Yes."

He signaled their waiter. "I'm concerned about Rod because of the long drive he makes back and forth to LA every day. I think it's getting to him." The waiter came just then and brought their drinks. Rand waited until he left and then continued. "I wish I could think of some way to help him."

Netty ignored his comment as she took a sip of her wine. "I think Saun should focus on her shop when he's gone."

Again, he let the affront against his brother slide. Her comments apparently meant more than she offered to share with him. She either didn't understand or didn't care that Rod was more important to Saun than anything else. He sighed. *Pal, you'd appreciate that kind of consideration from your wife, if you had one.* He pushed that idea into the recesses of his mind and observed Netty instead. Her voice held a sultry southern drawl that set his heart racing, especially when she called him cowboy or darlin,' as she did earlier when he gave her the flowers. At the touch of her hand on his arm he mentally shook himself out of his thoughts. "Sorry. What did you say?"

She threw back her head and laughed. "Your friend wants you to join them. See, he's motioning to you." She watched as he stood and strode quickly to the stage.

"You all give Rand Gray a real warm welcome." The young blond-haired lead singer spoke into his microphone. When the applause died down as Rand took his position at the keyboard, the man chuckled. "He's my boss Monday through Friday and he didn't know I was going to spring this on him. Please make him welcome so I have a job come Monday."

Rand waggled his eyebrows as the audience applauded even louder than before. Grinning he leaned into the mike. "Just wait 'till Gage finds out what I surprise him with on Monday!"

The crowd roared at their good-humored banter, Netty along with the rest of them as the band began playing "Lucky Man" a song made popular by Emerson, Lake and Palmer.

When Rand was featured at the end of the song, Netty stood with everyone in the place as some cheered, some clapped and others whistled.

A man standing behind her commented to those around him. "The regular keyboard player better not miss too often because this guy is much better. He's a good showman too."

"He's also very handsome!" A woman next to the man cooed.

After shaking hands with Gage and the other band members, Rand exited the stage as Cab approached him.

"Hey, man, that was great! I noticed you and Netty earlier but didn't want to interrupt. Rod told me you were celebrating your birthdays."

Rand burst out laughing. "A man can't have any secrets around here." He clapped Cab on the back as he started to walk away, but Rand caught his arm. "Who's the pretty lady?"

Cab grinned and glanced at his date. "This is Katie Lambert. She's a teacher at the school in Fire River."

Rand quickly scrutinized the petite young woman. She was a little shorter than Cab, even wearing heels. Her ash-brown hair lay in waves several inches below her shoulders. He briefly took her hand. "Nice to meet you, Katie. I'd better get back to my friend before she decides to leave without me." He grinned at Cab.

When he got back to his and Netty's table, Zeke Finn was sitting in Rand's chair.

Zeke stood when Rand stopped beside their table. "Those guys are good and you weren't bad either! Am I going to lose you when you all become famous?"

Rand clapped Zeke's shoulder. "You don't have to worry about me. I have too much fun to make a career of it."

Zeke heaved an exaggerated sigh of relief and nodded to Netty. "Nice to meet you Miss De Bois. Enjoy your weekend, Rand."

"You too." He called after his boss.

Rand reached for Netty's hand. "Are you ready to go?"

She slipped her hand in his and he ushered her out the door.

After parking in the alley behind her building, he escorted her up the steps to her apartment, unlocked the door and placed her keys in her hand. When she took them, he pulled her into his arms and kissed her forehead.

She tilted her head back and closed her eyes.

He kissed her cheek and then his lips gently brushed hers.

She wrapped her arms around his neck, slid her fingers in his hair and leaned into him as she deepened the kiss.

His heart pounded so hard he wondered if she could feel it. He cut the kiss short, took note of her sultry expression and put some distance between them. "It was fun tonight." He was sure the huskiness in his voice betrayed hm.

"It was and you were the center attraction." A provocative smile played on her lips while she ran her hand up and down the edge of his suit coat.

He tried to breathe when her fingers blazed a trail of heat through his shirt making his muscles tense.

"It's still early." She grasped his hand. "Come on in, I'll fix us something to drink."

He drew in a deep breath and shook his head. "I have to get up early for church."

Her eyes lost their sparkle as she released his hand.

"Would you like to come with me?" He gave her a hopeful smile.

"No!" She pivoted into her apartment, slammed the door and locked it.

His chest tightened and he stepped back as if he'd been struck. His lips pinched together and he descended the stairs. Going around the building, he crossed the street, entered the mansion and leaned against the wall. *Didn't finesse that well, pal.*

Six

Early Tuesday evening a large man with long, greasy hair and a dark scowl stepped into the Black Rose bar and grill in Montecito, scanned the interior, and chose a seat at the bar. He planned to find an insignificant place to park his bike and maybe get a room for a few nights. He'd found out the town had no place to stay that wouldn't be too conspicuous so he chose a place farther away, but not too far.

Two men sat a few stools over from his. "We can't let him get away with it." The first man with dirty-blonde hair growled. "The cops have been at my apartment twice asking questions." He complained.

"You ain't got a record to worry about so quit your belly aching." The other one remarked as he ran a large hand over his balding forehead. "We need to teach him a lesson he won't forget."

Intrigued by their conversation, the solidly built man nodded toward them, got off his stool and approached them. "Buy you two a drink?"

They both eyed his sleeveless black T-shirt with their mouths gaping open.

"Couldn't help overhearing your conversation. Maybe we can help each other. Interested?"

Together they quickly responded. "Yeah."

"How about we move where we can talk private like." The man with the serpent tattoo indicated a table in a back corner.

The three of them settled at the new location and the newcomer ordered a round of drinks.

The first man with blonde hair and shifty-blue eyes introduced himself. "Kane."

The other man with a heavy mustache and bulbous nose gave his head a quick bob. "Buzz."

He studied the two men while they waited for their drinks. He figured the heavier of the two was the brains. The other one, with the wiry looking frame, was eager to get even. He figured he could pretty much get them to do whatever he suggested. They were both ripe for revenge, and he could relate. He'd be happy to help them and then they could help him.

The bartender signaled the man with the tattoo, and he left the men long enough to collect three bottles. Setting them on the table, one in front of the other two and the last for himself, he sat and drank half of his brew before addressing Buz. "What'd he do to get the cops on your tails?"

"Young dandy fired us for no good reason!" Buzz growled.

He raised his bottle, exposing his bulging bicep. "So, you'd like to teach him a lesson?" He wanted to make sure he understood what he'd heard them say.

Kane squinted at the bartender and lowered his voice. "Yeah, but the cops have already been asking too many questions, like they want to pin something on us, and we ain't done nothing."

He raised an eyebrow and tossed his long ponytail over his shoulder. "This man you want to get even with have a name?"

"Yeah." Buzz almost yelled and then quickly lowered his voice to a near whisper. "Rand Gray." He added in a menacing voice that he barely kept low enough so he wasn't overheard.

The newcomer reared his head back and roared with laughter. "Drink up, boys. This is your lucky day."

"Hey, you got a name?" Kane wanted to know.

He speared him with a piercing glare. "Some folks call me Virg."

Seven

The following Saturday, Rand fixed a pot of coffee and let it brew while he took a shower. He emerged from his bedroom, wearing black leather pants, a long-sleeve denim shirt and an old pair of tan cowboy boots. Afterward he sat at the kitchen table, drinking from a mug as his gaze scanned the room. He was glad Rod chose to keep the old potbellied stove. It lent a little familiar warmth to the room. An exhaust pipe, attached to the back stretched two feet up the wall and then out through it.

He closed his eyes and his lips pulled down at the corners as an image of Vera Roe, the woman from his early childhood, crossed his mind. He could almost visualize her standing in front of the stove with her back to him. She and her husband, Ned met Rand's basic needs, but even though they called him, their boy, they weren't given to showing him much affection.

As he grew older, he began to think most of his difficulties were related to or as a direct result of his relationships with women. His ex-girlfriend, Claire, stole his heart and then tossed him aside like so much garbage when he asked her to marry him. When he first came to Fire River to find his mother, she barely tolerated him. Once she found out his name was Gray, she detested him as much as she did his dad and half-brother.

He was attracted to Netty, but was she only interested in him for fun and games? *Can any woman really care about you, pal?* He rubbed his chest with one hand while twisting his coffee cup in half circles. He shook his head and pushed away from the table. He grabbed his leather jacket from the desk chair in his room, left the mansion, hurried out the door and down the steps.

He retrieved his helmet and gloves from behind the seat of his truck, put them on, mounted his bike and left the village. The bent tire that he replaced last week served as a reminder to never underestimate the possibility of the unexpected. That lesson also taught him to wear leather clothes and gloves, especially when preparing for a race. He intended to spend the entire day riding in the mountains and practicing his skills.

Once away from the village, he slowed down to enjoy the ride. In the past he tried to fill the void inside him with challenging feats. He climbed mountains just to prove he could. He won a gold-plated buckle bronc riding at a local rodeo, enjoyed hang-gliding, para-sailing, and racing anything with wheels. Never one to brag about his accomplishments or trophies, he took pleasure in every opportunity to live life to the fullest. Eventually he found his exploits were futile because the exhilaration he received from them quickly vanished.

He spent the remainder of the day practicing how he'd handle the obstacles that the upcoming race would demand and paused only long enough for short hikes to stretch his legs. Toward evening he rode along Coyote Canyon Road, which eventually crossed Cochella Road and passed his property and Rod's on the way south to Fire River. He was in no hurry to return to the old otherwise unoccupied mansion.

He marveled at the rugged bluffs along the opposite side of the canyon. The towering rock walls appeared painted in varying shades of gray, brown, and black. A scrub-peppered slope descended on his right and a small stream ran along the base of the gorge. Wild grass grew in the midst of the gravel alongside the edge of the asphalt.

He spied a bird soaring effortlessly above the rugged terrain. 'To everything there is a season,' a Bible phrase from pastor Clark's sermon last Sunday, replayed in his mind along with, 'a time for every purpose under heaven', a line from a sixty's song by the Byrds. How many seasons did these mountains endure? Did time affect the condor, floating so lazily above him? Like the mountains and the bird, he'd forged through many phases of life as well. He glanced at the sky. "God, I'm ready for a change."

The tang of rock, dust, and moist air along with the scent of pine and manzanita teased his nose as a breeze swabbed chilling fingers over the skin on his face and neck. He connected with his environment and the creatures that lived here. He glanced to his right and caught the last glimpse of the sun before it sank below the horizon. A few moments later, he marveled at the burst of color, which painted the sky tangerine, mustard, and blood red before midnight blue swallowed it all. A light fog descended and plunged him into murky darkness. He slowed his speed, breathed deeply and focused on the road illuminated a short distance ahead of him by his headlight.

Suddenly around a curve in the road behind him bright lights glared in his rearview mirror and obstructed his view of the road ahead. He tapped his brakes as a signal to the driver that he was on the road.

The vehicle bore down on him with increased speed, caught up with him, and pulled alongside of him. The passenger door swung open. Quickly, he knocked it closed with his handlebars. His heartrate escalated and he drew short breaths. *What's going on?* The van swerved as it sped up and clipped his front fender. "Hey!" He yelled as he fought to stay upright. "Watch it!"

As if the driver heard his protest, he slammed on his brakes right in front of Rand. With his heart in his throat, he jerked his front wheel. It slid off the pavement. In his headlight, he spied a flash of green paint.

He jerked his right leg over to the left side of the bike. Laid it down. Shoved himself hard away from the back wheel. Tucked his head against his chest. He hit the ground on his side and slid in dirt and gravel. Momentum propelled him forward. He grabbed desperately at woody scrub, weeds or anything that would slow him down. Everything slipped through his gloved hands. He caught a brief glimpse of his bike as it summersaulted into the ravine. He fought to stay alert. Something struck his helmet. He lost consciousness and slid over the edge of the escarpment.

Eight

Monza and his two companions watched Gray in their rearview mirror before they scrambled from the van and hurried to stand on the brink of the canyon where they believed Gray's twisted and broken body lay hidden in the coal-black night far below. Monza threw his head back and laughed. He wished he could have seen Gray's face when he slid in the gravel and tumbled over the edge of the cliff.

"I'm only sorry it was too dark to see the fear on his face when he realized he was going to die and there was nothing he could do about it." Monza told the others. He laughed so hard that his entire body shook.

The two men with him looked at one another in stunned silence. They were dealing with a madman.

Monza crossed his arms, still laughing as he spoke his benediction. "I hope he was wide awake all the way down and each jab by every rock and stick hurt worse than the one before."

Suddenly there was an explosion. Startled they all ran back to the van and sped away into the night. They wanted to be miles away if someone heard the noise or spotted the flames.

Nine

A loud noise awoke Rand with a jolt. His heart rate skyrocketed. Someone, held his right hand. *Do not fear. I am with you.* When he opened his eyes, no one was there. His head throbbed, ears rang and everything around him seemed to spin. He barely made out the shape of his hand in front of his face. In his peripheral vision, he spied a fire in the distance. Red and yellow sparks twirled in eerie streaks into the inky-black night. *Where am I?*

He lay half immersed in cold gurgling water and was soaked to his skin. He shivered. *Breathe, pal.* Every inch of his body pulsated with agony. His right hip throbbed. He clenched his teeth, but could only manage small gasps of breath while anger incited his determination to survive.

Moving only his arms, he tried to pull himself out of the water. After several futile attempts, he lay helpless as one wave of nausea after another convulsed his body. Clamping his eyes shut, he willed the dizziness to pass. Finally, he was able to roll onto his left side and out of the water. Thankful the stream was shallow, he sat up slowly. Blood oozed down the side of his head beneath his helmet and further obstructed his vision. With trembling fingers, he discarded his useless gloves, carefully took off his helmet and dropped it beside him. He eased the bandanna from around his neck, carefully wound the material around his head and winced as he tied it in place.

Gingerly he touched his right leg and nearly passed out again. *Protect it, pal.* After a few minutes of trying to figure out what to do, he removed his tattered and water-logged leather jacket. Laying it aside, he shrugged out of his shirt, which clung to his skin. With shaky hands he wound it around his thigh. Clenching his jaw, he yelled as he tied it in a knot. Slowly he pulled his jacket back on while chills shook his entire body. Blood trickled down the side of his head and neck and oozed down his chest.

Rolling over with a groan, he pulled himself onto his knees and immediately collapsed. Every nerve in his entire body screamed in protest. With the side of his face pressed against the ground, he panted for several seconds before forcing his lungs to draw slow deep breaths to keep from hyperventilating. *Can't stay here, pal.*

Rising only on his hands he attempted to guess how far he fell. *Fifteen feet? Thirty?* He rested briefly before any attempt at the laborious climb. With his goal focused on the road above, he inched upward as he grasped clumps of scrub and rock. *Keep moving, pal.* He winced each time he managed a small thrust upward. He pushed with his left foot with what little strength he still possessed and dragged his useless right leg along as he went. Exhaustion overcame him after only a few inches. He sank to the ground and his chin plunged into a clump of scrub. He spit leaves and dirt. *Jesus, help me!*

With a moan, he resumed the relentless ascent. He clawed at dirt and gripped anything that would give him leverage. He pushed on and tried to ignore the spasms in his legs and hips while muscles in his arms and shoulders burned with over exertion. He pushed and pulled upward even though his strength oozed from his body along with his blood.

Minutes dragged by like eons or was it hours? Finally, he reached the dirt along the side of the road. He lay face down on his arms for several minutes, completely spent from the tortuous assent. *Stay awake, pal.* Every nerve and muscle in his body writhed in anguish. Turning on his left side he tried to sit up, but slumped onto his back in defeat. He squinted into the darkness and fought hard to remain conscious.

In addition to being half hidden by grass and weeds, all his clothing was black. *Send an angel!* He pleaded as moisture stung his eyes. With jaw set, he rolled slowly onto his side again. Somehow, he needed to make himself more visible without getting run over. His teeth chattered, his hands were almost numb and there was no feeling in his right leg or foot. A stabbing sensation in his hip took away his breath and everything faded to black.

Later a whimper invaded his semi-consciousness and something wet swept across his cheek. His mouth filled with bile as he stared into the face of . . . a wolf! He could scarcely breathe and had no strength left. But he would fight with sheer willpower if he had to defend himself.

A vehicle approached. The wolf ambled onto the road. He tried to prop himself up on one elbow. It made him dizzy and darkness again threatened to consume him. He tried to fight it off as he sank back onto the ground. Screeching tires and a yelp filled the stillness, but he couldn't summon enough energy to call for help.

Cab Martel was on his way home from visiting with a boy from the church youth group he led. His mind was occupied with the troubled teen whose parents had recently divorced. The youth was struggling with the separation.

A wolf ran in front of Cab's car and jerked him into the present. He swerved and it yelped when his front bumper clipped it. He stopped.

The animal favored a hind leg and limped to his door, stopped, stared at him and barked. He watched it run to the side of the road and come back to stare at him, whining. He rolled his window part way down while he tried to decide if it was tame or wild.

It appeared to be a German shepherd not a wolf as he first thought. It hung its front paws on his window and tried to put its head inside the car. Slowly he opened his door and the dog grabbed his jacket sleeve and tugged him out of the car. He laughed "Okay." He snatched his flashlight from the glovebox and turned to follow the dog to the side of the road where he found a man lying on his back.

Cautiously he dropped to his knees beside the man's body and shone the light on his face. "Rand!"

"Took, long enough. . .an-gel." His lips held an attempted, but crooked smile.

A grin passed quickly over Cab's cheerful face at Rand's attempted humor. Any other time, Cab would have laughed. "What happened?" He kept the light on Rand's face.

He squinted. "Got run. . .off. . .road."

Cab breathed a silent prayer for help. Quickly he assessed his friend's injuries, ripped off his jacket and shirt, tore off one of the sleeves and exchanged it with the dirty and bloodied rag around Rand's head.

Cab scrutinized him. "Can you sit up?"

"If. . .you. . .help." He managed between clenched teeth.

Cab peered down into the inky darkness. "What's burning?"

Rand stared at him as moisture pooled in his eyes. "Bike." He muttered between tight lips.

Cab's stomach churned and a shiver ran down his spine. "I'll be right back." He moved his car closer to Rand. Afterward, he opened the rear door and knelt at Rand's side. "Easy man, I'm going to help you onto the seat. Ready?"

Rand's brows furrowed and his chest heaved. "Yeah."

Cab put Rand's arm around his neck and as carefully as he could manage, hoisted Rand inside. It wasn't easy because Rand was six inches taller and several pounds heavier.

He squeezed his eyes shut as Cab eased him onto the rear seat.

Cab ran around to the other side, opened the door and carefully pulled Rand's body toward the left side of the car. That accomplished, he grabbed his jean jacket, rolled it into a makeshift pillow and put it under Rand's head. When he raised Rand's legs onto the seat, he passed out with a groan.

"Sorry, buddy." Cab closed the rear door and opened the front passenger one. After helping the dog inside the car, he scrambled into the driver's seat and sped down the road to Rod's house. "Thanks Lord, for the dog."

―――◈―――

Rod Gray was, sitting at the desk in his office. His pecan-brown hair fell across his forehead as he dipped his head to focus on the blueprint he was drawing when a car, speeding down the lane toward his house caught his attention. He leaped from his chair, rushed out of the den and to the front door. Turning on the outside light, he jerked the door open and stepped onto the porch as Cab's car came to a grinding stop beside the house.

He climbed out, yelling. "Call an ambulance!"

Rod spun around, ran to his desk phone, and dialed the emergency number. He was giving directions when Cab caught up with him.

He was panting. "Rand's been hurt!"

Rod's pulse escalated, he shoved the receiver into Cab's hands, and raced outside. He jerked open the rear passenger door, and climbed inside. "Rand." He whispered. Careful not to press against his brother, he gently grasped Rand's wrist and found a pulse. "Thank God."

"Here's some clean rags." Cab called from behind him. "Ambulance is on the way."

Saun, Rod's wife peered into the car. "What's going on?"

Rod wiped blood from Rand's face and pressed a clean cloth against the gash on his head. "Quick, bring some blankets." Rod ordered without taking his gaze off Rand's ashen skin.

Saun returned moments later with the blankets.

He took them, covered Rand, wound another cloth Cab gave him around Rand's head, and applied pressure to slow the bleeding. A siren wailed in the distance, but Rod didn't leave Rand's side.

The ambulance arrived and two medics leaped out of the back. "We'll take over sir." The first medic addressed Rod.

He backed out of the car and frowned as he observed them place a c-collar around Rand's neck. Afterward they used a back board to slide him from the car seat onto a stretcher and took him to the ambulance. Once inside, they fastened an oxygen mask over his mouth and nose, attached a blood pressure cuff and an intravenous pump. One medic rewrapped Rand's head with a clean bandage as the other medic cut away what was left of the leather clothes.

"How old is he?" The other medic asked Rod, who stood behind their truck and took note of everything they did.

"Thirty-one." Rod stared while they covered Rand with more blankets and applied metal clips to the stretcher to hold it in place.

The first medic nodded as he attached a cardiac monitor. "Any known allergic reactions to medication?"

"None to my knowledge."

The second medic closed the rear doors.

"We'll follow you." Rod shouted as he ran to Cab's car and they followed the ambulance.

Rod leaped from the car as soon as Cab pulled into the emergency entrance. The medics were talking to a doctor and two nurses when Rod entered the hospital.

"Let's get him to surgery." A doctor ordered.

A nurse addressed Rod, who was focused on the hospital staff, as they wheeled Rand down the hall. "Are you related to him?" She raised her voice.

Rod acknowledged her, but continued to watch the actions of the doctors with Rand until they disappeared around a corner. "He's, my brother."

"You'll need to check him in at the admittance desk." She indicated an area down the hall.

At the desk, he was bombarded by raucous noises. Patients were called to admitting stations, someone giggled, another moaned, a man swore, doctors were being paged over the intercom while in the background the glass door slid open and shut with a swish, swish.

"May I help you?" The admittance nurse sounded impatient when she thumped her stapler on the desk.

Rod's head snapped toward her. He'd been preoccupied, staring in the direction where he'd last seen Rand. Several minutes later with all the paperwork completed, he headed for the bank of elevators.

Cab tugged on an over-sized shirt he wore. "Saun gave me this." He remarked and pressed the up button.

Rod waited for the door to open and stepped into the elevator after Cab. When the doors opened again, he exited with Cab on his heels and they walked to the waiting area in silence. Rod chose a seat near the hall, sat down and rolled his shoulders. Someone paged a doctor and he observed the nurses who scurried along the hall. A staff member in dark blue scrubs pushed a metal cart loaded with towels and headed in the opposite direction from the nurse's station.

The murmur of voices as they exchanged information and instructions to staff came from there. Rod listened and hoped to catch news of Rand. A doctor stopped and spoke with those who were at the desk.

"If it wasn't for the dog, I would have missed him." Cab broke the silence between them.

Rod's gaze snapped to Cab's face, who sat in a chair next to him. "What?"

"A dog forced me to stop when I hit her."

Rod raised his eyebrows. "You hit a dog?"

Cab chuckled. "Clipped her. She was trying to get my attention."

"When? What dog?"

Cab grinned. "I'm trying to tell you. A dog was with Rand. She forced me to stop and nearly dragged me from my car. She led me to him."

Rod frowned. "What happened?"

Cab blinked. "I left her with Saun."

"To Rand not the dog." He growled.

Cab offered him a bemused grin. "He said he was run off the road. I found him beside Old Canyon Road."

Rod's stomach churned. "Run off the road. . .in a canyon?" He whispered hoarsely.

Cab rested his hand on Rod's shoulder. "We'll have to wait until he can give us more details."

Rod leaned forward in his chair with his elbows on his knees and clasped his hands. "He was losing a lot of blood. I think he was in shock, when you brought him to the house."

Cab's steady gaze held Rod's attention. "He's been in good physical condition and he's a fighter. He'll be okay, buddy."

Rod rubbed the back of his neck as he sat up straight. "I hope so." He pinched the bridge of his nose.

Cab gave him a reassuring wink. "Doctors perform all kinds of miracles these days and don't forget he's in the Lord's hands. He'll be okay, but it may take time, buddy."

Rod gave him a quick nod as he scrutinized the immediate area. "Please God, help Rand recover completely." He mumbled quietly.

Cab pulled a pack of gum from his pocket, extracted a stick and offered it to Rod.

He shook his head, got up and crossed the room to stare out a window. An emergency vehicle was heading down the street away from the hospital with its lights flashing. Cars pulled to the curb until it passed. A boy bounced a ball on the sidewalk. A woman and small child waited to cross the street. He frowned. The rest of the world continued as if nothing had happened, while Rand's life was severely altered. He turned away from the window, trudged back to the chairs, and sat next to his friend. He picked up a Newsweek Magazine from a nearby table and checked his watch. Only an hour passed since they arrived on this floor.

Cab stood, folded his wad of gum in the wrapper and stuck it in his pocket. "I'll get us some coffee."

Rod regarded him as a corner of his mouth lifted briefly. "You're wearing one of my shirts." It hung off Cab's shoulders, almost reached his knees, and the sleeves were rolled up to his elbows.

He grinned. "Yeah, Saun gave it to me at the house."

His smile faded as Cab disappeared around a corner. He leafed through a Time Magazine without reading anything and laid it on the table beside him. Picking up another one, he read an article about the second attempt to assassinate President Ford on September 22. After he finished that article, he searched for something else to occupy his mind as he waited for a report on Rand. He skimmed a few more stories, but unable to focus on them, tossed the magazine on the table with the others.

How long did Rand lay on the side of the road before Cab found him? Rod shuddered as his thoughts formed unwelcomed images in his mind.

Wings of Steel

Did something go mechanically wrong with his bike? He could accept that possibility, but still couldn't imagine anything serious enough to make Rand lose control.

He claimed he'd been riding for years and Rod didn't doubt him. Rand casually mentioned once that he raced trail bikes besides being able to do some trick maneuvers. Rod once spied some small trophies stashed behind the bench seat of Rand's truck. Rod was aware that his brother was adept at most everything he did, but wasn't one to brag about his accomplishments.

An image of Rand as he took charge of the renovation work on Candlewood passed through his mind. It was Rand who saved Tommy's life last year when he was hit by a car. His brother was good at handling emergency situations with calm self-assurance.

Cab returned with coffee in two Styrofoam cups.

Rod took note of Cab's somewhat comical appearance. What was he doing before he found Rand? He raised his head with a brief smile as he accepted the cup. "Thanks. How'd you happen to be on that road tonight?"

"I spent the evening with one of the boys in my youth group and was on my way back to the village."

Rod tried to focus on their conversation. The coffee was hot and strong and he drank it slowly more for something to do than for enjoyment.

"No word yet, I take it." Cab commented as he sat next to Rod.

He shook his head, finished his coffee and squashed the cup in his hand. He got up, walked across the room and tossed it in a trash receptacle. "I'll be back."

He meandered down the hall and entered the men's room. A toilet flushed and an older man emerged from a stall, walked up to the sink, washed his hands, and quickly left.

The room reeked of cleaners and bleach. Rod wrinkled his nose. A green stream oozed from the soap dispenser. The water-streaked mirrors needed cleaned and the sink counter was smeared with soapy goo. He glanced at his watch: 2:13 AM. They'd arrived on this floor three long hours ago.

He stood, and stared for a moment at his image in the mirror above the sink. When it blurred, he turned on a faucet and ran cool water over his hands and raised them to his face. He stood for several minutes with moist fingers pressed against his burning eyes. Once he received a measure of relief, he snatched some paper towels from the dispenser and dried his face and hands. Sighing, he tossed the paper at the overflowing trash receptacle, left the room, and took a deep breath. The hospital was apparently short-staffed on this shift.

In the waiting area, Cab sat with his head bowed. Quietly, Rod occupied the chair beside his best friend, thankful for his prayers. Rod tried to pray, but instead imagines of Rand losing control of his bike filled his mind. He stroked his upper lip with an index finger.

One of the things Rand seemed to enjoy most was riding mountain trails. Rod was aware his brother often sought for things that challenged his abilities. His brow wrinkled and he scowled at his watch: 3:24 AM. Another hour passed since he last checked. As if on cue, a doctor approached them.

"Mr. Gray?"

Rod cleared his throat as he stood. "How is he?"

"I'm Doctor Stockton." He extended his hand. "Your brother was in shock and experienced severe hypothermia when he arrived. His right leg is fractured along with several ribs and he has multiple contusions."

"How's his head?" Cab interjected, standing beside Rod.

"He has a concussion. We are monitoring for infection. Were you present when he was hurt?"

Cab shook his head. "I found him lying beside the road."

Dr. Stockton addressed them both. "Do you know how he was injured?"

"He mumbled something about his bike being run off the road." Cab answered.

The doctor's lips formed a straight line. "He's fortunate he wasn't hurt worse."

Rod swallowed against the dryness in his throat. "But he will recover?"

The doctor gave him a direct look. "We'll observe him for a few days until we determine the extent of nerve and muscle damage."

Rod frowned. "I'd like to see him."

"He's in ICU, unit 220, just beyond the nurse's station. We have him under sedation so he will not regain consciousness for several hours." Something behind them appeared to capture the doctor's attention. "If you'll excuse me." He responded and quickly left.

Rod raised an eyebrow.

"Go ahead. I'll wait." Cab cuffed his shoulder.

―――――⟨⚭⟩―――――

Rod entered Rand's room to discover an IV pole with a line was attached to his arm above his wrist. He was lying on his left side and the hospital gown had pulled away from his back above the sheet. Rod stared at the marks on his shoulders and gently covered his exposed skin. It appeared Rand had issues in his past that he had never mentioned. Beeps from the cardiac monitor and IV pump filled the room and mingled with the traffic and voices in the hall and adjoining unit. Rod moved a side chair and placed it near the head of the bed. The bed clothes were raised to revealed where the bandages, covered Rand's legs.

Rod surveyed the pale walls and large window with drawn curtains. The room contained a small sink, closet, bathroom, and a rolling table and nightstand with two drawers. Both side rails of the bed were locked in place. The acrid scent of cleaning supplies, astringent and over-bleached sheets brought back unpleasant memories.

He shuddered. He had occupied a room just like this one after being trapped in his bungalow by the fire that destroyed it and almost claimed his life. The room was also similar to the one Tommy was in while he recovered from being hit by a car. He had almost lost a leg, but God was merciful and answered their prayers for the boy. He would always have a limp, but even that became barely noticeable as his leg had healed, but Tommy wasn't as active as Rand or as old, not that thirty-one was old.

He reminded himself that Rand was generally optimistic about most things, like Cab. But Rand also felt things more deeply than he allowed most people to see. Rod's brow furrowed as he stroked his upper lip. He kept his own emotions closed to the outside world and guessed that it was a trait they shared. However, this was different from anything Rand had ever experienced, at least to Rod's knowledge. Was this one more thing he would not be able to shrug off or walk away from like his tussle with the dock workers? "God, help him rely on You for strength that he won't have right away." He whispered and raised his head when Cab entered the room.

He stood on the other side of the bed. "Apparently the doc didn't plan on coming back. The nurse at the desk told me he was scheduled to return in the morning around breakfast time."

He briefly acknowledged Cab and swallowed hard as he gazed at the cuts and bruises on Rand's face and hands.

Rand stirred as if he heard their voices and the covers slipped, exposing his shoulders again. The tie around his neck had come undone and the gown pulled away from his body as he thrashed in the bed with a moan.

Cab eyed Rod before pulling the covers up to Rand's neck as Rod had done earlier. "The doc mentioned contusions—"

"Bone bruises." He frowned as his body almost ached while he stared at Rand's pale and drawn features. He observed Cab, who placed his hand lightly on Rand's side and prayed for his strength and healing.

After praying, he peered at Rod. "I'll stay here if you want to call Saun. There's a pay phone in the hall near the men's room." He offered.

"Thanks." Rod gave him a curt nod and left the room. He stared at the clock on a wall near the phone: 4:27 AM. She'd be waiting for his call. He picked up the receiver and dialed. "Saun, he's out of surgery. In ICU. They won't be able to determine the extent of his injuries until they run some tests." He tried to swallow around the lump in his throat. "Pray he doesn't have muscle or nerve damage. Yes, Cab's still here, thanks. I'll call you after he awakes. I love you too."

When Rod got back to the room, a nurse was standing with her back toward him. She was adjusting the medication flowing into a line in Rand's arm, which was attached to a bottle hanging beside his bed. Rod regarded her in silence as she retied the opening of Rand's hospital gown.

When she finished, she studied Rod for a brief moment. "He'll be unconscious for a few more hours. You two should go home and get some rest."

Rod sat on the bedside chair. "I'm staying."

She checked Rand's chart at the foot of his bed. "I understand." She glanced at Cab and left.

Cab placed a hand on Rod's shoulder. "I'll be back later. Call if you need anything."

He nodded his head. The hospital staff did all they could do for Rand, but Rod couldn't bring himself to leave. He couldn't help wondering about his half-brother's past and the marks on his shoulders. "God, please heal Rand of his past and present."

Ten

Netty sat at her dining table, drinking her second cup of coffee late Sunday morning, putting off cleaning her apartment. She was still dressed in the clothes she'd worn the day before, a pair of orange short shorts and a black T-shirt with no shoes. She'd stayed up until after two, waiting for the sound of Rand's bike or a light to appear in one of Candlewood's windows, but fell asleep on her couch.

She peered through the window beside the table and scowled at his truck, which was parked in front of the mansion, but still no bike. She stared at the vase on her table, now empty of the poppies he gave her the night they celebrated their birthdays. They recently began spending more quality time together and he actually planned their special birthday celebration.

When he walked her to her door that night, he kissed her forehead, her cheek and then his lips briefly met hers. She'd responded, leaning into him, intending to prolong the kiss until they were both breathless and he was unable to resist spending more time with her. Her cheeks flushed just thinking about being in such close proximity to him. She touched her lips, remembering her ecstasy when he responded with like passion. She couldn't remember any man affecting her the way he did, but he'd pulled away too fast.

She huffed. Not only did he give her the brush off, but had the nerve to invite her to go to church with him, practically in the same breath. How quickly things happened totally opposite of what she'd planned. She drove to Sunnyside to visit a friend the next day in order to avoid him and stayed for the week. She'd returned to the village just yesterday afternoon.

A knock on her door interrupted her musing. She rushed to open it, found Cab standing on the fire escape outside, and her hand flew to her breast. "Did something happen to Rand?"

His smile wobbled as he gave her a once-over. "Can I come in?"

"Sure." She opened the door wider. She and Cab were friends, even though they mostly saw one another when either Rand or Rod were present. Cab never came alone to visit her. "I was just about to have another cup of coffee. Want to join me?"

"Thanks, I could use a nice strong cup." He followed her as far as her dinette table and sat down.

"Coming right up, just the way you like it." She took another cup from the cupboard, filled it for him and refilled her own. Taking them to the table, she sat across from him. "You look like you've been up all night." She appraised him over the rim of her cup. His eyes were puffy and his brow was unusually wrinkled for his care-free, happy personality. The smattering of scruff on his face was also an unusual addition.

"I spent most of the night at Lakeside hospital." He yawned as he reached across the table and covered her hand with his.

Her eyebrows rose. "Hospital!" Coffee sloshed on the table as she quickly set her cup down. "Rand?" She gasped and watched his brow crease even deeper. "Something happened to Rand?" She folded her arms over her stomach, which was suddenly queasy.

His head bobbed. "He had an accident."

She stared at him, blinking rapidly. "Is, is he alright? Why—why didn't someone call me?"

He shook his head. "It was late. Rod and I couldn't think about anything else. I'm sorry, Netty."

The coffee she'd just swallowed soured in her throat. "What happened? I bet Rod called Saun."

"He said he was run off the road and—"

"Run off the road ... on his bike!" She dismissed his explanation with a flap of her hand. "How?"

"We don't know. He was still unconscious when I left. I found him on Old Canyon Road sometime after nine o'clock last night. We were informed he has a broken leg, some fractured ribs and a concussion."

She took a small sip from her cup and folded her arms in front of her on the table. "I can't believe he lost control as meticulous as he is about that bike." She knew Rand kept a trophy behind the seat of his pickup. She'd taken the liberty to inspect it when he wasn't looking. She didn't ask how old he was when he received it, but his name was inscribed on it and he'd won first place in some kind of bike competition. "Have you ever seen him ride?"

"Just around the village." His expression grew thoughtful.

"I've watched him ride and even been behind him. You'd think he was one with that bike." She swirled coffee around in her cup.

"Maybe he overcompensated or something. Couldn't see well enough in the dark or maybe tried to avoid hitting something. A German shepherd forced me to stop, maybe the dog got in his way."

She frowned, trying to imagine Rand, the man who mastered practically everything he attempted, mechanically speaking at least. She couldn't fathom him making a false move on his bike. "Was anyone else involved?"

"Maybe the dog."

She stared at him with her mouth hanging open. "A dog! I guess that could explain it, but I think he'd have stopped instead of wrecked."

He reached in his pocket for a pack of gum and pulled out a stick. He offered it to her and she took it. "That's an interesting possibility. Rod and I were focused more on what happened than how. But that dog got so close to my car that I clipped it. I wouldn't have noticed him on the side of the road if it wasn't for her. I'm telling you, Netty, it was a miracle! It was dark and so were his clothes."

She crossed her arms and grasped them. "You found him on the side . . ." She paused and shook her head in disbelief. "How long will he be in the hospital?"

"Don't know. When I left, he was still unconscious. I knew you'd want to know, but for now his visits are limited to family."

"I'll just tell them I'm his sister." She told him with a smug expression.

He eyed her and finished his coffee. "I talked to Saun a little while ago and she told me Rod's still there. I'd better be going. I need to get back to the hospital." He stood and began walking toward the door.

She got up and followed him. "Thanks for telling me."

Netty's lips flattened as she sank onto her couch, grabbed the phone on the table beside it and dialed. Before Saun could even say, hello, Netty yelled. "Why didn't you call me? I was awake half the night worrying about Rand and wondering why he wasn't home."

"I'm sorry Netty. It got pretty crazy around here. Cab brought him, then called an ambulance an—"

"I get that, but why didn't you call me?" She fought back tears.

"Netty, please listen to me a minute. When the ambulance left, Rod and Cab followed it. Tommy and I were trying to take care of a dog Cab hit. Rod didn't call me until after four this morning. He asked me not to tell anyone until he received a report on the extent of Rand's injuries. I'm sorry, Netty, I—"

"I'm sorry too, Saun!" She hung up the phone with a bang before she said something she'd regret. "She never thinks for herself." She huffed. Tears rolled down her cheeks and she didn't try to stop them. Her chin trembled. They'd shut her out completely. Rand was a good friend. They were even in the process of developing a closer relationship. It was no secret, but they, no Rod, didn't approve of her and Rand being together.

The brothers became really close to each other over the last year since Rand showed up out of nowhere. She bit down on her bottom lip. She'd have to try and curb her anger toward Rod. She didn't want to ruin what little friendship they still shared since Rand became a Christian.

She sank onto the couch, snatched a pillow and buried her face in it and let her tears flow unchecked. When they were spent, she got up, went to the bathroom and washed her face. She'd wait until tomorrow and then go visit Rand whether Rod liked it or not.

That afternoon Netty was heading for her kitchen when there was a knock at her door. When she opened it, she drew in a breath. Rod was standing on her porch.

She whirled away from him, leaving the door open. He probably came to reprimand her for yelling at Saun.

"Netty, I am sorry. You can blame me if you like, but news like this is best told in person, not over the phone. Cab informed me that he stopped by, but I wanted to stop as well."

She slowly faced him. He had circles under his eyes and his clothes were unusually rumpled. He appeared sincere so she let it go. "Will he be alright?" Her chin trembled.

Rod nodded. "He's still heavily medicated so not very coherent when he is awake. The doctors are running tests and haven't yet been able to determine anything definite. Right now, visiting is restricted."

She sniffed. "Is there anything I can do in the meantime?"

"Would you mind keeping an eye on Candlewood? Cab and I are alternating times at the hospital."

Her lips puckered in a smirk. "Not at all. I kind of like the old place."

Rod smiled for the first time since he'd entered her apartment. "Either Saun or I will call as soon as he's able to have visitors. When you go, don't expect him to respond much." He took her hand in his and placed a key in it. "This will work for any door."

Netty peered up at him for a moment as she curled her fingers around the key. "I guess I owe Saun an apology."

His expression grew a little brighter. "I'm sure she would appreciate it." He turned toward the open door. "I'm going home to change and get back there."

As he stepped onto the balcony, she grasped his shirtsleeve. "Thanks for stopping."

He gave her a one arm hug. "Rand will be alright. It will just take time. Try not to worry."

She crossed her arms and studied him. "Good advice for you too, Rod." She emphasized his name.

A small sigh escaped his lips as he descended the steps.

After Rod left, Netty stood for several minutes and stared out her window at Candlewood. Just the thought of the old empty mansion made it difficult to hold back tears. What would she ever do with all the lonely nights or even the days for that matter? She swallowed hard as she focused on the key, which was clasped in her hand.

Was Rod intentionally vague about Rand's condition. Was he hurt worse than Rod said? She took into account Rod's expressions and the seriousness of his tone not to mention the condition of his clothes.

It was obvious to her that he tried to soften the blow, and tried to give her hope against hope. How many people survived a motorcycle accident? She glanced out her kitchen window and made up her mind to check on Candlewood at once. After all it had been at least twenty-four hours since anyone walked through those empty rooms. Just the thought of it made her throat constrict uncomfortably.

She rushed out the door and ran down the fire escape steps. It was Sunday afternoon and not even Willis would be working or be there to spy on her. She could cross the street, enter the mansion, and return to her apartment without anyone's knowledge. And if she decided to spend some time in Rand's room and went home after dark, who would know? The café was the only business in the village open on Sunday and it was only open until three to accommodate the after-church crowd.

She climbed the mansion's steps, let herself inside, and closed and locked the door behind her. She stood in the foyer for only a few seconds before she chose where to begin her search for anything that needed a woman's touch.

She couldn't pass Rand's shop. She opened the door and breathed deeply of cut wood and the scent of oils and other things he used to polish and perfect his creations. She smoothed a hand over pieces of redwood and pine that were sanded so that they felt like glass. Her eyes filled with tears as she touched a hammer, a T-square and his safety goggles.

She snatched a broom and a dustpan from a corner and swept up all the sawdust and small wood shavings, and emptied them in a trash can that was mostly full. Maybe she'd even empty it before she left. She pivoted slowly and tried to imagine Rand there working. She eyed the drill and pictured him steadily and precisely drilling each hole in the length of wood she held in her hands. Just holding something he recently touched made her feel closer to him.

She left his shop, strolled into the library and picked up a book he'd obviously been reading. She opened it to a page with a turned down corner and read a description for a preflight check. With a sigh, she recalled how they'd sat in this very room and he told her about a book he was reading. She tried to kiss him, but he wanted to talk about a pilot. She laid the book down exactly as she found it and continued her inspection in the kitchen. She found a dirty plate, coffee cup, fork and spoon on the sink along with a dirty skillet. The remnants of his breakfast before he'd left that day? She swiped a hand over her eyes and she proceeded to his bedroom.

She grinned when she observed the room. A pair of Levi's, a long sleeve shirt, T-shirt, and socks lay strewn around the room. She picked them all up and carried them to the laundry room, threw a load in the washer from the clothes bin and went back to his bedroom. She picked up papers and odds and ends. The things she couldn't find a place for she stacked on his desk.

She paused to study a black and white photo of an older couple and wondered who they were. After putting it back on the desk, she picked up a leather letter opener that was limp and cracked. She assumed it was a keepsake of sorts. She gazed at the picture and thought it could have belonged to that couple.

She turned in the desk chair and perused the rest of the room and inhaled Rand's scent, which still lingered. His bed was unmade and the covers hung over the side of the bed where he'd hastily gotten out of it. She'd also wash them before she left. He could come home to a clean room and a nice fresh bed. It was the very least she could do for him. Afterward she cleaned the bathroom as well.

When she finished cleaning, straightening and doing laundry it was late. She needed to get up early and have her shop ready before her first appointment at nine. She retrieved his shirts from the dryer and placed them on hangers in his closet, she spied his four cowboy hats on the top shelf, a white, a black, a tan, and a gray one.

She didn't even know he had a white one. He mostly wore the black or tan, and she remembered he'd worn the gray one a few times. He'd commented once that it was his favorite. She was partial to that one as well, because the contrast between his dark hair and eyes and that hat, did funny things to her insides. She snatched it along with a silver-blue long-sleeve shirt. She felt slightly guilty, but told herself she'd return them if...when he came home. She left the mansion, and locked the door behind her.

Back in her apartment she sank onto her couch, clutched the shirt to her chest and set the hat beside her. Tears streamed down her cheeks as the real possibility of his failure to recover struck her with full force. She sobbed uncontrollably. If Rand never came home, at least she had something of his to treasure forever.

Eleven

R and awoke to harsh florescent ceiling lights. Squinting he lay still and listened as a doctor was paged. Slowly he started to run his fingers through his hair and frowned. "Ow." He gently explored the bandage on his head, which throbbed. He eyed a bottle, which hung on a pole near him, lowered his hand and rested it on the cold side rail.

"My legs?" He whispered as he wiggled the toes on his left foot and drew a short-ragged breath. "Hurts." Unable to get any response from his right leg, he gripped the rail so hard that his knuckles turned white. He tried to sit up, but dropped back onto the pillow with a groan. Perspiration beaded on his forehead as he expelled a breath.

The last thing he recalled was Cab, lifting him onto the seat of a car. Memory of what happened came flooding back to him in three-dimensional Technicolor. His chest suddenly felt tight and he fought to breathe. *Hope you don't have to deal with just one leg, pal?*

A nurse entered the room. "Good morning, Mr. Gray, time for your meds."

He flinched at her unexpected presence. "My leg?" He tried to raise an eyebrow, which made his entreaty appear more urgent.

"You still have two." She smiled sympathetically and raised the head of his bed and then lifted the blankets over his feet and legs so he was assured of what she claimed.

Thanks God. He attempted to smile, but it felt like a grimace.

"Your recovery will take time and work, but you can do it." She smoothed the sheet and blanket back over his feet and gave him some pills and a glass of water with a straw.

He drank it thankful for a little reprieve from his dry mouth even though his throat burned when he swallowed.

"Let's get this bandage off your head." She carefully removed it and then lowered the head of his bed. "The medicine will help with the pain so you can rest."

"What time is it?" As the pounding in his head began to subside, his breathing returned to normal, but his stomach felt empty.

She replaced the bottle that hung beside his bed. "It's just past eight."

"I'm hungry."

"They're coming down the hall now with breakfast."

"Bacon, eggs over easy and toast." He was half joking, just swallowing water was difficult. "I think I could eat a twenty-ounce steak."

She shook her head. "Jell-O and chicken broth." She replied with a sympathetic smile and wrapped a blood pressure cuff around his upper arm, resting it between her waist and elbow.

He mentally gagged at the menu offering. "Coffee, skip the rest!" He griped not appreciating her attempted humor. *Jell-O and chicken broth, no way. you're hungry enough to eat a whole cow, pal.*

"Sorry, doctor's orders, no caffeine."

"When can I go home?" He surveyed the room, hoping for an escape route. *You'll starve if you don't get out of here soon.*

"Your doctor should be in around eleven. You can ask him."

He got a whiff of acrid smells as her movements stirred the air in the room. His mouth was dry as a desert and he swallowed several times. "Could I have some more water?"

She filled a pitcher, set it on the tray table, poured water in a small plastic glass and gave it to him.

"Thanks." He noticed the way she perused his chart as he drank slowly, hoping the moisture would soothe his throat and calm the nausea. "Is something wrong?" His heartrate began to pick up again.

She replaced the chart on the end of his bed and connected with his concerned expression. "Just checking when you're next meds are due." She threw over her shoulder and left the room.

———⋈⋈⋈———

As the nurse left, Rod, entered with a Styrofoam cup in his hand. "Good morning, sleepy head." He was relieved to find Rand awake and alert.

Rand gawked at him. "Your shaver broke?"

Rod quirked an eyebrow and tossed his hair out of his eyes with a quick jerk of his head. "I guess that bump on your head didn't affect you too much." He sat on a bedside chair and observed Rand intently.

Rand positioned himself so he was able to peer at Rod and a grin pulled at one corner of his mouth.

Rod appraised him over the rim of his cup. He knew his brother was up to something.

"You brought me coffee?"

"Yes, and I'm drinking it." Rod hid a quick grin behind his cup. *He's up to his old tricks so he must be better than he appears.*

"You're no help." Rand attempted a scowl and crossed his arms.

"What is that supposed to mean?" Rod took another drink.

"Just wait." He muttered something unintelligible.

A young woman with black curly hair in an orderly's uniform entered with a tray, which held Jell-O and a cup of light-yellow liquid. "Here's your breakfast, Mr. Gray." She set the tray on the moveable table and pushed it in front of him.

"Is there something else to drink?" He grumbled.

She tilted her head. "How about herbal tea?"

He wrinkled his nose. "Anything's better than chicken broth!"

She giggled. "Honestly, I don't blame you. I'll get you some tea."

When she left the room, Rod raised his eyebrows. "No caffeine?"

Rand mimicked a male voice he heard from the hall outside his door. "Give him coffee not chicken broth."

The orderly returned and appeared puzzled. "Did I hear Dr. Preston in here?"

Rand tried to quirk an eyebrow. "He's under the bed."

She started to stoop down, but stopped herself and laughed. "Oh, you're an ornery one! I'll have to keep an eye on you."

"Promise?" He winked, but it too was distorted.

She chortled. "Here's your tea, Mr. Gray." She placed a paper cup on his tray.

"No mister, sweetheart."

She winked at him. "Okay, Groucho."

He threw a glance at Rod. "She's good."

Rod smirked and took a drink from his cup. "Don't encourage him."

She grinned at Rand. "I'm Anita and I'll be back to check on you later, baby!" She gently patted his shoulder and left the room.

Rand eyed Rod with a wry grin. "She loves me!"

"Drink your tea." Rod got up, shut Rand's door, tossed his empty cup in a trash can and sat down next to the bed. "What happened that night?"

Rand was silent as he met Rod's direct gaze over his cup. "You mean last night?"

Rod crossed his arms and prepared himself for questions Rand would ask once he understood how much time had passed while he was mostly unconscious. "The night of your wreck."

Rand avoided eye contact. "Wasn't a wreck."

Rod leaned forward. "Then what went wrong with your bike?"

His nostrils flared. "It was done on purpose."

"What do you mean?"

He peered at Rod and shook his head slightly. "It was dark, happened fast."

Rod's jaw was set as he studied Rand. "What happened?"

"Got run off the road."

Rod breathed deeply and steepled his fingers. "Are you sure?"

He bounced a curled knuckle against his mouth. "Tried to knock me off balance first."

Rod pressed his lips together without a comment while he imagined the scene Rand described.

He met his direct gaze. "That didn't work so they slammed on their brakes in front of me." He paused and stared at the foot of the bed. His voice was thick with emotion when he muttered quietly. "It was Jess's bike."

Rod dropped his focus to the floor as he recalled Rand's quick trip to Arizona on his birthday to pick up his present. He could still remember the joy on his brother's face when he rode onto Rod's property the next day. Rand took him and Tommy for a ride and spent a large part of Saturday evening telling them stories of the rides and camping trips he and Jess enjoyed. "Do you think it was someone you know?"

Rand squashed the empty paper cup in his hand. "You hang around your cop friends too much." He tossed the cup at the trashcan and his teeth clenched with the effort. It missed and fell on the floor. A pained expression crossed his face. "I'm sorry. I shouldn't have said that, but you worry too much. They'll say I lost control and—"

"But if that isn't true?" Rod pressed his lips together.

"Can we just drop it?" Rand stuck a spoon in the Jell-O, and shoved the tray away. "Has the doctor talked to you?"

Rod gave him a curt nod. He'd changed the subject so Rod followed his example. "Your right leg is fractured and you have a concussion and some cracked ribs. They've kept you under sedation for the last few days, but your surgeon is confident you will recover with the help of physical therapy." He couldn't imagine how Rand would cope if he didn't recover completely.

His brow puckered. "They keep everything pretty numb and since it's wrapped, I can't tell how bad it is."

Rod stroked one side of his upper lip. "I wouldn't have let them do anything drastic without your consent."

Rand scrutinized him with furrowed brow. "Your shaver isn't broke." He studied Rod's face. "You've been here all night!"

He ran a hand over the stubble on his chin, aware that dark circles beneath his eyes were evidence of his lack of sleep. "Actually, Cab and I have been here for the last few days."

Rand's eyebrows rose. "How long have I been here?"

Rod's lips pressed into a thin line. "Since late Friday night. This is Thursday." The image of Rand lying on the back seat of Cab's car, flashed through Rod's mind and he dropped his gaze to the bed.

Rand drew an audible breath. "I've been here a whole week."

Unable to respond because of sudden dryness in his throat, Rod's answer was a mere nod.

"You should go home and get some rest."

"I am now that I've seen how you're doing." He stood, tightened his hands into fists and then flexed his fingers. "I'll come back later."

"Wait a minute. Did you say this is Thursday?"

"Yes."

Rand frowned. "You don't wear jeans and polo shirts to work."

"I took some time off. Netty will be coming to visit soon." It wouldn't surprise him if she'd already come.

Rand crossed his arms. "I appreciate the visits, but you don't need to worry about me. I'll be fine. I just need to get out of here."

Rod gently touched his shoulder. "Now that you're alert, we don't want you to stay any longer than necessary."

Rand grinned. "That's music to my ears."

Later that morning, Rod stopped to speak with Sheriff Gus Palmer.

Wings of Steel

The copper-haired lawman sat at his desk and was wearing his usual tan-colored uniform. He was going over some paperwork and raised his head as Rod entered. "Are you working from home these days or is this a social call?" His countenance held a wrinkled brow.

Rod stepped quickly to the chair next to the desk and sat down. "I don't know if you heard, but Rand's in the hospital." He hoped Gus wouldn't pass off Rand's wreck as insignificant like he suggested.

Gus frowned and shoved his paperwork aside. "I heard he wrecked his bike. How's he doing?"

Rod's lips flattened into a thin line at the sheriff's comment. "He said someone caused it. I would like to know who and why." He paused to take a deep, calming breath. "I just came from visiting him." He wished he had more details for Gus.

Gus leaned forward. "Is he okay?"

Rod gave him a quick nod. "He will be eventually. He has some fractured ribs among other injuries." He spoke through clenched teeth as he pictured the agony on his brother's face every time he attempted to move too much or too quick.

Gus sighed and picked up a pencil from his desk and rolled it between his thumb and forefinger. "So, you think it was intentional?"

Rod hesitated and weighed his words before he spoke. "Rand said it was." He remembered the way Rand bounced a curled knuckle against his mouth when he described the incident. Rod couldn't help wondering what if anything the gesture meant.

Gus rubbed the back of his neck without making eye contact. "Did he get a license number or can he describe the vehicle?"

Rod's jaw clenched. "It was a van. He said it was dark and all happened fast. There's a stream at the bottom of that gulley. Whoever ran him off the road likely hoped he'd drown if he survived the fall. We need to find out who did it and why."

Gus rubbed his chin. "Now don't jump to conclusions. I'll check on the two he fired from the docks a few weeks ago. But I have to level with you, Rod, I need proof of foul play before I can do anything."

Rod scrutinized the sheriff for several seconds before he got up and started for the door. "You know about the incident on the docks?"

"I have a friend who works for the Montecito police. They took the report and when Leo found out Rand lives in Fire River, he called me."

Rod stared at him as he opened the door. "Rand said it was intentional and I believe him."

Gus tossed the pencil on his desk. "I'll check into it and go talk to him myself. Maybe he'll have remembered more by then."

Rod nodded without a backward glance. "Thanks, I appreciate it." He closed the door behind him. For now, that was all he could expect from Gus.

After Rod left the hospital Rand went over the details of the incident, at least what he could remember. He studied his bandaged hands and thanked God that he was wearing leather gear or it would have been a lot worse. *But you've been here for almost a week, pal.*

He lay in bed with his eyes squeezed tight while he tried to recall every detail immediately after he awoke. He thought he heard a voice, but when he opened his eyes, no one was there and the pressure he'd felt on his hand upon regaining consciousness was gone. He pondered the real sensation of a person grasping his hand. His eyes flew open at the sound of footsteps and he focused on Cab's face.

"Hey, buddy, how're you doing?" He entered with his usual energetic step and customary smile. "Hope I didn't wake you." He pulled a chair beside the bed.

"More than ready to get out of here."

Cab bobbed his head and raised the Bible he was holding. "I thought you might like to have this. It could help you pass some time while you're here."

Rand stared at him with his mouth hanging open.

Cab leaned toward him. "What's wrong?"

Rand gave his head a slight shake. "I've been trying to figure out something."

Cab crossed his arms. "Anything I can help with?"

"I was thinking about how I woke up when the bike exploded and even though it startled me, I sort of ignored it. But before I opened my eyes, I thought someone was holding my right hand, which was stretched over my head. Also, a couple times while I tried to get to the road, I thought I heard a voice, but no one was there."

Cab grinned. "I'm glad I brought your Bible. It sounds to me like it was the Lord speaking to you. Do you remember anything you heard?"

Rand smirked. "Why would God speak to me?"

Cab reached through the rail on the side of the bed and grasp Rand's arm. "You belong to Him. He loves you and protected you from worse injury. He also sent you help."

"I think." Rand scrubbed a hand over his face. "I heard something like, don't fear or I'll help you. I'm not sure. I was really trying to focus on getting out of there."

Cab smiled and opened Rand's Bible. "Let me read something to you from the book of Isaiah, chapter forty-one. 'For I am the Lord your God, who upholds your right hand.'" Cab paused to give Rand a direct look and then resumed reading. "'Who says to you, do not fear, I will help you.'"

Rand stared at Cab, blinking rapidly. "Let me see that."

Cab gave him the Bible and pointed to the verse he'd just read.

Rand read it once, twice and then stared at the words until the page blurred. "Do you think He really held my hand?"

Cab's eyes twinkled. "The important thing is what you think."

Rand turned back a corner of the page and closed the Bible. "I was talking to myself the whole time, at least I thought I was. Does that mean He was listening?"

Cab's smile was even wider. "You called me angel when I found you. Did you ask Him for one?"

Rand couldn't think of a response, just opened his mouth and then closed it before jamming his fingers through his hair. "Jesus, You really did help me." He whispered.

Cab, grasped Rand's hand and closed his eyes. "Father, God, let Your words to Rand sink deep into his soul and help him to grasp how much You really love him." He opened his eyes. "I really should go and let you talk your Father." He stood. "If you need anything or have any more questions, call me anytime."

Rand peered up at him. "Thanks."

Cab stood. "See you soon, man."

It was almost three that afternoon when Netty drove her car into the hospital parking lot. She took a stick of gum from her purse and popped it in her mouth. She was wearing designer jeans, a pale-blue silk blouse, strappy navy-blue sandals and carried a matching purse. She got out of her car and rushed inside to find the reception desk. "Hi, can you tell me Rand Gray's room number?"

The woman behind the desk checked the admittance records. "His visitors are restricted to immediate family."

"I'm his sister." Netty cracked her gum.

"He's on the fourth floor, room 443."

"Thanks." She strolled to the bank of elevators and punched the up button. When it stopped on the fourth, she exited as soon as the doors opened, found his room and knocked softly.

A young orderly opened the door and pressed her forefinger to her lips. "He's sleeping, but you can come in. Are you, his wife?" She asked quietly.

Netty crinkled her nose. "Sister." She replied in a hushed tone.

The orderly left and Netty took a deep breath before she walked quietly to stand at the foot of Rand's bed. Her chin dropped, followed by rapid blinking as she stared at his reposed form. Even after both Cab and Rod warned her about his injuries, nothing could have prepared her for the actual sight of his lifeless appearance.

She drew in a sharp breath. His eyes were closed and there were dark shadows beneath them. He appeared vulnerable, so still except for the rise and fall of his chest when he breathed. She clutched her purse. Would he ever be able to do the things he enjoyed again? She bit her lip and wished he'd wake up.

She tried to hold back tears as she gaped at his pale skin, so foreign from his normal robust appearance. His beard was more prominent than usual. Under different circumstances, it might have been appealing, but she preferred just a sexy hint of facial hair. Why hide such strong features? Being a barber, her fingers tingled with desire to give him a shave and wash and trim his hair. Even his lips appeared dry and expressionless.

She caught her lower lip between her teeth as a tear escaped and trickled down her cheek. Quickly she brushed it away with her fingertips. She didn't want him to wake up and find her crying. Would he be in pain? His expression would reveal it if he was uncomfortable.

She was glad Rand was different from his brother in that respect. Her mouth pinched as she pictured Rod's face. She never could figure out what he was thinking, let alone feeling. Sometimes she doubted he felt anything at all.

Rand, on the other hand, was fun and exciting. Her lips would stretch into a wide grin and his wit often would often surprise her. She loved that about him. Sometimes she wasn't sure if he even possessed a serious side at all although it did show up from time to time and when she least expected it. The depth of his character intrigued her. She found him to be a mysterious combination of pensiveness and hilarity. His stories often compelled her to laugh until her sides ached and she had to beg him to stop his antics, which often accompanied them. She was tempted to place a gentle kiss on his lips. She stared at his mouth until unable to resist and then leaned over the rail and kissed him deeply. When she straightened up, she gasped.

The same orderly from earlier stared at her with a twinkle in her eyes. "Never saw a sister kiss a brother like that!"

"I, I—"

The woman winked at her. "I'll close the door." She picked up her clipboard and left.

Rands eyelashes fluttered and he gave her an uncertain grin. "What are you looking at?"

"You darlin.'" She bent to give him a light kiss on his cheek.

"How long have you been here?"

She winced at his raspy voice. "Not long."

"What time is it?" He asked with a yawn.

She glanced at her watch and her eyebrows arched. It felt as if she'd only arrived, but she'd been there nearly two hours. "Almost five. Do you need anything?" She was thinking, like a hug or maybe another kiss or two?

"Water."

Her lips pressed into a grimace and she filled his pitcher and the glass, gave it to him and set the pitcher on the bed tray. "Your lips are chapped. Don't they give you anything to put on them?"

"It's awful stuff."

"I'll try to find something you'd like better in the gift shop." She started to touch his lips but lowered her hand to the side rail.

He yawned again. "How'd you get in here? I thought only family was allowed."

She winked at him. "Told them I'm your sister." She took his hand folded it carefully in hers, bent over and pressed her lips against the bandage.

"Careful, sis, you'll have the staff talking." He chuckled softly.

She took note of his heavy eyelids. "You need to rest so I won't stay much longer. How are you feeling?"

"They keep me pretty doped up. Have a hard time staying awake."

"Sleep is good for you. It'll help you get better faster." She eagerly anticipated taking care of him when he got back to Candlewood.

"Don't worry. I'll be fine. Going home soon." He searched her face. "You don't have to come here."

Her chin trembled and she shook her head slowly, not believing he'd even suggest she'd stay away. "I came because I wanted to see you."

He gave her hand a light squeeze. "I didn't mean it that way."

She withdrew her hand. "It's okay. You seem a little out of it. Are you okay otherwise?" She wanted to sit on the bed, hold him close and kiss him until he was well again.

His eyelids drooped. "Sorry, Red, can't think straight."

She blinked at the nickname he used occasionally. "It's all right, darlin', I'll come back later." She drew his hand to her lips and gently pressed them in his palm. "Rest now, okay?" She traced his jawline with her forefinger and paused when she reached his chin. "Pleasant dreams, cowboy." She placed a gentle kiss on his mouth, was tempted to deepen it, but resisted instead. She peered at him as a smirk pulled at her lips. Wouldn't want him to go into cardiac arrest.

With eyes still closed, one side of his lips tilted upward.

She paused a moment longer and listened to his soft snore and once satisfied he was asleep, she left.

Twelve

The next day Rand had just finished his lunch and pushed the tray table to the side of his bed when he heard a gruff voice that he recognized outside his door.

"Knock, knock." Sheriff Gus Palmer grinned as he entered the room.

Rand eyed him. "How did I rate a visit from you?"

"Heard about your wreck, thought I'd check on you."

Rand raised an eyebrow. "Didn't think you took time for social calls."

The sheriff chuckled. "Got to keep tabs on the village's favorite sons."

Rand sneered. "Yeah, right."

He pulled a chair closer to Rand's bed and sat down. "Tell me about your wreck."

He glared at the sheriff. "Wasn't a wreck, Gus! Someone ran me off Coyote Canyon Road. When they approached me from behind, I flashed my brake lights. They tried to knock me over with the passenger door, passed too close, and then clipped my front fender. When that didn't work, they slammed on their brakes a few inches in front of me."

Gus's brow wrinkled. "What kind of vehicle was it?"

His lips pressed together. "A van. Only caught a glimpse of green paint in my headlight."

"Did you see the license number?"

Rand fingered the blanket on his bed as the incident replayed in his mind. "I was concentrating on staying alive, Gus." He raised his voice.

He squinted at him. "Obviously you didn't go over that ridge on the bike or you wouldn't be here."

He clenched his teeth. "Like I said, I tried to keep from rear ending him when he slammed on his brakes. I jerked my wheel and slid sideways in the gravel."

Gus' mouth dropped open. "How fast were you going?"

Rand pursed his lips, trying to remember. "Maybe thirty or forty."

The sheriff removed his hat, scratched his head, and then set it back in place. "You were doing thirty to forty and then what?"

Rand started to shake his head, but quickly changed his mind because the motion often made him nauseous. "Laid it down and pushed away from it."

Gus eyed him. "How did that work?"

Rand shrugged, choosing to ignore the sheriff's question. "I woke up at the bottom of the canyon when my bike exploded."

Gus narrowed his eyes. "Is there anything else you can tell me? Did you see who was driving? How many were in the van?"

Rand felt heat climbing up his neck. "Had to be at least two, one driving and one to open the passenger door." His voice faded to a mere whisper as he finished and stared at the foot of the bed. He swallowed hard. *I thought I was going to die.*

"Can you think of anyone who might have reason to harm you?"

Rand bit the inside of his jaw to keep from shouting. "All I know is they came to a dead stop in front of me and I had to get off that bike, quick."

Gus fixed a direct look on him and rephrased his question. "Think. Could they have wanted you to think twice before you crossed their path ag—?"

"They tried to kill me, Gus." Rand grasped the bed's side rails so tight his hands ached.

Gus stared at him. "Tell me about the fight at work."

Rand crossed his arms. "What's that got to do with—?"

"Tell me about it anyway." Gus leaned forward.

Rand's facial muscles tensed, he opened his mouth to protest, but inhaled a long breath instead. "Two longshoremen demanded to be paid for some hours they didn't work the week before because the superintendent dismissed them early for fighting. I reminded them they only got paid for hours worked and they jumped me."

"Anyone get hurt?" Gus peered at him intently.

Rand's lips pulled into a thin line. "Hollis pulled a knife and cut Sloan's side."

Gus focused on Rand's face. "Was Hollis aiming for you?"

He raised his chin, but maintained eye contact. "Yeah, but Sloan was hanging onto me. I fired them, they left, my boss called the police and they took a report."

"Okay, I'll check into it." He stood.

"Gus?"

He met Rand's gaze.

"I'd almost guarantee it wasn't either of them."

"What makes you think that?"

"They could get a job anywhere. What would they gain by running me off the road?"

"Good point." He turned to go.

"Gus?"

With his hand on the door, he regarded Rand with a raised brow.

"Thanks for coming." *Bet he doesn't believe you, pal.*

"Stop by my office once your home. Maybe you'll remember something else. Just SOP."

Rand's eyebrows knit together. "SOP?"

"Standard operating procedure." The sheriff waved and left.

"Thanks, for making me relive the whole blasted nightmare." Rand grumbled.

Back at his office, the sheriff drummed his fingers on his desktop before he picked up the receiver, dialed the number for the Church of the Way, and asked for Cab Martel. He snatched a pencil and scribbled some notes on his desk pad while he waited. "Cab, Gus here. Got a question for you. How far from Rod's house was Rand when you found him the night of his wreck? Thanks, that helps. Yes, I'll let you know if I need anything else." He hung up the phone and sat tapping his pencil on the desk, listening to his deputies discussing a case of breaking and entry they were trying to solve. The peck, peck, pecking of a typewriter and the zing of the carriage-return accompanied their conversation. At least they were following through and making out their report. Gus tossed his pencil on the desk and pulled his long legs from under the small desk. He exited through the back door of the municipal building.

Gus drove to the village fire department and found Pax Warner in the kitchen. He stirred a pot of something, which reminded Gus that he'd skipped lunch.

Pax wiped his hands on a towel, which hung on the stove's oven door and tossed it on a table. "Hey, Nate, wake up." He yelled into the next room as he grabbed a La Dodger's baseball cap and pulled it on over his short tawny-colored hair. "Come finish cooking." Pax grinned. "He isn't good at it either. Where we going?"

"Tell you on the way." Gus growled as he walked through the open doors. Once they were in his car and headed out of the village, Gus threw a warning glare at Pax. "Keep this to yourself."

Pax tugged on his ear. "Sounds serious."

"Rand claims someone ran him off the road." Gus grumbled.

Pax whistled. "How can I help?"

Gus parked on the side of Old Canyon Road, got out of his car and Pax followed. They began searching the area for signs of a disturbance when Gus suddenly dropped to one knee to inspect some dark-colored dirt. "Found blood. It's likely Rand's." He called to Pax.

"Over here." Pax yelled. "The brush and weeds are trampled and torn and it looks like maybe some blood too. From the looks of the embankment here, this looks like some kind of path."

Gus joined him. "Could either be where Rand went down or came back up. My guess is it's the latter. Too regular and methodical for a decent. Considering the amount of blood here and then over there, he's darn lucky Cab found him when he did." Gus scratched his chin. "I wouldn't have believed anyone could survive a motorcycle wreck let alone having rolled or tumbled down there to land in the stream. Whoever ran him off the road could have drug him back up and left him by the road. But why would they if the intent was definitely to kill him."

Pax paced back and forth on the rim of the canyon studying the location of the wreckage and pointed down in the ravine. "A bird's the only way to get her out of there, Gus."

He crossed his arms staring at the heap of tangled metal. "That's what I figured."

"I have a buddy who works for search and rescue over in Ventura County. Want me to call him?"

Gus scowled at him. "Yes, and I want this kept quiet. Tell him to put it in the police garage. I don't want the whole village getting in an uproar over this. Understand? Tell no one except your friend in search and rescue, got it?"

Pax took a deep breath and exhaled. "Gotcha. I'll contact him from home when I get off work tonight."

Gus headed back toward his car. "Let me know when he can get it."

Pax saluted. "If Willis finds out, he'll tell the whole village."

"Exactly." Gus hissed.

Pax tilted his head. "Do you think anybody's told Lucinda? After all, he is her son." He hunched his shoulders as Gus let him out at the fire department.

Gus scrunched his eyebrows. "Interfering in family affairs isn't in my job description. Besides, everyone in and around Fire River knows of Miss Warner's hatred for anyone with the name of Gray and to my knowledge Rand is no exception."

Thirteen

The following Friday morning Rand buttoned his shirt and gazed out the hospital window. He wished there was a clock in his room. It seemed like hours since breakfast.

A nurse came in his room a few minutes later. "Are you ready to go home?"

"And then some." He grumbled. "I'm waiting on my brother."

Rod walked into his room just as she was leaving.

"I'll get a wheelchair and be right back." She told Rod as she walked past him.

He glanced first at the departing nurse, then at Rand. "Sorry I'm late. I needed to talk with Tommy's teacher."

Rand thought he detected a note of worry in Rod's tone. "Everything okay at school?"

"Yes, it's school policy to be informed of any changes with student transportation."

Rand listened without commenting as he finished with his buttons.

"I asked Netty to keep an eye on Candlewood while Cab and I were here. She cleaned and did some laundry." Rod commented.

Rand hesitated to weigh in on the remark. Was Rod upset about that? He shrugged it off. *Don't think about how you left things, pal.* Still, his face heated at the thought.

Rod picked up Rand's Bible from the tray table and retrieved a duffle bag from the closet.

The nurse returned with a wheelchair, helped him into it and pushed him to the elevators while Rod walked beside them.

When the elevator doors closed, she eyed Rod. "Bring your car around to the front entrance and we'll meet you there."

Once outside, the nurse helped Rand into Rod's car.

He glanced at Rand as they left the hospital parking lot. "Saun's brother called Wednesday evening to say their father had a stroke. He asked her to go and stay with them for a while."

Rand frowned. "I'll pray for her and her family. You and Tommy going to bunk with me while she's gone?"

Rod's lips formed a brief smile. "I hoped you wouldn't mind. Tommy wanted to call and ask you as soon as she was off the phone."

"I'll appreciate the company." Rand caught Rod peering at him as he enjoyed the passing view.

"Don't let him monopolize your time. He can entertain himself after school. You need to rest. Some of the women from church will be bringing food so we won't have to worry about meals and Netty said she'd check on you too."

Rand scrutinized Rod's face. His tone indicated there was more to his earlier comment than his words conveyed.

Later that morning, Rod parked beside Rand's truck and retrieved a pair of crutches from the back seat.

Rand opened the passenger door and struggled to get out, trying to keep weight off his right leg. Using the crutches, he carefully crossed the cobblestone terrace and paused at the gate on the right side of the mansion.

"I'm right behind you." Rod spoke reassuringly as he reached around him for the gate.

Rand drew a deep breath and maneuvered through it. "I can do it."

Rod followed him as he started up the garden path toward the outside door to the library. "Just take it easy, okay?"

Rand shot a narrowed glance over his shoulder. "I've got it." As they reached the door, he pressed his lips together. "I'm staying in the library." He stepped inside and drew in a deep appreciative breath. There was no stinking antiseptics and stale air. He made his way around a corner alcove with two stuffed armchairs and a reading lamp with a table between them. He settled in his favorite spot, which included a semi-modern couch situated in front of the hearth. He sank carefully onto the plush cushions.

Rod waited for Rand to get settled. "I'll put your bag in your room."

Rand raised his head and with pinched lips forced a laugh. "Thanks." He appreciated his brother's concern, but didn't want anyone hovering over him.

He'd had enough of that in the hospital and it was a constant reminder of his temporary limits. *Can't let them see you as vulnerable or weak, pal.*

Without another word, Rod left the room.

Netty entered the library behind Rand and stopped beside him. "Welcome home, cowboy! Can I get you anything?"

Rand threw a quick glimpse at Rod, who'd just reappeared in the room. "Thanks, but I'm fine, Netty." He observed the glare she directed at Rod.

"There're sandwiches on the table and I made you a pot of coffee, darlin'. Since you're going to be here." She fired at Rod. "I'll go back to my shop." She bent over to kiss the top of Rand's head. "Call me if you need anything, darlin.'" She threw a scorching glance at Rod and left.

Rand stared at the cold hearth. "What was that about?"

Rod sighed. "It appears she's upset that I'm here."

Rand forked a hand through his hair as he reflected on Rod's remark. *Would you be better off at the hospital, pal?* He sighed. "I called dad. He has a friend who's a physical therapist and she's willing to come with him and stay here."

Rod nodded and steepled his fingers. "Even though Tommy's fourteen, I don't like the idea of him being at the house alone, especially when I get home late. He wanted to take off from school today but I assured him you would still be here afterward."

Rand rubbed the back of his neck. "I don't know when dad and his therapist friend are coming, but there's plenty of room for all of us."

Rod crossed his arms. "We'll see how it goes. I found some coffee in the pantry, a few boxes of crackers and some cereal, but not much else."

Rand raised an eyebrow. "I'm good for now if you have things you need to do. Netty left sandwiches and coffee."

Rod gave him a curt nod. "I'll be back shortly. I'm going to pick up a few things at the grocery." He said as he left the room.

Rand shook his head when the front door closed.

He snatched his crutches, took a deep breath and cautiously made his way to the kitchen. He found a cup of coffee and the plate of sandwiches. He dumped the cold coffee in the sink, refilled the cup and carefully took it to the table and sat down to enjoy his first real food and drink.

Wings of Steel

After eating, he headed for his bedroom. Rod left his suitcase on the desk so Rand opened it, thinking he'd put his stuff away, but changed his mind and picked up the phone instead. He sank slowly onto the desk chair, picked up the letter opener and twisted it in his fingers after dialing Netty's number. When she answered, he dropped the opener. "Hi, thanks for making coffee and sandwiches." He wanted to thank her for straightening his room, but he wasn't sure how to say it without giving her the wrong impression. His face grew uncomfortably warm even as he considered it.

"Of course, cowboy, do you need anything else?"

"Maybe later, but I'm kind of tired right now."

"Okay, darlin', let me know. Sweet dreams."

"Thanks." He hung up glad to be back at Candlewood. Here he could be alone with his thoughts at least for a little while. He lowered himself onto his single bed. After all the noise at the hospital, the silence here was soothing as long as there wasn't too much of it.

He lay on his back and stared at the ceiling. He and Netty often ate dinner here or at her apartment and spent the evening afterward together. *Jesus, please open her heart to You.*

Rand gazed at the off-white walls, the plain light-brown curtains at the window, the functional desk with a ladder-back chair, and the small bed and dresser. The simple lines of the furniture impressed him as serviceable and therefore more to his liking than the fancy antique furniture in the rest of the mansion.

His focus landed on the old portrait of one of their ancestors, hanging over the desk. The picture hid a wall safe, which held his and Rod's birth certificates among other legal documents. As he stared at the portrait, he recalled that his new life in Christ began in this very room. His lip hitched at the memory.

Someone entered the front door and before he could get up from the bed, a bark echoed through the mansion followed by the clicking of toenails on the floors. He laughed with delight as he swung his legs over the edge of the bed and sat up as the dog came running into his room. "You brought the dog!" He laughed.

She put one paw on his unbandaged leg and peered at him with such a happy expression that he couldn't help hugging her. "Hi girl!" He gazed at her with a wide grin on his face.

Rod was standing in the doorway with his arms crossed. "Here's your angel."

Rand raised his head and quirked an eyebrow at Rod. "Angel?"

"Cab told us you called him angel when he found you. Tommy thinks she was your guardian angel since she practically forced Cab to stop and help you. So, that's what we started calling her and she seems to respond to it."

"Huh." Rand studied the dog as he scratched behind her ears. "Angel, huh?" She licked his chin and he chuckled. "You saved my life." She licked his cheek and he hugged her again. "Good girl, Angel."

Fourteen

Netty busied herself early Monday morning and gave her shop a thorough cleaning. She didn't schedule any appointments for the day because she planned to spend it with Rand. Rod was upset with her when he came to Candlewood after work on Thursday and found she'd cleaned and re-organized Rand's bedroom. Rod acted as if she'd violated Rand's privacy because she'd straightened things up, did his laundry and organized things so he could find them easily.

When the phone on her desk rang, she sprang to answer it. "Sam's barber shop—You're leaving? Do you want me to come now or aft—? Fine! I'll be there in a few." If she dragged her feet, maybe he'd leave. Probably not because Rod wouldn't leave Rand alone even for a few minutes whether he was awake or asleep.

She carried the broom and dust pan to the storage room, picked up her purse from the desk, and locked her shop. She'd run upstairs, change, and hope Rod was gone before she arrived. She dressed up a little more than she did for work, wanting to appear she hadn't spent time deciding what to wear. She chose a pair of black tight-fitting jeans with a mint-green scoop-neck blouse and black flats. She added small pearl earrings and appraised her reflection in the bathroom mirror with satisfaction as she spritzed herself with perfume, then added a little blush and mascara.

———◈———

She took a deep breath as she marched across Chino Avenue, up the steps and was about to grasp the door handle when it opened. She moved aside when Rod exited and pulled the door closed.

"I fed the dog and made a pot of coffee."

She frowned at him. "What dog?"

"The dog that found Rand. We appreciate your willingness to help and he can have whatever he wants to eat. He hasn't had much of an appetite, so try checking with him every two or three hours. If you need anything, Cab's available. His office number and mine are on the wall next to the kitchen phone. Rand's medicine schedule is on the counter and he can have aspirin in between. Give him the first dose at seven with his breakfast. Dr. Mills is aware that he's home and will come if needed, but he basically needs to rest."

She narrowed her eyes as she met his unwavering gaze. "Your brother will be fine and I'm perfectly capable of taking care of him." Her voice rose with her words precisely pronounced.

Rod's lips flattened into a thin line. "Tommy can get himself up and ready for school and will come here afterward. I'll be back as soon as possible. W. T. informed me someone from our church will be bringing food."

She pushed against Rod's chest. "Just go on to work. I'll make sure Rand is well taken care of."

A wry grin appeared briefly on his lips before he descended the steps. "I'm sure you will."

She caught his mumbled response. She crossed her arms and watched his departure while tapping her foot. When he drove away, she marched inside.

She anticipated some real quality time with Rand and paused to scrutinize her image in the hall mirror located over an intricately-carved redwood table, which held an artificial bouquet of various colors of California poppies.

She entered the library and spied an afghan thrown over the back of a couch. She assumed Rand spent at least part of his time there. She folded it, left it where it was, picked up some cups, a glass, a crumpled napkin, and preceded to the kitchen. She hoped he didn't sleep the whole time. Maybe she could hold him while he slept, but told herself she'd better redirect her thoughts. He may not want to be worried over because he'd had enough of that from his brother.

In the kitchen she found his medicine on the counter and picked it up. The instructions were right on the bottle. She bristled at the idea that Rod figured she wouldn't bother reading the label and set the bottle of pills down hard. He said he fed the dog so she wouldn't give it another thought. It was a little after six and she hoped Tommy was the self-starter Rod claimed. She threw up her hands.

She was here for Rand and that was all. Before his accident he was usually up and gone before she started her day. Would he get up early even though his routine would be different? She knocked lightly on his door and when there was no response, she opened it just a crack.

He wasn't in bed so she stepped into the room to investigate, just to be sure he was all right. As she passed the desk, the bathroom door opened and Rand maneuvered into the room.

His gaze locked on hers and he froze. He leaned on a pair of crutches, was barefooted and seemed to be wearing only a bathrobe.

She gaped at him and her lips curled upward while she appraised him. "You didn't answer when I knocked. So, I thought I should check on you. Do you need help getting dressed, darlin'?"

His cheeks turned bright red. "No! But breakfast, would be good." His voice sounded strained.

She stood and stared at his bare muscular leg beneath the robe. At least the one not covered by a bandage. He was cute when embarrassed. "What would you like?"

His jaw clenched and he gazed at the floor. "Oatmeal's fine."

She backed up and stopped in the doorway. He'd caught her ogling him and his expression was anything but friendly. Was he angry or had she made him uncomfortable? "It'll be ready in about ten minutes." She winked and hoped his mood would brighten. "Whistle if you need anything." She slowly perused him again from head to foot. His dark expression only added to his appeal but when he made no attempt to move, she closed the door.

In the kitchen she prepared his cereal but couldn't get his image out of her mind. He'd stood there like some Greek god and his crutches along with the cut on his head, tugged at her heart. Her arms ached to comfort him even though his cold stare was anything but friendly. She tried to concentrate on breakfast preparations, but was distracted by the image of how he'd stood dumbstruck and glared at her as if she was an alien.

He entered the kitchen several minutes later and wore a dark green long-sleeve shirt. It hung loose over his Levi's, which had the right leg cut short, and he was still bare-footed. His injured leg was bandaged half-way up his thigh and down to his foot, which was covered except for his toes.

She stopped what she was doing. "Do you want to sit at the table?"

He shook his head. "Library."

She frowned and hoped Rod's grouchiness didn't rub off on him. "Do you need help getting settled?"

He shrugged and navigated into the hall.

She threw up her hands. Rand wasn't feeling well. She should've expected him to be somewhat gruff. She turned off the stove and followed him.

He stopped next to the couch, leaned one crutch against the end of it and with the other struggled to ease himself to a sitting position.

She reached for him, but he landed awkwardly before she was able to help. When he sat up straight, she stared at his wrinkled brow and wondered if he'd held his breath against the pain of his haphazard landing. At least it appeared painful to her.

Once situated, he stretched his legs straight out in front of him and leaned back against the couch, breathing heavily. "Guess I'll have to perfect my landing." He chuckled, as he peered up at her.

She grabbed the afghan she'd spied earlier from the back of the couch and covered his legs. "I'll get your breakfast. Are you okay?"

He removed the afghan and laid it on the couch beside him. "Netty, I'm not sick, just recovering from some broken bones that will heal. I appreciate you being here to keep me company, but I can take care of myself."

She crossed her arms, stared at him a moment, sighed, and then left the room. A few minutes later she returned with a bowl of oats on a tray along with two cups of coffee, his medicine and a glass of water.

She set the tray on the coffee table and chose the chair closest to him. "I thought you'd be in bed most of the day."

He shook his head. "Can't recover staying in bed. I'm able to get what I need. You don't have to stay, but if you want to eat breakfast and maybe lunch with me, I wouldn't mind that unless you have appointments. Otherwise, if I need anything, I can call you."

She smiled. "You can't get rid of me that easy, cowboy. Besides, what if you fell or something and no one was here? Rod would never let me forget it. Besides, he left me all kinds of instructions for your care."

His brows knitted. "What's going on between you two?"

She huffed. "He doesn't think anyone but him knows how to take care of you!"

"He has a lot on his mind." He gave a small shrug and indicated the crutches. "Except for the way I just landed, I'm good with these and I'll get even better with a little practice."

Her lips pinched together. He always made excuses for Rod. "Do you want more coffee?" Rand said nothing about her straightening his room, so she chose to disregard Rod's objection.

Rand stared at his empty bowl. "I could eat a couple eggs, ham, toast and potatoes, if it isn't too much trouble."

She smiled, relieved he didn't suggest that she leave again. "Sunny side up?" She raised her eyebrows.

"Yes, please." He winked at her, took the medicine, and then regarded her as he drank the water. "Will you let the dog in?" He asked as he set the glass back on the tray. "She can keep me company while you're in the kitchen."

She picked up the tray and headed out of the room. "I'll fix you a real breakfast, and then I'll join you."

He chuckled. "Now you're talking."

Her mouth fell open at the joy in his voice, but then she remembered Rod saying what Rand needed most was rest. In the doorway, she pivoted toward him. "After you eat, you should go back to bed for a while."

"I'm staying here, Netty."

She raised an eyebrow. His obvious struggle and ensuing discomfort when he sat or rather fell onto the couch crossed her mind. "At least let me help you lie down."

He shook his head and raised his feet onto the coffee table. "Need to be able to move around. It's easier if I'm sitting."

She sighed and retreated to the kitchen to fix the rest of his breakfast. At least he had a healthy appetite.

After eating, they spent the rest of the morning talking, and she took note whenever she asked what happened with his bike, he changed the subject. She was touched by the way Rand was attached to the dog and Angel seemed content to sit or lay close by his side.

She fixed grilled ham and cheese sandwiches for lunch and afterward when she let Angel outside, Rand's eyelids began to droop. She coaxed him into laying on the couch and when she covered him with the afghan, he promptly went to sleep.

Before she knew it, Tommy came bounding in from school.

Netty rushed into the kitchen just as the dog followed him inside. "Sshh, Rand's sleeping and get that dog out of here!" She half whispered.

Tommy spun around and opened the door for Angel. "Come on girl, I'll give you a treat." He gaped at Netty. "Is Uncle Rand alright?"

She put her hands on her hips. "He's fine."

"Are you staying for dinner?"

"I'll stay until either Cab or Rod come." Netty tapped his shoulder with her fingers. "There's a snack for you in the fridge."

"Can I see him?"

She smiled as she gave in to the boy's request. "Try not to disturb him." He was a sweet kid, always full of fun and energy. She could picture a younger Rand who could've been a lot like Tommy. She regarded him as he scurried quietly toward the library.

A few minutes later, he rejoined her in the kitchen. "Are you in love with Uncle Rand?"

She didn't have much interaction with teenagers so his question caught her off guard. She was tempted to tell him it was none of his business, but kept the remark to herself. "We're friends." She replied, hoping her response satisfied the boy.

Tommy gawked at her. "Don't you want to get married?"

"Not really." She didn't know about Rand, but marriage was the last thing on her mind. "We're just friends, Tommy!"

"I've seen you guys kiss." He smirked.

Netty rolled her eyes and tried to hide a smile. "Why don't you take your stuff upstairs and change your clothes. Then eat your snack and go play with the dog." She suggested, hoping to change the subject.

Tommy blinked and then abruptly pivoted toward the refrigerator.

She waited until he opened it and then headed for the library. She chose a chair and grabbed a magazine off the table beside it. She definitely wanted a more serious relationship with Rand. But marriage? She'd never consider that kind of commitment to any man.

A few minutes later, Tommy entered the library and stopped to stare at her. "I'm glad you're here. I wouldn't know what to do if Uncle Rand needed something." He whispered.

She studied him. "I'm glad you're here too." She responded quietly.

Tommy meandered out the library door and the dog greeted him outside.

She focused her attention on Rand who appeared restless. She stood close to him and lightly touched his arm. "Rand?"

He inhaled sharply and blinked several times. "Netty?"

Not expecting him to respond, she clutched her throat. "Is there something you need?"

He shook his head, tossed the afghan aside, sat up and slowly lowered his feet to the floor.

She stroked his warm, damp forehead and gently smoothed his hair away from his face. He was trembling. She clasped his hand. "Are you cold?"

His brows wrinkled. "What time is it?"

She glanced at the clock on the mantle: "4:45."

Frowning, he zeroed in on the outside door and rubbed the back of his neck.

"Your medicine isn't due until seven. Would you like an aspirin or two?"

He shook his head. "No, I'm fine."

"Are you cold? You're shivering."

"What I really want is a walk to the fountain."

She frowned. "I don't think that's a good—"

"You can come with me or I'll go—"

"I'll come with you."

He managed to get to his feet on his own. "Atta girl, Red. I need some fresh air and sun."

She watched his Adam's apple bob several times, leaned close to him and whispered. "Rand, what's wrong? Let me help you."

He eyed her for several seconds before he spoke softly. "You are helping me."

Barely able to hear him, she ran her fingers through his tousled hair and took note that it covered his ears. "You need a haircut and a shave."

He shook his head. "Maybe later." He crossed the room and managed to exit into the garden. They made their way toward the fountain, passed it and sat on the bench together.

He breathed deeply of the Jeffrey pine and fragrant purple, pink and white flowers which filled the garden, but stared at his bandaged leg and the crutches, which leaned against a nearby chair. They served to remind him that somewhere out there were at least two people who wanted him dead.

He rolled his shoulders and raised his head to peer through the trees at the bright blue sky. *Jesus, who wants to kill me? I know of one person and I just dreamed he found me. Must I pay for that one mistake my entire life?* He closed his eyes and swallowed hard. A soft breeze blew across his skin and gently lifted his hair so that it fell across his forehead. *Soon it will all be over.*

His eyes flew open and his gaze landed on Netty who was sitting quietly beside him. "Did you say something?" As soon as the words left his mouth, he knew the voice he'd heard was the same one that spoke to him that night in the canyon.

Netty touched his shoulder. "It's okay, darlin' just the breeze rustling the leaves on the trees. Do you want to go back inside?"

He shook his head. "I like being outside."

Tommy came running up to them with the dog. "Uncle Rand, you're up. Guess you're feeling better, huh." He stood in front of them, petting Angel's head. "I fed her and Ethan called to ask if I could go to his house for a couple hours. His mom said she could pick me up and bring me back."

"I don't know what time Rod will be here and I'm sure he'll want to see you and ask about your day." Rand automatically reached for Angel and she licked his hand and sat at his feet.

"He told me when he left this morning that he'd probably be really late getting home, I mean here. It's only for a couple hours, please."

Rand held Tommy's pleading gaze with a steady one. "Is your homework done?"

Tommy smiled. "I didn't have any, got it done in study hall."

Rand grinned. "Okay, pal. Have fun."

"Thanks, Uncle Rand. Bye Netty." He yelled over his shoulder as he ran toward the mansion.

Rand stared after him as a smile tugged at his lips and he absently scratched behind Angel's ear.

"Rand?" Netty touched his shoulder.

He startled and peered at her as heat crawled up his neck from under his collar. He'd temporarily forgotten he wasn't alone because she was so quiet. "Let's go inside and listen to some music." He reached for the crutches and stood.

"Rand." She grasped his hand. "Tell me what's troubling you. Is it the wreck?"

The hairs on the back of his neck bristled. "It wasn't a wreck, Netty. I did not just lose control." He responded in a matter-of-fact tone.

"Please, tell me about it then, I sense something is upsetting, you." She walked as close to him as she could without tripping over one of his crutches.

"I'm going to listen to some music and maybe grab a snack. Do you want to join me?" He also wanted to be near the phone in case Rod called.

Wings of Steel

Rand helped Netty start a fire on the hearth and then stacked some LPs on the bookcase stereo in the library. After listening to a couple by Dan Fogelberg, he whispered against her head, which was tucked against his neck and shoulder. "I'm a little hungry, are you?"

She smiled at him and kissed his cheek. "I'll be right back."

He was staring at the ceiling when she returned.

She had a small glass in one hand and a cup in the other and set them on the coffee table.

He eyed the cup. "That's not tea, I hope."

She chuckled. "No, it's soup."

He wrinkled his nose. "What kind?"

"Chicken."

He nearly gagged. "I'm not a chicken man."

Grinning, she raised her eyebrows. "He's everywhere! He's everywhere!" She danced about squawking like a chicken and flapping her arms as if they were wings.

He raised his eyebrows. "Whaaat?".

She laughed as she shook her head. "Never mind, I'll find 'Chicken Man' on the radio for you sometime. How about some coffee and I found apple pie in the fridge?"

He grinned. "Now you're talking and if there's any roast beef and potato salad left, that sounds good too."

She gave him a flirty smile. "Sounds like you're more than a little hungry. Do you want it here or in the kitchen?"

"Here's good."

"Okay, but first take the aspirin." She indicated the glass of water and the pill-bottle on the coffee table.

He shook his head. "You can take those back to the kitchen."

She frowned. "I'll leave them. You can take them while I fix our plates."

After she left the room, Rand made his way to the stereo and tuned in to a smooth listening radio station and left the water glass and pills on the bookshelf before returning to the couch. He was pleased that he had mastered, getting up from there as well as returning with more adeptness. He smiled to himself and mumbled. "Practice makes for perfection, pal."

Netty returned. "What did you say?"

"Nothing." He peered up at her. "Don't think I mentioned it earlier, but you look nice." He touched her sleeve as she sat beside him and a lopsided grin lifted one side of his mouth. "The color of your top makes your eyes sparkle."

She placed a tray, holding their dinner and coffee, on the low table in front of them. "You turned on the radio and I saw where you left the aspirin." She arched an eyebrow.

"That's for pain. I don't need it." His lip hitched before he gave thanks for their food.

Rod parked beside Rand's truck that evening and stepped into the library. He glanced at his watch: 9:35. Quietly he crossed the room to where Netty sat beside Rand. A flickering fire was their only light. "How's he doing?" He asked quietly.

"He's doing good." Rand responded.

"Did you take any aspirin?"

"He didn't want any." Netty glared at Rod.

Rod stood, studying his brother's furrowed brow. "What have you eaten today?"

She chewed on her lower lip as she glared at Rod. "He had eggs and—"

"Hey, I'm here!" Rand protested.

Netty stood. "Yes, you are. So, you can answer your brother's fifty questions, I'm going home!" She marched out the door and a few seconds later it slammed.

Rod crossed his arms and gave Rand a puzzled look. "Is that how your whole day went?"

Rand shook his head. "She was fine until," his eyebrows rose, "until you—?"

The front door closed again. "Rod, you're back!" Tommy came running into the room and skidded to a stop. "I'm sorry, Uncle Rand, I forgot—."

"It's okay, pal." He raised both hands, palms outward. "I wasn't asleep."

Rod glanced at Tommy and then at Rand.

Tommy kicked at the carpet. "Uncle Rand said I could go to Ethan's for a couple of hours, but we sort of lost track of time. The movie lasted longer than we thought."

Rod folded his arms. "When were you supposed to be back?"

He stuffed his hands in his jeans pockets and stared at the floor. "About an hour ago."

"Did you call and let him know you'd be late?"

"No, sir."

Rod frowned. "Would you have called if I was here?"

"Yes be…because you'd of been worried."

Rod cocked an eyebrow. "And you didn't think Rand would?"

"He doesn't worry about stuff like you do." He said the words so quietly they were almost whispered.

"Tommy, look at me." Rod fastened his gaze on Tommy's face. "The point isn't who worries about or who doesn't. You disrespected Rand's authority, not only by staying later than was agreed upon, but also by not calling and at the very least, letting him know you'd be late. From now on, come straight here after school."

"Yes, sir." He hung his head.

"Is that all you have to say before going to bed?"

"I'm sorry, Uncle Rand." He glanced at Rand and then at Rod. "Good night, Rod, Uncle Rand." He gave Angel a quick pat on the head and dejectedly left the room.

Rod sank wearily into an armchair. "How was your day? Did you get any rest?"

"I had a nap this afternoon. Netty stayed all day. I tried to tell her I didn't need her to stay. She has a business to run."

"Would you rather she didn't come?"

"I can manage, Rod. You said the church will be bringing food and I can call Cab if I need anything. I really don't want to be hovered over all day."

Rod sighed. "I apologize. I should have asked you first. You've improved quicker than the doctors expected and that's mostly due to your determination."

Rand smiled. "Give yourself a break. It could have been a lot worse and then the call about Saun's dad. I get it, okay. I don't know if I could handle things any better if the situation was reversed." He paused to think of something to lighten things up a little. "I think there's a fresh pot of coffee and some roast beef and potato salad unless you already ate."

Rod stood. "Do you know if there's any apple pie left?"

Rand smiled. "If there is, I'll join you with that and coffee."

Fifteen

It was nearly ten o'clock Thursday evening when Rod parked his BMW beside Rand's pickup. He got out of his car, went up the steps and entered the mansion as the murmur of male voices came from the library.

Rand and Cab both raised their heads as he stepped into the room. "Man, you're getting home later and later." Cab remarked, getting up from an armchair.

Rod nodded. "Hermann and I spent the day discussing a contract with a client and he still couldn't make up his mind on several points."

"And afterward you had the long drive home." Rand frowned.

Rod glanced at Rand and then Cab. "Stay here a minute." He indicated the chair Cab just vacated and directed his gaze at them with a slight tilt of his head. "I already told Saun when I talked to her on the phone earlier, but as of today it's official. Hermann purchased an office in Montecito. He asked me to manage it and also continue as the company's lead architect. Soon we'll be meeting at the LA office only as needed." Rod eyed each of their faces as he spoke.

Cab was quick to offer Rod his hand. "That's a real answer to prayer!"

Rand expelled a loud breath. "How soon will you be moving? You're wearing yourself out driving that far twice every day, especially since you've been getting back so late."

Rod scraped a hand across his face. "I'll be moving sometime within the next two weeks."

Cab started out of the room. "W. T.'s wife dropped off dinner earlier. I'll go warm some up for you, Rod."

Rod strolled across the room to where Rand sat on the couch. "How are you doing now that you're home and eating regular meals? I'm sorry I haven't been available much this week."

Rand peered up at him. "I've gotten used to the crutches, but will be glad to get rid of them."

Rod chose the armchair nearest Rand and leaned forward, regarding him for several moments. "Has Netty come over the past few days? She hasn't been answering her phone in the mornings."

Rand stared at the floor. "I haven't seen her since Monday."

Rod took note of his response and withheld further comment. Rand's feet were bare and his hair needed combed, but other than the nearby crutches on the floor and the temporary bandage on his leg, there wasn't much evidence that he'd been injured. "So, I gather you're doing okay being alone most of the day." Rod's brow wrinkled as he got a whiff of Rand's aftershave. He wished his brother would find a woman who appreciated him.

"You look tired." Rand countered.

Rod crossed his arms. "I've been working late on some blueprints in the drawing room this week." He sat quietly for several seconds, focused inward and blinked rapidly, before proceeding. "I was in the kitchen last night and heard you call out. When I came to check on you, you were asleep, but restless." He peered intently at Rand.

Rand's lips formed a straight line, his jaw muscles clenched and he lowered his gaze. "Must have been dreaming."

Rod appraised him for a few seconds. "I had nightmares for quite a while after the fire." With elbows resting on his knees Rod steepled his fingers under his chin. "I was trapped in a room with windows that wouldn't open and only a door that separated me from flames and most of the smoke. Along with the fire's roar, I could hear glass breaking elsewhere in the house."

Rand studied Rod's face intently. "What did you do?"

Rod's brow furrowed, as he considered the best way to answer. "The situation was grim and before losing consciousness, I told God I didn't want to die and He sent the firemen to rescue me. Once out of the hospital, I sometimes awoke and felt like I was choking from smoke. It often took a few seconds to realize it was just a dream."

Rand shot him a quick glance. "What made them stop?"

He stared at the afghan, which was lying in a haphazard way on the end of the couch. "I kept thanking God for getting me out of there and the dreams eventually went away."

Rand searched Rod's face. "I don't doubt that God was with me now, but at the time, I felt abandoned." He pulled on a corner of the afghan, which lay close to him. "When I saw the brake lights, I turned my wheel to avoid the van and pushed away from the bike. That's how I avoided, having my leg crushed or getting flung into the canyon with the bike."

Rod's head jerked upward and his eyebrows vanished under a lock of hair that fell across his forehead. "Quick thinking. Thank God you survived."

Rand shrugged. "Something Jess taught me a long time ago."

Rod shook his head. "Incredible."

Rand wiped his eyes with his shirt sleeve as he remembered Jess's words as clearly as if he'd spoken them yesterday. 'I hope you'll remember ole Jess when you ride. That bike's given us a lot of good memories.' He raised his head to glance briefly at Rod. "How am I ever going to tell him?'"

Rod nodded. "I remember that trip. You weren't even gone a whole day."

He sighed. "A little over nineteen hours to be exact, straight there and back." He blinked and pulled his mind back to the present. "I swear whoever was driving that van forced me off the road when they suddenly stopped in front of me."

Rod shook his head. "Jess gave you the bike and I think he'd be glad you used the skills he taught you. I'm also sure he'd remind you that a bike can be replaced."

Rand stared at the floor. "You're probably right."

Rod's brow wrinkled at Rand's dejected tone. "Could it have been the men who fought with you at work?"

He tipped his head back and glanced at the ceiling. "Gus said he'd check them out."

Rod tried again to distract Rand's train of thought. "Could it be someone you met before coming here?"

He recoiled then quickly shrugged. "I can think of only one person. If I thought it was him, I'd be on the next plane out of here." He crossed his arms and slowly shook his head. "But he wouldn't have waited this long."

Rod stood and placed a hand on Rand's shoulder. "Let's not borrow trouble from the past. It's likely someone local who's upset with you."

Rand doubled his fists. "I can't figure out who would hate me enough to kill me."

Rod observed his reaction. "I'll do some checking around myself."

Rand frowned, staring at Rod. "Laying there beside the road, I knew my chances were slim for anyone to see me. I asked God for an angel, but never imagined He'd send a dog!"

Sixteen

The next day Rand was ushered into a room at Lakeside Hospital and squirmed in his chair while waiting for his surgeon. Soon, the doctor entered and checked Rand's leg and ribs. "Everything looks good. You'll need to begin your therapy as soon as possible. I understand your family physician has recommended a physical therapist for you in Las Angeles. Continue taking the pain medication you have as prescribed. Any questions?"

Rand scanned the paper he was given. "No, thank you."

"Alright then, we'll get a cast on your leg and then you'll be free to go but in the interim keep moving carefully and deliberately and especially when you begin therapy."

After his leg was placed in a cast, he left the room to find Cab, who was in the waiting room.

He stood. "All set?"

Rand grinned. "You bet." Once in the passenger seat of Cab's car, Rand turned toward him. "I talked to dad on the phone last night. He has a friend who's a physical therapist and she's willing to come with him and stay at Candlewood. So," a slow smile turned up the corners of his mouth, "I'm not going to LA like Doc Mills suggested."

Cab smiled. "Great, that makes things easier for all of us."

Later that evening Rod parked in front of the mansion and went inside.

Cab and Rand were sitting in adjacent chairs in the library and Tommy was leaning on the wall with a basketball under one arm and Angel at his side.

Rand frowned at Angel as she padded over to him. "Tommy, why don't you take her outside? Maybe she'll play catch with you."

Rod's brow wrinkled as he tried to evaluate what Rand tried to accomplish.

"I'll try, Uncle Rand, but I bet she won't stay outside very long. Come on Angel."

She looked at Tommy and then at Rand, wagged her tail and sat next to Rand's feet.

Tommy's lip quivered. "I'm going to bed." He quietly left the room.

Rod regarded Rand and pushed an ottoman closer to his chair so he could rest his leg on it. "How long has that been going on?" He asked indicating Angel with his head.

"Pretty much since we've all been here. I think she gets use to just me during the day. I've tried to leave her outside, but she barks until I let her back in and then follows me everywhere I go. I feel bad for Tommy, but I don't know what to do. I can't make her go with him." Rand focused on petting Angel.

Rod crossed his arms. "When do you start therapy?"

"I talked to dad last night. He has a friend who's a physical therapist and she's going to come with him and stay at here at Candlewood. I called Dr. Mills and gave him the therapist's name. Doc said he'd make sure she's qualified to help me and afterward he'll cancel the LA appointment."

Cab stood and stretched. "It's getting late. There are some leftovers in the fridge from last night, Rod."

He nodded. "Thanks, but I stopped at a drive through."

"Guess I'll get going. Call if you need anything, Rand."

"Thanks, see you later."

Cab waved and left.

"I want to talk to Tommy before I turn in. Do you need anything?" Rod asked Rand as he headed for the door.

Rand shook his head. "I'm sorry about the dog. Maybe if you and Tommy went home and took her with you—"

"I'll get him a dog that will bond with him." Rod interrupted. "Don't worry about it."

———◊◊◊———*

Upstairs Rod knocked softly on Tommy's door. "Are you still awake?"

"Door isn't locked." He called from inside.

Rod entered the small room. "Mind if I sit down?" He asked gently.

Tommy avoided Rod's gaze.

He sat on the bed beside him. "Would you like to tell me about Angel and Rand?"

Tommy's lower lip trembled. "She's been following him around ever since we've been here. When I come in from school, she comes to see me and then goes and stays with him."

"How does Rand react?"

"He tries to coax her to come to me, but she just stares at him and stays with him anyway." He chewed on his lower lip.

Rod put a hand on his shoulder. "Would you like a dog of your own?"

Tommy's face lit up. "A puppy. Then he'd be all mine!"

Rod chuckled. "As soon as Saun comes home, we'll see what we can find. It will be your responsibility to house-break, feed and take care of it."

"Really?" His medium-brown eyes shone with delight. "You'll let me have a dog?"

Rod winked at him. "Whatever kind you want."

"Do you think it would pick me like Angel did Rand?"

He chuckled. "That's how you'll know the right one."

"Thanks, Rod. I really am happy for Uncle Rand now." Tommy gave Rod a quick hug. "Can I call Ethan and tell him I'm going to get a dog?"

Rod shook his head. "It's late. You can tell him tomorrow."

Some of the sparkle left his eyes, but he smiled. "I can't wait until tomorrow. Good night, Rod."

He stood then and after gazing at Tommy for a few minutes, before he quietly left the room.

Rod descended the stairs, thinking to check on Rand before going to bed. But the lights were all out downstairs so he turned and exited the mansion through the drawing room. The air held a chill and he was glad he'd not taken off his suit coat. He ambled toward the fountain and stopped at the wall to stare at the ripples on the water and the reflection of the moon's light.

It was times like these that he missed Saun. His heart ached for Tommy to accept them as his parents even though they would never be able to give him their name. Saun shared that desire with him and together they would face the heartache. He'd call her tomorrow and see how she felt about adding a dog to their household, but he was confident her answer would be affirmative. He longed to hear her voice, but it was late and he didn't want to disturb her family.

He hoped that promising Tommy a dog would show the boy how deeply he was loved. It had been a long time since he thought about his little boy, Terry. How he'd loved that little guy even after finding out he wasn't his own flesh and blood.

Rod raised his head to gaze at the sky. "Thank You, Father, that Terry never knew I wasn't his father, but we both know I was his daddy. Thank You for giving me another boy for a son. If it isn't too much to ask, could You show him I really love him and want to be his daddy." Rod drew in a deep breath. "Good night, Lord, and thanks for listening." Some words from a verse in Micah chapter seven came to him. 'My God will hear me.' A small smile lifted one corner of his mouth as he slowly walked back to the mansion with his hands stuffed in his pants pockets.

Seventeen

Netty glanced out her shop window Wednesday morning and spotted Rod as he walked up to his fancy BMW, opened the passenger door and bent over to put something inside and then closed the door. As he started to cross the street in her direction, she busied herself with cleaning the sink at her single station.

She propped her fists on her hips as he entered her shop. "I heard Saun is coming back today."

"That's right." His smile faded at the tone of her voice.

She plopped down at her desk. "Does that mean you're going back to your own house?"

He crossed his arms. "Yes. Do you have time for a haircut?"

"Have a seat."

He sat in the only chair for that purpose and observed her quietly in the mirror.

She inspected his face while she trimmed his hair and tilted his head to the right and then left. Rod's face held a softer appearance than Rand's. She'd bet Rod's mother was a beautiful woman with a sensitive face. His expressions were often sober and lacked any semblance of emotion, but Rand's expressions were often cheerful or playful.

Since his wreck he was guarded, more mysterious, more aloof, and his mind was often somewhere other than the present. He acted like he didn't even want her around and refused to let her help him with anything. He wasn't the least bit interested in anything resembling a close relationship. Had Rod's perception of her finally influenced Rand? Maybe she should just try to forget him altogether.

Rod's brows furrowed and then released.

"I used to kick myself for not recognizing the two of you were related right from the start." She remarked with a shake of her head. "But your personalities were so different back then."

Rod studied her face in the mirror without responding.

She blew a bubble, popped it and continued with her monologue. "I guess the differences are more subtle now."

He raised his eyebrows. "You don't like change, even if it's good?"

She huffed. "The vote's still out on that one." She'd closed her shop for a whole day just to be with Rand, but didn't even get one kiss from him out of the deal. He used to be so much fun. Maybe his 'fun emotion' got broke too.

When she finished, she whipped the cape off of Rod. "There you are." She began sweeping up the hair on the floor, and watched him from the corner of her eye as he left his money on her desk.

He sighed. "Thanks, Netty." He left her shop and crossed the street.

She'd wait until Rod left and then call Rand and give him something to think about.

———⟨⟩———*

At Candlewood, Rod stepped into the kitchen and spied Rand on the veranda through the window in the door. He was sitting on a deck chair with his legs stretched out in front of him. Rod stepped outside and watched Rand pet Angel, who wagged her tail. "There's dinner for you in the refrigerator. I picked it up when I stopped at W. T.'s to get gas."

Rand raised an eyebrow. "Thanks, I'll save it for tomorrow. Thought I'd order a pizza for me and Tommy. You get a haircut?"

Rod frowned. "Yes."

Rand stared at him. "And?"

Rod raised his hands in surrender. "I have no idea what's wrong with her. She was barely civil."

Rand's lip curled. "She's probably upset because she wanted to smother me up close and personal, but I don't like being pampered." He growled.

Rod raised an eyebrow. "It will be late when Saun and I get back. I'm planning to stay at the house tonight."

Rand peered up at him. "I figured you two would be tired and have a lot to talk about."

Rod gave him a brief smile. "I finished setting up my new office today so I need to go home and change."

"No problem. Is Tommy coming here after school?"

"No. He's going to the Cromwells and one of them will bring him here after dinner. They're celebrating Ethan's birthday. Either Saun or I will pick him up at school tomorrow and inform them he'll resume riding the bus." He clapped Rand on the back. "I'll stop by tomorrow."

Rand waved. "Enjoy your time with Saun."

Rand grabbed his crutches, got to his feet, and left Angel outside. He maneuvered through the kitchen, entered the library, and sighed as he sank onto an arm chair. He hoped Rod was able to spend some quality time with Saun. He knew he missed her. Rand stared blankly at the cold hearth. When the phone rang over an hour later, he couldn't imagine who would be calling as he picked it up on the first ring. "Hello?"

"Rand?"

"That's me." He smiled. *Maybe she isn't as upset as you imagined, pal.*

"I can't talk long. I'm getting ready to visit a friend."

His posture stiffened. "Okay?"

"My friend has family in Montecito and won't be in the area long."

He rubbed the back of his neck, but withheld any comment.

"Do you think I'm making this up?"

He bit his lip and kept his voice composed. "Why would I think that?"

She huffed. "Rod was upset with me when he stopped by my shop earlier so I thought—"

"Let's leave Rod out of it."

"Fine!" She snapped and let a few seconds lapse before she continued. "I haven't seen this friend for a long time and we used to be very close. I hope we can become even closer than before."

Unable to think of a reasonable reply, he offered the first thing that came to his mind. "Okay."

"Is that all you have to say?"

His jaw clenched and he shrugged even though she couldn't see him. "Yeah, I guess."

"I'm not sure how long my friend will stay this time, I'm hoping permanently." She raised her voice.

He frowned. "Enjoy your visit." His voice dropped to a quieter level.

"We have a lot of catching up to do so I'll probably get back late or maybe even stay all night. My friend doesn't like being alone."

"Have fun." *What's her point?*

"I'll call you when I get home, if it's not too late."

Wings of Steel

He forced a laugh. "Don't worry about it."

"Okay, bye!"

He winced as the receiver on her end banged in his ear and he let the phone dangle from his hand for a moment. Shaking his head, he hung up and tried to shrug off the conversation as he fixated on the hearth for several moments. *Did she just break up with you, pal?* Afterward he made his way to the drawing room and sat on the piano bench. He stared at the keys without seeing them and shook his head

---

Footsteps echoed in the hall. Rand grabbed his crutches and negotiated out the hall door as quickly as he could. He stopped at the bottom of the stairs and spied Tommy perched on the top step. "Come down here, pal." Rand coaxed.

"Okay." Tommy's hesitant response was laced with dejection.

Rand glanced at him as he descended the last step. "Let's go in the library so I can rest my leg."

Tommy silently followed him inside, and then sat beside him on one of the sofas.

He laid his crutches on the floor and propped his leg on an ottoman. "I didn't hear you come in."

Tommy lowered his eyes. "You were on the phone, so I started to go to my room, but—"

"Anything I can help with?" He took note of the teen's dismal expression. He didn't want to pressure Tommy if he didn't want to talk. "You've been spending a lot of time with Ethan since you've been staying here. Did you have a fight?"

Tommy shook his head. "Not exactly."

He zeroed in on his nephew's drooping lips. "Want to talk about it?"

Tommy eyed him as tears threatened to spill onto his cheeks. "His parents hug him and tell him all the time how much they love him."

Rand faced him. "That upsets you?"

Tommy dropped his focus to the floor. "Sort of."

"Sort of?" He cuffed Tommy's shoulder.

Tommy twisted a lock of his hair. "They try to include me."

He scrutinized Tommy's dejected expression. "Don't you want to be included?"

He shrugged. "Sure, but, when I get home—"

Rand wondered what his hesitation implied. The abandonment Rand experienced in his early years was permanently etched in his mind as if it happened yesterday. After Vera died, Ned became an alcoholic and Rand was pretty much on his own, except for Jess and Alice who encouraged him all they could. "When you get home, what?"

Tommy studied Rand's face. "I've been thinking."

He drew himself back to the present. "And?"

"You, Cab and me are all orphans."

He frowned. "Not exactly I have a dad." *And a mother even though she doesn't like you much, pal.*

Tommy nodded. "But not when you were a kid. Rod wasn't alone like us."

His brows rose. "Rod believed his dad died when he was only eight."

"Is that why he didn't like Grandpa Karl at first?"

Rand grimaced. "He didn't know Karl was his dad until recently."

"I thought he made up with grandpa."

"What're you trying to say, pal?"

Tommy was silent for a few minutes. "Saun was adopted and so were her brothers. So, all of us are orphans, except Rod. He lived with his real mom until he was an adult."

Rand tried to follow his logic. "Are you upset with Rod?"

"He doesn't understand."

Rand wrinkled his nose. "What doesn't he understand?"

"He's not like you. You care about people and ask if something's wrong and stuff."

Rand's brows rose. "So, you think Rod should ask questions if you seem upset about something?"

Tommy smiled sadly. "You noticed."

Ouch! Is he comparing us? "Rod and I are different, but that doesn't mean he doesn't care. He probably assumes everything is good unless he's told otherwise because he trusts people to tell him when something's wrong. Once he's aware of a problem, he does everything he can to solve it. Remember, he just told you he'd get you a dog? Why don't you talk to him?"

Tommy pouted and fixed his gaze on Rand.

"I'll bet if you tell Rod how you feel, you'll find out he cares about you more than you can imagine."

Tommy's mouth opened as if to protest, but instead he asked. "Do you think he'll let me call him dad?"

Rand's eyes stung and he bit the inside of his cheek. "Why don't you ask him?"

"I'm afraid he'll say no," Tommy's voice broke, "because of my grandpa's will."

Rand grabbed him and gave him a quick hug. "He can't adopt you because of that stupid will, but that doesn't stop him from loving you. I bet he's waiting for you to tell him that's what you want."

He played the piano quietly after Tommy went upstairs. Music always soothed him. When his fingers paused over the keys, an image of Vera rocking him when he was about preschool age flashed through his mind. He remembered her voice as soft rather than melodious as it wrapped around him like a warm fire on a cold night. He was surprised by the thought. He could almost hear her voice singing, 'you are my sunshine, my only sunshine.'

He went out the terrace door and leaned on his crutches as he gazed into the darkness. A wet nose pushed against his hand until he reached down to pet Angel's head.

She licked his hand and wagged her tail. When he continued to stare into the night, the dog pressed against him until he was forced to move or fall over.

One eyebrow rose as he peered down at her. "What girl?"

She turned around in a circle, pawed on the door and then stared at him. When he didn't move, she barked softly.

He chuckled. "You trying to tell me something?"

She wagged her tail and pawed at the door again.

He shook his head. "Are you part human, dog?" He made his way inside behind her, moved wearily into the library and sank onto the one of the couches.

Angel put her head in his lap and fastened a soulful expression on his face.

He began stroking her as the events of the day played on the screen of his mind. *Did Netty see the scars when you were in the hospital? Did they change her opinion of you, pal?* His throat constricted.

Angel nudged his hand and then stood on her hind feet and licked his cheeks making a soft whining sound. He leaned over and hugged her and she put her front paws on top of his uninjured leg and stared straight at him.

"Can you read my mind, girl?"

Rand awoke sometime later to Rod's voice as his hand gently shook his shoulder.

"Rand, wake up. You can't sleep here all night."

Rand raised one eyelid and spied Angel lying on the floor beside him. He sat up and tried to become alert as he squinted at Rod. "We need to talk since you're here."

Rod's eyebrows rose. "Are you alright?"

"It's about Tommy."

"I'll let the dog out first."

Rand patted Angel's back. "Probably a good idea." He got up, made his way to the kitchen, fixed a fresh pot of coffee and grabbed some leftover apple pie from the refrigerator while Rod attended to Angel.

He was sitting at the table when Rod came back inside with Angel at his heels. Rand gestured toward a chair. "Where's Saun?"

"Home in bed. I told her I wanted to check on you."

Rand frowned. "Can you spare a few minutes?"

Rod filled two cups, set one in front of Rand and sat in a chair across from him. "What's on your mind?"

"Tommy's upset because of his grandfather's stupid will. I advised him to talk to you."

Rod stroked his upper lip. "Thanks for telling me. I'll give him a little time to come to me first." He finished his pie and coffee. "It's late, I better be going. Do you need anything before I leave?"

"No, thanks. Go home and get some rest."

Rod stood and put his cup and plate in the sink. "Thanks for the pie and coffee."

Rand waved and contemplated their conversation as he finished his coffee and then headed for his bedroom, hoping to sleep without dreaming about a certain redhead.

Eighteen

Rand was in his bedroom on Friday when Angel tore off to the front door, growling and barking. "Angel, come." He commanded and she returned to his side immediately. "You have to stay in my room." He pointed inside.

She padded slowly into the room with her head down, tail drooping and pinned him with a woeful look once she entered.

"Stay." He commanded and closed the door. He maneuvered back through the kitchen and into the foyer. When he opened the front doors, two men were getting into a truck, which was parked beside his. He stepped onto the porch and uttered a shrill whistle.

The men got back out of the truck and one came up the steps and stopped in front of him, eyeing him with a curled lip. "You Rand Gray?"

Rand's jaw clenched. "I wasn't expecting you until this afternoon."

"Is there an easier way into this place?"

Rand pointed toward the garden gate. "Go through there to the veranda. You'll enter the kitchen and then follow the hall. I'll meet you outside the room where I want the equipment."

The man grunted. "Can I come in and check it out?"

Rand moved to the side and pointed to the arched doorway. "The room where the equipment will go is through there to your left, the hall is on the right."

The man walked to the doorway of the drawing room and then faced Rand. "Where do we come in?"

"Down the hall and through the kitchen."

The man rubbed his chin. "Mind if I go out that way?"

Rand shrugged as his gaze flicked upward. "Outside go to the right and through the gate."

The man strode down the hall and exited.

In order to avoid having Rod and Cab rearrange the room later, Rand made his way into the drawing room to supervise the placement of the equipment.

Once the men were gone, Rand released Angel from her temporary confinement. She licked his hand with her tail wagging briskly as he dumped his cold coffee in the sink, refilled his cup and let the dog outside. Afterward, he made his way to the library, carefully balancing a cup between his finger and thumb while managing his crutches.

That same morning, Lucinda Warner whisked into the post office. She searched the immediate area for Willis, who was nowhere in sight. "That lame-brain. I do wish they would hire someone more responsible for this job. I wonder how much mail gets lost or misplaced by that, that boy." She grumbled as she straightened her large frame and slapped the bell on the desk mercilessly.

"I'm coming, 'I'm coming. I ain't deaf! A body's gotta take care of person—" He stopped in his tracks and pasted a smile on his face. "Miz Warner, what can I do for you?"

She harrumphed. "Don't patronize me, young man! You can be where you're supposed to be. Post this and don't be asking foolish questions."

Willis gawked at the envelope and his eyes got so big it seemed they'd pop out of their sockets. "Do you have family in—?"

"Zip your mouth and put a stamp on that!" She ordered.

Willis grinned. "Yes ma'am. Have you heard about Rand Gray's wreck? He was in the hospital for a month. Been laid up at the ole mansion for a couple of weeks too. I ain't seen him since his brother brought him back there. I saw them come back myself. He was using crutches too and his brother stayed close like he was afraid Rand would fall. One of his legs has a cast on it too!"

Lucinda's glare flitted around the room before she fiddled with something inside her purse to avoid Willis's probing gaze. "What kind of accident?"

"He went over a cliff on his motorcycle. Guess he's plumb lucky to be alive. Golly, I wonder if he'll ever recover!"

Lucinda squinted at Willis, clasping her hands together. "You aren't telling a fib, are you, boy?" She looked down her nose at him over the counter.

"No Ma'am, I seen him and his brother get out of his BMW."

"Well, you mind your manners and don't go blabbing it all over the village. You hear me?" She supposed her warning was a little too late.

"Yes Ma'am."

Lucinda left the post office quickly. She had a mission to accomplish.

In the library, Rand set his coffee cup on the table next to the couch, propped his crutches against it, and carefully lowered himself onto a cushion. Once seated he raised his injured leg onto the coffee table, picked up his cup and raised his other leg. After finishing his coffee, his eyelids began to droop. He leaned his head against the back of the couch and with the empty cup still in his hand, fell asleep.

Sometime later his eyes flew open and his eyebrows rose as a familiar voice called his name.

"Randall, where are you?"

Slowly he shook his head in disbelief while an uncertain smile played on his lips. "In the library, Mother."

Lucinda bustled into the room. "What are you doing up? Shouldn't you be in bed? What's wrong with that brother of yours leaving you here alone?"

He blinked rapidly and then stared at her. "Mother, if I didn't know better, I'd think you were worried about me." He chuckled softly as his heartrate increased.

She sat on the couch beside him. "Why on earth did you do such a fool thing? You could have been killed!"

"Been talking to Willis, huh Mother?" He scanned her weathered face, which normally held a perpetual frown, but at that moment a softness lingered in the lines and planes of her skin that he'd never seen before.

"Don't you have any better sense than to ride one of those contraptions? Where's your common sense, boy?"

He sighed drowsily. "I'm kind of tired, Mother." *If she's going to lecture me, she can go, now.*

"Indeed." She got up and swung both of his legs onto the couch.

He winced at the sudden movement. "Mother, please." His protest died on his lips as she spread an afghan over him. With a sigh, he focused on her actions instead of his throbbing leg. "What're you doing?"

"Hush. Go to sleep. I'll fix you some lunch after you rest a while."

His eyebrows rose as her words penetrated his daze. *She's staying here? And fixing me lunch!* He frowned as he thought of Angel and the way she carried on when the equipment was delivered. "Whatever you do, don't open any outside doors besides the one you entered."

She put her hands on her hips, lowered her chin and appraised him over the top of her round wire-rimmed glasses. "Why?"

"My dog's outside and I don't know if I can trust her with people she doesn't know." *I could never forgive myself if Angel bit my mother.*

"How dreadful! I'll be sure to lock those doors. Now, you rest, young man." She added in a softer tone than she'd used before and briefly cradled his cheek in her hand before leaving the room.

The unexpected tenderness of her touch made his Adam's apple bob and he closed his eyes against sudden moisture. "I'm glad you're here, Mother." He managed to whisper before succumbing to sleep.

———)(○)(———*

He awoke sometime later, surveyed the room and tried to remember why he was lying down. He usually fell asleep sitting up because it was easier to rise from that position. He turned his head and flinched. His mother was sitting nearby in an armchair, knitting. *Am I dreaming?*

She quickly came to him. "Are you hungry?"

"I, yes. How long have you been here?"

"You've been asleep for a couple hours. I'll go fix your lunch'" She left the room.

Rand focused on the ceiling, smiling as a tear oozed down his cheek. *Jesus, You're amazing. If I had to get hurt to get mother to come to me, it was worth it.*

Lucinda returned in a short time, carrying a tray, which she set on the coffee table beside the couch.

A mouth-watering aroma made his stomach rumble. Eyeing her steadily, he held his breath, and watched her.

She propped him up against the arm of the couch with large pillows behind his back, moved the coffee table and then pulled a straight-back chair next to him. She placed a towel under his chin and over his shirt.

He stared with his mouth hanging open. "Moth—er?" His voice was thick as heat spread up his neck to his face. He wasn't sure if he was embarrassed or just hesitant to believe she was actually attending him. As he maintained strong eye contact, he found her deep-gray eyes were tender and full of compassion. His vision blurred and he lowered his gaze.

"Let me to do this for all the times I missed when you were..." She sniffed.

He raised his arm to protest, but changed his mind because of the tenderness in her expression. "Mother, you don't have to—"

"Hush now." The command was softly whispered. "Don't argue with me, Randall. Just eat. You need your strength. You're weak as a kitten."

He greedily absorbed her every movement. Her touch brought healing to the deep fissures in his heart as she fussed over him. He blinked rapidly. He wouldn't even think of refusing her. *She loves me. She really loves me.* After he ate every bite, she wiped his mouth with a damp cloth. Tears spilled onto his cheeks at her tender touch. "I love you, Mother." His voice was ragged.

"I love you too, son. And I'm proud of you. Both you and that brother of yours for all you've done for this village."

He wiped his face with the back of his hand as his Adam's apple bobbed. "I've waited so long to hear—" He choked out the words.

"Sshh, quiet, dear." She leaned over and enfolded him in her arms. "I've been an old fool, but things are going to be different now. I'm going to take care of you."

He held her close and drew in the scent of herbs, flour and something sweet. "Mother, I appreciate what you're—" He whispered hoarsely.

She pulled from his embrace and pressed her fingers against his mouth. "I won't do this again, but will always remember and treasure this time with you. You're a grown man after all. Thank you for allowing me this little time to cherish you."

He grasped her hand, pulled her close, and hugged her again. "You've made me very happy, Mother." His heart was so full that his words escaped his lips in a hoarse whisper.

She smoothed his hair away from his face. "Rest now. I won't be far if you need anything."

His brow wrinkled as he rubbed his jaw. "I have something to tell you. I hope it doesn't change anything because I want you, I mean, I need you in my life. The doctors say I have to do some physical therapy. Dad has a friend who's a therapist and—"

"Is your therapist a woman?" Lucinda removed her hand from his cheek.

Slowly, unsure of where she was going with her question, he swallowed and nodded his head.

"Is your father coming with her?"

His brow wrinkled. "Dad didn't think it would be good for us to be here alone even though we're both Christians. He insisted on coming with her."

She took his face between her hands leaned forward and kissed his forehead. "Then we will make the most of today and not worry about tomorrow. However, I'm glad you told me. I would not have wanted to encounter him." She got up and put the chair and coffee table back where they were and left the room.

His mind reverberated with her words. 'I will always remember and treasure this time with you.' He exhaled a deep sigh and closed his eyes as a smile teased his lips.

Footsteps in the hall alerted Rand that he had company. "In the library." He called as he sat up and began folding the afghan.

Rod entered the room with one eyebrow arched, shaking his head. "Miss Warner was leaving as I came up the steps. She asked me to call her if you need anything and she was nice about it."

Rand grinned, thinking that was the most surprise he'd ever seen on Rod's face. "Amazing, isn't it. Have a seat and I'll tell you all about it."

As he finished his tale, he dropped his focus to the floor unable to hide his emotion. "It's been kind of mind-blowing." He replied hoarsely. "Dad's coming sometime tomorrow with his therapist friend."

Rod stood. "Cab promised to check on you later since Saun will be getting dinner ready. Do you need anything before I go?"

Rand shook his head and tried to focus on Rod's face. "I'm good."

Nineteen

Rand spent Saturday morning reading the Fire River Gazette in the library. One article stated there was a collision of two subway trains in the Mexico City Metro System on October twentieth. Forty-three people were killed and more than sixty were injured. Rand shook his head and tossed the paper aside as Rod strode into the room with three bags of groceries.

"I'll put these in the pantry." He announced as he took a shortcut through the library. He made a few trips back to his car and it was several minutes before he joined Rand. Rod stood across from him and crossed his arms. "Tommy told me last night that he wanted to call us mom and dad, but was hesitant to approach me about it. Apparently, spending time with the Cromwells served to increase his desire for a closer relationship with us. I appreciate you encouraging him to talk to me."

Rand gave him a half smile while keeping steady eye contact. "I'm glad he finally came to you."

Rod regarded him soberly. "I didn't want to pressure him if it wasn't what he wanted." He lowered his gaze with a sigh. "I have some errands to run so if you are—"

"I'm good." Rand gave him a two-finger salute. "Thanks for the groceries. I have no idea who'll do the cooking. Guess we'll figure it out when they get here."

"When are they coming?"

He shrugged. "Sometime today."

Rod started to leave but paused. "Have you seen Cab?"

"He said he might stop by again later."

Rod nodded. "Hopefully we'll cross paths soon."

He leaned forward. "Are you coming here after church on Sunday?"

Rod glanced at his watch. "It all depends on what Saun has planned. Aren't you coming?"

"Planning on it, hopefully at least dad will come with me."

"If you need a ride, I'll come and get you." He headed out the door into the hall.

When the door closed behind Rod, Rand leaned his head back against the couch and started humming the song, "Green Eyed Lady." It had run through his mind off and on all morning. He smiled at the memory of Netty's eyes the first time he sang that song to her.

Later that day Angel leaped up from where she laid beside the couch and emitted a low growl. "Stay!" He commanded as he picked up his crutches and got to his feet.

She stared at him and whined, but obeyed.

He made his way out of the library, closed the door behind him and eagerly maneuvered into the foyer. As he opened the front doors, he observed Alfred helping a young woman and then his dad out of a black limousine.

Rand hadn't expected Alfred, Karl's chauffeur, but it made sense since they weren't planning to fly and his dad didn't drive. Standing on the columned porch to greet his visitors, he stole a glance across the street and caught a glimpse of Netty peeking out her shop window.

He shook his head and focused on his dad, who was the first one up the steps. Karl Gray was a stocky-built man with salt and pepper hair. His friend, Miss Germayne, was a petite blond.

"Hi, Dad!" Rand greeted him with outstretched arms.

Karl welcomed his embrace. "I'm glad you're mostly in one piece."

Rand chuckled and appreciated that his dad's hug lingered a little.

"This is my good friend, Brooke Germayne." Karl stepped back. "She's Arlo's niece. In case I didn't tell you, he's my long-time friend and business partner."

"Nice to meet you, Miss Germayne." Rand greeted her as he grasped her hand. "Thank you for being willing to come and help me."

She clasped his hand. "My pleasure. It's nice to finally meet you, Rand. Please call me Brooke." She held his attention, giving his hand a warm squeeze before releasing it.

He found her grip firm and it made him curious what his dad told her about him. Her sparkling cobalt-blue eyes made him think of mountain concha flowers.

Alfred Drummond, who had gray hair and a precisely-trimmed mustache and beard, cleared his throat.

Rand jerked his attention from Brooke's eyes. "Alfred" He quickly accepted the man's outstretched hand. He was a slender man, about his dad's age with some gray in his light brown hair and he spoke with a slight English accent. "Welcome, I'm sorry we didn't get much chance to talk when you were here before."

He chuckled. "You were concentrating on getting acquainted with your father. I understood completely."

Rand swept his arm in a broad arc. "Come on in." As the four of them went inside, Rand gestured down the hall. "Through the second doorway is the stairs. Alfred, please show Brooke the rooms upstairs and you can all choose the one you want. Brooke, you're welcome to explore inside as well as out. My dog, Angel is—"

"Angel?" All three guests spoke in unison with eyebrows raised.

Rand coughed a short laugh. "She's the German shepherd who adopted me so I'm not sure how she'll react to strangers." He directed his next comment to Brooke and Alfred. "If you don't mind, I'd like some time alone with Dad"

"Capital idea." Alfred remarked and pivoted toward the front doors. "I will see to our luggage. Karl, may I assume you and I will occupy the same rooms as before?"

Karl gave him a curt nod.

Brooke bounced from one foot to the other, while her face shone. "You really don't mind if I explore? I love old mansions!"

Rand grinned at her excitement. "Just be careful if you go to the third floor. The restoration up there isn't finished."

Her expression became serious. "Thank you, but I really should check the therapy equipment first."

"It's through the arch and double doors"" Rand appreciated her focus on the reason she was here even though it was obvious she was eager to explore. He observed her as she headed in the direction he indicated. She could just be the distraction he needed to keep from thinking about a certain redhead. He watched the sway of Brooke's hips as she moved gracefully in heels that seemed too high for comfort. Her navy skirt swirled around her knees with each step. She sashayed through the arch and stopped in front of the open doors.

"What a lovely room." She turned and smiled briefly at him before disappearing into the drawing room.

"Son?" Karl chuckled. "Where do you want to have our talk?"

Caught in the act of staring, Rand's ears heated. He swallowed dryly, realizing his heart was beating rapidly. "Let's, let's go to the garden. I'm tired of being inside. I'll hold Angel until I see how she's going to behave with you."

Karl indicated he'd wait in the hall.

Rand entered the library, sat on the edge of a chair, and grasped Angel's collar. "Okay, Dad, come in slowly."

Karl carefully approached Rand and Angel.

Her tail thumped on the floor as she appeared to smile at Karl.

"This is my dad." Rand spoke softly but firmly to Angel. "Be nice to him."

Angel stretched her head in Karl's direction as her tail wagged furiously.

Karl patted her head and Angel licked his hand.

Rand squinted at him while a slow smile lifted a corner of his lips. "She likes you. I hope she accepts Alfred and Brooke as easily."

"Seems like a friendly dog. I don't think you need to worry."

"I hope not." Rand considered the dog that was obviously enjoying Karl's attention.

"Are you up for that walk now?" Karl asked.

Rand gestured toward the door and followed Karl outside. When they reached the fountain, Rand gave him a tentative smile that broke into a full grin as Karl sat beside him on the bench instead of in one of the chairs. "I'm really glad you came, Dad." He raised his head to gaze at the tops of the black oak and California palms and inhaled the warm earthiness of their surroundings stirred by a slight breeze. "I hope you can stay even after Brooke leaves."

Karl rested his arm on Rand's shoulders and peered into his eyes. "That's music to these old ears. There's a lot about you that I don't know. Do you ever think about the place where you grew up? Will you ever go back there?"

"We can talk about that some other time. I'm just glad you're here."

Wings of Steel

After dinner, Rand and Karl sat on a couch while Brooke chose an armchair in the library. Alfred retired to his room and the rest talked until Karl yawned and checked his watch. "It's 9:45. I think I'll turn in for the night."

"Okay, Dad, sleep well."

"Alfred gets up early, so he'll have breakfast ready by eight unless you'd like me to tell him to another time."

"That's fine. I'm usually up by five. I'll have coffee ready for anyone who wants it before breakfast. I didn't mention it earlier, but would you like to go to church with me tomorrow? It starts at ten so eight will work for breakfast. Rod and I attend a church in Montecito."

Karl squeezed Rand's shoulder as he stood. "I'll let Alfred know. I will want to go with you and I'm sure he will also. Brooke can decide for herself. Good night." He acknowledged them and left the room.

After he left Brooke responded. "I'd love to go to church with you. Uncle Arlo and I rarely miss." She rubbed her arms. "It's kind of chilly in here. Do you mind if I light a fire?"

He started to get up. "I can—"

"No, sit still. I do it at home all the time. Cedric, Uncle Arlo and I enjoy evenings in front of a fire. I honestly don't mind."

"If you're sure it isn't too much—"

"No trouble at all." Her voice was soft and gentle.

Rand watched her with an amused grin, thinking she'd get her clothes dirty. To his amazement a fire crackled cheerfully a few minutes later and the only thing dirty was her hands.

She promptly wiped them on a cloth that was left on a stool near the hearth.

Angel nudged her arm as she finished and she hugged the dog's neck. "You're a beautiful girl, and so loveable and your name is even on your collar."

"That was my nephew, Tommy's, idea."

She hugged the dog again and got a lick on her chin in response. She giggled as she chose the same chair she sat in before Karl left them. She crossed her ankles and faced Rand.

"You'll get to meet him at church tomorrow long with my brother and his wife."

"You mentioned this dog adopted you. I'd like to hear that story."

He leaned back, stretched his legs out in front of him and rested his outstretched arms on the back of the couch. He appraised her honey-colored tresses, which cascaded over her shoulders and his gaze traveled to her pink lips that framed a cute smile. Suddenly, he became aware that he'd been caught staring. He rubbed a hand over his hair as his cheeks heated. "What did you say?"

She focused on Angel, stroking her head. "You said there's a story about this girl."

His eyebrows rose. No one commented when he mentioned it earlier so her curiosity intrigued him. He told the story taking note of her rapt attention as he spoke. She appeared genuinely concerned about his injuries and seemed interested in every detail. Her deep-blue eyes sparkled in the firelight and her face shone with joy. *It might be fun having her here, pal.*

Brooke continued petting Angel as he told her how the dog helped rescue him. "Angels are God's messengers of comfort and help so the name fits her, but I bet you don't make a practice of calling your male friends angels." She giggled.

He chuckled and tilted his head to the side. "Since you brought it up, God's angels have male names, at least the ones in the Bible."

She regarded him with a thoughtful expression. "You know, I think you're right."

He met her direct gaze. "Where did you go for your training? What made you choose physical therapy?"

"I received my degree at Chapman University. My mother had polio as a child. She loved having her legs massaged and it helped her get around a little better."

He raised an eyebrow. "How old were you when you first started helping her?"

"I was around five, but it wasn't until I was nearly ten that I was strong enough to do her much good."

"How is she doing now?"

Brooke chewed on her bottom lip for a few seconds before answering. "My parents died in a boating incident when I was twelve."

Rand took note of her downturned lips and wished he could offer more than soothing words. "That must have been hard for you."

She blinked several times. "Uncle Arlo took me in and treats me like I'm his own daughter. My faith in Christ has helped as well."

Rand sympathized with her loss. If they were better acquainted, he might offer the comfort of his arms. "I'm glad your uncle was there for you. Do you have sisters or brothers?"

She shook her head. "I have Uncle Arlo and your father who has been like a second uncle to me."

"That would sort of make us cousins." He winked at her, hoping to lighten her mood.

She laughed as her face flushed a pleasing pink. "I guess you could say that."

He leaned forward as his grin stretched wide. "I think I might like having a cousin for a therapist."

"Okay, cousin, it's my bedtime. Let's plan to start therapy on Monday at ten. I'd like to work for an hour to start with and we'll go from there. I'm glad you're already up and around. It will speed your healing process."

"That's the plan. Sleep well."

"Good night, Rand." She patted Angel's head. "Good night, Angel."

The dog licked her hand before resting her head on her paws again.

When Brooke left, the room suddenly didn't seem quite as bright. He picked up his crutches, got to his feet and maneuvered to the kitchen. He let Angel out for a few minutes and stood gazing out the veranda door until she barked. He let her back inside and headed for his bedroom, hoping for a good night's sleep.

Changing his mind, he made his way back to the main hall. Once there he stood and stared at Netty's second floor apartment, but there was no light in the windows. *Good night, Netty. Hope you enjoyed your time with your friend.* He sighed and headed for his room.

Twenty

Early Monday morning, Rand whistled as he maneuvered into the kitchen, let Angel out and filled her dishes with food and water. He came back inside as Alfred stepped into the room.

His eyes twinkled. "Good morning. Shall I start breakfast?"

Rand's eyebrows rose. "Aren't you on vacation too?"

"No sir. Your father is my friend, but also my employer. Cooking and chauffeuring are part of my responsibilities and I happen to enjoy both"

"Okay, but dad is the only 'sir' around here." Rand poured himself a cup of coffee before carefully making his way to the table. "I don't want to interfere with your arrangement with dad, but I can't enjoy the benefits of your helping dad without offering to pay for whatever you do for me."

Alfred crossed his arms. "I assure you, Karl compensates me quite well, but if it'll make you more comfortable, why don't you discuss it with him?"

Rand smiled as he sat down at the table. "Fair enough."

"Would you like me to set the dining room table for breakfast?"

"Here's fine with me, unless dad objects, but I'd like you to eat with us."

"As you wish." Alfred conceded.

Later after they finished eating, Alfred cleared the kitchen table as Rand, Karl, and Brooke enjoyed their coffee. Karl was the first to finish. "Do you have the Gazette delivered or do I need to go get it?"

Rand lowered his cup. "It should be on the front porch. Lenny delivers it. He goes to school with Tommy and drops it off on his way there during the week. I used to count on money from my paper route when I was his age so I pay him for bringing it."

Karl nodded. "I'll be in the library. Don't let him slack on his exercises, Brooke." Karl winked at her.

She laughed as her brows wrinkled. "I won't."

"She'll have to slow me down." Rand smirked.

Karl shook his head as he left the room while Alfred started washing dishes.

Brooke pushed her chair from the table. "If you're finished, we should get started."

Rand turned away from the table and stood. "I'm ready."

Rand left the kitchen and moved slowly to the drawing room with Brooke following him. He sat on the end of an exercise bench and she gave him weights to lift.

"We'll work on your upper body first. We need to strengthen your arms and shoulders so they bear most of your weight while you're using the crutches. Are you having any trouble with them?"

"They're a little awkward, but I manage to get where I need to go." He raised and lowered his arms several more times than she required.

She appraised him. "Good, we'll keep increasing the weights for your arms."

"I have a set in my room."

"I'd like to see them and then we'll go from there. For now, let's move to the massage table. I need to assess the extent of your injuries and the progress of your healing up to this point."

He sat down on one end of it, swallowed and rubbed the back of his neck. *No one mentioned any massages to me.*

She took the crutches and put them aside before helping him raise his legs onto the table, one at a time.

He grimaced when she lifted his right leg and blew out a couple of short breaths when she helped him lie down on his back.

Her brow wrinkled and she leaned toward him. "I'm sorry. I didn't expect that to hurt you. You need to be more careful about putting weight on your injured leg. That's why we're starting on your upper body. I contacted your surgeon and he sent me a full report of your injuries. The ones on your back and shoulders appear older. Do they still bother you?"

He sat up too quickly and winced. "I understood this therapy was for my legs." *No one else mentioned old injuries. Why her? Why now?*

She studied him with raised eyebrows. "It is, but your back and shoulders appear tense. Massage therapy would be good for those as well as your leg. You seem like the type who's physically active. The tightness in your upper body is likely due to the extra stress on your arm and shoulder muscles because of the crutches."

He blinked rapidly and slowly sank onto his back as sweat beaded on his forehead. When she began to examine his thigh, he flinched. *I can't do this.*

She eyeballed him with drawn brows. "Tomorrow we'll start with some exercises for your legs, but try to limit the amount of pressure on the injured one."

He closed his eyes and inhaled slowly. "I'll do my best."

She crossed her arms, scrutinizing his face. "By learning to manage the amount of stress you put on it, you'll heal much quicker, Rand." She smiled as she lightly touched his shoulder.

He flinched reflexively, lowered his gaze and gave her a curt nod.

She raised her eyebrows. "I'm sorry I startled you." She reached for his crutches.

"I wasn't—" He started to make an excuse for his response, but changed his mind. "It's all good."

She observed his face for several seconds. "Don't you trust me?"

He dragged his fingers through his hair, giving himself time to think, and stared into the distance. "It isn't . . . let's just focus on my leg." He remarked as he slid off the table. grabbed his crutches and headed for the double doors.

"Rand." She called after him. "May I see your weights?"

His head bobbed as he continued to his bedroom.

After showing Brooke his weights, Rand spent more time catching up with his dad on the events of their lives since they'd been together last. He gave Karl a brief summary of the incident with his bike and how Angel found him and forced Cab to stop and help him.

"Is there something wrong, son? You've been distracted even though you've done most of the talking."

He forked his fingers through his hair. "Just have a lot on my mind."

Karl studied him. "What do you think of Brooke?"

Rand took his time getting to his feet, careful not to put unnecessary weight on his injured leg. "She's smart."

Karl's brow wrinkled. "Isn't that a good thing?"

"Too soon to tell." The words were mumbled.

Karl beamed. "She is a rare gem indeed, has a heart of gold." He paused, looking at Rand as if waiting for a response.

He shrugged. *She's sharp. Be on your guard around her, pal.*

Karl frowned. "Alfred and I are going to Montecito. I have some things I want to pick up. Is there anything you need while I'm out?"

Rand shook his head. "No thanks. Is Alfred going to be doing stuff for all of us or just you?"

Karl's eyebrows rose. "Has he said anything to you?"

"No, I mentioned it to him. I have no idea what his job is or what you expect of him. I don't want to interfere with your arrangement with him."

Karl chuckled. "I never gave it a thought."

"But if he's going to be cooking and cleaning besides what he does for you personally, I'd like to pay him extra."

Karl nodded. "I understand your concern. If you wish to give him a little extra you may, but he's well compensated."

Rand crossed his arms. "Okay, I'll see you later." He left the library and made his way to the drawing room where he closed the doors. He crossed the room to the massage table and stared at it for several moments as his nostrils flared. He flung one arm out and over it. *Not happening, babe.*

Finally, he turned to the piano, carefully sat on the bench and laid his crutches on the floor next to him. He ran his fingers over the keys and began playing a classical piece, pounding on the low bass notes, but half-way through changed to some popular country and western tunes.

Brooke finished her walk in the garden and when she came back inside, piano music filled the mansion. She recognized "Rachmaninoff's Concerto no. 2" immediately and was lured to the drawing room doors. The music changed abruptly and she was familiar with the songs Rand began to play and was delighted to hear him sing a line or two of each one. His voice was pleasant and his pauses between phrases emphasized his emotion. She could empathize with the unconcealed emotion in his voice and it brought tears to her eyes.

She put her hand on the door, but sensed he wouldn't be pleased if he knew she was listening. She could feel his agitation when he struck the keys with vengeance. A thundering discord startled her so that she scurried into the library lest he discover her. She couldn't help wondering if he'd ever broken a string.

Karl was no longer present and the paper he'd been reading lay folded neatly on a side table. She peered out the windows and discovered the limousine's absence. She slipped outside and hurried along the path to the fountain.

She vowed to never give her heart to another man, but there was something about Rand Gray, which captivated her. Actually, several things took her by surprise, his talent both as a pianist and a singer, the diversity of his musical sensibilities and his complex personality. Those traits could prove to be a dangerous combination. This was a job and she'd best not forget it.

Later Rod parked his car in front of Candlewood and Angel came to greet him when he entered. "Hello, girl. Where's Rand?"

The dog padded down the hall toward the kitchen as Rand made his way into the hall.

Rod met him there and observed Rand's pinched lips. "What's wrong?"

"Nothing." He snorted.

Rod squinted at him. "Sit down. I'll get us a glass of water." Angel whimpered and he let her outside to avoid any distraction while they talked.

Rand was sitting in an armchair, tapping his fingers on his knee when Rod entered the library,

He shut the door, crossed the room, gave Rand a glass of water and sat on a chair adjacent to him. "Do you want to talk about it?"

Rand stared at the floor. "What happened while I was unconscious in the hospital?"

Rod crossed his arms. "What do you mean?"

Rand stared at him. "No one mentioned anything to me about massage therapy."

Rod put his glass on the side table next to his chair and steepled his fingers. "Did your therapist recommend it?"

"Yeah." He took a deep breath.

Rod leaned forward. "Why don't you call your surgeon?"

Rand eyed him. "I just might do that."

He studied Rand's angry expression for a few seconds, waiting for a further response. When he made no indication of continuing the discussion, Rod gave him a quick smile. "I wanted to see how therapy is going."

His gaze bounced around the room. "Fine." He drank until the glass was empty and set it on the table. "Thanks for checking on me."

Rod meditated on Rand's terse answers. He seemed furious about the massages, which made Rod wonder about the reason for the marks on Rand's skin. "Have you spoken with Clayton?"

"Why would I call him?" He growled.

Rod shook his head, picked up their glasses, left the library, took them back to the kitchen and set them on the sink.

The veranda door opened and Rod swung around to find the petite blonde woman, who he'd met briefly at church yesterday. She was staring at him with her mouth hanging open. He extended his hand. "I'm Rod Gray. We met yesterday. Brooke Germayne, isn't it?"

She clasped his hand. "Yes. I noticed the resemblance even before Rand introduced us. Have you been here long?"

"I stopped to check on how his therapy is going."

She gave him a wry smile. "Physically, he's doing fine."

Rod raised an eyebrow. So, she picked up on his reluctance? Not one given to being overly speculative, he filed the observation for future investigation. He'd witnessed his brother's surliness firsthand and her comment increased his concern. "Has he told you about the kind of work he did before his injury?"

"No and I haven't asked him, but I discovered he plays the piano exceptionally well. I guess I assumed—"

"I'll let him tell you." Rod considered her response. "Do you have someone in mind who can continue with his therapy when you leave?"

She tilted her head to the side. "I plan to stay as long as my uncle doesn't need me."

Rod stroked his upper lip with his index finger, frowned and lowered his arm. "My wife and I will be praying for your success as well as Rand's. It has been a pleasure talking with you, Ms. Germayne."

"Please, call me Brooke. Since you're Rand's brother and Karl's son, I hope we can be friends."

Rod nodded. "Let me know if there's any way I can help. I'm on my way to a meeting with a client so I'll see you next time."

As soon as Rod left, Rand picked up the phone and dialed Dr. Mills. The receptionist informed him the doctor would return his call as soon as possible. Rand sighed as he hung up the phone and raised his head when the hall door opened.

Brooke poked her head inside. "May I join you? I think we need to talk."

His head bobbed curtly.

She entered, but left the door ajar. "I sense you're anxious about me being your therapist. May I ask why?"

He weighed his response for several seconds before scraping a hand through his hair. "As I already said I will gladly do the exercises you recommend."

She regarded him for several seconds. "You don't appear to be the bashful type. You've spent time in a hospital recently so several people have worked with you in various ways. If this is too personal because it's just you and me, you're welcome to have your father pres—"

"I need therapy for my leg, that's the reason you're here."

"My desire is to help you," she pleaded, "not make you uncomfortable. I noticed you flinched when I barely touched your shoulder. I don't understand why you reacted that way because you don't strike me as untouchable. Quite the contrary, you seem like a guy who isn't afraid of much of anything. I think there's more to your reaction, but I respect your privacy. However, if something is troubling you that much, maybe you should think about getting some counseling. It won't get any better or easier unless you do. I'll pray you find someone to help you."

Rand blinked at her directness. "Thanks."

She sat down beside him on the couch. "Okay, we'll proceed with your leg therapy. I would count it an honor if you told me what's troubling you, but even if you don't, please find someone you can talk to."

"Got it." His cheeks flushed and he pressed his lips together. The memories, parading through his mind were as real as if they happened only moments before. He swallowed hard, trying to dislodge the dryness in his throat.

"I can tell you're deep in thought about something and I really want to help you." She whispered.

He bit the inside of his cheek. "I'm good." His voice was barely audible.

Her brow wrinkled. "We'll do it your way, nothing but physical exercise, okay?"

He blinked and met her direct look. "Okay."

She sighed. "That's a start."

The next day after breakfast, Rand made his way into the drawing room, sat in an armchair and waited for Brooke to finish eating and talking with Karl and Alfred.

Angel pushed open the terrace door, padded into the room, placed her head on Rand's knee and focused her warm brown eyes on his face.

He petted her, glad for the distraction.

Brooke entered the room, leaving the door open behind her and stopped in front of him.

Angel removed her head from Rand's knee and stared at Brooke.

Rand continued to pet her as she eyed Brooke.

She smiled. "Your dog almost seems to be protecting you."

He slowly released a deep sigh. "Maybe she is." One side of his mouth hitched, as he focused on Angel and gently stroked her. "I told you she found me after my wreck. Didn't you, girl." He leaned over and pressed his face against Angel's head. "She's rarely far from my side."

Brooke blinked several times as she rubbed her arms. "Okay, let's get started with the leg exercises I showed you yesterday."

Several minutes later he finished them, puffed out his cheeks and released the air. "I'm ready to move on to something more difficult."

"Please rate your pain for me on a scale of one to ten with ten being the most difficult."

"Maybe three." He frowned.

She placed her hands on her hips. "I don't think you're ready to move forward just yet. Like I told you earlier, stressing it too soon will slow the process rather than speed it up. Please repeat those only slower this time."

His brows pulled in, but he repeated the exercises as she requested.

When he finished, Brooke made some notes in a little book and then peered up at him. "Repeat those five sets again tonight and we'll see if you're ready for more on Thursday."

On Thursday, Rand's jaw was set as he repeated the scheduled exercises and breezed through a new set without even thinking about them. He wanted to avoid going to LA at all cost and it was more convenient for everyone that he continued his therapy here.

Brooke eyed him. "How do you rate your pain today, Rand?"

His intense gaze held hers. "Zero."

Her eyebrows arched. "Seriously?"

He regarded her with a challenging expression.

"All right then, let's try this." She demonstrated the movement.

He followed her motion, but winced when he raised his injured leg.

She rushed to his side. "Let's try that again only much slower."

He raised the leg slowly, but it dropped to the floor quickly as he drew in short breaths and expelled them.

"Will you let me help you raise and lower your leg?"

He fisted his hands, giving his head a short jerk.

She grasped his cast just below his knee and slowly raised and lowered it.

His forehead broke out with sweat. "Let me try it."

"Just take it slow."

He raised and lowered his leg fourteen times. *You can do this, pal.* But the next time, he released a breath he'd been unconsciously holding and couldn't lift his foot off the floor.

She focused on his face. "How do you rate your pain now?"

He stared at the floor. "Maybe five."

She appeared to weigh his response. "Alright we'll try that again tonight and I want to be with you when you do these exercises."

He pressed his lips together and wiped his forehead with his sleeve. "Okay."

Twenty-One

On Halloween night at a prosaic bar near Summerland, a scraggy bartender strolled over to a large bulky man with a long pony tail who was sitting alone at a table. Neon orange lights draped over the rafters above it and paper witches and goblins hung on strings between the lights. "I'm closing, man. It's time to leave."

The customer raised his head and glanced around the empty room. "Gimme a bottle of your house whiskey for the road."

The bartender crossed his arms. "You able to drive, man?"

The outsider stood, knocking the chair over he'd been sitting on. "You'll find out if you don't get me that bottle."

The bartender backed off, holding up his hands. "Take it easy. I'll get your whiskey. Then you can pay for it and get outta here." He swaggered around the bar and set a bottle on top of it. "That'll be—"

"On the house." The large man finished for him as he grabbed the bottle off the bar top. "Next time I come in here, if you're real nice, I just might pay." He swung around and headed for the door.

"Hey!" The barman yelled. "Not so fast. You can't leave until you pay for that!"

The intruder whirled his two hundred sixty pounds around to face the man with his switchblade drawn. "I ain't in the mood for arguing!"

An hour later, he shook his head at the man lying on the floor. "Told you I wasn't in the mood for arguing." He left the bar, stuck the bottle in a saddle bag on his Honda and rode off.

After clearing the town and leaving all trace of civilization behind, he pulled off the road and hid his bike in the bushes. He hiked a considerable distance from the road, cleared a place to build a small campfire, laid out

Donna Noblick

his sleeping bag and sat down with the bottle to stare into the fire. After he'd consumed half of it, he began to weep as he drank. "I miss you so much, little brother. It ain't the same without you. Our old man's gone too." He began to sob. "I'm all alone now, but I got rid of him who killed you, like I promised." He fell on his face as sobs racked his entire body.

Twenty-Two

The next morning Rand made his way into the drawing room just as the phone rang. He picked it up. "Hello."

"Good morning, Rand."

He expelled a huge breath as he recognized Dr. Mill's voice. "Morning."

"Doctor Stockton, your surgeon, ordered those x-rays. As a precaution, he sent a thorough report to the therapist you chose."

He frowned. "Does anyone else know—?"

"It's doubtful that any of the other staff would have seen the x-rays."

"Rod and Cab were at the hospital. Could they have seen—?"

"The x-rays are viewed only by your surgeon and his staff. Is there a problem?"

Rand rubbed the back of his neck. "Just that no one mentioned—" He sighed. "Thanks, I appreciate the call."

"You're welcome. If you have any other questions, don't hesitate to call."

Rand hung up the phone and pivoted toward the door as someone approached it. He stiffened when Brooke entered the room.

"Are you ready?" She greeted him warmly.

He studied her as he silently went over his conversation with the doctor. He nodded, rolled his shoulders, grasped both crutches, and made his way to the exercise bench.

She sat on the massage table. "I'll just observe this morning. I want to make sure you don't push yourself too hard."

Later when he finished, he leaned against the bench and wiped sweat from his forehead with a towel, which was left there for that purpose. "I've been cooped up long enough. How about a break for lunch?"

She crossed her arms and appraised him. "It's too soon for you to drive."

He frowned. "My truck is a standard shift. Do you know how to use a clutch?" He studied her and wondered if she would even be able to see over the dash.

"My car's a standard." She gazed at him with a mischievous twinkle in her eyes.

His lips pressed together in a straight line. "Let's check it out." He headed for the door.

"Wait for me."

He paused on the porch at the note of panic in her voice, but continued down the steps with his crutches as a corner of his mouth quirked upward.

"What's so funny?"

He pinned her with a lop-sided grin. "I was thinking what could happen if you tried to keep me from falling. We'd probably end up in a heap at the bottom of the stairs." The scene he imagined made him tug at his collar.

She playfully swatted at his arm and reached for him. "That's not funny."

He avoided her hand. "I can do better on my own."

She lowered her arm to her side. "Just be careful, please."

He eyed her with a smirk. Once on the stone terrace he crossed it with no mishap, opened the driver's door of his truck, and waited for her.

She climbed inside, checked the shifter, instrument panel and pedals, and then moved the seat forward. "As they say 'piece of cake.'" Her lips twitched and she grinned. "When do you want to go?" She took the hand he offered to help her step down.

"I'd like to grab a shower first. Can you be ready in half an hour?" He took note of her small hand still enclosed in his and released it quickly.

Her face turned pink. "I'll be ready."

Rand waited for Brooke in the drawing room. He sat at the piano with his hands resting on the keys until thoughts of Netty crossed his mind. He played the first song that came to him, "Can't Help Falling in Love." He stopped abruptly.

Brooke clapped from behind him.

He swallowed his emotion and then spun around on the bench to face her. His jaw dropped open at her stunning appearance. "Your sweater matches your eyes." He hadn't meant to comment, but the sparkle in her dark-blue orbs captured his attention.

"Thanks." She appraised him with a smile. "You're very talented. Do you play professionally?"

He turned away from her to run his fingers randomly over the keys. "Depends on what you call professional."

"Do you get paid for it?" She asked.

"Sometimes." He crossed his arms.

She huffed. "Are you going to make me guess?"

He shrugged. "Played some in bars. No big deal."

"Should I assume then that Rachmaninoff is for your own enjoyment?"

He turned to face her again as a slow smile raised the corners of his mouth. "That wasn't what I just finished."

She giggled. "I know." Her gaze quickly dropped to the floor.

He rubbed his chin with his thumb and peered at her with raised eyebrows. She'd been listening before. After a few moments, he picked up his crutches and stood. "Ready to go?"

Rand started down the steps.

Brooke clutched his arm. "Careful."

"I got it." He removed her hand and managed the descent. On the ground, he crossed to his pickup, put his crutches in the bed, and hopped around to the passenger door. As he lifted his injured leg inside, he threw a glimpse at Brooke.

She caught up with him and eyed him curiously from the open driver's door.

He blinked. "What?"

"I think you're going to recover quicker than I expected."

He crossed his arms over his chest with a smug look and handed her his keys.

She tossed him a sideways glance. "You don't think I can handle this, do you?"

He adjusted his position, but his lips twisted in a grimace when he stretched out his leg.

"I have a Maserati." She told him with a smirk as she started his truck.

His jaw dropped. "No way!"

She nodded her head. "A blue one. Better fasten your seat belt." She retorted.

"Lady, you're full of surprises." He shot her a crooked grin and secured his belt.

She winked at him. "Someday maybe I'll give you a ride you'll never forget."

He raised an eyebrow. Hard enough to believe she could drive his truck, let alone a Maserati. He stared out the passenger window and caught a glimpse of Netty, gawking at him from her shop window. Quickly he jerked his head toward the windshield. *Women!*

Brooke drove them away from the village and they rode in silence for several miles.

When they drew near to the mountains, he pointed ahead. "Soon we'll pass one of my favorite spots."

Brooke slowed down when he indicated the place. There was no one behind them so she stopped and fastened her attention on a narrow upward path. "It's almost invisible."

"Yeah. I leave my bike—truck by the road. The view's incredible up there."

She smiled. "You'd love Uncle Arlo's chateau. The formal living room has windows from the ceiling to floor and the mountain peaks often have snow on them."

He imagined the view she described and it intrigued him. There was something about the mountains that called to him more than the ocean or beaches. Not that he would openly admit it, but it was likely because of where he'd spent his youth. "I take it you still live with your aunt and uncle?"

"Just Uncle Arlo. My aunt died when I was very young. Cedric, my uncle's driver and housekeeper sometimes stays with us."

After they'd driven several miles, he pointed toward the windshield. "The restaurant's just up ahead around the next corner on the right. You can park in the back."

Brooke parked behind the restaurant.

Rand got out and retrieved his crutches from the bed. He opened the restaurant door and allowed Brooke to enter first.

———⟪⚭⟫———

Brooke surveyed the restaurant's log cabin interior. The place was family friendly with tables and long benches in a large open room. The decor upheld an old west theme with wagon wheels and various equipment of that era displayed on the walls.

The hostess approached them. "Table for two?"

Rand's head bobbed in response.

"Follow me." She led them to a small corner table with a window view of the nearby beach. She laid their menus on the table. "Your server will be with you shortly. May I get you something to drink?"

"Coffee, thanks." Rand answered promptly.

"I'll just have water, please." Brooke responded.

The waitress returned with their drinks. "Are you ready to order?"

He crossed his arms. "I'll have a loaded burger."

Brooke appraised him with a smile. "I think I'll have the steak salad."

The waitress noted their order on her pad. "Will there be anything else?"

Rand shook his head. When the waitress left, he eyed her with a whimsical grin. "There's an ice cream shop just around the corner so save room for dessert."

She studied him curiously. Was he flirting with her? "Thank you for the heads up. I'll probably need a to go box because I usually skip lunch."

After the waitress brought their food, Rand met Brooke's gaze across the table. "My treat." Afterward, he took a bite of his burger.

Brooke watched him eat with gusto. "When Karl told me about your wreck, I knew right away I wanted to help. It was a perfect excuse to meet you. Last year when he came home, you and your brother were all he talked about for weeks." She busied herself with her salad and hoped she wasn't overly enthusiastic. Her heart beat faster at the appreciation, which shone on his face. "Do you come here often?" She blotted her lips on a cloth napkin.

"Couple times a month, maybe." He dipped a fry in some ketchup on his plate.

"I spoke to Rod briefly on Monday before he left the mansion. He asked about your progress. It seems the two of you are really close." Brooke contemplated the wistful expression that passed over Rand's face when she mentioned Rod but she sensed it was none of her business. "Even though Karl told me he just found out about you last year, he didn't share a lot of details. May I ask how that all came about?"

He frowned, finished chewing, and swallowed. "I came to Fire River to find my mother and also found Rod and then dad."

She appraised his face, especially his eyes. At times like now, they appeared to hold deep feelings she couldn't identify. At other times they held something akin to mischief and sometimes such sorrow that she found it difficult to breathe as she studied him.

He finished eating. "What are you interested in, besides your work?"

Thrown off guard by his sudden question, her thoughts turned in a completely different direction. She considered how to best answer his question. "I enjoy playing piano, mostly classical music. I like to ski. I love going to street fairs and open-air markets to hunt for antiques. On the quieter side, when I have time, I like to paint."

His brow rose. "Paint what?"

"Scenery and occasionally portraits. What are your hobbies?"

"Hiking and riding—" His face sobered briefly. "I especially like wood carving."

She frowned. There it was again, an almost reference to his motorcycle. She focused instead on the twinkle in his interesting eyes, which appeared slightly different in color. She lowered her gaze lest he catch her staring. "What kinds of things do you carve?" She raised her head to peruse his square jaw and high cheekbones.

"I helped restore some of the mansion's woodwork, but I make mostly small items. I like to choose a piece of wood and imagine what it can be. I've also made a few animals for little ones."

He had a soft spot for children. "Karl told me you haven't been here long. Where were you born?"

Rand's gaze dropped to his plate. "Arizona."

She took note of the tightness around his mouth at the mention of his birth place. "Why did you come to Fire River?

"To find my mother."

"How did you find out she was there?"

"She left some letters with the couple who raised me."

Her breath caught in her throat at his tender expression when he mentioned his mother. "So, you found her here."

"I did." His face beamed with joy as he focused on his plate. "We didn't really hit it off at first, but since I got hurt . . ." His voice dropped almost to a whisper.

When he didn't offer anything more, she became even more determined to try and get him to talk about it. It was clear to her that he was disturbed by some aspect of his past and she wanted to find a way to help him deal with it. She finished with her salad and when she focused on his face, he appeared to be waiting for her.

Wings of Steel

"How about that ice cream?" He waggled his eyebrows.

"I'll wait for my box if you want to go pay the check." She was forking the last of her salad into a box when he returned.

"All set?" He asked and pulled out her chair when she nodded.

---*

"We can walk to the ice cream shop. It's only a couple blocks." He told her while they crossed the street.

"Are you sure?" She asked with a glance at him.

He smirked. "Positive."

They walked three blocks to a cute little shop with colorful candy treats displayed in the window.

"So, it's more than an ice cream shoppe." She teased.

He grinned. "Guess I forgot to mention the extras." He made his way to the counter.

"Hi, what'll it be?" The pretty brown-haired clerk sang out as they approached.

Rand reached for Brooke and ushered her to the counter. "I told her you have the best homemade ice cream there is."

She grinned. "You want your usual, Rocky Road on a sugar cone?"

He winked at the clerk. "You bet."

She placed two scoops of thick chocolate on a cone and drizzled hot fudge over it. "Here you are. What would you like?" She asked Brooke.

"One dip of vanilla topped with whatever you just put on his, please."

"Coming right up." The clerk smiled, fixed Brooke's cone and gave it to her. "What happened to you?" She asked, pointing at Rand's crutches.

He raised an eyebrow and paid for the treats. "Nothing serious." Afterward he hurried Brooke out the door.

"Take care." The clerk called to him.

Rand gave her a backhanded wave and maneuvered to a nearby table that had a chair on either side. He sat down and laid his crutches next to the storefront out of the way of other pedestrians. Quickly he licked his cone when it began to drip.

Brooke sat in the other chair and focused on her ice cream. "How long have you been coming here?"

"I found this shoppe shortly after coming to Fire River." He concentrated on his ice cream. When he finished, he grinned at her and pointed to his nose.

Her cheeks turned pink and she quickly swiped at her appendage with her napkin.

He shook his head. "You missed a spot."

She scrubbed with the napkin until it was almost in shreds and made quick work of her cone. When she finished, she leaned across the table and stared at him. "You have some chocolate on the side of your mouth."

He swiped his lips with his tongue. "Where?"

She giggled. "Other side."

He pushed his tongue to the other side of his mouth while she stared at him with an intensity. "Is it gone?" He asked with a crooked smile.

"Yes." Her cheeks turned red and she lowered her gaze. She pushed away from the table and headed in the opposite direction from the way they came. "Let's go."

"Wrong way." He called after her.

She pivoted slowly in his direction.

He chuckled to himself. Poor girl, she embarrassed herself twice in less than ten minutes. Soon they were back at his truck. He put his crutches in the back, climbed in the passenger seat, and tried to give her time to regain her composure.

His jaw clenched. "I've enjoyed this. It's been a while." He was preoccupied with his thoughts as he stared unblinking through the windshield for several minutes. "I've been thinking, I wouldn't blame you if you didn't stay—"

"I'm okay with—" She touched his arm.

"What I'm trying to say is," he quirked an eyebrow, "I found out you were shown things that no one besides the doctors know and—"

"Your secrets are safe with me." She considered him soberly. "I know only that you were injured previously, honest."

He dropped his gaze to the dash. "I believe you." His Adam's apple bobbed as he swallowed noisily. "I'm sorry, I acted like a jerk."

"Apology accepted." She continued to drive in silence for several moments. "Let's get you back home and settled in the library where you can prop up your leg."

Twenty-Three

Wednesday after lunch Rand sat in the library and drummed his fingers on the arms of his chair. He and his dad talked intermittently while they shared sections of the Fire River Gazette. Rand caught a glimpse of Brooke when she passed by in the hall on her way to the kitchen. He waited a few minutes and when she didn't return, he figured she went out to the garden. They reached a mutually agreeable patient and therapist relationship once she agreed to limit his therapy to exercise only.

Karl fell asleep with the newspaper on his lap, Alfred disappeared, and Angel was outside. Rand assumed she followed Brooke. Not an inside person by nature, he wrestled with his physical limitations. Slowly, he managed to exit the mansion, stood on the porch, and took a deep breath of fresh air.

He began to whistle while he carefully descended the steps. He proceeded east along the sidewalk away from Netty's shop and crossed Chino Avenue directly opposite the post office. When he entered the building, a bell on the door banged against the glass. His brows rose in surprise. When had Willis added that? Rand made his way to the counter, hit the desk bell repeatedly, and grinned.

Willis came running from the back room. "Hey, Rand. How're you doing?" Willis grabbed the bell and slammed it under the counter.

Rand eyed him with one eyebrow raised. "Not bad." He chuckled at the quick action of the quirky little man. Many of the villagers didn't care for his slow-to-respond nature, but he enjoyed ribbing the postal worker just to observe how he reacted. Sometimes, like now, he was pleasantly surprised. Willis was a major source of village gossip, but Rand didn't hold that against him. After all, no one was perfect. "Do you have anything for me?"

"A box came from Arizona this morning. Want me to take it over to the mansion for you?"

An idea struck Rand while he peered over Willis's shoulder. A mirror on the back wall in the mail room would let him see when someone entered out here. "Thanks, just put it inside the front doors."

"I'll do it as soon as I finish sorting today's mail. Who's the pretty lady and the two men with her? I saw one guy carry several suitcases up the steps."

Rand winked at him. "My dad's friends."

"The lady sure is a purty little thing. How long they staying?"

He shrugged. "See you later, Willis."

Slowly Rand swung toward the door. The box from Arizona must be from Jess. He bit his lip and promised himself he'd call his friend as soon as he could think of a way to tell him what happened. *You can't lie to him, pal. He'd never believe you lost control. And if you told him the truth, he'd only worry.*

Rand stopped beside the driver's door of his pickup, thinking he could keep busy by making something from some of the wood stored in his workshop. He leaned his crutches against the side of his truck, opened the door, and reached inside for a tool he left behind the driver's seat.

"Hello, Rand."

He jerked upward, hit his head on the top of the doorframe, and nearly lost his balance.

Netty gripped his waist from behind him. "Careful, you don't want to hurt yourself again."

His muscles tensed and he pivoted to face her, which forced her to remove her hands. He retrieved his crutches and shut his door.

"Sorry I startled you." She snickered. "Will you be able to fully recover from your wreck?"

He chewed the inside of his cheek. He was tempted to yell. It wasn't a wreck. "Definitely."

"Good, then we can go wind surfing or hang gliding to celebrate."

He rotated away from her to avoid her unwelcome intrusion into his personal space. *She's trying to rile you, pal.* Without a word, he started up the steps.

"She isn't your type. You'll destroy her." Netty yelled after him.

He flinched, but continued upward as if the remark didn't affect him. Once inside with the door closed, he felt light-headed. He wasn't sure whether the dizziness was a result of the effort to control his temper, the bump on his head or his rapid ascent of the steps. Murmured voices came to him through the closed library door so he shuffled into the drawing room.

He wanted to sit and pound out his frustration on the piano keys until—until what? He closed the doors behind him, slumped against them, and squeezed his eyes closed. He was trembling. He couldn't believe he let Netty get to him that way.

"Rand?" Brooke's voice was a mere whisper. "Come and sit down. I'll get you a glass of water."

He shook his head trying to erase the impact of Netty's remarks.

Brooke rested a hand on his shoulder. "Did you hurt your leg?"

"No, I'm okay."

She gently brushed his hair away from his face. "You're very tense. Do you want to tell me what's wrong?"

His jaw clenched as he took a deep breath, removed her hand, enclosed it with his and gazed intently at her. "Did I interrupt what you were doing?" His voice was a hoarse whisper.

She slid her hand from his. "I can finish later."

"You can finish while I play." He indicated the piano with a slight nod of his head.

She studied him directly. "I'd like that, if you're sure you don't mind."

He sat at the piano and began to play randomly.

She moved quietly to a corner out of his line of sight.

Nearly an hour passed when a familiar voice along with Alfred's reached Rand's ears. His fingers paused in mid-air when he focused on Brooke, who stood nearby. "I thought you left."

"You invited me to stay." She lowered her gaze.

"I didn't mean—that's my boss in the hall. Will you ask him to come in here, please?"

"Of course." She left immediately.

Rand faced the hall doors, but didn't move from the piano bench.

Zeke Finn entered the room and offered Rand his hand. "How are you doing?"

Rand briefly clasped Zeke's hand. "Better."

"Glad to hear it and I'm sorry to have to tell you this." He tugged on the beard that covered his chin. "I wish I could hold your position open—"

"No problem, I figured you'd have to fill it."

"If there's anything I can do for you, let me know. I'll be more than happy to give you a good reference."

"Thanks, Zeke."

He shifted his stance and backed up a few steps. "I hate to bring bad news and run."

Rand met his gaze with a steady one of his own. "I understand. I'm sure you're busy."

"It's the least I could do. Good, honest men, like you, are hard to find. I've enjoyed working with you. Take care of yourself."

"Thanks, I will." He waved and then expelled a huge breath.

———*———

A few minutes later Brooke returned. "The postal clerk brought a box for you while Mr. Finn was here. Where would you like me to put it?"

He raised his head. "Leave it in the hall. I'll get it later."

"I'll tell Alfred to put it in your workshop. Your boss told me why he came. May I ask what kind of work you did?"

He sighed. "I was a stevedore."

"Your brother suggested that I ask about the kind of work you were doing."

He closed his eyes and enjoyed a sudden release from his dock responsibilities. "Basically, supervised the transfer of equipment to and from the docks and ships." He took a deep breath. "Truthfully, I won't miss it."

She pinned him with a pleased smile. "I like your attitude. I think you've got a lot more to offer than physical labor that didn't seem very satisfying anyway."

"What do you mean?" He snorted.

"You're intelligent and talented. I'm sure you'll be able to find work that will be more suitable." She stared at him with a wrinkled brow.

"I hope so." He pivoted around to the piano and began to play a Tchaikovsky piece with vehemence.

Saturday afternoon, Rod opened the door to Sheriff Palmer's office and let Rand enter first.

Gus raised his head as they stepped inside and set aside a stack of documents on his desk. "Paperwork, wish there was a better way to do things. Thank you both for coming. Grab a chair."

Rod eyed Rand as they both sat on the chairs in front of the sheriff's desk.

Rand blinked at Rod.

He nodded, assuming Rand wanted him to initiate the conversation. "Have you found out who caused Rand to wreck?"

Gus frowned at Rand. "I asked you to come once you were out of the hospital. Since you didn't, I told Rod to bring you here. So, I expect you to answer my questions."

Rand rested his crutches against the desk and stared at Gus. "I've tried to figure out who could've run me off the road." He shrugged. "I have no more idea now than I did before."

"What do you mean, you don't remember any more? It's been five weeks since your wreck." Gus took a pencil from a glass on his desk.

"Six, but who's counting." Rand expelled a long breath. "I already told you all I know." He glanced at Rod.

Rod narrowed his eyes at Rand. If he suspected someone, why didn't he tell Gus? He turned his focus on the sheriff.

Gus peered at them and crossed his arms. "I would have told you earlier, but it took some juggling to get your bike, or what's left of it, out of the gulch."

Rand raised his hat and swiped his sleeve across his damp forehead. "Was there something that led to—?"

"We found green paint on the bike. It matched an abandoned van near a vacant lot over around Summerland." Gus tossed the pencil on his desk. "We placed your bike in a simulated position with it according to what you told me. The van had a black streak of paint that matched the scratch mark on your bike's fender, which was found several feet away from the wreckage. The impact would have been enough to make you lose control."

Rand expelled a long breath. "I hope you find out who did it." He avoided eye contact with Rod.

"I get the impression that isn't all you found?" Rod crossed his arms as he pinned the sheriff with a penetrating stare.

Gus cleared his throat. "There were no tags on it. I called you both in here to let you know I'm doing everything I can to get to the bottom of this. I checked out the two dock workers you fought with last month. They both have solid alibis."

"I, told you that." Rand growled. "Like I said, they could get another job almost anywhere. So, why come after me?"

Gus crossed his arms. "Unfortunately, that's all I have right now. If it was locals, they haven't left much evidence."

"What about the vehicle identification number?" Rod asked as he took a small notebook from his pocket and wrote something in it.

"The man it was titled to died last year." Gus rubbed his chin.

"So, it's a dead end." Rand scoffed.

Gus frowned. "I'll pretend I didn't hear that. We'll find them." He growled.

Rand's jaw clenched. "You mean you don't think whoever did it is one of your upstanding citizens?"

Gus's face turned red. "I didn't say that! I figure it probably is a local. You boys stirred up quite a lot of folks last year and not everyone was happy with the results even though most of the village business owners were happy with their settlements. By the way I appreciated all you both did to help get that situation wrapped up."

Rod stood then. "Are you telling us that this may be a result of last year's resolution?"

"Don't go getting all riled up. I'm only stating a possibility. I have to check every angle."

"We're not upset with you." Rod responded. "We realize you're doing all you can."

Gus glared at Rand. "If you think of anything and I mean anything—"

"Already told you all I remember." Rand snarled.

"Call us when you find out anything else." Rod responded as he helped Rand to his feet and handed his crutches to him.

"That's why I called you in here." Gus growled.

Rand tipped his hat with a smirk as Rod opened the door. "Afternoon, Sheriff." He stepped carefully out the door.

Rod gave Gus a tight-lipped smile. "We'd appreciate being informed of any further information." He closed the door behind them.

Twenty-Four

Rand turned off his drill Tuesday afternoon when Tommy stepped into his shop. He smiled and raised his safety goggles. "Hey, pal. Good to see you."

Tommy returned his smile. "What're you making?"

"A hutch for my mother."

"Oh." He shifted from one foot to the other. "Did dad tell you I got a puppy?"

Rand chuckled at his excitement. "Yes." He was glad Tommy no longer called Rod by his given name and hoped that meant the teen now felt like a real part of the family.

"Sparky's a black and white border collie and he picked me just like Angel did you!"

Rand grinned. "That's the best way."

"Dad said Sparky can sleep in my room as soon as he's housebroke." He stared at the different pieces of wood scattered around the room in neat stacks. "What's this going to be?" He picked up one long flat board.

"A shelf. The rest of them are over against the wall." He pointed to a heap stacked on a long table.

Tommy ran his hand over the wood in his hands. "Do you always make them this smooth?"

Rand measured another piece of wood with a layout square. "Depends on what I'm making."

"Could you show me how to make something?" Tommy crossed his arms.

Rand threw him an amused grin. "You have something in mind?"

"Maybe something pretty for mom?"

He marked the wood with a pencil and glanced at Tommy. "What does she keep her tea in?"

"Plastic bags. She don't have anything big enough to hold it all." He was silent a moment. "Could you help me make her a wooden box for her tea bags?"

Rand grinned. That's exactly what he'd thought of, but gave Tommy the opportunity to come up with the idea. "Would she like light or dark wood?"

"I don't know."

"Guess you'll have to do some investigating. Look for things she sets on shelf or table tops. They can give you some ideas. Where does she keep it now?"

Tommy stared at the floor for a few seconds before he raised his head. His eyes opened wide and then he scrunched his nose. "In a drawer."

Rand straightened and winked at Tommy. "Then you ought to make something she'll be proud to show off."

Tommy bounced on his toes. "Could you show me how to make Indian designs on it? Mom likes her blankets and pottery and jewelry and stuff."

Rand grinned. "You can get some good ideas from those."

"Do you think we could finish it before Christmas?" He clapped his hands.

"Shouldn't be a problem."

Rod entered the shop. "What do you want to finish by Christmas?"

Tommy pivoted toward him. "Uncle Rand's going to show me how to make a wooden box for mom's tea."

Rod placed a hand on Tommy's shoulder. "She'll really appreciate something you've made." He switched his attention to his brother, but didn't remove his hand from Tommy. "How're you progressing with therapy?"

"Alfred drove Dad and Brooke to Montecito. She said she'd get me a cane while they're out. I'm more than ready to get rid of the crutches."

Rod nodded. "That's good news. Do you need anything from Beck's Hardware? I plan to stop there after work tomorrow." The store, located in Montecito was not far from Rod's new office, and held a combination of plumbing supplies and lumber.

"More wood for this project but I can ask Alfred or Brooke to take me."

Rod watched him measure another shelf and mark it. "I can always pick up whatever you need and drop it off on my way home."

Rand stopped and stared at him. "You're more relaxed now that you're not driving back and forth to LA every day."

Rod smiled. "I am." He gave Tommy's shoulder a pat before releasing him. He observed Rand's hands as they almost caressed the wood as he sanded it. "Are you ready to go, son? Dinner will be ready soon."

He peered up at Rod. "Can I say good-bye to Angel first?"

"Just a few minutes, we don't want to be late for dinner."

Tommy scrambled down the hall.

Rod chuckled when Tommy ran out the door. "Is that a hutch you're making?"

Rand responded with a bob of his head. "Mother's running out of room for her knick-knacks."

Rod crossed his arms as he continued to watch Rand. "Do you think you'd enjoy being a carpenter?"

"It's a thought. I forgot to tell you Zeke stopped by last week. He hired someone to take my place on the docks." He forked his fingers through his hair. "I thought about quitting anyway."

Rod's brows wrinkled while he pondered Rand's comments. "The third floor here still needs some work."

Rand considered the piece of wood he'd been sanding. "It's a shame the village didn't catch our vision for it. The old place has a lot of character. It's a waste not to use more of the space, even with dad, Alfred, and Brooke here. And I don't want to stay here indefinitely, in the mansion, I mean."

Rod stroked his upper lip. He was glad Rand clarified his statement, but began to pace a few steps away from him. "I haven't completely given up on the project. Do you think you'd like to manage it? At least the historical society tabled their desire to raze it."

Rand snorted. "For now. That was largely due to mother's belief we don't intend to make it another inn. Do you really think we should give it more time and effort, not to mention money?"

Rod stopped and crossed his arms. "Why don't we meet soon and exchange some ideas. We might be able to make an investment of it. I'm sure if we put our heads together, we can come up with something. Preferably, one that would benefit the community as well."

Rand shook his head. "You're always thinking of ways to benefit others here."

Tommy bounded back into the makeshift shop. "I'm ready, Dad."

Rod studied Rand's face. "I'll look forward to hearing your ideas about my suggestion."

Rand acknowledged Rod's comment, but focused his attention on Tommy. "Don't forget to check out Saun's decorations."

"I won't, bye Uncle Rand."

Rod nodded and followed Tommy out of the shop.

Friday morning, Brooke finished her stretches as Rand entered the drawing room. She studied his face and hoped she could memorize the way his eyebrows rose and the slight upward curve of his lips, which waited to impart a cheeky grin. She gently bit her lip. "Good morning. Do you think you're ready to use a cane?"

"Sure, but maybe not ready for any marathons." His lip hitched. "Still have a little limp but the strength exercises will take care of that soon."

"They should." She stretched to one side and then the other. "You've improved quicker than I expected." She enjoyed working with him, and would miss his musical abilities and also his spirited attitude, which she found delightful. Her stomach rumbled and her face heated.

He chuckled. "Breakfast's ready. Alfred sent me to get you. They're already at the table."

"Okay, we'll do your exercises afterward. She took a deep breath, put on a cheerful face, and hoped he'd continue to progress after she left. "When we're finished, I have something to tell you."

"Okay, let's go, I'm hungry." He followed her from the room.

A little later, when they were all finished with breakfast, Brooke suddenly pushed her chair back. "If you gentlemen will excuse us, it's time for Rand's exercises. Breakfast was delicious as always, Alfred, thank you."

Rand finished his exercises in record time and took note of Brooke's subdued mood. When he finished his cool down, he tilted his head and observed her. "I'd like to get some fresh air if you don't mind." They took the path to the fountain.

After they passed it, Brooke sat on one end of the bench. "Please sit down."

He sat near the other end and turned toward her. "Is something wrong?"

She turned sideways and faced him. "Not with you. It's good that you're confident but please continue to be careful."

He winked at her. "I'm always careful. That's how I stay alive." His brow wrinkled at her downcast expression. He swallowed his mirth. "Whatever you're going to say, must be serious."

Her smile seemed forced. "I got a call from my uncle's driver while you were outside yesterday. Uncle Arlo isn't doing well and Cedric, his butler, encouraged me to return home as soon as possible."

He winced. "Wasn't he ill when you came?"

She nodded. "He hasn't been well for some time. Cedric told me Uncle Arlo was admitted to the hospital. I'm his only family and—" She wiped a tear from her cheek. "I hope you understand."

He focused on his empty hands and kicked at a stone. "When are you leaving?"

"Alfred will drive me to Montecito in about two hours. From there I'll catch a flight to LA and then on to San Francisco."

His gaze caught and held hers. "I'm sorry about your uncle. If there's anything I can do, I'm only a phone call away."

"Thank you, Rand. Even though I'm your therapist, I feel like we've become friends. I believe you can continue the exercises on your own."

He sighed. "Don't worry about me. I'll be fine."

Briefly she touched his arm. "Perhaps you can come to San Francisco for a visit sometime."

He swallowed dryly at the hopefulness of her tone. *You aren't crazy about big cities, pal.* "Maybe."

She pulled her bottom lip between her teeth. "I guess I'd better go. I still have a few things to pack." She stood.

He caught her hand, knowing his response disappointed her, but he refused to give her false hope. "Don't forget I'm a good listener."

She leaned over and kissed his cheek. "I'll remember."

He let her hand slip out of his. She quickly pivoted away from him but he caught sight of a tear that escaped her eye. While he stared after her, he hoped he hadn't led her to believe there was more than friendship between them. He was determined to continue therapy on his own and would keep the equipment and exercise the way she instructed until he regained his strength.

Twenty-Five

Late Monday afternoon Rod parked beside Rand's truck and ascended the steps. Piano music, which Rod recognized as a classical piece came from the drawing room. He entered quietly and closed the door behind him when Rand switched to some moody love song. Rod was familiar with the tune but couldn't recall its name. He stood silently and listened for several moments.

Rand suddenly tuned his head, stopped playing, and pivoted on the bench to face Rod. "How long have you been here?"

Rod crossed his arms. "Long enough to appreciate your skill."

He shrugged. "Chalk it up to years with not much else to do. Are you on your way home?"

"Yes, I stopped to check on your therapy's progress. Dad told me Brooke went home and you left church yesterday before I could talk to you."

Rand met his brother's direct gaze. "I have a cane now and will continue with the exercises for the time she suggested."

Rod nodded and drug a chair close to the piano and sat down. "Have you considered my suggestion about the renovation?"

Rand raised his head. "I don't have any immediate plans so I can do whatever you want. Will you be involved?"

"Some but you'd be in charge here. I made some notes and sketched a few things to consider." He gave Rand a folder. "Go over these when you get a chance and after you look over the list we can discuss how to proceed."

Rand opened the folder and scanned the pages. "Seems doable."

"I told Tommy I'd help him with his homework after dinner tonight."

"I envy you."

Rod sat up straighter. "Why?"

He ran a finger lightly over the piano keys. "You and Saun are in tune with each other and—"

"Are you thinking about Netty or Brooke?"

He shrugged. "Neither, since the bike incident—" He dropped the subject, embarrassed that he'd brought it up.

Rod frowned at Rand's obsession with Netty to the exclusion of other possibilities, like Brooke. He leaned toward him and held his gaze. "Has Netty said anything to you recently?"

Rand threw his hands up. "Every time we cross paths—"

"Have you tried talking to her?" Rod stroked his upper lip.

His lips pinched together. "Why would—forget I mentioned it."

Rod stood, put the chair back, offered him a small smile and briefly touched his shoulder. "I'll see you later."

———)◆(———*

Rand exercised after breakfast the next day and kept rigidly to the program Brooke set up for him, but added to it. He wanted to progress more quickly than she allowed him and was confident he knew his body well enough to do more. Karl and Alfred left soon after breakfast so Rand took the opportunity to up his regimen. When he finished, he showered, put on Levi's, a dark green long-sleeve shirt, and brown cowboy boots. He snatched a tan cowboy hat from his dresser and the cane, which was propped next to it.

He stood on the porch and stared at the barber shop across the street. An older man left her shop. Rand figured if he went to her, he would have the option to leave if things didn't go as he hoped. In any case, the appearance of one of her customers might also prove beneficial.

He adjusted his hat lower on his forehead, carefully made his way down the steps, and crossed Chino Avenue. He took a deep breath, opened the door to her shop, and stepped inside. He glanced around the immediate area. It appeared she hadn't swept up after the man who left a few moments earlier. She must be in the back. From his peripheral beside the door, he observed her enter the shop from the storeroom. He slowly pivoted toward her. *Lord, help her listen.* He peered at her face from under the brim of his hat. "I'd like to talk to you."

She raised her chin, planted her feet wide, and plopped her fists on her waist. "Your little girlfriend left you, huh. So, you come crawling back to me!" She hissed through tight lips and took a step in his direction.

He spread his feet. "Netty, I—"

"No! You listen to me." She yelled. "You're the one who started this." She pointed her finger at him. "You pushed me away, remember? Or did it mean so little to you that you shrugged it off just like you do everything that doesn't really concern you." She took several steps toward him.

He didn't move. "What are you talking about?" He ground out the words between clenched teeth. He rested one hand on his cane and fixed her with a level stare. "I thought we were friends."

"Ha, that's a joke!" She crossed her arms. "What's your idea of a friend?"

He pushed his hat farther back on his forehead. "Someone I trust to have my best interests in mind just like I do theirs."

She gaped at him. "What about the way you kissed me?" She hissed as she observed the red color, which appeared on his neck and ears. She stomped her foot. He's embarrassed because he doesn't even remember.

"If you're talking about the night we celebrated our birth—"

"Oh, ho! You're so good at giving mixed messages." She spat at him as heat engulfed her entire being.

"You're an attractive woman. What did you expect?"

"Your wreck obviously damaged your brain as well." She took several more steps, entered his personal space, and gave his chest a shove. "You're nothing but a tea—."

"Back off, Netty!" He took two side-steps while his lips formed a straight line and fire flashed in his eyes.

She drew back her arm, intending to slap him, hard.

Quick as a whip, he grabbed her wrist. "You really think I'd let you hit me?" His eyes were flinty. He ground out the words between clenched teeth and his voice sounded low and gruff.

"Let go of me!" She snarled. She refused to let him see he frightened her. So, she speared him with a dark scowl.

He flung her arm away from him and adjusted the position of his cane.

"Get out, Rand!" She backed up several steps and wrapped her arms around herself. She could tell he wanted to hit her. His whole body screamed it. "Go ahead, hit me. I dare you. But you'll be sorry, mister." She growled with all the bluster she could summon.

A vein throbbed in Rand's temple. He snatched one last glimpse at her. His lips curled as he left the door open behind him and navigated to the sidewalk. *I wanted to try and work things out, but all she wants is a fight.* He flinched when the door slammed behind him. The finality of it momentarily shook him as he stepped off the curb. He had the same kind of feelings she had. *Didn't mean you needed to give in to them, pal. Didn't mean you didn't want to either.* The screech of tires penetrated his thoughts and his heart leaped into his throat.

"You want to get run over, man?" A young man hollered from his mustang. "Get out of my way!"

Rand stopped and waited for the youngster to leave. Afterward he cautiously crossed Chino Avenue and navigated to the garden gate at the side of the mansion. He let himself in, closed it behind him, and made his way along the path until he reached the fountain where he sank onto the stone wall surrounding it. Netty's venomous, *get out, Rand,* reverberated in his head like an echo in a large empty room. His muscles quivered and his cane slipped from his hand. It made a ringing sound when it hit the ground and lightly bounced on the stones at the foot of the fountain's wall. *You almost hit her, pal. God forgive me, I wanted to.* He snatched his hat from his head and sat staring at it as he turned it in his hands.

Rod's warning that Netty wasn't a woman to trifle with came tiptoeing into Rand's self-incrimination and added guilt to his misery. He'd been totally honest with her. Her comment about celebrating his recovery with wind surfing still irked him. *Is all I am or was to her fun and games?* He squeezed his eyes tight and unconsciously rubbed his chest, attempting to ease the heaviness there.

---*

Rod had rounded the corner from Fountain Street and caught sight of Rand as he opened the garden gate. Rod observed him as he entered and closed it while parking his car. Hastily he made his way toward the gate, unlatched it, and proceeded in the direction his brother went. He slowly approached Rand, who sat on the fountain wall with Angel's head on his knee.

Rod stopped some distance away and studied his appearance. He was staring at his hat as he turned it in circles. His usually erect shoulders were rounded and the cane lay haphazard near his feet. Rod approached him slowly and his heart clenched at the vacant expression on Rand's face when he raised his head. "What's wrong?"

Rand blinked rapidly several times. "Why aren't you at work?"

"I just finished a meeting with a client here in the village and came to ask if you'd like to get a cup of coffee."

Without meeting Rod's gaze, he shrugged. "Sure."

Rod silently questioned the cheerless response. He picked up the cane, gave it to him, and paused to pet Angel.

Rand gripped his cane. "Can we go somewhere besides here?"

Rod caught a fleeting glimpse of Rand's lips, which were stretched into a thin line. He hoped to find out what was troubling Rand before they parted company. They made their way back to the side gate, Rod opened it, and followed Rand through it. He continued to silently observe his brother.

Rand opened the passenger door of the BMW, slid inside, leaned his cane against the seat beside him, and closed the door.

Rod got in and drove away from the village, The ride to the coffee shop in Summerland was filled with silence.

———⁂———

Rand got out of the car when Rod parked and headed for the outside tables surrounded on three sides by a picket fence. When Rod caught up with him, they went through the open gate and sat on either side of the nearest wrought-iron table.

A waitress soon approached them. "What can I get you guys?"

"Coffee." They answered simultaneously.

"Coming right up." She scurried away.

Rand gave the area a once over. "You come here often?"

Rod placed his arms on the table and regarded him. "Once in a while."

Rand avoided Rod's steady scrutiny. "Nice place, peaceful."

Rod folded his arms. "You didn't answer my question."

Their waitress returned with two cups. "Do you guys want to order now?"

"I'm good." Rand replied as he reached for his cup.

"We may like more coffee eventually." Rod offered her a small smile.

"Would you like me to bring a pot?" She batted her eye-lashes at him.

"Yes, thank you." He responded at the slight bob of Rand's head.

Rand smirked at her attempt to flirt with his brother even though he appeared totally unaffected.

She nearly bounced away from their table.

Rod raised an eyebrow.

Rand snickered. "She likes you."

Rod frowned, opened his mouth to make a retort, but refrained.

In the blink of an eye, the perky waitress brought a metal pot of coffee and set it in the middle of the table. "Can I get you anything else?" She directed the question at Rod.

He picked up his cup while his elbow rested on the table against his other fist. "No, thank you."

"My name's Candy. If you need anything else, just wave." She pointed. "I'll be right over there."

"Thank you." Rod replied over the rim of his cup.

She raised her hands. "Enjoy." With a quick backward glance, she scurried off to wait on another table.

Rand chuckled. "Candy, huh."

Rod stared at him. "You still haven't answered my question."

Rand quirked an eyebrow. "You hid your ring."

Rod frowned and took a slow drink from his cup. "Did you talk to Netty?"

He frowned and mumbled. "Tried."

Rod set his cup down and fastened his gaze on Rand's face. "What happened?"

He shrugged. "Not much."

"Did you fight?" Rod crossed his arms on the table.

"More or less." He traced the iron design of the table top while his neck heated beneath his collar.

Rod scrunched his eyebrows. "Did it get physical?"

Rand shook his head. "Didn't give it a chance."

Rod momentarily contemplated his response. "She tried?"

He swallowed hard. "Caught her wrist." His lips formed a straight line and he stared at the tabletop. "I almost hit her." His voice was unsteady, but he met Rod's scrutiny without wavering.

Rod placed a hand on his arm. "I'm sorry I suggested you to talk to her."

He shrugged and clenched his jaw several times. "I can't believe, I almost hit her." He spat the words out through gritted teeth.

"Are you giving up on her?"

"Yes . . . no . . . maybe." He shrugged. "I don't know."

"If there doesn't seem to be a solution—"

"I should have listened to you in the first place." *But your heart has ideas of its own, pal.* He filled his lungs and expelled a breath. "Guess I'll have to find another barber."

Rod steepled his fingers in front of his chest. "There's one in Montecito where I go occasionally. He does a decent job."

Rand shrugged and twisted his cup in half-circles. "I'll be driving soon so I can go anytime I want." His gaze shot to Rod's face. "I mean, I won't have to wait for a ride." He didn't tell anyone, especially not Rod, how many times he thought about leaving, but he had family here, roots. And while they weren't always quite what he longed for, they were enough, for now.

Twenty-Six

Friday morning, Rand and Karl sat in the library while he showed his dad the folder Rod left with ideas for completion of the work on the mansion. Rand pointed to the third-floor blue print. "Do you have any suggest—"

"Anybody here?" Gus Palmer's thunderous voice filled the foyer.

"In the library." Rand's brow wrinkled as he glanced at his dad. "He never knocks."

Gus strode into the room and eyed Rand. "I need to talk to you."

"Dad, meet our renowned sheriff, Gus Palmer."

Karl stood and offered his hand. "Nice to meet you, Sheriff."

Gus grasped the older man's outstretched hand. "Likewise, Mr. Gray." He then confronted Rand. "I have more information on the green van."

Rand crossed his arms. "I thought the owner was dead."

"He is, but was Buz Sloan's uncle. Sloan claims it sat abandoned on the vacant property after his uncle died. Since both Sloan and Hollis have solid alibis for the night of your wreck, there's nothing I can do unless one of them does something outside the law. Just the same, I advise you to stick close to the village until we find the responsible party." He rotated his large frame and swaggered out of the library.

Rand shuffled after him. "Gus."

The sheriff stopped and threw a scowl at Rand. "Make it quick. I'm on my way to continue a murder investigation in Summerland."

Rand stiffened. "When did that happen?"

Gus tugged on the brim of his hat as his lips formed a tight line. "Halloween. The man was stabbed several times. There's been a rise of violent deaths in the area in the last month."

Rand's breath caught in his throat and he broke out in a cold sweat.

"You alright? You look a little pale."

"Must have been something I ate." He rubbed his stomach with a jerky hand and then jammed both hands in the pockets of his jeans.

"I repeat, stay in the village. Take care, Rand."

He gave the sheriff a two-fingered salute. "Always." He stood and stared at the floor while Gus's words about the increase of violent deaths in their area played over again in his mind. His legs started to tremble and tingles ran up his spine to the back of his neck. Rand quickly squared his shoulders when Karl stepped into the hall.

"I heard part of what the sheriff said. Does he think the dead man is somehow connected to your wreck?"

Rand shrugged to mask his apprehension at the thought of recent multiple deaths in the area. He wiped his forehead with his sleeve. "I'm going out, need some fresh air." He headed for the side door.

"The sheriff appears to take a personal interest in your welfare. It's always a good thing to have the law on your side." Karl called after him.

He gave his dad a backhanded wave and escaped to the garden.

After nearly an hour of speculation over Gus's warning and the reason behind it, Rand made his way back inside and managed to slip into his workshop undetected by either his dad or Alfred.

His gaze darted around the room in search of something to distract him from his troubled thoughts and the images they invoked. With furrowed brow, he snatched one of the boards for a shelf he started to make for Netty. He snorted. *You're always attracted to women who cut you to the quick, pal.*

Later as he used an electric sander to smooth out a board, he spied Tommy as he cautiously stepped into the shop.

"Hey, Uncle Rand. What are you making now?"

He smiled. "School out already?"

"Yeah, we got out early since it's the last day before Thanksgiving break. Dad told me this morning to wait for him here."

Rand shut off the sander, wiped his hands on a rag that hung from his carpenter's belt, and picked up a coffee cup that was on his workbench. "I could use a break"

Tommy ran his hand along the wood. "Smooth as silk. What color you going to paint it?"

Rand almost spewed the coffee he'd just sipped. Not even lukewarm. He wiped his chin with the back of his hand. "Not paint, varnish. Don't want to hide the beauty of the wood, but enhance it."

"But what color is it going to be?"

Rand set the cup on the bench. "Think gloss or shine, Tommy, not color. I want the beautiful grain, the character of the wood to be exposed."

"I like the way you explain things."

Rand chuckled.

"How long have you been making stuff?"

"Since I was around eight, I guess."

"You learned a lot from the guy you lived with, huh."

Rand stared as if in a trance while the corners of his mouth drooped. He should be thankful for what he learned from Ned. He'd been a craftsman before becoming an alcoholic. He flinched when Tommy rested his hand briefly on Rand's arm.

"When can we start on mom's tea box?"

Rand focused on Tommy. "How about over Thanksgiving since you're out of school?"

"Will that be enough time?"

"It'll only take a couple days, three if we take it slow."

"Great! Today was the last day of school till December."

Rand chuckled. "Did you check out Saun's decorations?"

Tommy's eyes opened wide. "Yeah, there's dark wood statues and colorful little plaques with Bible verses and flowers, a wood napkin holder and a spice rack in the kitchen."

Rand stared at his workbench with his brow scrunched. "Did you find any ideas for decorating the box?"

Tommy shuffled his feet and gazed at the floor. "I sort of borrowed one of her favorite pots. It has a neat design on it. I hid it in my duffle bag and hope I can get it back where it belongs before she misses it."

Rand quirked an eyebrow. "You have it now?"

"Yeah."

"Let's make a sketch of the design and then you can put it back." He examined the surface of the wood he'd been sanding.

Tommy studied Rand's hand as it glided over a board. "Who's that gonna be for?"

"Netty." Rand picked up his cup and drained it even though the coffee coffee was beyond cold and left a bitter taste in his mouth, which matched his mood.

Tommy scrunched his nose and tipped his head to the side. "I heard dad tell mom she broke up with you. How's come you're still making it?"

"I promised." His posture stiffened and he set the cup back on the workbench.

"She promised dad she'd take care of you when you got out of the hospital, but—"

"People don't always do what they promise, Tommy." Rand crossed his arms.

Tommy stared at him with a blank expression. "But you're keeping your promise. Why bother? She didn't."

"I keep hoping—" He blinked rapidly a few times. "Someday maybe she'll understand that she needs Christ. If I could show her—" He exhaled heavily. "Maybe one day she'll be able to receive the love and acceptance I've found in Christ."

Tommy stared at him as tears filled his eyes. "You really love her, huh, even though she's mean to you?"

Rand shrugged. "Keeping my promise might show her Christ's love." He took a deep breath and muttered to himself. "Even if it means we're never together." He winced when Tommy suddenly grasped his arm.

Tears slid down his cheeks. "Can Jesus make me love people like you do?"

Rand's eyebrows rose. "No. He won't make you do anything, but if He's in your heart you'll want to."

"If you didn't have Jesus, do you think you'd still make it for her?"

Rand's brow wrinkled and he stared at the floor while he searched for an honest answer. "I learned it's important to keep my promises as a boy. So, I'd have made it out of determination to keep my word." *And you wouldn't have cared whether she noticed or not, pal.*

Tears slid down Tommy's cheeks. "I want to ask Jesus in my heart. But I've done mean stuff and had bad thoughts about Rod and even Saun sometimes."

Rand put his arm around the teen's shoulders. "What do you mean, Tommy?"

"I listen to Pastor Clark and dad and mom talk, but I thought it was just them. You know, the way they've always been, but you're different. I've seen you change."

Rand winced. "You have?"

"You used to smoke and stuff when you first came here and you kinda kept to yourself a lot. But since you accepted Jesus, you're easier to talk to and stuff. I like spending time with you. I can tell you anything and you understand."

Rand sucked his bottom lip between his teeth at Tommy's assessment. Maybe the rejection he encountered from some of the villagers, especially his mother, made him withdraw more than he realized. *Lord, what am I supposed to do here?*

"Will you pray for me?" Tommy pleaded. "I want what you have."

Rand rubbed the back of his neck. "You can talk to Jesus in your own words just like you've been talking to me. He hears you."

Tommy nodded and squeezed his eyes tight. "Jesus, I'm sorry for all the bad stuff I've done and thought. Please forgive me and come into my heart like Pastor Clark says. I want to care about others the way Uncle Rand does, even when they're mean to me." He started sobbing.

Rand wrapped his arms around Tommy and held him. Joy he'd never experienced before filled his heart and made his vision blur.

Karl stepped into the room. "Is everything okay in here?"

Rand bobbed his head in response.

Karl cleared his throat. "Rod just called. He said he'll be late and Saun is spending the evening with a woman whose husband is ill. He said he'll pick Tommy up on his way home."

"Okay." Rand responded with a quick glance at his dad.

Karl nodded and disappeared.

Tommy pulled away from Rand and peered briefly at him. "Sorry. Old Abe always told me real men don't cry." He scrubbed at his damp cheeks with his fists.

Rand smiled. "It's nothing to be ashamed of, pal. We've all shed a few tears at times, if we're honest."

Tommy stared at him. "Even you?"

He mussed Tommy's hair. "Even me." He grinned, and patted Tommy on the back. "Tell you what, I have a whole selection of different kinds of wood under a tarp on the plaza. Let's go pick out something for Saun's tea box. I have a polaroid camera. You can put it in your back pack and maybe you can take some pictures of her artifacts when she isn't looking."

"Cool! Maybe I can get dad to distract her if she gets home before us."

Donna Noblick

"Once you choose your wood, I'll show you the steps you'll need to do to make it."

Tommy gave him a side hug. "You're the best uncle anybody ever had!"

Netty picked up her broom that afternoon as her customer left. "Thanks, Mr. Winters, say hello to your wife for me." She sighed, he was her last appointment for the day, but before she could lock the door, Willis entered.

"Miss Netty, I know you're supposed to close now, but I just got off work and I need a haircut. See, I have a date tonight and I want to look my best. Please, Miss Netty, I know I'm supposed to have an appoint—"

"Sit, Willis! I could have finished it by now." She chuckled. The entire time she cut his hair, Willis continued with his monologue. She basically tuned him out because her mind was busy with her plans. When she finished, she whipped the cape off him. "Do you think your girlfriend will approve of your hair being so short?"

"Oh, yes ma'am! She likes it this way."

She raised her eyebrows. "You've been out with this girl before?"

He grinned. "Yes, ma'am, we're going steady. How much do I owe you since I didn't have an appointment?"

She pressed an index finger against her cheek and pretended to think about it. "How about we make a deal?"

He tilted his head. "What kind of deal? You know I don't do anything dishonest."

She laughed. "I'm very glad of that Willis. I'm planning to leave the village but I don't want anyone to know until Monday. Can I trust you to keep my secret until then? Just to prove I trust you to keep it, you don't need to pay for your haircut."

Willis scratched his ear and then rubbed his chin. "I don't have to pay for my haircut?"

She crossed her arms. "Can I trust you to keep my secret until Monday?"

He tugged on his ear. "I can tell whoever I want on Monday?"

"You can tell the whole village, in fact, I hope you do."

Willis's eyes almost popped out of his head. "Golly, Miss Netty, that's a big job. What am I supposed to tell everybody?"

"Tell them I left the village and you don't know if I'll be back." She tried to remain patient, but sometimes she wondered if the man understood anything he was told.

"Sure, Miss Netty, I can tell everybody you left, but when are you coming back?"

"I don't know, Willis, maybe I won't. Look, I have things to do now. You need to go so you can get ready for your big date." She quickly ushered him out of the shop as she spoke. She locked the door after him and turned her sign to, closed.

She swept the floor and made sure everything was straightened up and put in its place. She dropped into her desk chair, picked up her phone and dialed her friend's number. "Paige, it's Netty. Got a question for you." She paused. "No, nothing like that. I wondered if you would like some company for a while?" She held her breath. "I don't really have a time frame." She drew a shaky breath. "Yes, we had a fight. He threatened to hit me! No, I'm okay, for now. I can leave tomorrow morning if that's not too soon." She managed to say between angry sniffs. "Thanks, see you then." She hung up and stared at her door as tears streamed down her cheeks. She swiped at her face with one hand and drew up a quick 'for sale' sign. She'd put it in the window right before she left on Sunday.

After a few moments, she stomped up the fire escape, into her apartment, and began snatching clothes from her closet and dresser and placing them in a suitcase. If Rand didn't want her, she'd have no trouble finding someone who did. She didn't need him anyway. He could keep his religious self for some poor excuse of a woman. He wasn't man enough to suit her anyway. She could no longer stay here and hold her breath, because she was afraid, he would come back to hit her like she knew he wanted to do. She'd lived with that kind of fear before and wouldn't do it again.

Twenty-Seven

Early Thanksgiving afternoon, Rod watched Tommy exit the house and join the adults. His son's gaze sought his face.

"Dad, will you guys shoot some baskets with me?"

Rand glanced at Rod with a quirk of his lips. "Your dad hasn't run for years. How about you, Cab?"

He chuckled. "I'm a youth leader. I have to stay in shape for self-defense." He jumped to his feet. "I'm in."

"Okay." Rand's brow wrinkled as he appraised Cab, Rod and Tommy for a few seconds. "How about Tommy and I take on you two?"

Rod winked at Saun. "She'll be on our team." He eyed Rand. "How's your leg?"

He flexed his knee. "Good. You afraid we'll beat you?"

"We can take them, Uncle Rand." Tommy shouted as he ran back into the house.

"Okay, Cab, Saun. Let's see if Mr. Confidence can prove his boasting." Rod exchanged high-fives with Cab and Saun before they stepped off the deck and started around the house to the basketball hoop. Their house included a large two-car garage with an amply paved driveway at the end of a mile long lane.

"This I've got to see." Karl rubbed his hands together with a snicker as he picked up a lawn chair and followed the others. "How about you Alfred?"

"It should be a jolly good game." Alfred chuckled and trailed behind Karl with another chair.

"I need to change my shoes." Saun called as she headed back inside.

Tommy came back with a ball and began to dribble it.

Saun joined them a few moments later. She'd changed into shorts and tennis shoes the same as Rod and Cab. "Okay, let's play ball." She rubbed her hands together.

Rand gave her the once-over. "Rod and Cab need all the help they can get. Dad, you and Alfred are referees."

"Wait!" Tommy tossed the ball to Rand. "I'll get my whistle."

Rand dribbled toward the basket, jumped and slam-dunked the ball.

"Lucky shot." Rod yelled cheerfully.

"Too bad it doesn't count!" Cab added with hands on his hips.

Saun grabbed the ball when it dropped to the cement and dribbled it as she ran toward the basket, tossed it up, and it rounded the rim and dropped through.

"Nice." Rod shouted.

"I'm glad you're on our team." Cab trotted over to her and they exchanged a high five.

"That doesn't count either." Rand countered. "The refs aren't ready."

Cab playfully punched Rod's arm. "We've got him worried."

Tommy reappeared. "Here Grandpa, you can use this."

Karl took the whistle and blew it. "Play ball."

Rod retrieved the ball after Saun's shot and began to dribble it.

Rand blocked him.

Rod leaped to the side and passed the ball to Cab.

Cab leaped in the air, threw the ball, hit the backboard, and the ball dropped into the basket.

"Two points." Rod shouted as he lunged for the ball.

Tommy was quicker, snatched the ball and launched it to Rand.

He hurled it from where he stood and missed. "Sorry Tommy."

"No problem, Uncle Rand."

Rod got the ball and threw it to Saun.

She dodged Tommy and made a basket.

Tommy retrieved the ball and tossed it to Rand.

Rand heaved it in a high arc and it dropped through the basket.

"Yeah, Uncle Rand!" Tommy clapped. "Two points."

Rod got the ball next and Rand slammed into him. Rod stumbled but stayed on his feet.

Karl blew the whistle. "Foul!"

"Sorry." Rand panted.

Rod retrieved the ball and shot a glance at Rand. "You alright?"

Rand bobbed his head. "Yeah, you?"

"Yes." Rod frowned and stood in position to make the foul shot. It dropped in the basket.

"Yes." Cab yelled.

Rand retrieved the ball, jumped to make a slam-dunk, and mis-stepped. He expelled a low groan as he recovered his balance.

Rod frowned at the brief twist of Rand's mouth.

"Yeah." Tommy yelled. "Way to go Uncle Rand!" They exchanged a high five.

When they'd played for over an hour, Rod observed Rand, trying hard not to favor his injured leg. Rod bent over and breathed hard while he snatched a glimpse at Cab and then Saun. "Sorry guys, I'm beat. It's been a while since I've played this hard."

Tommy ran over to him. "You okay, Dad?"

He winked at his son and whispered. "Yes, but we need to quit."

Tommy nodded, bounced the ball and made a bank shot.

"Two points" Rand shouted. "You guys play a pretty mean game." He leaned over with hands on his knees and breathed deeply. He stared at Saun. "You're pretty good for a girl." He panted.

She laughed and eyed him with her hands on her hips. "You forgot. I grew up with two brothers. Dinner will be ready shortly."

"I'll help with that." Rod put his arm around Saun's waist as they waited for Karl and Alfred to follow them inside.

Tommy trotted over to Rand. "Are you okay?"

"Yeah, fine."

"Dad quit and so did mom and Cab so we won. Nice game, Uncle Rand."

He grinned. "We make a good team, pal." He grasped Tommy's shoulders for a quick side hug.

As they headed inside after the others for the Thanksgiving meal, Tommy faced Rand. "Can I spend the night with you? I don't have school until Monday."

Rand chuckled. "I'm okay with it if Rod and Saun are."

"Can I, Dad, Mom?"

Rod wrapped one arm around Saun and nuzzled her cheek. "What do you think?"

She laughed. "I don't have any objections."

"Yeah!" Tommy yelled. "I'll toss some stuff in my gym bag."

Wings of Steel

Later that evening Rand carefully maneuvered up the steps as Tommy scampered ahead of him and went inside.

Alfred and Karl followed more slowly.

When Rand entered, Tommy gave him an envelope. "I found this taped to the door."

Rand glanced at the familiar handwriting and stuck the envelope in his pocket.

"Can we stay up all night?" Tommy turned right into the library.

"Depends." Rand began to whistle. His leg was a bit achy. He'd try to rest it tonight and go easy on the exercises for a day or two. In any case he intended to show his nephew a good time.

"I think I'll turn in for the night." Alfred said as he strode past the library door.

Karl followed on his heels. "Good night boys. See you in the morning." He called to them.

"Good night." Rand and Tommy responded together.

"There's two couches in here." Tommy glanced around the spacious room. "Can we can sleep in here if we get tired?"

Rand crossed his arms. "I bet you even want a fire and maybe some marshmallows to roast."

Tommy's eyes flew open wide. "Cool! Do you have any?"

He laughed. Tommy's excitement was contagious and he was glad the teen wanted to spend the night. "Might be able to find some."

"Did you and Netty ever sit by the fire and roast them?"

Suddenly Rand's desire to whistle faded. "Has anybody ever told you, you ask too many questions, pal?"

Tommy grinned. "I have lots of questions. Can I ask you anything I want?"

Rand stopped and stared at him with one eyebrow cocked. *Should have known the kid would be asking twenty questions, pal.* "You can ask, but doesn't mean I'll answer."

"Okay. Can I leave my bag here?"

"Sure." Rand proceeded to build a fire and winced. *Better take some aspirin, pal.*

"Could we sit on the floor and play chess close to the fire?" Tommy interrupted his speculation.

"Sure."

"Can we turn all the lights off? It'll sort of be like camping."

Rand grinned. "Have you ever camped?" He began to whistle again.

167

Tommy plopped down on the floor. "Nope, grew up in LA."

Rand frowned as he observed how easily the youth's body landed on the floor. "Maybe we can go sometime."

"You mean it?"

"We'll see." He chuckled. "I'll get the marshmallows." He resumed whistling as he left to grab them from a kitchen cupboard. When he returned to the library, Tommy sat Indian style in front of the hearth. Rand gave him one of the sticks he'd retrieved from the terrace, sat down beside him and set the marshmallows on the floor between them. He stretched his feet out, roasted and ate three golden-brown treats. He grinned when Tommy ate twice as many. "How about that game of chess?" He pushed up from the floor. "You set up the board and I'll get us some real food."

"You want white or black?"

"You choose." Rand called over his shoulder as he stepped into the front hall and stopped to peer through the windows. Netty's shop was dark and no lights were on in her apartment. He sighed as his lips pulled down at the corners. *Did she spend Thanksgiving alone?* Unconsciously, he rubbed his chest as he made his way to the kitchen. He rummaged in the refrigerator and cupboards until he found some lunchmeat, cheese slices and a loaf of bread. He spread them on a tray with two bottles of soda.

Back in the library he whistled softly as he set it all on the coffee table.

"I'm hungry." Tommy said as he got up and made a sandwich, stacked high with meat and cheese. He sat back on the floor, ate with one hand and moved his white knight with the other. "Your turn." He took a big bite of his sandwich and washed it down with Pepsi.

Rand studied the board for a few seconds and then moved a pawn before putting together his own sandwich.

They continued to play until the game ended in a draw.

Rand chuckled. "You're pretty good, pal."

Tommy beamed. "You are too. We have a chess club at school and so far, nobody has beat me."

Rand raised an eyebrow. "Holding out on me, huh." His mouth stretched into a cheeky grin. "Next time, I'll concentrate harder."

Tommy peered intently at him. "Where did you live before you came to Fire River?" He asked as he began putting the chess set back in the box.

Rand's cheek twitched and his eyebrows rose. He stared at the fire and tried to figure out how much he wanted to reveal. "Grew up in Arizona. Once out of school I spent some time in New Mexico, Texas and Colorado before coming here." Rand observed Tommy, who leaned back against one of the arm chairs. The firelight reflected in his medium-brown eyes as he focused on Rand.

"What did you do, I mean you had to work, right?"

Rand scrunched his eyebrows as he tried to think of a way to describe his travels. "Went from one town to the next and if I couldn't find work on a ranch, I could usually win enough shooting pool to survive in between ranches. I never stayed anywhere long. Most ranch work is seasonal."

"Were the towns like here?"

"Each one was kind of unique, People aren't so different though, no matter where you go. Most didn't take too kindly to strangers, especially pool sharks."

"Wow! You're a pool shark? Can you teach me to play?"

Rand frowned. *Shouldn't have let that slip, pal.* "I was sometimes accused of cheating though I never did. When there's money on the table, people can get pretty ugly if they don't win. Sometimes I had to leave in a hurry." He stared at the hearth as he spoke. He enjoyed the aroma of wood as it burned and the pop and crackle of the flames as a log shifted. "Few times I didn't get away quick enough."

"Did you ever get hurt?"

"A bullet grazed my shoulder once, and I got jumped by four guys after I spent some time with a girl that was with one of them."

Tommy's chin dropped. "Was she married?"

Rand shook his head. "Don't know. Said she wasn't, but they came after me.

"How'd you get away"

"She found me in an alley and drove me to a nearby town."

"Did they come after you?"

Rand chuckled. "Didn't stick around to find out. Drove clean out of the state."

"Doesn't sound like you had much fun."

"None that lasted." He scoffed at his past.

"Did you have lots of girlfriends?"

Rand was silent for some time as a few faint images of nameless women paraded through his mind. His cheeks heated and he slowly shook his head at the life he once lived. He gave Tommy a realistic snapshot of his experiences, hoping it would discourage him from choosing a similar lifestyle. "Traveling alone isn't much fun. Met a lot of interesting people, but none wanted to get involved with a drifter." He rubbed the back of his neck as Claire crossed his mind. It was mostly because of her that he'd kept on the move.

"Did you ever have a serious girlfriend?"

"Most wanted the same thing I did, someone to keep them company for a short time." He reached in his pocket for a toothpick.

"Didn't you get tired of being alone?"

He shrugged. "Just kept moving on to the next town, hoping to find whatever I was missing." He stuck the toothpick in his mouth and chewed on it.

"Did you ever go back home?"

Rand clamped down on the toothpick. It snapped in two and he flicked it into the fire. *Those aren't memories you want to relive, pal, especially not with him.* "Went back last year to pick up my bike."

Tommy nodded. "I never knew who my dad was and my mom was a druggie and a prostitute. Sometimes her guy friends could be pretty mean so I spent a lot of time on the streets in LA. Rod found me a few days after she died and took me to my grandpa's house in San Diego. I guess ole Abe told Rod not to visit me. I wish Dad could adopt me, but something about grandpa's will and stuff says he can't."

Rand slouched against the nearest couch, the tension in his shoulders diminished while Tommy shared his story. "I wasn't adopted either, but—"

"Rand?"

"Hmm?" He pulled another toothpick from his pocket.

"Why did you come here?"

He blinked at the unexpected question. "To find mother."

"Did you?"

"Yeah." He responded with a grin around the toothpick in his mouth. Warmth spread through his chest at the memory of her gentle touches and tender care after he was injured.

"Where is she now?"

"Seabreeze Inn." He held his breath and waited for Tommy's response.

"Lucinda Warner is your mom?" The boy's eyes nearly perfect orbs.

Rand's head bobbed and his lips quirked at Tommy's expression.

"Have you seen her?"

He withdrew the toothpick as he nodded when a wide smile pulled his lips into an upward curve.

"Does she like you?"

The toothpick in his fingers broke in two. "She does now."

"Cool!"

"I'm not proud of my past, Tommy, but I've accepted Christ. Now I have family that I love and I think they kind of like me too."

Tommy scooted closer to Rand and put his arm around his waist. "I think you're the coolest grown-up I know, except maybe for dad."

Rand gave Tommy a quick side hug. "Thanks, you're pretty special too." He reflected on Tommy's face for a moment, then turned to gaze at the fire, and sighed. *Glad he mentioned Rod first. That's how it should be.* He cleared his throat and blinked several times. He wondered if Rod had any idea how lucky he was or knew how much this young man loved him. "You're something else, pal." He flipped the tooth pick pieces into the fire.

Tommy grinned. "Rod's lucky to have a brother like you."

Rand sucked air into his lungs when he scrambled to his feet. He'd stressed his injured leg. "We'd better get to bed. Alfred and dad get up early."

"Do we have to?"

"You want to start on Saun's tea box in the morning, don't you?"

"Sure!"

Rand couldn't help but envy Tommy when he scrambled to his feet with utmost ease. "We'll make a few sketches from the pictures you took."

"Great! Uncle Rand?"

"What?"

"Me and Ethan talk about stuff sometimes, but it's neat to talk man to man with someone besides dad."

Rand winked at him. "Your dad loves you very much." Rod had a good woman who loved him like crazy and a kid who admired him. *What more could a man want, pal?* He rubbed his chest and tried to ease the ache there.

After Tommy went to sleep, Rand carefully maneuvered into his room and sat on his bed. His leg throbbed when he sat on his bed and then tore open the envelope, which held familiar handwriting.

Willis had written. *Netty's leaving and not coming back. Do you know why?*

Rand's shoulders sagged. His lungs seemed to deflate like a balloon when all its air had escaped. He crumpled the paper in his fist and pushed himself to his feet. He trudged into his bathroom and took two aspirin.

Donna Noblick

Afterward he shuffled back to his bed and lay staring at the ceiling. He drew a deep breath, puffed out his cheeks, and exhaled slowly. He reached for the radio on his bedside table and turned it on at low volume. *Gonna be a long night, pal.*

Twenty-Eight

The following Saturday, Monza pulled up to a little bar in Ash Springs about a hundred miles east of Fire River and climbed off his motorcycle. After walking it around to the back of the bar, he left it behind a large trash bin, walked in the opposite direction, and swaggered inside. He stood, feet spread with his beefy hands propped on his hips and scanned the entire place. His gaze landed on a woman sitting alone at one end of the bar and he sidled over to her while keeping an eye on the rest of the patrons.

No one moved or paid him any mind. He took the seat next to her and crowded her space.

She glared at him. "A bull like you needs a table to hisself!"

He roared and slapped her on the back so hard she spilled her drink. "Hey barkeep." He bellowed. "Give the lady here another drink and while you're at it, bring me whatever she has."

The bartender, no small man himself, crossed his arms. "Six dollars. Put it on the bar and you'll get your drinks."

Monza put his arm around the woman's shoulders. "What's his name, babe?"

She sneered at him. "Mac and if you don't want your fingers busted, you'd better do as he says, Mister, and get your hands off me!"

He grabbed her off the stool and held a knife to her throat. "Mac, you'd better bring those drinks to our table pronto. And you." He grabbed the woman's wrist, twisting it so that she was forced to walk to a table with him. He pulled out a chair and shoved her onto it. "We're gonna have a drink and then a nice little talk, upstairs."

She bared her teeth. "Over my dead body!"

He shook his head. "Now that would be a shame, wouldn't it. Mac over there just might miss you. Ain't that right Mac? What's you name babe?"

"Why should I tell you?"

The other patrons cleared out of the bar.

"Cause you and me are going to celebrate and Mac over there is going to fix us a real nice dinner, ain't cha, Mac." He turned to glance around the entire room and the last two men sitting at a corner table got up and left. His grin was menacing. "Time to lock up, Mac. We're going to have us a private little party."

Two hours later Monza grabbed two bottles from the supply behind the bar and raised first one and then the other in mock salute to the bodies lying on the floor. "Sorry you two had to leave before the party was over." He threw back his head and laughed while he strode toward the rear door and left it open behind him.

He retrieved his Honda from its hiding place, hopped on, left in a cloud of dust, and three hours later found a suitable place to stop. Sitting on the ground, he drank from one of the bottles he'd taken from the bar. "Ain't got nobody to have Thanksgiving with, little brother." He sobbed until he was exhausted and then laid down and slept.

Twenty-Nine

On the first Friday in December, Rand called to confirm that his exercise equipment would be picked up later that day. A knock at the front door caught his attention. Angel, who was lying at his feet, barked and wagged her tail so he figured the visitor was someone she knew.

He approached the double doors and froze. Netty stood on the other side. He took a deep breath, opened one door, and blocked the entrance with his body. He gazed at her with eyebrows squished together. The episode of her raised hand and razor-sharp words when she screamed at him replayed in his mind. *This might not go well, pal.*

She gave him a tight-lipped smile. "I came to apologize."

He inhaled sharply. "For?"

She ogled him for several seconds. "Can we still be friends?"

He shrugged. "Thought you weren't coming back."

"Maybe I changed my mind."

He expelled a half laugh, half huff. "About what?"

She shifted from one foot to the other and suddenly flashed a dagger like glare at him. "At least I'm trying."

He studied her face for a moment. "Now isn't a good time for either of us. Not sure there ever will be." A tight fist constricted his throat as he spoke the words quietly.

She sneered. "Just so you know, you're the one who started this whole thing."

He raised his palms. "Until you believe I care, there isn't much hope." His words spilled out in a flat monotone.

"Fine, have it your way! You always have to have the last word." She turned on her heels and sashayed down the steps.

He shut the door with a whispered snick, shook his head and trudged down the hall into the kitchen where he fixed a strong pot of coffee.

He was sitting at the kitchen table drinking his coffee with eyes closed, taking intermittent deep breaths when Angel began to bark. It took several moments for him to pull himself out of his recent encounter with Netty. He hoped it was the men, coming to pick up the exercise equipment instead of her. He was in no frame of mind to be dragged into another argument.

He marched to the foyer and opened the doors just as the men reached the terrace. They crossed it to their truck as he stepped onto the porch. He whistled sharply. "I think you forgot something, gentlemen." His eyebrows pinched when he called to them.

The men trudged back up the steps and inside. They both held smug expressions on their faces as they hefted the equipment outside and down the steps without a word. When they were finished, one of them climbed into their truck while the second man came back with a clipboard in hand. "You need to sign this, Mr. Gray."

Rand scrolled his name on the line indicated and received a copy of the invoice. "Thanks." He pasted a smile on his face.

The man threw a glance at Rand. "Did you have to do that again?"

Rand raised his eyebrows. "What?"

The man growled. "That stupid whistle."

"Oh, this?" He whistled again as the man covered his ears and descended the steps. Rand waited until they drove away, clenched his jaw and shut the door. *Is everyone in a bad mood today or is it just you, pal?*

The next day, Rod stood in the doorway to the library with his arms crossed while he observed Rand, who was on the phone. When Rand ended his call, Rod stepped into the room.

Rand raised his head and studied Rod. "Aren't you working today?"

One corner of Rod's mouth lifted. "How about some lunch? I'm sure you could use a break from all the silence while dad and Alfred are out."

Rand shrugged. "Sounds good."

Rod raised an eyebrow. "Tell me about it while we eat."

"Can we go someplace where we can talk?" He asked as he got up from an armchair.

"We can go to the café in Montecito and sit outside."

Wings of Steel

Rand was thankful for his jean jacket and long sleeve flannel shirt a short time later when they sat at a small table near the beach. The sun was shining brightly, but the breeze coming off the water chilled him. He picked up a menu from the middle of the table.

Rod broke the silence that was between them all the way there. "Who were you talking to on the phone?"

"The exercise equipment company. They wanted to make sure I was satisfied with their service."

A waitress stopped at their table. "Good afternoon, guys, may I get you something to drink?"

"Coffee." They both responded.

"Are you ready to order?"

"I will have the house salad with house dressing." Rod replied.

"And what would you like?" She asked Rand.

"Steak sandwich, rare and fries." Rand added as he gave her the menus.

"Coming right up." She scurried off to place their orders.

Rand stared at the waves rolling toward the beach. "Netty stopped by yesterday."

Rod frowned. "What did she want?"

Rand crossed his arms and rested them on the table in front of him. "She attempted to apologize but I think she really wanted to argue."

The waitress returned with their coffee and left again.

Rod placed his elbows on the tabletop and steepled his fingers. "Did she try to get physical again?"

Rand shook his head. "I told her we need to take a break and cool off." He stretched his upper lip thin over his teeth and chewed on the bottom one. "Seemed like she just wanted to argue."

"What about?"

Rand rubbed the back of his neck. "No clue."

"Here's your lunch, guys. Enjoy." Their waitress interrupted. "Can I get you anything else?"

"More coffee." Rand replied.

After she left, Rod's brow wrinkled as he peered at him. "There are some attractive young women at church if you want to date."

Rand took a bite of his sandwich and chewed for several moments before he swallowed. "Not interested." He growled.

The waitress appeared, refilled their cups and quickly left.

When she retreated Rod quirked an eyebrow at Rand while cutting up his salad.

"What?" Rand asked.

Rod focused on his plate. "Saun waited a long time for me to realize we were more than friends. We met when I was still married to Taryn. She was aware of the way Taryn acted and what I went through when she and Terry were killed. She was also there when I was going to propose to another woman, who went back to New Zealand the same day I lost my job." He grinned as his face flushed. "She never gave up on me and she never pressured me. She just kept waiting and being available when I needed her." He smiled at Rand.

He stared out over the vast ocean and imagined having dinner with a woman who really loved him for who he was. Absently, he rubbed his chest.

Rod spoke and redirected his attention. "What are you doing the rest of the day?"

With brows raised, he met Rod's gaze. "Haven't given it much thought."

"Did you tell Brooke you're no longer using a cane?" Rod speared a bite of his salad with his fork.

Rand bit into his sandwich and shook his head as he chewed. "How are you getting along in your new office?"

Rod took a drink from his cup. "Things are coming together. We're all enjoying me being closer to home."

Rand chewed and swallowed. "Me too."

Rod regarded him as the corners of his mouth lifted slightly. "I appreciate the time you spend with Tommy. You're good for him. I'm not always able to give him as much time as I'd like."

"He's never complained to me. He thinks you're the greatest."

The corners of Rod's eyes crinkled. "He admitted that he still struggles with not being able to claim Gray as his name, but I think he understands that has nothing to do with the love Saun and I have for him."

"I still don't think the old man was fair to make that part of the agreement."

"He trusted me enough to raise Tommy, but not enough to manage his inheritance without a legally binding will. I understand his reasoning. He didn't really know me."

Rand's brow wrinkled. He didn't understand but there was no sense arguing with his brother because it was none of his business.

Rod nodded, as he concentrated on Rand's face. "Tommy asked me to thank you again for helping him make the tea box for Saun. Have you thought anymore about resuming work on Candlewood?"

Rand focused on his plate. "I don't know what I'm going to do once I'm released to go back to work."

Later that afternoon Karl met Rand and Rod at the mansion's front door as they stepped inside. Karl addressed Rod. "I'm glad you came in instead of going straight home. Brooke called a few minutes ago and asked me to come back to San Francisco. Arlo isn't doing well and Cedric would like me to be there. Arlo's chalet has ample room for Rand as well as Alfred and me."

Rand exchanged a worried glance with Rod.

Rod flashed a grim smile at them both. "I'm sorry to hear Arlo isn't doing well. I will be happy to take Angel home with me if you want to go with them."

He eyed Rod and then Karl. "Unless you really need me, I'd like to be here for Christmas with Rod's family."

Karl placed his hand on Rand's shoulder. "Cedric and Alfred will be there, so if you'd rather not come, I understand. Alfred and I have already packed and are planning to leave around five in the morning. We'll stop for breakfast along the way."

Rand gave him a curt nod. "I'm always up early so I can at least see you off."

Rod prayed for safe travels and for wisdom for them once they arrived. "Keep me posted. Saun and I will be praying for all of you."

Karl gave Rod a side hug before he left.

That evening, Rand stood and stared out of the windows in the foyer. Netty's apartment lights were on and she was dancing with a man wearing a cowboy hat. He stared at the silhouettes on the shades and a lump lodged in his throat that he couldn't swallow.

Karl came up behind him, put a hand on his shoulder and stood for a moment with him. "She's obviously moved on, son. Maybe it's time you did too. Brooke would appreciate your company if you change your mind."

Rand shook his head slowly. "Sorry, not interested."

Karl squeezed his shoulder before releasing it. "At least she would be gentle with your heart." He remarked quietly and then headed for the stairs.

Rand sighed deeply and forked his fingers through his hair. *What good is gentleness without love?* He pivoted away from the windows and Angel pressed her nose into his palm.

Thirty

The following morning, Rand was up and had coffee brewing before either Alfred or his dad came downstairs. Angel barked at him through the glass in the veranda door. He stepped outside, filled her food and water bowls, and scratched her back.

He stepped back into the kitchen and paced the small space between his bedroom and the table. He stopped pacing and his brows drew together when Rod entered the kitchen. "Didn't expect to see you before church." Rand stared at him.

He strolled to the cupboard and took out two cups. "Saun was sleeping when I left and I didn't want the aroma of coffee to wake her. Tommy was sick and we were up with him most of the night." He filled the cups and set them on the table. "What's wrong?"

Rand crossed his arms. "What do you mean?

"Were you were counting the steps from your room to the table?" Rod smirked as he pulled out a chair and sat on it.

Rand growled under his breath.

Rod picked up his cup and smiled up at him. "Good morning to you too. You still didn't answer my question."

Rand puffed out his cheeks and expelled his breath before sitting in the chair across from his brother. "Dad seems really worried about his friend."

Rod observed him with a grin. "Are you concerned about him or Brooke?"

He glared at him, but raised his gaze to Alfred as he appeared from the corner of the hall. "Where's dad?"

Alfred headed for the coffee pot. "He'll be down shortly. Good morning, to you both."

Rand took a drink, hiding his smirk. "He didn't want to wake his wife so he came here for coffee."

Alfred sat across from Rod. "Karl wants to leave as soon as he comes down so we'll be eating our breakfast on the way."

Rod nodded with a quick glance at Rand. "Good idea. You won't have as much traffic to deal with until later."

Karl entered and quietly occupied the fourth chair.

Rand nearly knocked over his chair as he tried to stand before Alfred, who started to get up. "Dad, would you like some toast with your coffee?" He snatched a loaf of bread from an open shelf and set coffee in front of Karl.

He picked up the cup, took a small sip, and peered at Rand. "This is fine. We need to leave soon."

Rand sat on the end next to him and scrutinized his face while he was preoccupied with stirring his coffee. Karl's face was pale and his features were drawn. There were dark circles beneath his eyes that weren't there yesterday. Rand raised an eyebrow and watched Alfred down his coffee.

He pushed away from the table and stood. "I'll take our luggage to the car." He told Karl before leaving the room.

"Alfred's a good man to have around, Dad." He wanted to trust the man would watch out for Karl especially since his friend seemed seriously ill. He didn't respond so Rand grasped his arm. If you need me just ca—"

"I'll keep in touch." He grasped Rand's shoulder. "I'm sorry my future plans are so uncertain at this point." He pushed his chair back and stood. "I'll check my room before we leave."

———❈———*

Rand's brow wrinkled as he too rose from the table, intending to help Karl. He almost changed his mind about staying when his dad left the kitchen with a limp that was more pronounced than usual. "Dad appears older somehow. Why didn't I notice it before?" He whispered and flinched when Rod grasped his shoulder.

He frowned and removed his hand. "I've observed his limp is more obvious when he's overly tired. Alfred is aware of the situation and I'm sure he'll call and let you know—"

"Absolutely." Alfred interrupted as he entered the room. "I apologize for leaving last night's dishes but—"

"No problem." Rand smiled at him. "I'll miss your cooking."

A slight smile appeared and quickly vanished from Alfred's mouth. "Thank you. I'm sure you'll do fine without me."

"I hope you come back if dad—"

"Thank you I've enjoyed being here." Alfred interposed.

Rand shook his hand while he peered intently into the older man's eyes. "Have a safe trip." He wanted to add, take care of dad, but out of respect for Karl who just reappeared, Rand kept the comment to himself.

Alfred regarded Rand for an instant and quickly slipped a small piece of paper in the palm of his hand. "Take care of that leg."

Rand met his serious expression with a slight nod of his head.

When Karl stopped beside Rand, he wrapped his arms around him. "Take care of yourself, Dad."

After Karl and Alfred left, Rand sank onto a chair at the table and stared at the scrap of paper in his hand. Alfred had written, I will call if Karl needs you.

Rod refilled their cups and sat across from him. "I'm glad you stayed here."

Rand moved the salt and pepper shakers in a do-si-do pattern while his eyebrows scrunched with concentration.

Rod observed him over the brim of his cup. With elbows on the table, he held it between his hands. "What's on your mind?"

Rand squinted at him before he quickly focused on the table. "Dad appeared to be struggling because of his friend's situation and I'm sure he's also concerned about Brooke. I got the impression he doesn't expect Arlo to recover. I could have gone, but figured I'd only be in the way." Rand absently continued to move the shakers.

Rod watched him. "Are you second guessing yourself?"

Rand shrugged. "Dad just seems older, I guess, and sort of lost."

"So, you're considering going—"

"Only if he needs me."

"Just be aware. Grief can cause people to be vulnerable and sometimes they lean on others for comfort and support. I'm glad Cab and Saun were there to check on me when I lost my son." His Adam's apple bobbed. "Brooke could mistake your presence for more than friendly concern, especially if she finds Karl, whom she seems to depend on, has his own struggles. One or both of you could end up hurt."

Rand's jaw clenched as he stared at the table without commenting.

"It's apparent that you like her."

Rand switched places with the salt and pepper shakers again, several times. "We're barely friends." He growled.

Rod considered Rand's irritated response and stood. "Something to remember if you do go."

Rand chewed on his lip. "I'm not interested in Brooke or anyone else. And, I haven't given up on Netty... exactly."

"Saun and I pray for you both. Do you want me to pick you up on my way to church? Saun is staying home with Tommy."

Rand shook his head. "Thanks, but I'll drive." He continued the dance with the shakers on the table.

Rod stood and put his empty cup in the sink. "Are you coming to our house for dinner tonight?"

Rand raised his head and smiled for the first time since Rod arrived. "If Saun doesn't mind feeding an extra mouth. What about Tommy?"

"He'll be fine. I'll tell Saun to expect you. See you at church." He called over his shoulder as he stepped into the hall.

Thursday morning Rand made his way down the front steps and climbed into his pickup. He backed out and headed east around the square and left Fire River. When he got to Montecito, he searched for East Valley Road and parked in the lot for Clayton Mills' office. Before getting out of his truck, he took a deep breath.

As he strode around the building to the entrance, he straightened his shoulders and tried to breathe deeply. He glanced quickly at the door, looked away, and slipped a hand into his jacket pocket. He stepped inside and approached the receptionist's desk.

"I have an appointment with Dr. Mills." He avoided the gray-haired woman's curious scrutiny.

"The doctor will be with you shortly, Mr. Gray. Have a seat and fill out these forms." She passed him a clipboard and pen.

He took them, sat in a chair, and completed the paperwork. The area was small with a large picture window facing the street. The reception desk occupied at least a third of the space and a shoulder-high counter ran along beside it, hiding him from her view. When he was finished, he returned the forms and pen. Before he sat down again, a door opened and the doctor approached him.

"Good morning, Rand, come on in." Dr. Mills followed Rand into the room and shut the door.

"I called on Monday, but you were at the hospital." Rand informed him.

"I'm sorry I wasn't here when you called. Have a seat. Esther told me you said it was urgent."

Rand took off his hat, grasp the brim, and held it like a shield against his chest. "Not exactly." He shifted his position in the plush leather chair. "I, Rod advised me to get some counseling." He took a deep breath and expelled it slowly.

"Clayton. I think we've known each other long enough to skip the formalities. I do have some counseling experience, but I may need to refer you to someone else." He gave Rand an amicable smile. "Tell me what you're struggling with and we'll go from there?" He leaned against the side of his desk near Rand's chair and crossed his arms.

Rand curled and uncurled his fingers around the brim of his hat. "I'm not sure where to start."

Clayton pulled a chair directly in front of him, sat down, and gave Rand his undivided attention. "What's the first thing that comes to your mind?"

Rand closed his eyes and took a calming breath. "March 16, 1961, I was hunting when a girl's screams caught my attention. When I found her, she was being attacked by a guy about my age. Her shirt was ripped open and one of her eyes was swollen. He drew back his fist to hit her again and I jerked him backward. The girl screamed and covered her face. I spun around and stared at my best friend lying on the ground with blood oozing from his head. I couldn't wake him so I drove him to the hospital."

Clayton held Rand's gaze without wavering. "How old were you?"

Rand stared at his hands and sighed. "Sixteen and a half."

Clayton's eyebrows drew together. "What happened then?"

He tried to ignore the heaviness in his chest. "He died of a brain hemorrhage the next day. I was arrested, spent a year in jail waiting for trial, and then was sentenced to five-years' probation."

Clayton pursed his lips. "Did the girl tell the authorities you were defending her?"

Rand snorted and shook his head. "A friend told me her dad and her disappeared before the authorities were able to question her."

Clayton frowned. "What did you do during your probation years?"

His laughter held an edge. "God was looking out for me even though I didn't recognize it then. There were two men who lived near me and they pretty much raised me even though I didn't live with them.

"Jess Ferris somehow became the official person I needed to report to during my probation. He taught me many skills, including motorcycle racing and safety. Frank Sims was the rancher who hired me before I started in first grade. He actually paid me even though I wasn't technically old enough to work. He took me to town on paydays and made sure I spent my earnings on things I needed like clothes and stuff. He'd let me have a few dollars for things I wanted, but I'd have to save the extra money for a whole month. So, he taught me to spend it wisely too. Now, I thank God for those men. They supported me through the things that happened. I never had a real dad, but according to what I heard, they were better to me than many of the dads of the kids I went to school with."

"What was the most difficult memory you have of your childhood?" Clayton rested his arms on his knees and leaned toward Rand.

Rand's chest was suddenly heavy. "I found Vera, the woman I lived with, face down in her flower bed one day after school. When I told her husband, Ned, he made me help him dig a hole in her flower bed and bury her. I don't think he ever reported it to the authorities and no one ever asked me where she was except Alice Ferris. I told her Vera got mad at Ned and left because I was afraid the sheriff would put me and Ned both in jail."

Clayton placed a hand briefly on Rand's shoulder. "How old were you then, son?"

"Eight." He responded in a quiet monotone voice.

Clayton slowly shook his head. "How have you dealt with your friend's accident?"

He blinked several times. "I try not to think about it. And sometimes have nightmares about him, asking me, why, Rand?" He whispered.

Clayton studied him. "Guilt is a poor companion. Have you ever shared this with anyone?"

Rand inhaled and expelled his breath through lips pressed into a thin line. "Rod knows some of it. Jess and Frank lived nearby."

Clayton smiled. "I'm glad you shared with Rod."

Rand nodded.

Clayton shook his head. "Some things are just too difficult to handle alone."

Rand lowered his gaze against the doctor's scrutinizing appraisal. "No kidding." His voice was a mere whisper.

Clayton eyed his watch and placed a hand on Rand's shoulder. "I think that's enough for today. I want you to come in again next week. In the interim, I advise you to find Scriptures that tell you about God's forgiveness. Start with Ephesians, chapter one and verse seven."

Unable to speak, Rand bobbed his head and put on his hat.

Once outside, he drew several deep breaths and tried to get his heart rate back to normal. He strode quickly to his truck, slid in, and closed the door. He leaned his head against the seat, took off his hat and wiped the sweat from his forehead with the sleeve of his jean jacket.

Thirty-One

The following Friday Rand began getting excited about spending Christmas with Rod and his family. Mostly alone since his dad and Alfred left, he spent more time in his shop, making Christmas gifts. He chose a small piece of Aspen wood from his supply, which he kept in a corner of his shop. He picked up his scriber knife and began to fashion a box for his dad's watch.

The phone rang and he picked it up on the first ring. "Hello? Dad?" Rand pressed the receiver close to his ear because Karl's voice was barely audible and held a slight tremor. "Are you alright?"

"Arlo passed away last night. Brooke is upset and stays in her room. Could you come and keep her company until after the funeral? I have a lot to do as the executor of his estate and Cedric is busy with things here at the chalet."

Rand heard the sorrow in his dad's voice and knew he was dealing with his own grief. "I'll be there as soon as I can."

Karl paused, apparently trying to retain emotional control. "I know it's short notice, but the funeral is on Monday. If you could be here beforehand, I'd appreciate it. I'm concerned about Brooke. She's taking it very hard. Arlo hasn't been well for quite some time, but we just didn't expect—"

"Okay, Dad." Rand struggled to control his own emotion. "I'll be there as soon as I can get a flight."

"Call when you have your flight scheduled and I'll have either Alfred or Cedric meet you at the airport."

"Okay, I'll do it right away."

"Thank you. I know you want to spend Christmas with your brother and his family, hopefully you still can."

Rand frowned and wished his dad could be here for Christmas.

"See you soon, son."

"Take care, Dad." Afterward he called and secured his plane tickets and then left a message for his dad. When he finished, he clambered down the front steps and hopped in his pickup.

A little later Rand entered Rod's office, sat in a chair, and waited until his brother got off the phone with a client. Unable to sit still, he swiveled the chair slowly from side to side and scanned the office. The walls, which needed a fresh coat of paint, were a drab off-white. The only decorations were two pictures on a credenza: Rod and Saun's wedding picture, and another of them with Tommy.

Rod contemplated Rand a moment after he hung up the phone. "I get the impression you're here on a mission."

Rand steadily held his brother's scrutiny. "Dad's friend passed away and the funeral is on Monday. I made flight arrangements out of LA for tomorrow evening. I couldn't get the connector between Montecito and LAX for tomorrow, but I was able to get it on the return trip."

Rod made a note on his desk calendar. "I'll drive you to LA. What time is your flight?"

"Six forty-five tomorrow night."

"When will you be returning?"

"I'm leaving there Tuesday morning."

Rod leaned back in his chair. "Would you like to come and eat dinner with us tonight?"

Rand shook his head. "I would, but I have some things I need to finish before tomorrow." He planned to stay up late in order to finish the gift he was making for his dad.

Rod nodded. "I'll pick you up around two and we can grab a quick bite to eat before you have to catch your flight."

"Sounds like a plan, thanks. Sorry to run, but I've got lots to do before tomorrow." He gave Rod a two-fingered salute and left.

It was late that night when he finished Karl's gift and he paused at the front door to stare in the direction of Netty's apartment. Again, there were two silhouettes on the shades, one with a cowboy hat. Rand rubbed his chest and heaved a deep sigh. *Guess she really did move on, pal.*

Rand was thankful that Rod came alone on Saturday for the drive to Las Angeles. His warning was never far from Rand's mind since Karl's call. Reluctantly he'd agreed to help Brooke, but didn't think he could offer her anything except his time and presence. Karl was Rand's primary concern. He hoped his dad didn't leave Brooke entirely up to him. He caught Rod's profile from his peripheral view and took note of the crinkles at the corner of his mouth.

"Saun, Tommy and I are painting my office on Monday. Too bad you'll miss out on the fun."

Rand grinned. "Your idea or Saun's?"

Rod nodded. "Both actually. I planned on doing it myself, but she insisted we make a family project of it."

Rand snorted. "I'll bet Tommy liked that."

"He did actually. In fact, he helped pick the colors."

"I can't wait to see it." Rand hooted.

Rod tapped his fingers on the steering wheel. "You'll be surprised. He's so excited about the tea box that it's already wrapped and under the tree. Thank you again for helping him make it."

They both were amazed that Tommy insisted on giving Saun a special gift.

But it didn't matter how hard Rod tried to distract him, Rand's mind kept circling back to his concern for his dad and how much time he'd spend alone with Brooke.

"Have you made an appointment with Clayton?" Rod asked.

"Yeah." He responded absently.

Rod's brow wrinkled and he quickly glanced at him. "Is he helping?"

Rand shrugged. "I've only gone twice."

Once they arrived at LAX, Rand received his tickets and checked in his suitcase. He parted company with Rod when boarding for his flight was announced. The flight seemed longer than he expected while he brooded over his dad's grief at losing a friend.

His eyes lost their focus as his thoughts followed the death of his own best friend from high school. *Will you ever be able to get over feeling guilty, pal?* He viewed the puffy clouds outside the window of the plane with disinterest and tried to imagine what he would do once he arrived at Arlo's chalet.

"Ladies and gentlemen, this is your captain speaking. We will be landing at San Francisco International in a few minutes."

Rand didn't hear the rest of the announcement because an attractive flight attendant sat next to him.

She gave him an alluring perusal. "San Francisco is my destination too. If you need assistance when we land, I have some free time, Mr. Gray."

He scowled at the wall in front of him and wished for his cowboy hat to shield his face against the attendant's suggestive scrutiny. "Thanks, but a friend is meeting me."

She placed her hand on his where it rested on his knee. "Francine Massey. I'll be happy to show you to the baggage area. That's usually where people meet."

He moved his hand and adjusted his position so that her hand slid off his leg and hung limply over the seat. "Thanks anyway, I'm sure I can find it." He tried to focus on the activity outside his window as his body tensed. It appeared to be a huge airport even from this height. He was confident he could find his way around, but suddenly clenched his fists as Gus's warning reminded him there'd been a rise of violent deaths in their area in the last month. He was glad he didn't promise to remain there as Gus suggested. He breathed deeply and released a long breath.

The stewardess grasped his arm. "We'll be fine. Landings are sometimes a bit rough. Is this your first time flying?"

He responded with a quick nod as the wheels touched the ground and the plane taxied down the runway.

Francine grasped his arm. "We'll be the first ones off the plane."

He was thankful he'd flown first class, but didn't appreciate the intrusion of his privacy. He did his best to hide the tension in his shoulders as he retrieved his leather jacket from the overhead compartment. He tamped down his frustration with the woman who hovered at his side while he tried to ignore the sensation of hairs lifting on the nape of his neck. The possibility of being followed caused his heartrate to race.

She walked beside him down the ramp and led the way to a bank of elevators. When they reached the baggage floor, she guided him into a large open area where several luggage carousels were circling and stopped next to one, which was just beginning to fill.

"What color is your luggage?"

He frowned at her close proximity as he grabbed his suitcase from the carousel. "I've got it." He told her while he raised his gaze to search the immediate area.

Just then Alfred approached them with a broad smile on his face. "Hello, Rand."

He expelled a huge breath as he acknowledged Alfred's greeting with a bob of his head and outstretched hand. "I wasn't sure who to expect."

"Karl thought it best if I came since Cedric wouldn't recognize you. He insists that Brooke be driven wherever she needs to go."

Francine's eyebrows arched as she briefly considered both men. "I see you're in good hands, Rand. I hope you enjoy your stay in San Francisco."

"Thanks." He replied absently.

"Here's my business card." She grasped his hand when he released Alfred's. "Call me sometime." She winked at him when she placed it in his hand and then sashayed away before he could respond.

Alfred grinned. "I gather you didn't invite the lady's attention."

Rand shook his head with a smirk. "How's dad holding up?" With a quick glance he noted the direction Francine went before he followed Alfred out of the area.

"Karl's soldiering through it. Brooke stays in her room." Alfred replied while they strolled toward the exit.

When they arrived at his dad's limousine, Alfred opened a rear door and waited for Rand who shook his head.

"I prefer to ride up front with you." He placed his suitcase on the rear seat along with his jacket. As he climbed in the front passenger seat, Alfred's chuckle reached his ears before the chauffer closed the rear door.

"Did Karl tell you we are staying at Arlo's chalet" Alfred asked as he started the car.

"He mentioned it." He glanced at the older man. "You've known dad for a long time. He asked me to help Brooke, but I would rather help dad with his needs."

Alfred's smile appeared forced. "Karl has his hands full with the funeral parlor's arrangements, Arlo's attorney for the settlement of his estate, and his will. That's in addition to consoling their mutual friends and business associates. Just between you and me, Karl is quite stressed, but I am used to handling difficult situations with him and have it under control. So, his only remaining concern is Brooke."

Rand briefly peered at Alfred, without turning his head. "I'm glad you've been here to help him through this."

Alfred's lips pulled into a tight line. "Miss Brooke tends to put people in categories known only to her and she's used to having things her way."

Rand sighed as he remembered her stubborn insistence on massage therapy until he flatly refused. "No kidding."

"If things get too difficult, Cedric has known her for most of her life and you can trust him. You definitely aren't getting the simplest task."

He chewed the inside of his cheek and was preoccupied with his own thoughts for the remainder of the trip.

"We're here." Alfred informed him after what seemed a lengthy amount of time.

Rand glanced at his watch in somewhat of a daze: 9:40 P.M.

Alfred quickly opened the rear door and grabbed Rand's suitcase before he could protest. "Can't have Cedric thinking I don't do my job properly." He winked at Rand and gave him his jacket.

Once Rand was inside, Alfred directed him to a library where a gas fire flickered on the hearth. "Would you like a hassock?"

"No thanks." He responded, as he sat on a plush sofa.

Alfred appraised him with slightly raised brows. "Karl has been busy trying to settle things with Arlo's attorney and informed me he would retire early. He will see you in the morning. May I get you anything?"

"Thank you, Alfred." Brooke interrupted as she entered the room. "Cedric went home so you can take Rand's things to his room."

Alfred gave her a curt nod. "Yes, ma'am." He left quickly.

Rand took note of her smugness toward Alfred and swallowed his words of protest.

She wore a tan suede-like pantsuit with a pale-yellow silk blouse. Her high heels perfectly matched her blouse. He glanced at his Levi's and green-plaid flannel shirt and shrugged. *You don't dress to impress. you are who you are, pal.* But he was glad he brought the suit he'd worn to Rod's wedding for the funeral, but that was out of respect for his dad. Rand redirected his attention to what Brooke was saying.

"Forgive me for not greeting you right away." She smiled at Rand. "Thank you for coming on such short notice."

He met her direct gaze. "No problem. I'm sorry for your loss."

"If you'll excuse me for a moment, I'll be right back. In the meantime, please make yourself comfortable." She exited the room.

Rand shook his head and stared at the floor to ceiling windows at the far end of the room. It was dark and unidentifiable shadows existed in the distance. He stood and stretched his legs and then his back before strolling to a large ornate bookcase to the left side of the room. He gazed briefly at several awards and trophies, one of which was the figure of a woman on snow skis. At the clicking of her heels on the marble floor, he pivoted toward the interior of the spacious room.

Brooke seemed to appraise him as she crossed the room. She carried a tray and placed it on the coffee table in front of the sofa. "I'm glad you brought a jacket. It can get quite cold here at night. Was your flight uncomfortable?"

"It was okay." He recollected the flight attendant. *At least your seat was comfortable, pal.*

"I found the seats a little confining, so I always fly first class." Smiling, she pulled an afghan from a chair back.

He drew a deep breath and it expelled it slowly. "The color of your blouse reminds me of the sugar cookies in the window of the sweet shoppe in Montecito."

"Is that the one where we went?" She grinned when he nodded his head. "Please," she gestured toward the sofa, "sit down."

When he did, she placed the afghan over his legs.

Rand's brows rose as he laid the blanket aside. "I didn't come here for you to—"

"I'm sorry, I'm used to doing that for Karl and my un-cle." She paused to blot away a tear with a lacy handkerchief, which she retrieved from her jacket pocket. "Karl's reaction was similar the first time I covered his legs." Her smile was tight.

Rand caught a glimpse of a tear on her cheek, before she pivoted away to sit on the other end of the sofa. He frowned. "Are you comparing me to dad?"

She observed him while she tilted her head to one side. "You are definitely more appealing."

Rand opened his mouth to respond with a wisecrack, but Alfred returned and interrupted him. "Will there be anything else, Miss Brooke?"

"No, thank you, Alfred, I know you're helping Karl tomorrow, so you may retire for the evening."

He responded with a curt nod. "Good night." He left and closed the door behind him.

Rand repressed the desire to spit and wished he'd stayed home. His blood pressure rose but he determined not to let her pompous attitude make him forget he was here because his dad asked him to come. In spite of the circumstances, he was somewhat hungry so he focused on the contents of the tray. It held a half dozen small sandwiches, slices of apples and oranges, a small dish of fresh pineapple along with dipping sauce, some chocolate chip cookies, and a small stack of Oreos along with a carafe and two cups.

Brooke's eyes twinkled at him as she poured their coffee. "I fixed this while I waited for you. It gave me something to do and something more pleasant to occupy my mind."

He ignored her comment as his stomach growled. "I guess I am a little hungry." He raised one eyebrow. "The chocolate chips look homemade so what's with the Oreos?"

Her head tilted slightly to the side as a beguiling smile played on her lips. "Oh, those are for me. They're my favorite."

"I like them too. I'll trade you two chocolate chips for an Oreo."

"No need to trade. I'll be glad to share with you, that is if you don't mind if I join you." She smiled wide, displaying perfectly spaced and brilliantly white teeth.

He smirked. *Wonder how much her perfect smile cost, pal.* "I won't eat all this myself.""

"I don't think I mentioned while I was at Candlewood how thrilled my uncle and I were when Karl told us he accepted Christ. He said you and your brother helped get him through a dark time in his life while he was there."

Rand examined her expression. He had little knowledge of the struggle Rod went through with their dad when he came to Fire River. "I don't know much about dad's life before I met him there. I guess you'll have to settle for his explanation."

She sipped from her cup with her gaze fixated on him. "I'm glad you came. I know Karl's busy with the details of my uncle's will and all. I didn't want him to worry about me on top of everything else but this has been really hard for all of us. Cedric is like family and Alfred is very close to Karl. My uncle's passing wasn't really a surprise, but—" She lowered her gaze and took a few deep breaths. "I'm sorry, his, passing seems to hit me in waves."

She blotted her eyes with her handkerchief. She exhaled a half giggle and half-sob, which then became near hysterical crying. "Would you—?" Her voice waivered in a futile attempt to hold back tears. "Never mind." She shot to her feet and bolted for the door.

Rand leaped from the sofa, caught her arm, and ushered her back to sit next to him. "You don't need to run away. I promise I don't bite." He murmured softly.

She studied him as tears streamed down her cheeks. "I'm sorry." She hiccoughed.

"Sshh." He patted her back somewhat awkwardly while offering her a small smile.

She leaned on his shoulder. "Is this, okay?"

"For a little while." He whispered as his pulse picked up and his muscles tensed. In spite of Rod's warning and her superior attitude with Alfred, her grief spurred his compassion and a desire to soothe her loss. After what seemed like a lifetime to Rand, Alfred returned.

He appeared somewhat flustered. "I'm sorry I didn't think of it sooner, Miss Brooke. Here are the pills the doctor prescribed for you. They'll help you rest." He offered her a small glass of water and some pills.

She sat up and took them like an obedient child before turning to Rand. "I'm so sorry." her lips quivered.

Rand caught Alfred's concerned gaze. "I'll stay with her a little longer."

Alfred gave him a small smile. "If you like, I can remain until she's ready to retire to her room."

Rand shook his head. "You have your hands full with helping dad. We—she'll be fine."

Alfred's brow wrinkled. "I'll leave a light on in your room. It's just down the hall on the right after you pass the formal dining room."

Rand nodded and watched Brooke set the glass on the coffee table when Alfred left the room. "Better?" He asked peering at Brooke's downturned mouth.

She avoided his eyes. "Maybe we should turn in for the night."

"Do you think you can sleep?" He took her hands in his.

"Could you hold me again? I'm so cold." She still avoided his steady gaze.

He scanned the room for something to cover her, spied the afghan on the floor, and reached for it. "Let me get this." He shifted her position so he could reach it, draped it around her shoulders and then pulled her into his arms.

"I'm sorry, I . . ." She whispered in a shaky voice.

"Sshh, relax."

She nestled her head against his shoulder. "Thank you."

He leaned back against the sofa as he held her close. "Close your eyes." He whispered.

She laid her hand gently on his chest and peered intently at him.

He considered her not-so-subtle scrutiny and found it somewhat unsettling.

Her lashes fluttered as she fought to withhold more tears. "Sometimes I get a fleeting glimpse of sorrow in your eyes." She drew her bottom lip between her teeth. "It's very similar to the expression Karl's face frequently held when he began coming here to visit my uncle."

Rand recalled the gravity in his dad's voice over the phone and found it difficult to swallow.

She placed her hand on top of his. "Let Jesus heal those dark places, Rand."

He met her gaze without flinching. *She lost her uncle and she's trying to comfort me.* "I think it's time for you to get some rest. You have a big day ahead of you tomorrow." Rod's warning that grief could cause some people to be vulnerable, tiptoed through his mind. "Come on." He stood, and offered her his hand.

"I'm sorry." She searched his face. "I've kept you up late. You must be tired. I'm sure Alfred hung up your clothes. Your room has a private bath and is stocked with everything you might need. It gets cold here at night so there're more blankets if you need them on the shelf in your closet. I'll walk there with you." She led the way. "Cedric comes at six and will fix breakfast for us. Karl will join us if he can."

He scanned the long wide hall with doors on both sides. "Thanks. I'll keep that in mind."

"This is your room." She stopped in front of an open door. The room was bathed in soft light from a bedside lamp. She waited in the hall while he stepped in to survey it.

He slowly turned to face her. "Thanks, it's nice. I'll see you in the morning." He spoke in a near whisper.

She giggled. "Karl and Alfred's rooms are upstairs so you don't have to worry about disturbing them." Her lips brushed his cheek with a featherlike kiss. "Sweet dreams, Rand. See you at breakfast."

He stood in the doorway, chewing on the inside of his cheek until she disappeared around a corner. He closed the door quietly and brushed his cheek with his fingers. An image of Netty's passionate kiss at her door the night, they celebrated their birthdays replayed in his mind. He rubbed his chest and his Adam's apple bobbed several times.

Thirty-Two

The next morning Rand awoke to the aroma of coffee and bacon, which made his mouth water, as he headed for the shower. After putting on a pair of Levi's and a black long-sleeve shirt, he strode to the kitchen where he found a man with gray hair and assumed he was Cedric. "Smells good in here." He remarked as he drew an appreciative breath.

"Good morning, master Rand." Cedric, who wore a uniform, greeted him with a wink.

Rand cocked his head with upturned lips. "Good morning." He scanned the massive room and took note of a small table in a corner nook that was surrounded by windows on three sides. He strolled across the inlaid marble floor to join Karl, who was seated across from Brooke. "Morning, Dad, Brooke."

Karl wore a dark suit, and a pale-yellow shirt with a matching dark tie. He raised his head at Rand's greeting. "Morning, son, sorry I wasn't up when you arrived."

Rand's head bobbed. "No worries. Is there something I can do to help you today?"

Karl gave him a cursory smile before taking a drink from his cup. "I'd like you to stay with Brooke. Cedric will be busy with his duties and Alfred will be with me."

Rand swallowed his retort and shot a glance at her. "How're you this morning?" He took note of her puffy eyelids. Her face was free of makeup and her attire was more casual than last night. She wore navy slacks and a lavender sweater. He caught a glimpse of slippers that matched her sweater when he approached the table and took his place.

Her cobalt-blue eyes held a far-away look as she offered him a small smile. "I'm fine. Glad you joined us for breakfast."

Cedric placed large plates of eggs, bacon, breakfast rolls and mixed fruit in the center of the table along with a basket of toast. He filled Rand's cup from a carafe and then set it on the table between him and Karl. "Would you like me to take care of the matter you mentioned earlier or would you prefer I wait until you finish eating, sir?"

Karl's brow wrinkled as he met the man's gaze. "Please go now. I want you here later to assist those who'll be checking on arrangements. I left a list on your desk of those who may either call or stop by."

"Very good, sir, I will return as promptly as possible."

From his peripheral view, Rand observed his dad's anxious grimace.

Karl acknowledged Cedric's response before turning to Rand. "How was your flight?"

He shrugged. "Okay."

Brooke filled their plates from the platters in the middle of the table, and passed one to each of them.

Rand raised an eyebrow at the extra portion she gave him, but withheld his protest.

She gave him a coy smile. "Would you ask the blessing please, Rand?"

After a short prayer he took a bite of his omelet, closed his eyes, and savored the spicy flavor. "Umm, perfect." He opened his eyes in time to catch her conspiratorial wink at Karl.

"Exactly the way your father showed Cedric how to make them." Her expression was filled with mirth as she appraised Rand's face. "Would you rather have a mug?"

Rand scrutinized the fancy teacup at his fingertips. The cup appeared expensive and fragile. "This is fine." His lips pinched into a flat line. and he swallowed the remark that flashed in his mind.

She jumped up from the table and hurried to the cupboard over a counter that stretched along an entire wall. "We'll use mugs if it's okay with you, Karl."

He concurred with a mumble as he buttered his toast.

She set three mugs on the table, and transferred their coffee to them. "Better?"

"Thanks." Rand drew his hand into a fist under the table and then released it. He took a drink from his cup to hide his grimace. *Going to be a long visit, pal.*

Wings of Steel

When they finished eating, Brooke was the first to stand. "You can either relax in the library or on the terrace." She directed her comment to Rand. "The terrace will be cold so you might want your jacket."

"I don't know about dad, but—"

"I won't be going to church this morning." Karl got up slowly. "I have several things to attend to before tomorrow. I hope you two enjoy your day."

Rand's mouth fell open slightly. "Will you be gone long?"

"Unfortunately, most of the day." Karl replied and traipsed from the kitchen.

Rand's brow wrinkled at his dad's abruptness. "I'm good with either one. What about you?"

She smiled. "I prefer the library. The only time I don't mind being cold is when I'm skiing."

"Are the medals on the bookshelf yours?"

She nodded. "Some of them."

"I've skied some in—"

"But you can't—"

"If you'll excuse me." He stood abruptly and left the room. He refused to listen while she listed things, she felt he could no longer do.

"I'll bring a fresh pot of coffee to the library before I finish getting dressed."

"You don't have to—"

"You only had one cup." She protested.

He shrugged. "Okay, thanks." He wandered into the library and settled on a couch near the massive gas fireplace.

She entered with a tray, which held some sweet rolls, a carafe, and a mug. She set them on the coffee table in front of him. "Is there anything else I can get for you?"

Rand peered up at her and blinked. "No, thanks."

She paused to study him. "I won't be long."

His brows rose. "Take your time." After she left, he exhaled heavily as thoughts of Netty entered his mind and how comfortable they were with each other's lifestyle. *Does she miss you at all, pal?* He shrugged and tried to dismiss the image of them sitting across from each other at the table.

Cedric came in the room and lit the fireplace. "May I get you anything else, master Rand?"

He shook his head. "I'm Good, but I'd appreciate it if you could just use my name."

A broad smile stretched across the man's face. "I sensed earlier you were uncomfortable with formality, but it wouldn't have been prudent to mention it in public."

Rand grinned and instantly liked the small, but heavy-set man.

"I will close the door for your privacy. Another of those formalities." He gave Rand a sympathetic wink and left the room.

Rand sighed. *Closed doors when no one else is here? Can't wait to go home, pal.*

A short time later, the clicking of high-heels on the floor in the hall captured Rand's attention and he turned to observe Brooke as she entered the library and closed the door behind her.

She stopped next to him. "May I sit beside you?"

He moved over to provide a comfortable space between them. He tried not to stare, but she wore a dress with elbow length sleeves and a skirt that fell softly to her knees. It was the color of rosé wine. Netty's preferred drink. He frowned at the intrusive memory.

Brooke stared at the floor for several seconds before she raised her head to focus on him. "My parents were my best friends. We went everywhere together. My father taught me to ski and my mother taught me piano. They also taught me the value of respecting others, no matter how young or old." The color of her cheeks nearly matched her dress. "What was your childhood like?"

His shoulders tensed as he briefly met her unwavering gaze. He squinted and stared through the windows at the picturesque mountains capped with snow. Unaffected by the sight and having no desire to invite her scorn or pity, he chose his words carefully. "I basically grew up on my own." He rubbed his jaw. "I learned a lot from a friend who was a carpenter by trade and worked on a neighbor's ranch."

Blinking, she studied him for several moments. "I admired some of your work while I was at Candlewood. You told me you worked on a dock before your accident and apparently had no desire to return there. Will you look for carpentry work?"

It wasn't lost to him that she failed to even acknowledge his work on a ranch. "Rod and I have discussed continuing restoration on Candlewood."

"Were you an apprentice to the man who taught you carpentry?"

"I learned the basics from him. The rest I pretty much picked up from others along the way."

She crossed her arms, as she appeared to listen intently. "You're an artist then. A self-taught one if I understand correctly."

He shrugged. "I find an interesting piece of wood, study it, and visualize what it could be."

She clapped her hands. "I go through the same sort of process when I study a blank canvas and I usually have a finished painting in mind."

His eyebrows rose. Could they really share a kind of commonality even if only in a creative sense?

Her eyes sparkled with unshed tears. "I'm glad you were willing to come, especially since it's so close to Christmas." She caught his gaze and held it. "Karl told me you won't be staying long. Do you mind if we don't go to church?"

Her quick change of subject influenced him to respond with scrupulosity. "Whatever you're comfortable with. Is there something I can do for you while I'm here?"

She shook her head and focused on her clasped hands for a few moments. When she raised her head, tears were no longer apparent. She swallowed visibly. "Sometimes I feel guilty for not being as preoccupied as Karl about all of this. Perhaps it's as much about the responsibility of settling my uncle's estate as it is about actually missing him. Uncle Arlo always said if or when I marry, my future husband will need to agree to a prenuptial agreement." She laughed. "I guess he was afraid someone would take advantage of me."

Rand couldn't identify with her situation, but on some level was able to understand her lack of emotion. She was likely in denial and the funeral would awaken her to reality. In any case, he would be here if either she or his dad needed him. "Dad is planning to stay and help you with some of it so, you won't be going through it alone."

"I know he wants to return to Fire River eventually."

His lips quirked at her bravado. "Maybe you should think of this as an opportunity to make your own way."

"Would you mind, terribly if I came to Fire River?"

He crossed his arms, careful to neither encourage or discourage such a move. "That's a possibility if you think you could be happy living in a smaller community with a slower pace."

She raised her head and stared at him. "I wouldn't want to impose—"

"Sometimes a person just has to be willing to take a chance." His lips flattened as he recalled his own journey. He had nothing but an old letter from his mother to guide his future.

"I do have a lot of loose ends here even aft—" She blotted her eyes with a tissue she pulled from a box on the coffee table and then held it crumpled in her fist.

"You don't have to make any major decisions today or tomorrow or even next week."

She drew in a ragged breath. "Thank you for having confidence in me that I can do this. How long are you staying?"

"My plane leaves at seven Tuesday morning."

She placed her hand on his arm and gazed longingly at him. "I wish you didn't have to go so soon."

He stared at her, at a loss for words. Tuesday morning couldn't come soon enough for him.

"But you've given me hope. It's time to make a fresh start." She smiled. "Would you be willing to go out later?"

His shoulders released their tension and he leaned back against the couch. "What do you have in mind?"

Her face shone with excitement. "Tadich Grill. I think you'd find it a comfortable place. It's the oldest restaurant in California. They always have fresh seafood and their steaks are delicious."

"Perfect." A corner of his mouth hitched. "What time?"

She tilted her head. "How about six?"

"Sounds good."

That evening Rand stepped into the two-car garage behind Brooke and his breath caught in his throat. Parked near the door was a sky-blue Maserati. His mouth dropped open as Brooke headed for the driver's door. She mentioned it while in Fire River, but he didn't exactly believe her. "This is your car?"

She laughed. "I'd let you drive, but you aren't familiar with the streets and they can be tricky."

He whistled as he rounded the fastback coupe. The hood reminded him of a shark's nose with pop up headlights. The white leather interior consisted of plush sport seats separated by a console with a five-speed gear shift.

Rand found ample room beneath the dash for his long legs. He studied Brooke's intense expression as she backed out of the garage.

She threw a quizzical glance at him before fixing her attention on the road ahead. "Do you like roller coasters?"

An impish grin tugged at his lips. He took note of the streets Alfred drove through on the way to the chalet last night. He leaned back and gazed out the passenger window.

She made a sharp right and they plunged down a steep hill.

His stomach felt like it lunged into his throat. He resisted the urge to grab the dash as they shot up the next hill. It appeared as if they would fly right off the crest of the hill and sail through the air. He hoped she could handle the machine. When she finally parked, he silently expelled a relieved breath.

She giggled. "I hope I didn't scare you."

He shrugged. "Not a chance." He eyed her mischievously as he climbed out of the car, strolled around the front, and offered her his arm. If only he could reciprocate. He'd give her a ride she wouldn't soon forget.

She was still laughing when she stood on the pavement. "Your expression tells me you'd enjoy a payback."

"Nah." He ducked his head and wished again he'd brought his cowboy hat while they walked toward the restaurant. He opened the door for her to enter ahead of him.

Inside along one wall there was a long counter with stools. Tables for two or more were surrounded by wood-paneled walls with a large mirror on the wall beside each table. He pulled out a chair for Brooke and sat across from her.

A waiter brought them menus and took their drink orders.

When he left Rand inspected the choices and was pleased by the variety. "I think I'll have the ribeye with shoestring potatoes. What about you?" He appraised her over the top of his menu.

She captured his attention as she coyly peered around her menu at him. "I'll have the broiled Perales sole."

The waiter came back with their coffee and Rand placed their order.

After he left, she studied Rand. "Don't you like trying something different?"

His mouth fell open slightly, but he responded quickly. "The crab and jumbo prawns sounded good but I'm in the mood for steak." He scanned the tables covered with white cloths and napkins with a large bowl of lemon wedges in the middle of each one. The aroma, which filled the atmosphere, made his mouth water in anticipation. He appreciated she'd chosen a restaurant that didn't exude a romantic atmosphere. All at once, he became aware that she was staring at him. He cocked an eyebrow. "What?"

She focused on the table as a blush stained her cheeks. "Can I ask you a question?"

He blinked and tilted his head to the side. "Sure."

She pulled something from her purse, gave him a small card and studied him with a curious expression. "Is this yours?"

He flipped the card over and read the name imprinted on the front, Francine Massey. His brow furrowed. The flight attendant. "Where did you get this?"

She winced. "I . . . found it in the foyer near the front door."

He shrugged. "You can throw it away."

She blinked. "Aren't you going to call her?"

He squinted at her. "Not my type." As soon as the words were out of his mouth, he wanted to take them back.

She smiled and dropped the card on the table. "What is your type, Rand?"

He immediately thought of Netty and gazed at the wall opposite them. "I guess I'll know when I find her."

"What about her didn't you like?"

He shrugged. "Her perfume was too strong."

Brooke was quiet on the drive back to Arlo's place.

If he said or did something to offend her, he refused to apologize unless she pointed out the offense.

They were late getting back to the chalet and she left Rand in the library while she went to find out if anyone else was there. When she returned, she found him studying a gold medal on the bookcase near the hearth. She brought two frosty glasses filled with iced coffee. "I'm thirsty and thought you might be too." She set one on the coffee table for him before sitting on the couch near the fireplace. "Thank you for turning on the heat. I didn't think of it until just now but perhaps hot chocolate would have been a better choice. It is kind of chilly in here."

She watched him as he stood with his back to her, staring at the flickering gas fire. For their dinner he changed from his Levi's to a navy-blue pair of dress slacks with a claret cashmere sweater and his ever-present black cowboy boots. She thought he was appealing and wondered how he'd look in a suit. When he didn't respond or move away from the hearth, she got up, crossed the room, and slipped her hand into his. "Come sit on the couch with me." She gave his hand a gentle tug.

As he turned to face her, she sensed she'd intruded on his private thoughts before he schooled them away behind the ghost of a smile. She tuned into some piped-in slow jazz music on the chalet's music system and turned it down to play softly in the background.

She waited until he was seated and then sat close to him. The gas flames from the hearth shone on his hair and she resisted the temptation to run her fingers through the unruly waves, which appeared as black as a raven in the firelight. Was it as soft as it appeared? After enjoying just being with him for several minutes, she gathered enough courage to whisper. "I had a good time tonight. Did you?"

"Umm-hmm." He responded quietly, staring at the floor. "The steak was excellent."

She peered at his mouth as he spoke and her gaze traveled along his chiseled jaw to the shadow of a beard over his lips and around the edges of his chin. She leaned her head against his shoulder. "I'm not really looking forward to tomorrow. My uncle's passing hasn't registered yet, but I'm afraid the funeral—" All at once there were tears in her eyes and her throat was too dry to swallow, much less speak. She set her glass on the table in front of them because her hand was so unsteady, she feared she'd spill the contents.

The motion seemed to draw Rand away from what she assumed was introspection and he put his arm on the back of the couch. "Tomorrow may not be easy for you. You should probably try and get a good night's rest." He started to help her stand but she placed a hand on his chest.

"Please." She managed to whisper. "I don't want to be alone right now and I'm not a bit tired."

"Okay." He whispered softly, chose a more comfortable position, and settled against the cushions with his feet stretched out under the coffee table.

She took note that he hadn't touched the iced coffee and snuggled against him. "Please hold me, Rand." She whispered.

He moved his arm from the back of the couch to around her shoulders. When she leaned into him, he closed his eyes and rested his head against the couch.

She tilted her head to gaze up at him. After nearly an hour passed with neither of them speaking, she tentatively brushed his cheek with an index finger. She enjoyed the rough and smooth texture of his face as her finger moved back and forth. She expected him to flinch. But his lip hitched slightly upward so she cradled his cheek in the palm of her hand and was intrigued by the strength of his jaw. Her thumb traced his cheekbone and then the stubble along his chin.

He exhaled a small sigh.

She traced his soft relaxed lips with her fingers, gently exploring them and toying with a desire to experience a kiss from him.

He didn't move or even bat an eyelash.

She took his lack of response as an open invitation and slowly slid her fingers into the thick waves of his hair. When he moaned softly, she tentatively touched his lips with hers.

His arms enfolded her and he deepened the kiss.

She responded eagerly, drawing him closer with her arms around his neck. As her fingers slid to the back of his neck, she experienced a kind of tenderness she'd never felt before.

His eyes flew open. He sat up quickly and set her off to his side. "I, I'm sorry, I must have been dreaming." He scrubbed his hands through his hair. "I'm sorry, Brooke, I—"

"No, I'm sorry, I don't know what came over me. I . . . I just wanted, I was afraid I'd never see you again and I'd always wonder if. . ." She leaped up from the couch.

"Hey." He spoke softly as he grasped her arm. "Come back and sit down."

She sat, but was unable to look at him. "I'm sor—no, I'm not sorry. If you're upset with me, you can consider it a good-bye kiss."

He raised an eyebrow with a quizzical expression. "You want me to think, kissing me was a bad thing?" He chuckled.

She shook her head. "Of course not. But I've never done anything like that before, ever!"

He took her hands in his. "You're all keyed-up about tomorrow and probably weren't thinking clearly. No harm done." He tapped the end of her nose with his finger. "It's okay."

She stared at his masculine features as if to memorize them. She'd never be able to think about him without remembering that kiss and that he didn't seem upset that she'd done it and those thoughts endeared him to her all the more. She couldn't even imagine what it would have been like if he'd initiated the kiss. "I've treated you badly and for that I am sorry."

He placed his finger under her chin and raised it until their gazes met. "I shouldn't have fallen asleep. Let's just forget it, okay?" He raised an eyebrow.

She nodded, unable to respond or do what he suggested. She doubted she'd forget that kiss as long as she lived. She drew a deep breath and stood. "See you in the morning." She called over her shoulder as she hurried from the room.

He blinked rapidly at her abrupt exit and was tempted to call a taxi and leave, right then. He made his way quietly to his room, closed the door, and locked it. He took off his sweater, hung it up, stretched out on the bed and stared at the ceiling. He couldn't get Netty off his mind and was dreaming about her when Brooke kissed him. *Netty's moved on. Why can't you, pal?*

He drew his hand across his mouth. He hadn't invited Brooke's kiss, but couldn't escape the memory of it. *It was soft and tend—No!* He sat bolt upright. *You will not go there, pal.* He jammed his fingers in his hair and pulled on it.

Still have tomorrow to get through. God, I need help, here. He got undressed, slipped beneath the covers and closed his eyes. But the tenderness in Brooke's kiss and her gentle caresses invaded his sleep, what little he was finally able to get.

Thirty-Three

Monday at the funeral parlor Rand stood between Brooke and his dad while Cedric and Alfred stood on opposite sides during the viewing. Rand appreciated the esteem his dad received among Arlo's friends and their business associates as Karl introduced him to the stream of well-wishers.

At the grave site, Brooke sobbed and Rand wrapped his arm around her shoulders to support her. When she and Karl stepped forward to toss a handful of dirt on Arlo's grave, she stumbled and nearly fell. She cried through both services and the entire drive back to the chalet.

Once there she retired to her room and Karl and Cedric also disappeared, which left Rand to do as he pleased. He changed into Levi's and a long-sleeve flannel shirt.

Rand sat in the library and made himself intentionally available if either his dad or Brooke needed him. He was reading his Bible when Brooke entered the room.

"What are you reading?" She peered at the book as she sat beside him.

He pointed to the first few verses of Matthew chapter five.

She read verse four. "'Blessed are those who mourn, for they shall be comforted.'" She sniffed and wiped a tear from her cheek.

He put his arm around her shoulders and read verse five. "'Blessed are the gentle, for they shall inherit the earth.' You're a gentle person, Brooke."

She studied him for several moments. "I've never met anyone quite like you, Rand. You make me feel very special!"

He winked at her. "You are special to God." His voice was a mere whisper.

Her cheeks turned a soft pink and she picked at something on the sleeve of her cream-colored cashmere sweater. "I wish you didn't have to leave so soon." When he didn't respond, she settled against his side and leaned her head on his shoulder. "Rand?"

"Hmm?" He murmured against her silky tresses. A memory of her kiss tiptoed through his mind but he quickly disregarded it.

She stared into his eyes. "There's an office building downtown with a life-size display of the manger scene with people, animals and angels. Uncle Arlo and I always went every year on Christmas Eve when most everyone else was at home with their families. I'd love for you to go with me before you lea—"

"I'd like that, but I'm leaving in the morning." He rested his arm on the back of the sofa behind her.

She sat up quickly. "That's right!" She jumped up and grasped his hand. "Let's go now!"

A corner of his mouth lifted. *She's cute when she's excited.* He searched her expressive features and little turned-up nose. His gaze traced the soft curve of her cheeks and lingered on her full pink lips. His mouth was suddenly dry.

She giggled. "Do you want to go?"

One of his brows hitched as he allowed her to pull him to his feet. "Go where?"

She licked her lips. "The manger scene, silly."

Distracted by the memory of her kiss, he blinked when her words finally registered. "Manger scene?"

"Yes." She gave his shoulder a playful nudge. "I'll put on some jeans and change my shoes."

He watched her leave the room and slowly shook his head, momentarily disoriented. *You almost kissed her, pal.*

The drive into the city wasn't as hectic for him as the previous night because of his familiarity with her driving skill.

After she parked, he helped her from the car, and they walked half a block to the Nativity scene. The wind was blowing and he guessed the temperature to be somewhere in the low forties. He shivered and pulled up the collar on his leather jacket to ward off the chill and watched Brooke button her wool maxi-coat around her neck.

She pointed to the various animals as they huddled together and enjoyed the scene along with the soft music piped outside from one of the nearby buildings. The Mary and Joseph statues peered down at the baby Jesus with the shepherds and wisemen further away.

Rand inspected the detail on each figure and shook his head in appreciation. "These are incredible!" They were so realistic he half expected them to move, speak or make animal noises.

After a few moments, Brooke began to sing "Silent Night" and he joined her. They drew the attention of a few passers-by, who paused briefly to listen. They sang every carol they could think of until they were both shivering even though wrapped in one another's arms. Reluctantly, they left the peaceful scene and started strolling toward her car.

"Do you want to drive?"

He exhaled a bark of laughter. "Are you sure you trust me?"

She snickered. "It's only fair after the ride I gave you yesterday."

With one arm still around her shoulders, he drew her close as they walked. *Careful, pal, she's affecting your resistance.*

Early the next morning at San Francisco International Airport, he squeezed Brooke's hand.

"Thank you for coming and for giving me some good memories during this time." She told him as they waited for the boarding of his flight to be announced. The announcement came and she grasped both of his hands. "May I kiss you good-bye?"

Instead, he drew her into his arms for a quick hug. "If you need anything, I'm only a phone call away."

"Okay, thank you."

Boarding for his flight was announced again and he bent to kiss her cheek, but she leaned away from him.

Their gazes locked and they stood still for a moment and then he lowered his head and she rose on her toes to touch his lips with hers.

He wrapped his arms around her and pulled her close as she slid her arms around his neck. "I hope you have a happier New Year." His voice was a husky whisper as he focused on the joy, which shone in her eyes. Reluctantly, he released her and began walking backwards away from her.

She kissed her hand, blew the kiss to him, and then waved.

He reached up to tip his cowboy hat. *Left it at home, pal.* He completed the motion with a wave and as he hurried onto the ramp, he forked his fingers through his hair.

"Hello, Rand. Your seat is ready for you." Francine, the airline attendant, greeted him when he stepped inside.

"Thanks, I'm looking forward to a nice nap."

"There's no one sitting beside you so I'll make sure you're comfortable."

He took the aisle seat, stretched out his legs to block access to his row, and closed his eyes. The entire flight to LAX, he fought with disappointment that his dad made very little time for him. He was already gone when Rand arose that morning so he was obliged to leave Karl's Christmas gift on his dresser without so much as a good-bye.

He tried to focus on Brooke's kisses and the feelings they stirred within him, but longing for lost time with his dad pushed those thoughts into the background. He wondered if Karl would ever return to Fire River or choose to stay in San Francisco to watch over his friend's niece. Perhaps his dad's health was worse than he would admit.

———⋈———

Later that same morning in Montecito, Rod was clearing off his desk in preparation to close for the holidays when the door of his office opened and Hermann Coolidge stepped inside. "Merry Christmas, Rod."

"Merry Christmas!" Rod closed the drawer on his desk, stood and walked around it to greet his boss.

Herman was a jolly sort of person with salt and pepper hair and a mustache that barely stretched the width of his upper lip. He was a robust man, about Rod's height with a few extra pounds. "You've already painted and decorated. The two-color pin stripes on the walls are a nice touch."

Rod smiled. "I can't take the credit it was Saun and Tommy's concerted plan. I originally intended to use only tan, but he liked orange while Saun insisted on off white." He picked up the sign, which was upside down on his desk. "I planned to close today at noon and reopen on the fifth of January as you suggested."

Hermann's eyes twinkled. "Excellent! You told me over the phone you have something to show me. Is it here?"

"No, actually it's in Fire River, the mansion that belongs to my family. Rand restored the wood on the first floor and a large part of the second. I took pictures before beginning the project and you will be able to view his finished work first-hand. I mentioned to you that he took over the management of the project while I was recovering from the fire.

"It's my desire to help him find work in his area of expertise since he will not be returning to his former position. I hoped you might have some suggestions. I have the pre-renovation pictures in my briefcase. Candlewood mansion is about forty minutes from here."

Hermann clapped Rod's shoulder and chuckled. "I have looked forward to seeing it. What a splendid name. How long has it been in your family?"

They stepped outside and Rod shut and locked his door. "It was purchased by my great, great grandfather, Alexander Gray, in 1850."

Hermann chuckled as they started down the sidewalk. "Remarkable. I will enjoy viewing the magnificent edifice." They stopped next to his Lincoln town car. "Hilda and I are leaving for vacation on Friday. We will return on January tenth, but will not open until the following Monday."

Rod smiled. "Are you leaving the country?"

"We are. We wanted to visit family in her home town of Bonn for quite some time and this holiday fit with both of our schedules. Everything is current and I have postponed beginning any new projects until after we return. We will have our yearly office gathering the following weekend. I took the opportunity to stop and see you today since I have an appointment in Oxnard."

Thirty-Four

Early that afternoon, Rand exited the twin engine plane, went down the steps to the tarmac at the small airport in Montecito and made his way into the terminal.

"Hey mister!" A child's voice called close by. "You dropped this."

Rand spotted a little dark-haired girl who smiled up at him. He took the envelope, which held his used boarding passes, from her outstretched hand and grinned. "Thank you, little lady." *Apparently, they fell out of my jacket pocket where I hurriedly stuffed them after boarding the flight to Montecito.*

"Mandy, you get back here!"

Rand chuckled. "You'd better hurry before you get in trouble."

"Bye, mister."

He watched her run to a woman, walking toward him with a small boy in her arms. "Rand Gray? I'm Shirley Warner. My husband, Pax, is your cousin. I believe you helped me a while back when a wheel came off Billy's stroller in front of your mother's inn. Did I remember to thank you?"

He scrunched his eyebrows and tried to pull back the memory. "Yes ma'am. You're Pax Warner's wife?"

"Yes, I heard about your wreck. How are you?"

"Fine. Tell Pax I appreciate his help with getting my bike."

"I'll do that. Sorry, but I gotta run before Billy starts fussing. You take care."

He scrubbed his hand over the lower half of his face. *I tried to avoid anyone connected with mother back then because she hated everyone with the name Gray.* He shook his head. He'd been up late last night and this morning since daybreak. *Leaving dad there during Christmas hurt more than I expected.*

While he waited for the baggage to be unloaded from the plane, he searched for a pay phone. He rounded a corner and almost ran into Rod.

"There you are." Rod backed up a step. "How did it go?"

Rand snickered at his surprise. "Better than I expected. Dad appeared to be dealing with the reality of it by the time I got there."

"Good, I'm glad." Rod clapped his shoulder. "I'll take you home with me and you can stay until after Christmas."

Rand grinned. "I would except I have one present that isn't quite ready. If you drop me off, I can finish it, pack the rest in my truck and come a little later today."

Rod led the way to the baggage area. "Just make sure you come in time for dinner, Saun is expecting you and so is Tommy."

Rand grinned. "Got it."

They collected his suitcase and Rod dropped him off at Candlewood.

Christmas Day, Rand admired the love Rod and Saun expressed for each other while his own heart ached with longing for such a relationship. He put on a happy face equal to the occasion and with reasonable assurance thought he managed to be convincing. Even though his mother and Cab were also there, Rand felt strangely alone.

Early that evening, Cab stood when they finished singing Christmas carols. "I need to get back to the village. I have an early morning meeting with my pastor."

Lucinda peered at Cab over her glasses as she pushed up from her chair. "It is getting late." She proceeded to follow Cab toward the door. "Saun, thank you very much for inviting me. Come along Randall, it's almost my bedtime."

Rand, in no hurry to leave, moved slowly toward the door and almost regretted that he'd offered to pick up his mother instead of letting her drive her own car.

Rod grasped his arm just before he stepped outside. "Call her."

Rand raised an eyebrow.

Rod chuckled. "It's written all over your face."

He frowned. "Call who?"

Rod nudged him with his elbow. "I believe Saun and I are the only ones who noticed."

Rand sighed. "I kept wondering how their day went."

"I can't imagine much enjoyment for the holiday after such a loss." A slight frown crossed Rod's features. "A call from you just might help."

He knew Rod inferred Brooke, but chose to ignore the comment. "I'll call dad tomorrow. He goes to bed early."

Later that evening back at the mansion, Rand sat in an armchair in the library, staring at a cheerfully crackling fire. The day's excitement and laughter paled now that he sat alone in the cavernous mansion. His posture slumped and his hope of ever having a relationship like Saun and Rod's evaporated as memories of past experiences played upon his mind.

He never believed love like theirs existed until he witnessed it for himself. *No woman in her right mind will ever love you that way, pal.* He reached for the phone to dial Arlo's chalet and paused. Maybe Rod was right and Brooke needed someone to brighten her day. He hoped his dad would answer. At least he'd get to talk to him and ask if he'd opened his present. He dialed the number.

"Hello, Germayne's residence."

He released his breath, swallowed his disappointment, and avoided the impulse to wish her Merry Christmas. "I hope it isn't too—"

"No, it's perfect timing. Cedric and his family left this afternoon and Karl and Alfred went upstairs a few minutes ago. Did you have a good time with Rod's family?"

He heard the smile in her voice. "Tommy entertained us all and even my mother laughed at a few of his tricks."

"I," she paused uncertainly, "don't recall that you ever mentioned your mother."

He blinked at her unexpected comment. "We just re-connected before you came to help with my therapy, but it's a long story." *She doesn't remember you told her about your mother, pal.*

"That sounds difficult for you." She paused. "I'm sorry, I don't mean to pry."

He frowned. "How are you doing?"

She sighed. "Can I be honest with you?"

He sat up straighter. "I'm listening."

"It's been too quiet since you left. I miss you."

His mouth stretched into a thin line. "Have you thought about what you're going to do as you move forward?"

"Uncle Arlo's will made it clear that I should sell the chalet. I'm so overwhelmed that I'd just like to run away and let someone else make all the decisions."

"Dad's there and Cedric. I'm sure they will help with whatever you need."

"Of course, but I don't think I'd like living alone."

He recalled the meager possessions Ned and Vera left him. So, he couldn't identify with Brooke's sentiment or the choices she faced. Would his dad choose to stay with her?

She paused, waiting for him to respond, but when he didn't, she continued. "I've never lived anywhere else since my parents . . . Would you ever consider moving here?"

He tried to be honest without being too abrupt. "Big city life isn't for me."

"Oh, I assumed your preference for western clothing was just a passing fad."

His eyebrows drew together as his cheeks heated. *What you wear is who you are, pal.* He disengaged from the conversation and let the silence between them linger. He could still hear her breathing into the receiver, but not having anything else to say he kept silent.

"I got the impression when you were here—never mind. Rand, are you still there?"

His lips pressed together. "Yes." He pondered her unsolicited comment about the way he dressed and that she had completely forgotten that he'd told her about his mother.

"I hope we can always be friends." She stifled a yawn. "I have to go now. Talk to you soon."

He was relieved she ended the call before he could no longer resist the scathing retort he held back. He placed the receiver on the base. The dying embers on the hearth echoed his current state of mind and he suddenly felt completely chilled. He pushed up from the chair, headed for his room, and toed off his boots. Dropping onto his bed, he stared at the ceiling and absently rubbed his chest to ease the tightness within while he waited for the sweet relief of sleep.

The next morning, he wandered from the kitchen to the library to the drawing room. He missed his bike and the ability to ease his restlessness by riding. Riding and hiking in the mountains were an integral part of how he spent his free time. The box that came from Arizona entered his mind.

He frowned when he recalled that Brooke told Alfred to put in his shop. His insides fluttered and his palms were sweaty as he entered and lifted the box from a workbench. He plopped onto a chair and began to whistle as he used his pocket knife to quickly open the box. It felt like Christmas all over again. The first thing he found was the motorcycle helmet that once belonged to Jess. The whistling died on his lips.

He turned the helmet over with hands that trembled. An image of the bike sailing over the cliff entered his mind. He shook himself and ran his fingers over Jess's engraved name on the back of the helmet.

Jess raced bikes before joining the marines and taught Rand all he knew. He remembered the trips they took when he stayed with Jess and his wife, Alice. Rand's eyes narrowed and he swallowed hard. He grew up without real parents, left with friends of his mother not long after his birth. Jess reached out to him even though he lived with the Rows until—*Don't go there, pal.*

Jess and his wife knew the Roes and encouraged and supported Rand as much as they could. Jess taught him how to take care of himself in an unfriendly world. He could almost hear Jess say, don't let anyone take that away from you, Rand. Before he put the helmet back in the box, he discovered a note and read it.

Rand, remember how I let you use my helmet while I taught you to ride? I hope you never forget the good times we had, riding and camping together. Love, Jess.

Rand's jaw clenched several times as he remembered Jess often spoke to him about his Savior. He carefully put the box back on the bench and with helmet under his arm, hurried to his bedroom. He slipped into his new black leather jacket, a Christmas gift from Rod and smiled as he left with the helmet in his hand.

Outside he climbed into his pickup and headed for a motorcycle dealer in Montecito. As soon as he entered the building, a salesman approached him.

"What can I show you today, partner?"

"Where are your used bikes?" Rand asked as he glanced at the new ones. If he found something that appealed to him, he'd buy it.

"Any particular one you're interested in?"

Rand shrugged. "Just checking them out right now."

"All of our used bikes are out back. Go out that door over there." He pointed at a side door. "I'll give you a few minutes to look around and then join you. My name's Benson if you have any questions."

"Thanks." Rand headed for the door the man indicated. He took his time inspecting the various specifications of several bikes, but kept going back to a white and black 1971 Harley-Davidson, which appeared to be customized. From his peripheral view, he saw Benson coming and stopped next to a 1973 Honda. "How much is this one?"

Benson checked the sticker. "Sticker says twelve hundred ninety-nine, but I can let you have it for twelve hundred fifty plus tax and title."

Rand shook his head. He moved over to the Harley that caught his eye. "How about this one?"

A predatory grin split Benson's face. "She's a honey, isn't she? The sticker says nine hundred ninety. Do you want to take her for a ride? I assume you have a motorcycle license."

Rand showed it to him.

Benson slapped a temporary tag on the back fender. "Go ahead and take her for a spin."

Rand circled the bike once, held onto the handle bars, swung his right leg over it and settled on the seat. He smiled to himself. *Not even a twinge in your leg, pal.* His adrenaline kicked into high gear as soon as he revved the engine. He drove off the lot and rode up and down several side streets in the area before he drove into an empty parking lot.

He got off and checked the bike over thoroughly back to front and then remounted and spun it around the large lot just to get an idea how it handled on tight turns and quick stops. He also forced the front wheel off the ground to test the balance. *This is it!* He smiled to himself as he returned to the dealer's lot.

Benson stood with his hands on his hips. "Well, what do you think?"

Rand surveyed the other bikes as he gave the key back to Benson. "It's okay."

Benson grinned. "I can let you have it for nine hundred fifty including tax and title."

Rand's shoulders slumped. "Thanks anyway." He swung around and started to leave.

"Hey, wait a minute. I think we can make a deal we both can live with. How much are you willing to pay for it? She's a real honey, you'll have to admit."

Rand glanced at the bike and then at Benson. "Seven hundred."

"Aw, man, that ain't even reasonable. I can let you have it for eight hundred ninety-nine."

Rand lowered his gaze and studied the bike carefully for a few seconds. "It needs new tires, seven hundred fifty."

"Seven hundred fifty, you've got to be kidding, man. It's got low mileage, no major damage, and the tires are still good."

Rand bobbed his head. "Thanks for your time, Benson." Again, he started moving away from the lot.

"Hey! Make that seven hundred seventy-five plus tax and title and she's yours."

Rand crossed his arms and considered the guy's offer. *That's close.* "Throw in the tax and title."

"Aw, man."

Rand frowned.

"Okay, okay." Benson raised his hands, palms out. "Seven hundred seventy-five including tax and title. Do we have a deal?"

Rand's face lit up. "Deal."

"You drive a hard bargain, man. Come on in and we'll fill out the paperwork."

An hour later, Benson helped Rand load the Harley onto his pickup and he drove back to Candlewood. *Could've got it for seven-fifty if you'd pushed harder, pal.*

After a quick bite for lunch, he headed out of the village. He spent the remainder of the day enjoying his new bike, but even the renewed freedom left him somewhat despondent. He enjoyed the time with Brooke, but he wasn't interested in pursuing a relationship with her even though she did share his faith.

He concentrated on the ocean breeze as it teased his nose with its briny scent. A gentle wind pulled invisible fingers through his hair and danced over the skin on his face and hands as he rode, but his heart still yearned for something he believed he would never have. He practiced jumps with the bike over hills and rocks and across a small stream. The increase in speed on the road over the older bike excited him, but the easy maneuverability over rough mountainous terrain exceeded his expectations.

Jess's admonition to keep his skills honed encouraged him as he rode for the sheer enjoyment of challenging himself. He wanted to win the upcoming race and give the trophy to Jess to show his appreciation for all his years of support.

Back in Fire River, he rode through the alley where Netty usually parked her car, but it wasn't there. *Maybe you should just give up on women completely, pal.* It was nearly dark when he parked his new bike beside his truck. Even though he enjoyed the freedom of riding again, he grew increasingly anxious as the sun began to set and darkness fell. He dismounted as a van pulled in beside him.

Cab parked and climbed out as he eyed Rand's bike. "Nice ride. I was starting to get a little concerned. I saw your truck and stopped several times to look for you inside."

Rand snatched a glimpse at Cab. "Bought it earlier today and needed to test drive it."

"She's a beauty, man."

Rand smiled. "Thanks."

Cab crossed his arms. "Is Brooke coming back with Karl?"

He raised his head and gazed at the sky. "You hungry?"

Cab started walking toward the steps. "I already ate."

Rand followed him into the kitchen and grabbed a pizza box from the fridge, took a piece and set the box on the counter. "There's enough for you too." He mumbled as he chewed.

"No thanks, man. I stopped to tell you Katie and I are going to a New Year's Eve party. She has a friend who wants to come, but doesn't have a date. Would you like to join us? Rosey just moved to the area last week and doesn't know anyone yet."

Rand cocked an eyebrow as he opened the box and reached for another piece. "For what?"

"A New Year's party." Cab pulled out a chair and sat across from where Rand leaned against the sink. "What's wrong, man?"

One side of his mouth lifted slightly as he studied Cab's face. "Nothing."

Cab's brow scrunched. "You sure?"

Rand gazed through the glass in the door for several moments. "First time I've rode since—It was—" He searched for a word to describe the feeling, "strange."

Cab raised his eyebrows. "Strange, how?"

He took another bite of pizza lost in concern over his anxiety as the sun began to set.

Cab stared at him. "Was it a good ride or not?"

Rand finished the pizza and dropped the box in a trash can. He shrugged.

Cab waited several minutes and when Rand made no further attempt to engage in conversation, he stood. "Call me if you decide to go with us."

"Thanks, I'll think about it." He tossed over his shoulder as he washed his hands at the sink. Rand hesitated a second too long and Cab left without another word. *Should you accept the invitation, pal?* Netty's voice yelling, get out, Rand, still ricocheted in his mind. Not that he ever considered her as more than a friend, but still he enjoyed her company until the bike incident. He once believed she really liked him and missed the comradery they used to share. He shook his head. *Nah, you're through with women, pal.*

Brooke briefly stirred something within him, but she couldn't see past his appearance or his lack of a professional occupation. He expelled a breath in a whoosh, edged away from the sink, headed for the outside and wished for Angel's company. *At least she likes you, pal.*

Rod parked his car, got out and gave Rand's bike a brief inspection before he ambled toward the gate. As he approached the fountain, he spied Rand leaning forward with his elbows on his knees and hands clasped in front of him. Rod brought Angel and she bounded toward Rand and nearly knocked him off the wall backwards into the pond when she tried to jump onto his lap.

He laughed as she licked his face and danced around him on her back legs. "You missed me, huh girl." He chuckled as he ruffled the fur around her neck.

Rod sat beside him.

Rand straightened and stared at him as a slight grin pulled one corner of his mouth upward. "Cab send you to check on me?"

Rod shook his head. "How did it go up north? You didn't say much about your trip yesterday at the house."

"I would have stayed longer, but between Alfred and Cedric, I didn't feel dad needed me there too."

Rod studied his brother. "Have you talked to Brooke since you came home?"

Rand blinked. "Yeah."

Rod's brow wrinkled. "Do you think she'll stay there?"

Rand kicked the ground with his heel. "She likes her life there just fine."

Rod sighed and wondered if Rand's comment revealed more than he intended. "Hermann stopped by my office Tuesday and I gave him a tour of the mansion. He was quite impressed with your craftsmanship and the restoration you did."

Rand crossed his arms. "Did you ask him here to show him Candlewood or my handy work?"

Rod tried unsuccessfully to stifle a grin. "A little of both. He and his wife have a New Year's party for all of his employees and their families every year in January. This coming year it will be Saturday the seventeenth. Would you like to go with Saun, Tommy and I?"

Rand frowned. "Nah, sounds like a family thing."

Rod smiled. "You would certainly be welcome. Hermann and Isabella would be glad to have you."

Rand shrugged. "I appreciate the thought, but I'll pass."

"I checked out your new bike. How do you like it?"

"It's faster than," Rand stared into the distance, "the one Jess gave me, road-worthy too."

Rod gently clapped Rand's shoulder before getting to his feet. "I'm glad you bought another one. Angel came back here twice looking for you so I thought I'd drop her off on my way back to the office."

Rand peered up at him. "I would have brought her home last night, but mother—why are you going back to your office this late?"

"I had a new client drop by last Monday and I forgot some paperwork I wanted to study during the holidays."

Rand raised an eyebrow. "You spend your evenings working at home?"

Rod chuckled. "Not usually." He stood momentarily staring at Rand's sober face. "What's on your mind?"

Rand shoved his hands in the pockets of his Levi's. "You're a lucky man. Don't ever take Saun for granted."

"Never." Rod smiled and gave Angel's head a quick pat. "Take good care of him, girl." He shot Rand a quizzical grin. "See you at church if not before." He called as he headed for the path.

Rand watched him go until Angel pressed her nose against his leg. "Don't you start, dog. You don't get another chance to knock me in the pond. Come on, let's go for a run."

Thirty-Five

Monza swung his black Honda 750 onto the road leading into Cove Creek cemetery. He drove along the paved road, which wound in between graves and past carved headstones, some old and some newer. He passed the well-manicured plots and on toward the more neglected ones. It was New Year's Eve and after midnight. The temperature was below freezing and he was glad for his leather jacket, but he needed to get some warmer clothes soon. He climbed off his bike and grabbed his rolled sleeping bag as the scent of earth and rock wafted around him in the frigid wind.

With his gear slung over his shoulder, he glanced to the right and left, but there wasn't another soul present and the darkness closed in on him, making his spine tingle with apprehension. Did ghosts really exist or did the spirits of the dead haunt such places? He trudged around dead trees, bushes and crumbling, discolored headstones.

He stopped at the base of the one marking the place where his brother's remains were decaying beneath the dry earth. His dad's stone lay on the ground next to the larger one. He dropped his gear between the two graves as tears began to roll from his eyes, down the sides of his face to drip off his chin. "I miss you, little brother." He ran his fingers over the letters and dates. His brother was born January 1, 1945, died March 17, 1961. "You would've been thirty one on your birthday this year. You were too young to die, little brother. It was supposed to be him not you." He wailed.

He stared at the flat stone on the other side of him. His father was born July 6, 1901, died March 18 1963, His's lips trembled. "Old man, why did you have to leave me too?" He fell on his face between the graves and sobbed. "I got rid of him like I promised and now I don't know what else to do."

The next day, he swaggered into the Cove Creek, Arizona post office, up to the counter and rang the bell.

A young woman with green and brown streaked hair gave him a toothless grin. "I heard you was in town, Virg, been saving this here letter for you." She held it toward him with outstretched arm, keeping as much distance between them as possible.

He glanced at it, frowned and then scrutinized the postmark and the return address. "This is postmarked November third!"

She started to smile, changed her mind and crossed her arms protectively as she backed away from the counter. "You said you wanted to know about any mail going to or coming from him." She hesitated. "So, I kept it for you."

He gave the woman a snide grin as he folded the unopened letter and put it in his shirt pocket. "Ya did good, scarecrow." He frowned with renewed purpose, knowing he needed to make sure he finished what he'd started.

Thirty-Six

Saturday morning, Rand strode into his workshop and stood with arms crossed staring at the display shelf he made for Netty. His throat tightened at the remembrance of their most recent encounter. *She acts like you committed a crime, pal.* He shook his head and picked up his mother's curio shelf, which he finished last night. At the front doors he came to an abrupt halt when he spied Netty, leaving the post office. Once she disappeared inside her shop, he carried his mother's gift down the steps to his truck.

After securing it on the seat, he strolled across the street, entered the post office, and checked his personal box. He snatched the single envelope from inside, shoved it in a back pocket of his Levi's and closed the box quickly.

Willis shuffled up to the counter. "I just talked to Ne—"

"Gotta run, Willis, mother's waiting." He pivoted on one heel and marched out the door, hoping his hasty reference to his mother would soften any hurt feelings Willis might have. He received ridicule from locals, but Rand treated him with respect, even though he did enjoy ribbing the young man on occasion.

As Rand opened his truck door, Willis called to him from the doorway of the post office. "It's okay, Rand!"

He tipped his hat, got in his truck and drove away. A few minutes later, he parked behind Sea Breeze Inn, took the shelf off the seat and carried it inside. He traipsed through the lobby and the inn's office.

Lucinda opened the door as he raised his hand to knock and her hand flew to her chest. "Good gracious, Randall! You startled me."

He tried to stifle a smirk. "Sorry, Mother. I wanted to give this to you before Christmas, but I didn't get it finished in time. I left for a few days before the holidays."

She crossed her arms, as her brow knitted. "I expected you to spend some time with your father in San Francisco."

"Didn't go there to visit, Mother, I—"

"I heard you broke up with that, that red-haired barber. I could have told you she was trouble."

His focus dropped to the floor. The last thing he needed was a discussion about Netty with his mother. "We were only friends." He mumbled.

Lucinda took his chin between her thumb and forefinger, raised his head and appraised his face. "She hurt you, didn't she?"

He backed up with a shrug. "Brooke's uncle and dad's best friend died so—"

"Merciful heavens!" Her hand flew to her lips. "Two men died?"

"No, Mother, Arlo was dad's friend. He asked me to go there for the funeral."

"Who is Brooke?"

"She was my therapist." He stood with feet spread, holding the shelf between them.

"Are you in love with her?" Her eyebrows rose with a hopeful expression.

He frowned. "I went to help dad."

"Does she come from a good family? She won't be after your money like that redhead, will she?"

He heaved a sigh. "Where do you want me to hang your shelf?"

Lucinda gently pulled him out of the doorway so she could inspect the shelf he'd made. "Set it over there. "Once it was on her desk, she ran her hands over the smooth surface and studied the intricate carvings on each side and along the top while she traced the designs with her fingertips.

After several minutes of scrutinizing every line and detail, she gaped at him with misty eyes. "It's the most beautiful piece of craftsmanship I have ever seen, Randall. It's obvious you spent a lot of time on this. Every little detail is meticulously carved. This will be an heirloom for your grandchildren's children. I've never seen anything finer anywhere." She rotated toward him and hugged him tightly, kissing first one cheek and then the other. "I will cherish it always and even overlook you not spending more time with me over the holidays."

He chuckled. "I'm glad you like it, Mother."

She hooked her arm in his. "Come, I'll show you the exact spot where I want it hung."

"You really need some work done around here. Since I'm no longer working on the docks, I could do some of it."

"What all do you think needs done?"

His brow knitted. "The lobby needs painted and also your suite for starters. I'll inspect the guest rooms upstairs and let you know if I find anything that needs attention."

She put her hands on her hips as she watched him secure her shelf on her living room wall. "Make a list and I'll decide how much I can afford and we'll proceed from there."

He finished hanging the shelf. "I'll give the upstairs a quick inspection before I go."

After leaving his mother, he drove back to Candlewood, entered the mansion, strode straight to his room, snatched a small rubber ball from his desk, and stepped out on the veranda. Angel needed a break from the garden and he needed something to distract his thoughts, which still lingered on Netty, Karl, and by extension Brooke.

"Come on, girl." He whistled for Angel as he started down the path. There were so many shrubs and flowers in the garden that the park would be a better place for playing catch with her. As he began throwing her the ball, he noticed a boy, shooting a basketball on the court.

A short time later, the teen called. "Hey mister," as he ran up to him. "You dropped this back there by the swings." He gave Rand an envelope.

He took it from the boy's outstretched hand. "Thanks."

"What's your dog's name?" The boy's face shone with pleasure as he gaped fondly at her.

Rand smiled. "Angel."

"Are you Tommy's uncle?"

His head bobbed. "And you're, Cory Yarrow?"

"Yeah. You brought dad home once." He dropped to his knees to pet Angel.

At that moment, Rand eyed the envelope and his hand trembled at the sight of unfamiliar writing. He had difficulty swallowing and cold fingers wrapped around his heart. His dismal thoughts were invaded by Cory's voice.

"You don't look so good, Mr. Rand."

Wings of Steel

His brow wrinkled as he gawked at the envelope. The return address held Jess's wife's name. Imagining the worse-case scenario, he wished he could turn back time and talk to Jess. He swayed on his feet.

Cory grasped his arm. "There's a bench over here, maybe you better sit down."

Wrestling with news the letter would reveal, he forked his fingers through his hair. His mind raced with possibilities of the letter's content while he followed Cory to the bench. Vaguely aware of the boy's presence, he tore open the envelope.

The teen dropped to the grass nearby.

With trembling fingers, Rand pulled out a sheet of notepaper and began reading.

Dear Rand, Jess told me he sent you a letter telling you of the latest report from his doctor. He died in his sleep on December eighth. During his illness, he asked me not to tell you he was gone until after the funeral on December eleventh. He knew you'd want to come and it would only cause more trouble for you and he didn't want that. If you'd like to contact me, I've moved in with my sister in Phoenix. Her phone number is below my signature. Jess's last words for you were he loved you like you were his own son. I'm so sorry to have to tell you this way, but I couldn't find your phone number. Love Alice

Moisture filled Rand's eyes and he crumpled the note in his hand. *Never got that letter.* His shoulders slumped as he leaned forward with the wadded note clutched in his fist. He rested his arms on his knees and stared at his empty hands as the paper drifted to the ground. He flinched when the boy touched his arm.

"You dropped this." Cory placed the wadded note in Rand's hand. "Are you okay?" Cory whispered.

A tight smile briefly pulled at Rand's lips and his Adam's apple bobbed. Unable to answer, he nodded. He took a measure of comfort from the boy's quiet presence, while he continued to pet Angel without moving from his position near the bench. After a few moments Rand stood slowly and began to walk with heavy steps toward the garden gate.

Cory stayed beside him with Angel close by his other side. "Will you be alright?"

"Yeah." He opened the gate and followed Angel inside, glancing briefly at the teen as he closed the gate. "Thanks." He trudged down the path and entered the side door into library. Once inside he sank into an armchair.

Sometime later, he went through the motions of feeding her and refilling her water dish on the veranda before grabbing his leather jacket from the chair in his bedroom.

He left the mansion, mounted his bike, and set off to ride for the rest of the day. Not wanting to talk to anyone, he stopped at a gas station outside Fire River. He sped along rough roads and dirt trails deep into the woods, jumping streams and every hurdle he found. He misjudged once and landed in a heap in some weeds, but afterward headed up into the mountains to practice riding on the narrow rocky trails. Energized by the adrenaline rush he always got from riding, he planned to be prepared for the upcoming trail bike race in May. He worked on improving his riding skills to help diminish his grief over losing Jess.

Later that evening Rod parked his car in front of Candlewood and entered the mansion. He stepped into the library to find Rand, slumped in an armchair with his head laid back, eyes closed and not a single light on in the entire mansion. As he approached his brother, the heaviness of Rand's mood permeated the room. Angel even raised her head to give him a soulful look with a quiet whimper.

Rand's gaze fastened on Rod without speaking as he stopped in front of him.

Rod picked up the wadded piece of paper from the floor flattened it out and scanned it before laying it on the table next to Rand's chair and turning on a lamp. "When did this come?"

He stared at the cold hearth. "Today." He responded in a flat monotone.

"Is that why you weren't here earlier?" Rod studied him, paying close attention to his posture and the tone of his voice.

He swallowed a couple of times, "I thought about visiting him before—" his voice broke, "my injury." He finished quietly.

Rod pulled over a chair and sat, facing him. "Did you know he was ill?"

Rand drew a deep breath, slowly shook his head and exhaled.

Rod considered his response. "Is he the one in the picture on your dresser?"

Rand shook his head. "The couple I lived with."

"How long did you know Jess?"

Rand met his scrutiny without wavering. "Not long enough. We were almost inseparable before I started traveling."

Rod regarded him, silently.

Rand grimaced and riveted his attention on the floor. "Mother has some things that need attention." He forced the words through tight lips. "Seabreeze isn't in real bad shape, but there's a lot of little things that need repaired."

Rod nodded, realizing his brother no longer wanted to talk about his friend. "I can put you in touch with some of the crew who worked on the renovation here if you need help."

Rand flashed him a wry grin. "Thanks, I only knew them by their first names."

"I can either call you when I get home or give you the list tomorrow at church."

Rand sighed. "Whichever is better for you, mother doesn't seem in a hurry to get anything done. How'd you know I was here? I didn't bother with the lights."

Rod's brow wrinkled. Rand's truck and bike are in their usual spot. Why wouldn't he know Rand was here? He was obviously more upset about his friend than he was willing to admit. "Let me know if you want to talk."

Rand shrugged and peered at the now flattened note on the table. "How are you guys doing?"

Rod crossed his arms. "We're fine. Did you have a good time New Year's Eve with Cab and Katie and her friend?"

Rand raised his head to meet his brother's steady appraisal. "Didn't go."

Rod scrutinized him with a quirked brow, but let the unenthusiastic comment go by. "You should have called. Saun and I were home all evening."

Rand shrugged.

"I stopped to ask if you want to have lunch with us after church tomorrow."

Rand tilted his head. "What're you having?"

Rod smiled for the first time since he walked in the room. "Your favorite." He started out the door.

"Hey!" He rose from his chair.

Rod stopped in his tracks and slowly pivoted to face him with one eyebrow quirked.

Rand stood with hands on his hips. "Which one?"

Rod stifled a grin. "Come and find out." He continued out the door, and congratulated himself that he managed to redirect Rand's thoughts, at least for a few moments.

Thirty-Seven

A week later, Lucinda entered the front door of her inn and caught a glimpse of Rand as he rounded the corner to her office with a hammer in his hand. She left her coat in her office and hurried to see what he was up to.

He shot a glance in her direction as she entered the kitchen. "Good afternoon, Mother. I stopped by this morning, but you weren't here. Rod gave me the names of some men who can help with repairs."

Lucinda crossed the room and stopped next to him. "I trust your judgement, Randall. I know you supervised a lot of the work on that old mansion. If you need some of those men to help, we can make plans toward that end, but just keep in mind that I don't have a lot of ready funds available. Have you eaten?"

"I'm trying to figure out the materials I need before making a trip to Montecito."

"Sit down, and I'll fix you a nice lunch. You need to keep up your strength."

He did as she asked while he watched her cut up some potatoes and slice some ham. "Will you join me? I hate eating alone."

She didn't miss his imploring gaze. It made her long to know what was going on in his mind. "Of course, I'll join you." She fried the meat and vegetables and then set them on the table along with a cup of coffee for him. When she finished, she sat across from him and prayed over their meal.

He focused on his plate while he ate.

She studied his furrowed brow over the rim of her cup. Was he worried about something? She discovered either eating or drinking coffee seemed to be when he talked most freely about his concerns. Therefore, she made a habit of drinking coffee with him instead of having her usual cup of tea, unless like now, they were eating. She waited.

He finished the last bite from his plate and then drank the rest of his coffee. "I want to ask you something, but don't want to offend you." He got up, refilled his cup, and offered her more.

She declined while, pondering his earnest face. She became so attached to him after his accident that she'd do her best to give him whatever he wanted. "What is it, dear?"

He sat and focused on the table, twisting the salt and pepper shakers, and exchanging their positions. His eyes pleaded with her. "Would you tell me why you left me with the Roes?"

She dabbed at her mouth with her napkin. Curious as to whether he wanted to understand or condemn her actions. She grasped her cup with both hands. "When I told Vera my father kicked me out because I was pregnant, she offered to let me move in with them. It didn't take long to discover they weren't doing well financially. I felt guilty for accepting the meager provisions they were able to share with me so, I wrote to my father's sister and she offered to take me in and put me through college. I didn't tell her I kept my baby. What I did was selfish even though I intended to send for you when I could support us."

She paused and adjusted her glasses, which gave her time to gather courage to continue. She grasped Rand's wrist to stop his dance with the shakers. "By the time I reached that goal, Vera stopped answering my letters."

Rand patted her hand before shifting his position to rest his elbows on the table. "I don't blame you. Cove Creek is no place for an intelligent woman like you, Mother. Thanks for telling me."

She wiped tears from her cheeks with a handkerchief she kept in her apron pocket. "Can you ever forgive me?"

One corner of his mouth hitched in that charming way she'd grown so fond of. "I already did, Mother, and haven't changed my mind. I love you and always will."

She got up and went around the table to stand behind him and put her arms around his broad shoulders. "I love you too, Randall."

He tilted his head back to look at her. "And now I have you and, and a brother." Unsure about his position with Karl, he neglected to mention him, in part out of respect for his mother's feelings.

She shook her head. "I'm sorry I judged both of you boys so harshly. You've proven to be good and honest men."

He kissed her hands where they rested against his chest. "Thank you, Mother, your approval means a lot."

Later that afternoon, Rand returned from Montecito with some materials for his mother's inn, parked his truck in front of Candlewood, checked on Angel and then called two of the men from the list Rod gave him. The electrician agreed to meet with him the following week at Seabreeze so they could assess the work needed.

Afterward he left the mansion and parked behind Seabreeze. Finding the rear entrance locked, he strolled around the side of the building to the front.

He spotted a little dark-haired girl riding a tricycle on the sidewalk and pedaling fast toward the corner beyond the inn. Rand scowled as he scanned the immediate area. Why was she out here alone?

Suddenly one of the rear wheels wobbled, toppled the tricycle over, and threw the girl into the street.

Rand raced toward her and grabbed her into his arms out of the path of an oncoming car. His heart pounded in his chest as the car skidded to a stop.

A teenage boy leaped out and ran to where Rand held the hysterically sobbing girl.

"Is she hurt? Did I hit her?" The teen's eyes were full of fear and he was breathing hard.

"A wheel came loose and threw her. She's a little scrapped up, but more scared than anything." He recognized Cory as the teen he recently encountered for the second time.

"I'm sorry I scared you." He told her as he patted her back and then gazed at Rand. "I hope your little girl's okay. I'm sorry I scared you both." He studied Rand for a few more seconds before he climbed in his car and drove away.

"Remember me? I saw you and your mom at the airport. Where do you hurt, princess?" Rand spoke softly, trying to calm them both.

She guided his hand to her ribcage.

He winced at the scrapes on her little hands and knees. Carefully, he carried her inside to enlist his mother's help. He grumbled to himself when the frightened child clung to his shirt and sobbed on his chest.

He opened the door and strode inside the inn. "Mother, where are you?"

Lucinda rounded the corner from her office. "What in heaven's name?"

"A wheel came loose on her trike and threw her. She says her ribs hurt." He spoke softly over the little girl's sobs.

"Bring her into the kitchen."

"Where's her mother?" He spat out the words.

Lucinda put hands on her hips. "Shirley asked me to watch her today and she was told to stay in the lobby until the cookies were done. Put her on the table so I can reach her better."

He tried to sit the little girl on the table as instructed, but she refused to let go of him.

"I want you hold me." She whimpered.

He fastened a pleading look on his mother.

Lucinda took the little face in her hands and spoke with quiet authority. "Mandy, I'm going to wash off the dirt and put medicine on it and then you can have some cookies and milk."

"Don't want cookies and milk, want him hold me." She pouted

Rand sat on a chair and put her on his lap. "I don't mind holding her. Maybe you'll want cookies and milk when you feel better, princess." He winked at Lucinda over Mandy's head

She proceeded to wash Mandy's scrapes. When she reached for her hands, which suffered the worst of her fall, she buried her head against Rand's chest, and screamed. "It hurts!"

"I'm sorry, dear, but I have to clean the dirt out or it won't stop hurting." When Lucinda applied antiseptic on her scraped skin, Mandy screamed so loud that even Lucinda's eyes were moist.

Rand held her a little tighter wanting to comfort the child. Rocking her gently in a straight back chair, he began to sing. "Hush little princess, don't you cry, gramma's gonna bake you an apple pie."

Mandy stopped crying, sat up straight, and placed her fingers on his chin. "How'd you know I like apple pie?"

Rand eyed his mother and winked. "It's written right here." He drew an index finger across her forehead. "It says, I like apple pie."

Lucinda shook her head. "My son, the charmer."

"Can you fix my bike?"

"I sure can, princess."

She giggled and hugged his neck. "I not a princess."

"Could have fooled me." He set her on her feet. "I'm going to go now and fix that wheel. You stay here and enjoy your cookies and milk, okay."

"Kay." She climbed up on a chair. "I ready for cookies and milk now, Gam-maw."

Rand exchanged a glance with his mother and gave Mandy a gentle pat on her head before turning to leave the kitchen. "Don't forget to check her ribs."

Outside, Rand found Cory, working on the tricycle wheel. "You don't need to do that, pal, I can fix it."

"I'm sorry I scared your little girl. The wheel's bent pretty bad. Whoever put it on didn't do it right. Guess you'll have to buy a new one."

Rand knelt beside him and noted Cory's clothes appeared faded and overly worn. "Are you old enough to be driving?"

"Not exactly, it's my dad's car."

"If the sheriff catches you, you'll be in trouble."

"You won't tell him, will you?"

"Depends, where's the car now?"

"In our garage where dad left it. I rode my bike back here."

"Were you trying to fix the wheel to keep me from telling the sheriff?"

"No, I just wanted to help. Figured you'd be busy taking care of your little girl. I won't drive it again, I promise."

Rand stared at him and recalled that night, weeks ago when he met Cory's dad and took him home. "Can I trust you to keep your word?"

"Yes sir, I'll even give you the keys."

Rand shook his head. "Give them back to your dad when he gets home."

"Can't, he ain't coming back. You live in that big old place on Chino, don't you?"

He bobbed his head. "Where's your mother, Cory?"

"Home, drunk. I wanted to stop her from going to another bar."

Rand frowned as he considered Cory's situation. "How do you know he's not coming back?"

"Got tired of her drinking so he left."

Rand expelled a long breath. "When did that happen?" He eyed Cory closely. The teen was too thin.

Cory ducked his head. "Couple days after you brought him home that night."

Rand finished taking the wheel off the trike. How long since Cory ate a decent meal or got new school clothes? His shirt sleeves and pant-legs were too short. "I have a friend who can help you. Come on, he's just across the street."

"Not that preacher, dad hated him!"

"Not the preacher. Cab works with teens and he'll understand your situation. His mother was an alcoholic too, besides he's a good friend of mine."

"For real?"

Rand chuckled. "You bet. Let Cab know what you need and if he can't help you I will. Do you still have my number?"

"Yup."

"Good. Anytime you need something, whatever it is, call me."

When Rand stepped into Rod's house that evening, he drew in a deep appreciative breath of fresh baked bread and something barbequed.

Once they finished eating, he and Rod sat in the family room while Tommy helped Saun clean up the kitchen. "Have you talked to Cab recently?" Rand asked his brother.

"Not since Thursday. Why?"

Rand focused on the electric fireplace while he gathered his thoughts. "I've run into a boy, who might go to school with Tommy, a couple of times recently. I wanted to introduce him to Cab today but he wasn't available."

"What's his name?" Rod asked, leaning forward in his chair.

"Cory Yarrow. He said his dad left around a couple months ago and his mom may be an alcoholic. He appeared to have outgrown his clothes and he's too skinny for his age."

Rod crossed his arms. "Tommy, would you come in here a minute?"

Tommy entered with a dish towel in his hands. "Can I finish helping mom first?"

Rod smiled and nodded.

Tommy started to leave the room, but Saun entered and took the dish towel from him. "I'll finish, Tommy. Stay here and see what your dad wants."

"Thanks, Mom."

"Do you know Cory Yarrow?" Rand asked.

Tommy kicked at the carpet. "What's he supposed to have done this time?"

Rod frowned. "Are you being disrespectful?"

"No sir. It's just that every time something bad happens at school, he gets the blame for it."

Rand bit his lip. "Why's that?"

"Some of the older kids pick on him."

"Why?" Rod and Rand asked at once.

"Because he doesn't have a dad and his mom's a, a—"

"An alcoholic?" Rand interrupted.

Tommy's lips twisted. "Or worse."

Rod studied his son. "How long have you known him?"

"Only since September. They moved here last summer."

Rand sighed. "Have you seen him do anything wrong?"

"No." Tommy shook his head. "Some older guys are always doing things and making it look like Cory did it."

"What kind of things?" Rand rose to his feet.

"They broke a window in the lunchroom last week. Threw a rock through it when no one was in there. Cory was sent home for throwing a spitball at the art teacher and hitting him in the head, which he didn't do."

"Do you know who threw it?" Rod wanted to know.

"Ted. I saw him and told the teacher. Mr. Wilks didn't believe me because Cory's my friend. Cory told me, when he left to go home, he saw Butch throw a rock at the window and since he was supposed to be in class, Cory got the blame again."

Rod frowned. "I'm going to school and put a stop to this."

Rand's ears began to turn red.

Tommy's face paled. "Don't do that. Those guys will pick on him even worse. I know because I—" He lowered his head. "I just know."

Saun stepped into the room then and gave Tommy a disapproving look. "I've been listening to this conversation from the kitchen. Didn't you tell me last week that you ripped your shirt when it got caught on a locker door in the hall?"

Tommy's head drooped. "Yes, ma'am."

Rand grabbed Tommy's shoulders. "What really happened?"

Rod got out of his chair and walked across the room and placed a hand on Rand's shoulder. "Easy, Rand, sit down and let him finish telling us what's been going on and then we can figure out how to deal with it."

Rand's lips stretched into a thin line as he resumed his seat.

"Continue, Son." Rod instructed as he took his seat also.

Tommy's lower lip trembled, but he sucked it in between his teeth for a moment. "They've been making fun of him since the first day of school this year, but it got worse right before Christmas. That's when they—"

"Wait a minute." Rand interrupted. "Who's they?"

Tommy swallowed hard. "Butch, Ted and a couple of their friends whose names I don't know."

Rod nodded. "Alright, go on."

"They started doing things like throwing spitballs, writing dirty notes to girls using Cory's name, putting toads in teacher's desk drawers and then Butch broke the lunchroom window. Before they started doing stuff to get him in trouble, they were always picking on him and making fun of him. They call him names because of his clothes and stuff. They know his dad left and I heard them say some of their parents have seen his mother in bars and stuff. When they do stuff to get him in trouble, they always get some girl to say she saw Cory do it. Most of the kids are afraid of them and will do whatever they say."

Rod crossed his arms. "Did your shirt get torn defending Cory?"

Tommy nodded and looked at the floor. "I'm sorry I lied to Saun."

"I hope you let the other guy have it." Rand snorted.

Tommy tried to hide a smile. "I gave him a bloody nose."

Rod glared at Rand. "Violence doesn't solve problems, Tommy."

"I was defending myself, Dad. I told Butch to leave Cory alone and he knocked me into the lockers so I hit him back."

"Did you get in trouble?"

"No, my teacher, Miss Lambert, saw the whole thing and he got in trouble for once."

Rod brushed his upper lip with his index finger. "I don't expect you to stand there and let someone push you around, but we need to find a better solution than violence."

Rand scowled at Rod. "Only one way to deal with a bully. Don't back down."

Rod studied him with elbows resting on his knees and fingers steepled. "I agree, but it doesn't have to involve fists."

Rand doubled his fists as he jumped up from the chair. "It doesn't make sense to give him permission to defend himself unless he knows how. But this is your problem so do what you want." He strode down the hall, through the laundry room, into the garage, and out the side door. Once outside, he climbed into his truck and drove off in a spray of gravel.

Wings of Steel

When Rand started up the steps to the mansion that evening, he eyed Cab who was waiting on the top step. Rand drew in a deep breath. "What do you want?" He sounded more growly than he intended. "Did Rod send you?"

Cab stood with hands up in a position of surrender. "No, man. I need a favor."

Rand opened the door. "Why didn't you wait inside? Lose your key?"

Cab followed him into the hall. "No, but I'll leave if you want after you answer my question."

"What?" Rand pivoted sharply.

Cab backed up three steps and studied him. "What's up with you, man?"

Rand growled. "Nothing." He crossed his arms. "What do you need?"

Cab stared at him. "They're renovating the church annex and making it into a space for the youth to meet so I need a place to stay."

"You're welcome to the whole second floor. Apparently, dad isn't coming back anytime soon." He snarled.

"I'd like to move in today if it's okay with you."

"Suit yourself." He turned and started walking down the hall.

"Whoa, wait a minute." Cab hurried to rest a hand on his shoulder. "Something's wrong. What is it, buddy?"

Rand studied him while he struggled to reign in his anger. "Go get your stuff. We'll talk when you get back."

Cab met Rand's direct gaze and bobbed his head. "I won't be long."

When Cab left, Rand made his way to the kitchen, gathered Angel's food and water bowls, filled them and set them on the veranda. He petted her as she began to eat. "I'll let you back inside in a little while, girl." He strolled into the library and sank into a comfortable chair. *Jesus, You know Cory needs to know how to defend himself and so does Tommy. I can't wait for something to happen to either one or both of them. If Rod goes to the school, it will definitely make it worse for them.*

Less than half an hour later, Rand listened as Cab made two trips from his van to one of the rooms upstairs. Afterward, he joined Rand in the library. "Did you get everything?" Rand asked when Cab sat adjacent to him in another chair.

"All I have are my clothes, sax and a few books and stuff."

"There're linen closets in the hall. Help yourself to whatever you need. How long are you planning to stay?"

Cab grinned. "Until you get tired of me?"

Rand eyed him. "The opposite's more likely."

Cab chuckled. "Will you tell me what had you so bent out of shape earlier?"

Rand stared at him. "Rod."

Cab's eyebrows raised. "Uh oh! What happened?"

Rand gave him a detailed account of the entire issue. When he finished, he leaned his head against the back of his chair. "I had to get out of there before I did something stupid."

Cab sighed. "I'm glad you left. I agree with you the boys do need to know how to defend themselves. You and I both know that, but Rod isn't entirely wrong either. Let's start with the fact that we all want to prevent Cory and Tommy from getting hurt. You in?"

"Yeah." Rand snarled "If you can make Rod underst—"

"Let's stick to basics. Rod, you and me all want what's best for the boys. Right?"

Rand sighed. "I guess."

Cab smiled. "You and Rod don't know each other as well as you think."

"What's that supposed to mean?" Rand grumbled.

"He may have forgotten, but when he was younger, he stood between me and a guy, who was twice my size. When he threatened me, Rod told Eric he'd have to go through Rod to get to me. Eric was a druggie and a thug, but he backed off from Rod."

Rand scrunched his eyes. "No way!"

Cab nodded. "It's the truth, man." He stood. "I'll be back. I'm going to go talk to Rod."

Rand squinted up at him. "Lots of luck."

———※———

Cab drove to Rod's house and sighed with relief when he saw the light on in Rod's office. Slowly, he got out of his car, walked up to the door and knocked.

Saun opened the door. "Am I glad to see you. Rod is in his office and I have to say it's been a while since I've seen him this upset. He and Rand—"

Cab raised his hands. "I know. I just talked to him."

Saun smiled. "That was a quick answer to prayer." She stepped aside to allow Cab space to enter. "I'll make a fresh pot of coffee."

Cab grinned and gave Saun a one arm hug. "Thanks." When she headed for the kitchen, he turned toward Rod's office and knocked on the open door.

Rod raised his head from the blueprint he was staring at. "What brings you here at this hour?"

Cab sat in one of the chairs and focused on Rod's face. "Two things. First, I just moved in with Rand because the church is renovating the annex. Second, Rand told me what happened earlier."

Rod crossed his arms and sighed deeply. "Rand needs to calm—"

"Let me finish. I agree with you, fighting isn't the best way to deal with most situations, but sometimes there's no other way to begin with. Remember how you stood up to Eric that time he threatened me?"

Rod frowned. "Yes, but I didn't expect him to—"

"You have to admit, you didn't know in that instant how he would react. You're a planner, Rod, and there's nothing wrong with that. In fact, it's one of the things I admire most about you." Cab shook his head. "I don't think you know Rand as well as you think. He's spontaneous, thinks quickly on his feet, and in the moment. He had to learn that to stay alive. Remember the scars we saw on his shoulders while he was in the hospital. I saw marks like that before on some kid I went to school with and was told his dad beat him with a studded belt. Rand feels things deeply and sometimes, in unguarded moments, his face reveals the hurt he holds inside."

Rod crossed his arms. "I know he's had it rough, but—"

"Fist fighting doesn't usually solve anything, but when you're dealing with bullies, if you don't know how to defend yourself, they will take advantage of you. Rand doesn't want that for Tommy or Cory, neither do I, and I know you don't either."

Rod frowned and crossed his arms. "What's to stop them from fighting just to prove they can?"

Cab shook his head. "Have faith in me and your brother. Do you think either of us has that kind of mentality?"

Rod shook his head. "Rand has a temper and if I'd been on my feet when he left here—"

"And that, my friend, is exactly why he left. I don't believe he would ever hit anyone he cares about no matter how upset he gets."

Rod shook his head again. "He told me he almost hit Netty."

Cab met his direct gaze. "The key word there, buddy, is almost. Rod, you need to put away your preconceived ideas of who your brother is. He would never intentionally hurt anyone, especially someone he cares about."

Rod put his elbows on his knees, folded his hands, and leaned his chin against them. "I hope you're right."

Cab stood. "How about the three of us get together tomorrow after church to come up with a plan we can all agree on? What do you say?"

Rod crossed his arms. "What time?"

Cab's brow wrinkled for a moment. "How about three at the mansion?"

"I'll be there."

Cab stood. "Good. See you then."

Thirty-Eight

Sunday afternoon Rand made a pot of coffee and paced on the veranda as he waited for Cab. They planned to eat a quick lunch before Rod joined them. Cab insisted the three of them get together to make a plan for teaching Tommy and Cory the art of self-defense. Rand stopped pacing and sat on the step to pet Angel.

Soon he spied Cab strolling along the garden path toward him. "Give me a couple minutes to change and then we can go the café and grab some lunch."

Rand glanced up at him. "Thought we could grab a sandwich here. Coffee's ready."

Cab paused before stepping onto the veranda. "Rod will be okay with this. You'll see."

Rand shrugged.

"Just remember, he doesn't want those boys to get hurt any more than you do. How about that coffee?"

Rand gave Angel a final pat and stood. "Sounds good." Inside he grabbed two cups, filled them, put them on the table and grabbed a chair.

Cab pulled slices of roast beef and cheese from the refrigerator and a loaf of bread from a shelf. He placed them all on the table, sat across from Rand, and prayed for their simple meal. Afterward, he stacked beef and cheese on two slices of bread smeared with mustard and took a bite of his sandwich.

Rand twisted his cup in half circles on the table.

Cab's eyes opened wide. "You aren't going to eat?"

Rand took a drink of coffee. "Maybe later."

"You worried about Rod's reaction to teaching the boys to defend themselves?" Cab offered around a bite from his sandwich.

Rand shrugged. "I told him what happened to me when I was about their age."

Cab frowned. "Did you learn from the experience?"

Rand stared at the table. "The hard way." His voice was barely audible.

Cab's face softened. "Even more reason for him to agree."

Rod entered the kitchen as Cab finished. "Agree to what?" He poured himself a cup and offered to refill Rand's.

He shook his head, moved his cup aside and reached for the salt and pepper shakers.

Rod sat beside Cab and drank from his cup.

Cab got up and moved to the chair on the end of the table so he sat between the brothers.

Rod stifled a grin and Rand raised an eyebrow.

Cab gave each of them a direct look. "Rod, you never did tell me what happened the night Eric busted your lip. Did you hit him back?"

Rod crossed his arms. "I stopped his second attempt and then he passed out. What does that have to do with the current situation?"

Cab nodded. "Just wanted to clarify we've all dealt with bullies in our own way. How about you, Rand?"

He moved the salt shaker around the pepper.

Rod clasped his wrist. "You don't have to go there."

Rand eyed him for a second. "I think I do for Cab's benefit. I shoved a kid too hard away from a girl he was hitting. He lost his balance, hit his head on a rock and died the next day." His jaw clenched as he resumed the dance with the shakers on the table. "I was angry and I shoved him harder than I intended. I never want Tommy and Cory to experience what I felt that day. They need to learn to defend themselves, but also be prepared to defend others if needed. Reacting in anger is dangerous for everyone involved. It's very hard to control your reactions when angry. They're immediate and often without conscious thought." He avoided Rod's direct gaze.

Cab glanced at Rand and then Rod. "Tommy and Cory need some guidance and a little training. They're dealing with some bullies and they need to have a skill set to help them so they aren't taken advantage of. I know some defensive moves I can show them and Rand does too. Neither of us goes looking for a fight, but we know how to deal with one when brought to us. That's what we want for Tommy and Cory. Can we all agree?"

Rod nodded. "As long as you stress, fighting as a last resort."

Rand grimaced. "Sometimes it's the only choice you have."

Rod crossed his arms. "In that case I want them to know how to defend themselves when necessary."

Cab nodded emphatically. "Good. Rand has some weights. I have a punching bag and between us we can show them some simple defensive moves. Can we clear a space here maybe in the drawing room for some practical training. I'd also like to proceed and end each session with prayer and a time to discuss any questions they may have."

Rod nodded. "What sort of time frame are we talking about?"

Cab drew his lower lip between his teeth. "How about Saturday morning? We can see how it goes and decide as we go how long to continue."

Rod stood. "Let me know what time. I'll talk to Saun and make sure she agrees." He placed his hand on Rand's shoulder and gave it a firm squeeze. "See you Saturday if not before." He nodded at Cab and left.

Rand met with a plumber at his mother's inn at noon on Tuesday and then returned to the mansion and parked his pickup. Then he slipped into his leather jacket and gloves, fastened his helmet to the back of his seat and mounted his bike. He rode out of the village and headed for the mountains. The weather was mild and the breeze drew its breath like fingers through his hair as he rode.

An hour later he turned off the highway and stopped long enough to secure the helmet on his head before he entered the first of many trails. He spent the next few hours practicing in order to familiarize himself with each of them. He wanted to be as prepared for the upcoming race as possible. It would be a grueling one and he was only one of exceptionally skilled riders who would be competing. There were steep climbs, rocky areas, small stream beds and vast descents to navigate with a minimum of guided markers.

Today as he rode, he was totally on his own since most of the other riders practiced on weekends. Spotting a rattlesnake sunning itself on a rock, he swerved to avoid it and leaped his bike over an embankment and landed several feet below his previous trail. He jumped a fallen tree and crossed a dry and rocky stream bed. He spied a raccoon as it skittered across his path and caught a glimpse of a condor as it sailed high above in the distance.

He was relentless in his pursuit of his goal, nothing and no one was going to come between him and that trophy. It was the only way he could think of to appease his guilt for the years he'd wasted the things Jess taught him by drifting aimlessly from place to place. He planned to spend hours each day the rest of the week, riding and practicing every strategy Jess taught him and some he'd picked up on his own. *You have to win that trophy, for Jess, pal.*

The wind picked up as he slowed down to head for the open road below. He took some time to enjoy the scenery while carefully descending the narrow trail. There were juniper, oak, and maple trees. Pine, brittlebush, and manzanita shrub also filled the lower altitude. It was nearly dark when his wheels touched asphalt and he headed back to the village.

Suddenly a car appeared around a curve in front of him and veered across the middle line toward him. He swung his front wheel onto a dirt trail on the steep embankment and sped upward. As the car tires squealed, Rand drove onto a narrow bike trail and veered off into thick foliage.

His heart palpitated rapidly as images of his previous experience flashed through his mind. Under cover of the brush, he turned off his engine, dismounted and paused to listen for any sound to indicate he was being followed. He quietly navigated to a concealed place where he could view the road without being seen. He huffed while squinting into the distance. "Nothing in sight." He turned and hiked quickly to where he left his bike in the bushes, mounted it and rode back down to the road.

The sun had already set and he felt chilled to the bone. He kept a sharp eye on his rearview mirror as well as the distance ahead, straining to make out any moving object. He tried to focus on his immediate surroundings when darkness overtook him, hoping to have enough warning if another vehicle approached from either direction. By the time he reached the outskirts of the village, he was nearly drenched with sweat.

He parked his bike between his truck and Cab's car. After dismounting, he glanced in every direction while the skin on his neck prickled as if someone watched him. He crossed the terrace and carefully climbed the steps on shaky legs. Once inside, he pulled the helmet off and then his gloves. He cut through the library and strode quickly toward his room. As he passed through the kitchen, the veranda door swung open and Rand automatically assumed a position of defense.

"Whoa!" Cab yelled with his hands held up with palms outward. "It's just me, man. Why so edgy?"

Rand blew out a breath, pulled out a chair and nearly collapsed on it. "Someone tried to run me off the road about an hour ago."

Cab's forehead wrinkled. "Are you okay?"

"Yeah. I barely avoided the car and then waited until I was sure it was gone."

Cab shook his head. "Maybe you should call Gus."

Rand cracked his knuckles one at a time. "And tell him what? I didn't see who was driving, I'm not sure what kind of car it was and I didn't get a license number. So, what do I have to tell him?"

Cab stared at him before crossing the kitchen, opening the refrigerator and pulling out a dish. He dumped the contents into a pan and set it on the stove to heat. "I had dinner at Rod's house and Saun sent some leftover casserole for you."

Rand sat staring at the table while he waited for whatever Cab heated on the stove. "Don't say anything about that car."

Cab shook his head. "I'll keep it to myself, but only if you tell Gus."

He picked up the salt shaker and set it back down, hard. "Fine. I'll tell him tomorrow for all the good it'll do."

Cab dished out Rand's dinner and set it on the table in front of him. "I could use a cup of coffee. How about you?"

Rand nodded and ate in silence.

The next morning after Cab left, Rand lingered over his coffee while he mentally prepared for his visit with the sheriff. Once he felt ready to face the lawman, he hopped in his truck and drove around the square to the police department. "Hey, Manny." He called to one of the deputies as he stepped into the squad room. "Is Gus here?"

The jolly Mexican-born deputy nodded. "He's not in a good mood."

Rand tipped his hat. "Thanks for the warning." He strolled through the room to the back where Gus's office was located and rapped on the door with his knuckles before entering.

Gus raised his head with a frown, but it disappeared when his gaze landed on Rand. "You come to apply for the position on the board at the post office?"

Rand smirked as he took the chair in front of the desk, turned it around and sat with his arms resting on the back of it. "You wish."

Gus leaned back in his chair and crossed his arms. "It would be nice if you waltzed in here with some good new—"

"Thought you'd want to know, someone tried to run me off the road again last night."

Gus's upper lip curled. "Who? Where?"

Rand pushed his hat upward a notch. "Old Canyon Road, again. Before you ask. It was dark, I didn't get a look at the driver and all I can say about the car is it was a dark colored Ford, maybe a sedan. The guy headed across the middle line into my lane and I took off up a dirt trail to avoid a head on."

Gus snorted. "You have a knack for getting into trouble while riding your bike. Why don't you just give it up?"

Rand tugged the brim of his hat lower and stood. "Can't. Practicing for a race on May eighth that I intend to win. Just doing my duty as a responsible citizen and reporting the incident." He walked over to the coffee pot which was located on a small shelf in the corner, poured a cup, and set in in front of Gus. "Have some. Appears you need it." He tipped his hat, went out the door and closed it quietly behind him.

Manny raised his head from his paperwork. "Did he throw you out?"

Rand shook his head. "Didn't give him a chance."

Manny chuckled. "Smart man."

———⋘⋙———

After leaving the sheriff's office, Rand parked his truck in its usual place and set his hat low on his forehead before strolling across the street to the post office. He checked his personal box. It was empty again. Stepping up to the counter, he punched the bell several times.

Something fell along with grunts that came from the back room and shortly afterward Willis appeared from a corner of the doorway. He stopped and stared at Rand with hands on his hips. "Why does everybody think they have to hit that thing so many times? I ain't deaf!"

Rand chuckled. "Maybe you should have a mirror back there so you can see when someone comes in."

"Hey, that's a great idea!" Willis was so excited he was practically dancing.

Rand smirked, knowing he did it just for the fun of riling the little guy. "I want to close my box."

"Why?" He frowned. "Are you moving?"

"No, just tired of an empty box."

Wings of Steel

"People seem to think all I have to do is stand here and wait on them." Willis mumbled as he reached under the counter for a form. He slapped it on the counter. "Fill this out and sign it. You got your key?"

Rand raised an eyebrow as he slowly drew it out of his shirt pocket. Willis must be having a bad day. He was usually pretty cheerful. He filled out the form and signed it, taking note how serious Willis took his job. He was sorry he'd teased him by pounding on the bell. "What you need is a sign that says, 'ring bell for service', but don't put out the bell. I'll get a mirror and hang it on the back wall for you so you can see them come in."

Willis giggled. "Sorta like a pay back. That'd be great." His smooth brow wrinkled as he reached under the counter again. "This just came on the truck this morning. I didn't even have time to put it in your box. I don't understand. Look at the postmark!"

Rand picked up the letter as his mouth dropped open. *It's from Jess.*

"Is it bad news?" Willis leaned across the counter. "You don't look so good."

He tugged on his cowboy hat, pulling it down to shield his eyes. "I'm fine." He pivoted his body slowly and navigated his way across the street. It was posted October thirtieth, but Jess died on December eighth. Where had it been? He climbed the mansion's steps like his boots were filled with sand.

He shuffled into his room and stopped, took off his hat, tossed it on the desk and shook his head. He sank onto the chair in front of the desk, and forked his fingers through his hair. Picking up Ned's old leather letter opener from his desk, he stared at it with unfocused gaze. His breathing slowed and there was thickness in his throat as he slit open the envelope, and read the half written and half printed words on the page.

Dear Rand, I was hoping to get out there to see you, but some things have come up that prevent me from traveling. We both know it would not be good for you to come here. I tried to call you the other day, but I lost your number. I've been more forgetful lately. Alice tries to keep track of my stuff, but I have a habit of putting things where neither of us can find them. I miss you, son, more than I can say. Please call when you get this. I'd like to hear your voice. Love, Jess

Rand's sight blurred when he glanced at the date the letter was written. October twenty-ninth. It was postmarked the following day. He leaned forward with his elbows on his knees while the letter dangled from his fingers.

Where was it all this time? Should have called him when I had the chance. If I'd known he was sick, I'd have made the trip.

"Rand?"

Rand raised his head and his gaze locked with Cab's.

"What's wrong, buddy?"

Unable to trust his voice, he shook his head as his Adam's apple bobbed.

Cab entered the room and stood near Rand. "Who's that from?"

He handed him the letter, avoiding his penetrating gaze.

Cab was silent long enough to read it. "Who's Jess?"

Rand took a few deep breaths. "He died the eighth of December. This was mailed in October. It just got here today."

"I'm sorry about your friend, man."

He spoke quietly once he found his voice again. "It's just—getting this so long aft—"

"I'm sorry, buddy." Cab cuffed his shoulder. "Come in the kitchen. I'll make some coffee."

He followed Cab into the kitchen and sat at the table staring into space with an unfocused gaze.

"I saw your truck and bike so I figured I'd ask if you wanted to catch some lunch. But we can talk while I find something here and then I need to get back to my office."

Rand shrugged. "Sounds good." He rested an elbow on the table, bumped his fist against his mouth, and watched Cab throw together a couple of ham sandwiches and pull a dish of pineapple from the refrigerator. "I stayed with Jess a lot." His voice was quiet as though thinking out loud. "He was an ex-marine and taught me everything I know about riding bikes and just about everything else I can think of." *Jess encouraged you to always face your fears, pal.* Rand hung his head. He'd never stopped running, until last year. Didn't even visit Jess, except to get his bike. *Are you through running, pal?*

After they finished eating, Cab put the dishes in the sink and faced him, frowning with concern evident in his silver-blue eyes. "I need to go, are you alright?"

Rand sighed as he rose from the table. "Yeah."

Cab grasped his shoulder. "If you need anything, I'm here, buddy."

He gave him a curt nod. "Thanks."

Thirty-Nine

After breakfast Saturday, Rand went to pick up a large mirror and smiled at Willis as he entered the post office. "This won't take long."

Willis followed him to the back wall, watched as Rand installed it, and then stood staring at it with his mouth hanging open. "Go walk in the front door. I want to make sure I can see you." He bounced on his feet with excitement.

Rand strode toward the front, went out the door and then returned to stand at the counter.

Willis came running, snatched the bell off the counter and threw it underneath. "I could see you from everywhere back there! Thanks Rand. You're a real friend."

He touched his hat with a forefinger. "Glad you like it, pal."

When he finished there, he stopped on the sidewalk, changed his mind and cut through Riverdale Park to La Mirada Street and walked to Seabreeze. As he entered the lobby, his mother stepped through the employee's entrance at the rear of the building.

Lucinda crossed her arms. "Where have you been?" She trounced the length of the lobby as she scolded him. "I thought you were going to do some work around here!"

"I'm trying to hire some professionals, Mother. I met with an electrician on Tuesday while you were out." He placed his hand on her back as he opened her office door and ushered her inside. "I asked Rod for some advice too."

Lucinda rotated so abruptly that he grasped her arms to keep from bowling her over. "Just don't forget with all your planning, this is still my inn. I'll not have you speaking to anyone on my behalf!"

He raised an eyebrow. "I'll be doing a lot of the work myself. And I wouldn't do anything without your approval."

She glared at him. "You better not!"

He sucked in a sharp retort as he squeezed past her into her kitchen and slowly shook his head. "Mind if I make coffee?" He called over his shoulder.

"I've missed you." She pouted.

He cast a glance at her beneath the brim of his hat as he spooned in some grounds and then filled the percolator with water. He strolled across the room and sat at the table to wait for the coffee to perk. "Are you going to join me?" He raised one eyebrow.

She perched her hands on her hips, pursed her lips and peered at him over the top of her wire-rimmed glasses.

He snatched his hat off and tossed it on the chair next to him. Avoiding her disapproving glare, he moved the salt and pepper shakers in the usual do-si-do fashion on the table.

"I didn't sleep well last night." She set a cup filled with coffee in front of him. "I think I'll have a cup of tea instead."

He frowned "Was it because you're worried about the repairs?"

"I realize there are things that need fixed around here, but I don't have a lot of ready cash to waste on unnecessary upgrades."

"You said that before and I promise to keep that in mind, Mother. Casper's an excellent electrician and Rod assured me his rate is reasonable."

She crossed her arms. "Just make certain you're here whenever any of those men are. I don't like the idea of strangers roaming around the premises when I'm here alone."

Rand scowled. "If you're going to scrutinize everyone who comes here to help, maybe you'd be happier choosing the workers yourself."

"Don't patronize me, young man! You just make sure you're present when there are strange men here."

"I'll do my best." He finished his coffee with one gulp, set the cup on the counter and snatched his hat. "I'm going to take some measurements." He set the hat on his head as he started out the door, but paused with his hand on the doorframe. "If Casper comes, I'll be upstairs." He winked at her and left. *If she is that afraid of strangers, maybe she should see a counselor.* He chuckled.

After a thorough check of the rooms and suites on the second floor of Lucinda's inn, Rand met Casper as he entered the front door. They toured the upstairs and assessed the needed repairs. "Write an estimate for me and I'll talk it over with my mother and let you know what she wants to repair now. We may have to do this in small sections so she doesn't feel overwhelmed."

The wiry man, who had dark hair with a dusting of gray, nodded before jotting some notes on a clipboard that he brought with him. "You have my number. Either have Mrs. Warner call me or contact me yourself. I won't be able to get anything done for at least a month. My company is pretty busy with several projects."

Rand rubbed the back of his neck as he avoided the man's direct gaze. "That's probably a good thing. It'll give her time to figure out how much she wants done."

Casper frowned. "Tell her not to wait too long because I'll have to figure a way to schedule her around our other projects."

Rand hated to seem so evasive, but it wasn't his decision to make. "I'll let you know as soon as possible and we can take it from there."

Casper tucked the clipboard under his arm and shook Rand's hand. "I'll look forward to hearing from you or Mrs. Warner." He turned and exited through the rear door.

Rand sighed, he'd deal with his mother later, but right now he needed to get back to Candlewood for his and Cab's session with Cory and Tommy.

He was met by Angel when he entered Candlewood's gate and she seemed unusually excited to see him and stuck so close that he nearly tripped over her while she ran alongside him. When he stepped onto the veranda, she whimpered. He frowned at her strange behavior and entered the kitchen cautiously.

As he closed the door, he heard loud noises coming from the other side of the mansion. He stiffened. The boys weren't due for an hour and Cab told him before he left that morning that he might be a little late. Rand made his way stealthily and quickly through the dining room, which was the shortest distance through the building from east to west.

When he reached the drawing room doors, he spied Cory beating the tar out of a punching bag. His face was scarlet, his lips were drawn tight and with every blow he spit out a curse.

Rand entered the room quietly and grabbed Cory around his waist from behind him. "Whoa, pal. You're going to hurt yourself." He took note of the boy's bloody knuckles and held him tight as he squirmed.

"Let me go!" He yelled. "I'll kill him!"

Rand gripped him tighter. "We aren't going through with this if this is how you're going act. Nothing is accomplished with anger, Cory. That isn't the way to defend yourself. You'll end up hurting yourself and doing more damage than you can even imagine."

"Then show me how to hurt them so they'll leave me alone." He yelled.

"No." Rand turned Cory around to face him. "The point isn't to hurt anyone. But to keep you from getting hurt with the least amount of injury to others."

Cory's lip was bleeding. "You see what he did to me? I want to punch his lights out!"

Rand drew Cory tight against his chest as the boy flailed at him with his fists. "I know how you feel, pal, but anger isn't the way to deal with it."

"I hate you!" Cory yelled when Rand pinned his arms against his sides.

Rand winced, but held him even tighter, knowing he needed to spend his anger. "You didn't mean that, pal. You know it and so do I." He responded quietly.

Tears filled Cory's eyes and his lower lip quivered.

"It's okay, pal. I'm here." Rand whispered against the boy's head.

Cory stopped struggling, and turning wrapped his arms around Rand's waist, and sobbed. "I hate him! He's mean and I hate him!"

Rand didn't say anything else, but held Cory until his tears subsided and he rested limply against Rand's chest. He pulled over a chair and helped Cory sit down. "The first thing you need to learn is fighting when you're angry will only get you or someone else seriously hurt. You lose control of your body when you're angry and that can get you into more trouble than you ever dreamed."

Cory glared at him. "How do you know?"

Rand swallowed hard. "I've seen people get in trouble with the law for responding in anger."

Cory studied him. "You?"

Rand held his attention. "Maybe."

Cab, Rod and Tommy entered the room on those last two words.

"What's going on?" Rod glanced at Rand.

"We were just having a little discussion." Rand said as he crossed his arms.

Tommy frowned at Cory. "Did Butch hit you?"

Cory hung his head. "He was waiting for me when I left my house."

Rod exchanged a look with Rand and then Cab. "I have some things to do. I'll pick Tommy up on my way home." He turned abruptly and left.

Rand shook his head. "Tommy, Cab and I can show you two some defensive skills, but if you don't learn to control your emotions, especially your anger it won't help you much."

Tommy nodded. "That's what I've been trying to tell Cory."

Forty

Tuesday afternoon, Rand rubbed the back of his neck while he stood staring at the shelf he made for Netty. They hadn't spoken since the day she came to Candlewood and attempted a half-hearted apology, which escalated into another confrontation and she made her choice and moved on with another man. His muscles tensed. *Might as well take it to her.*

He reached for his gray hat on the shelf in his closet and his mouth dropped open. Only the tan and white ones were there. He leaned out of the closet and spied the black one still on his desk. *Where's the gray one?* He kept them all lined up on that shelf except whichever one he currently wore.

Grumbling to himself, he set the black one on his head, retrieved her shelf, carried it outside and down the steps. He tugged the hat lower to shield his eyes from the glint of the sun, which reflected off the barber shop window. As he crossed the street, Netty's shouted, get out, Rand, rang so loudly in his mind that his ears tingled with the memory of it.

He paused as he reached the door to her shop. *This will be the last time you come here, pal.* Once the shelf was delivered, there was no further reason to see her because he now went to a barber in Montecito. His belly knotted as he imagined her yelling at him even louder than before.

"Get out!"

He stopped abruptly. *You've really lost it, pal.* He opened the door, stepped quietly inside and set the shelf on the floor near the door. His head snapped up as action within her shop materialized before him. Netty stumbled backward and landed awkwardly on the barber chair. He paused and allowed his brain to catch up to the mayhem, unfolding before his eyes.

A strange man dressed in a black pin striped suit drew back his fist as he approached Netty. "I'll teach you—"

With nostrils flared Rand lunged at the man, spun him around and twisted his wrist.

Wings of Steel

The man dropped his gun.

Rand slammed a fist into his abdomen.

The man crumpled to the floor.

Rand kicked the gun out of the man's reach and speared Netty with a concerned frown. "You al—?"

Bang! A shot pierced the silence.

A quick snap stung Rand's upper arm. The unexpected force knocked him off balance.

Netty threw a bottle of something from her sink and busted the man's head open.

The contents splattered a shower of liquid in his face. He screamed and covered his eyes.

Netty put on a glove, picked up a small hand gun and hurried to Rand's side. "Let me help you."

"Don't worry about me. Get a rope." He panted as he slumped against the wall. Intense white hot burning spread through his shoulder, chest, and arm, which hung limply at his side. Blood saturated his shirt and dripped onto the floor.

Wavering for a half second, she disappeared into the storeroom and quickly returned with a length of heavy twine.

"Who is he?" Rand managed to growl as he knelt and helped her tie the man's wrists together behind his back.

"Jacque LeVet." She spit out the name while they finished securing their attacker. "Now, let me help you." She ushered him to the barber chair and waited until he sank onto it. She grabbed a towel from the sink and pressed it against his wound. "Hold this." She threw him a wary gaze, ran to her desk phone and dialed. "Manny, it's Netty. Quick! My shop! Call an ambulance!" She dropped the receiver and ran back to Rand.

He glared at the man on the floor, drew several breaths, and tried to clear his mind. "What happened?"

She grabbed another towel from a drawer and pressed it in place of the other one, which was already saturated. "He had a gun in his boot."

Rand attempted to stay focused on their prisoner. "Why's he here?" He tried to ignore the muscles cramping in his shoulder and chest.

Netty huffed. "Revenge."

Rand winced and tried to ignore the pounding in his head while his arm tingled. His brow wrinkled as he studied the bruise that began to color her cheek. "You alright?"

"I am now, thanks to you. What're you doing here?"

Her question caught him off guard. He swallowed hard and wished for his hat to hide the sting of her words, but camouflaged it with a frown instead. "Brought your shelf." He managed to reply, between clenched teeth. *Could rescuing her change things between us?*

She crossed her arms. "He hit me when I refused to leave with him." Tears filled her eyes. "I've been such a fool." Her chin trembled.

He gazed at the thread like streams of mascara, streaking her face. "Now you're hurt." Her chin trembled.

He grasped her free hand. "It's just—"

"What's going on here?" Gus bellowed as he charged into the shop with his gun drawn and the medics behind him.

Netty raised her head. "Over here!"

Rand squinted at Gus and indicated the man on the floor with his chin. "He attacked Netty." The hoarseness of his voice surprised him.

Gus scowled at the stranger while he retrieved the gun from the floor and directed his attention to the medics and pointed at Rand. "How bad is he hurt?"

"We'll need to get him to the hospital." The medics wrapped Rand's arm, helped him lie on a stretcher and carried him to the ambulance.

"I'm going with him." Netty yelled as she followed them.

Later Rand avoided Netty's eyes when she entered his room in the emergency area. "Guess I was in the right place at the right time." One side of his mouth curved upward, but his face felt overly warm. "What'd you do to him?"

She laughed bitterly. "I guess I deserved that, I—"

"That's not what I meant." He growled. "What does he have against you?"

"You'd find out sooner or later." She sat on the chair beside his bed and studied something on the floor for several moments as she chewed on her lower lip. "I used to work for him, some might say." Her chin quivered. "I'm sorry for trying to persuade you—"

"Don't." Rand grasped her arm and gazed at the darkening color on her face. "Did they give you ice for that?"

She blinked rapidly. "While I was waiting for you, but you're the one who's hurt."

He tugged on her arm until she moved to sit on the side of his bed.

"When I said I used to work for him, I meant—"

He placed a forefinger against her lips. "Guess we both have a past we'd like to forget."

"I don't deserve your friendship. I'm sor—"

"Let's let the past be past."

Her intense look probed his. "Can we still be friends? I could sure use one."

He winked at her. "You got it." He ran an index finger softly along the edge of her bruised cheek. "Are you okay otherwise?"

She grasped his hand. "How can you care about me after the way I . . ." She stared at the room's partitioning curtain and lowered her voice. "The doctor said he'll release you if the x-rays don't show any broken bones. How are you feeling?"

"A little woozy, but okay." He huffed. "I'd like to get out of here."

"Gus called a little while ago. He's coming to get us."

Rand peered over Netty's shoulder when Gus entered. The throbbing from his wound affected his sight causing the sheriff's face to be shrouded in a haze.

"I just spoke with your doctor. He'll be coming to release you in a few minutes."

Netty pivoted toward Gus. "He'll be okay then, no broken bones?"

"No permanent damage. Seems your luck's still holding, Gray." Gus's chuckle lacked humor.

Rand sighed. "No such thing as luck."

Gus tugged on his hat and smirked. "Yeah, so I've heard."

"You can go now, Mr. Gray." The doctor informed him as he entered the room. "There are no broken bones, but you need to rest for at least twenty-four hours. If you have any inflammation, come back right away. You can pick up the prescription for pain at the desk. Otherwise take aspirin if you need something more. Do you have any questions?"

Rand slowly shook his head to avoid getting dizzy again.

The doctor nodded to Netty and turned to leave. "Sheriff." He acknowledged him in passing.

Gus reached for Rand's uninjured arm. "Come on, I'm taking you to Netty's place. She'll make sure you rest."

Once they were all in Gus' car, he regarded Rand and then Netty in his rearview mirror. "So, which one of you is going to tell me what happened?"

"The man is Jacque La Vet. I knew him in New Orleans. He was—I worked for him."

"I got that from his complaints on the way to jail." Gus grunted in response. "Why did he follow you here?"

She sneered. "You could say I was partially responsible for him losing his livelihood along with four other women."

Gus huffed. "Where are the others?"

She shook her head. "I don't even know their real names. But Le Vet is wanted by the police in New Orleans."

"Your record is clean and your reputation will be protected by this department as long as you stay out of trouble."

She breathed with a whoosh. "Thanks, you won't be sorry."

"Little late for that." Gus growled and then winked at her in the mirror. "I took some pictures of the crime scene. An empty shelf was just inside the door. You make it, Rand?"

He raised his head to peer at Gus. "Yeah."

Gus shook his head. "Shame, there's a slug imbedded in one end. I left it because it wasn't easy to get out without doing a lot of damage. I found another one on the floor. It apparently hit the lock plate on the door, ricocheted off and ended up there. I brought paperwork for the two of you to fill out. The sooner they come and get that scumbag, the happier I'll be." He growled. After a quick stop at the drugstore for Rand's medicine, they proceeded to Netty's apartment. "Are you alright, Netty?" Gus asked as he parked in the alley behind her building.

"I will be." Netty leaned against the seat.

"Good." Gus handed a form to her and pointed to the spaces he wanted her to fill in.

He took a long look at Rand. "Are you going to tell your brother about this?"

Rand snatched the form Gus handed to him. "Why?" He found concentration difficult as he attempted to fill the spaces on the paper, which was attached to a clipboard. He finally finished and signed it.

Gus frowned as he took the clipboard from Rand. "We contacted the authorities in New Orleans. They're sending someone to pick up Le Vet as soon as they can. Glad you're both okay." Gus helped Rand out of the car and ushered him up the steps to Netty's apartment. He waited until she unlocked the door. "I'll check on the two of you later." He tipped his hat and made his way back down the fire escape.

Netty opened the door to her apartment, clasped Rand's uninjured arm, walked inside, and closed the door behind them. "We'll get your hat later; it fell off when you hit Jacque. That was a powerful jab, Cowboy! You probably broke his ribs." She chuckled.

He staggered a step or two, breathing heavily.

She reached for him. "What's going on? You're really pale."

"Feeling a little dizzy." He whispered as he glanced at the chair, which was just inside the door and then squinted at the couch. He stumbled around the chair and leaned against a wall.

She hastily began grabbing at the pile of clothes on the couch. "I'm sorry. I was sorting through these before work and—"

He blinked and stared at her blankly while he slowly slid down the wall to the floor.

"Rand, you're scaring me." She reached for him. "Were the stairs too much for you?" She sank to her knees beside him. "What's wrong? What can I do for you?"

"Dizzy, cold." He shivered.

"I'll be right back." She ran into her bedroom and grabbed pillows and a blanket. When she returned, he was lying on his side with his back to the wall.

She knelt beside him, lifted his head and placed a pillow beneath it and then covered him with the blanket. "Is there anything else I can get for you?"

"I'm good, thanks." He responded in a mere whisper.

"Hang on!" She jumped up and ran to her bathroom, grabbed the medicine and a small glass of water. Kneeling beside him, she raised his head. "Here, cowboy, take these and drink some water." When he finished, she gently placed his head back on the pillow and set the glass on the coffee table behind her.

He moaned softly and snuggled deeper into the pillow.

She smoothed his hair away from his face and placed a gentle kiss on his forehead and felt him shiver. "Are you still cold?"

His eyelids were heavy. "A little." He responded through clenched teeth.

She lay down close beside him, gently stroked his forehead, and slid her fingers through his soft wavy hair. She traced his eyebrows and the lines between them with her fingers.

In a little while, he began to snore softly.

She continued to peruse his chiseled jaw and five o'clock shadow, which framed his mouth and chin. His prominent eyebrows slanted slightly inward and tilted upward at the outer edges. Her gaze followed his long straight nose and stopped to linger on his sensuous lips, which often hitched on one corner when he was being particularly playful. She put her arm across his waist, pulled him close and kissed his hair, but was careful not to jostle his injured arm.

Hours later he awoke momentarily perplexed by his surroundings until his gaze landed on Netty's face so close to his. He was startled until he remembered her chair and couch had been cluttered. He'd been exhausted and unable to remain on his feet long enough for her to move her stuff. The last thing he remembered was swallowing some aspirin and drinking some water.

He observed her relaxed features while she slept, absently rubbing a length of her silky ginger-red hair between his thumb and forefinger. Her scent reminded him of a mix of floral and spice and he often needed to guard against being tempted by it. He sighed, she was beautiful inside and out and was a match for his humor and adventurous spirit. She could also hold her own when faced with danger.

It wasn't like him to jump into a situation without some forethought like he'd done earlier. He shuttered to think what might have happened if Netty was too scared to come to his rescue. *Thank You, Jesus, that the man who attacked her was a poor shot.* He knew anytime a gun was involved; the probability of a good outcome was not good.

He was suddenly too aware of her scent, which clung to his shirt and filled his mind with ideas that weren't wise to entertain. Her warmth was more comforting than he dared admit, but her soft breath on his neck was making him extremely uncomfortable. He sucked in a sharp breath and gently shook her shoulder. "Netty, wake up."

Her arm around his waist tightened and he stifled a groan.

"What's wrong, cowboy?" She whispered groggily.

He chuckled. "Wake up, sleepy head." He didn't dare focus on what her closeness was doing to him.

Her eyes flew open and she quickly backed away from him, sat up and ran her hands through her hair. "What time is it?"

He checked his watch. "Six forty-five."

She scrambled to her feet. "I'll fix us something to eat, but first let me get my stuff off the couch." She grabbed the bundle of clothes and carried them from the room. Afterward she offered him her hand to help him up. "Come on, cowboy the couch will be more comfortable."

He allowed her to help him to his feet, took a few steps and sank onto the couch.

"I haven't been to the store this week. How does homemade gumbo sound?"

A corner of his mouth hitched. "Good." *Like coming home.* He leaned against the back of the couch, closed his eyes and listened to pans being set on the stove, the clanking of silverware and the refrigerator being opened and closed along with cupboard doors. *You could get used to this, pal. Familiar and comfortable, like an old pair of boots or a time-worn saddle.* He sighed, content to enjoy the moment.

Later after they'd eaten, the throbbing pain in his arm coupled with the emotional trauma of the entire experience made it next to impossible for him to remain alert."

"You need more rest, cowboy, and more pills."

He scrunched his nose. "Maybe."

She got up and took their dishes to the kitchen and returned with more pills and some water, which she placed carefully in his hands. When he was finished, she set the glass on the coffee table and gently pushed him down on the couch, put a pillow beneath his head, raised his legs onto the other end and covered him with a blanket. "I'll be right here if you need anything."

Grateful for her willingness to let him rest, he soon drifted off to sleep. After a while he began to toss about on the couch, mumbling in a half asleep, half-awake state. "No." He yelled, sat up and nearly toppled onto the floor.

Netty leaped off her chair and dropped to her knees beside the couch. "It's okay, darlin'. You were dreaming." She rubbed his arm.

He propped his elbows on his knees and let his hands hang loose between them. It couldn't be happening again. But his buddy's voice was as loud as if he had been sitting next to him asking, why Rand? He groaned.

Netty put her arms around him. "What is it, cowboy?"

He shook his head and stared at the floor. His thoughts plunged him into a familiar pit of despair. His insides grew cold with the realization that he could never escape the nightmarish reality.

"What's wrong? Talk to me." Netty drew him closer with one arm and smoothed his hair with her other hand.

Slowly he crossed his arms over his chest while avoiding her gaze. "It happened a long time ago. I stopped a girl from, from being hurt by, my, my best friend. It was an accident, but he—" He hung his head and closed his eyes.

"It was an accident. You didn't mean to hurt him." She pulled him into her arms and held him until he breathed normally again.

His lips formed a straight line. "He hit his head on a rock. The next day he . . . died."

"Sshh." She covered his lips with her fingers. "Did what happened with Jacque stir up those memories?"

His gaze dropped to the floor. "We were like brothers." He whispered. "I can still hear him asking, 'why Rand?' He was wearing a baseball cap backwards, so I didn't recognize him from behind." He took a deep breath and expelled it slowly.

Netty placed her hands on his cheeks. "You didn't do anything wrong. You saved the girl!"

"If you really knew me . . ." He responded quietly.

She leaned into him and kissed his cheek. "I do know you, cowboy." She gently pushed him back until he was resting against the pillows again and then she got up and raised his feet so that he was lying on his back. "Try to go to sleep. I'll be right here."

She pulled an armchair close to the couch next to his head, rested her hand on his chest and clasped his hand. She caressed his face and hair until he relaxed. Before long he was asleep, but restless. The sleeve of his shirt, which the medics cut away to attend his wound slipped off his shoulder, exposing it and part of his upper arm that wasn't wrapped in the bandage.

Her pulse quickened and she drew in a deep breath. For a moment she was tempted to touch his skin, but drew back her hand when she spotted a long scar at the top of his shoulder. Quickly she carefully pulled the blanket up under his chin, trying not to disturb him. She held her breath, hoping he wouldn't wake up as she held her tears in check. "There's much more to you, Rand, than I ever imagined. I finally understand what you tried to tell me. You care about me and you're determined to treat me like a lady and I intend to treat you with the respect you deserve." She whispered. Her eyelids began to droop while she stared at his handsome face and she was content, listening to his steady breathing. Before long, she fell asleep, leaning her head against the back of her chair and imagining their hearts beating together.

When he awoke, he searched Netty's face, which held so much tenderness that it made his heart ache. He could get lost in the deep pools of her blue-green eyes as the fragrant scent of her perfume permeated his nose and made him nearly dizzy with longing to hold her close. He licked his lips

"Hey." She whispered, gently squeezing his hand.

His gaze slid to her lips. *What if I kissed her, really kissed her? Careful pal, those kinds of thoughts can lead to trouble.*

She stared at him for several moments. "I'll go make us some coffee."

He grasped her hand. "Don't leave, sugar." He pleaded, catching her hand and holding it against his chest over his heart.

She inhaled sharply even though her hand rested on the blanket.

He appraised her reaction intently, feeling heat coursing through his entire body. "You were here the whole time I slept?"

She studied him. "Mm-hmm."

"I'll bet that was entertaining." He quirked one eyebrow.

"Interesting, at least." A small smile toyed with her lips.

"Do I talk in my sleep?"

"Maybe." She teased.

"You watched me sleep?" He scrubbed a hand across the stubble on his chin as his heartbeat rapidly. He wanted to taste her soft lips and inhale her spicy scent. *Better change the subject fast, pal.* "I'll make you another shelf and change the appearance of it so you won't have to be reminded—"

"Are you kidding? That shelf stays. It will be a constant reminder of you risking your life for me."

He chucked her chin with his knuckles. "You didn't do so bad yourself, Red."

"A girl has to protect what's important to her." She winked at him and licked her lips.

"Is that right?" He stared into her eyes, hoping she really meant she was beginning to feel the same way he did.

"I'm going to make us a snack and fix some coffee."

"Okay." He sighed, wishing she'd stay, but glad she wasn't at the same time.

She jumped up from the chair and hurried from the room.

Sitting up was a struggle, but he managed and picked up her phone and dialed. "Hey Cab, can you do me a favor? Grab a T-shirt from my room and bring it to Netty's apartment. Tel—when you get here. Thanks." He hung up the phone, rested his head against the back of the couch and stared at the ceiling.

Letting her take care of him wasn't such a good idea, but he knew she needed to focus on him to help her recover from the earlier ordeal. *But being here is playing havoc with your defenses, pal.* As he scrutinized the small living room, his boots standing next to the opposite wall snagged his attention. She must've taken them off at some point. He drew in a ragged breath, very much aware that things could get out of control if he wasn't careful. *How could I have thought we were history?* He continued to survey the room and caught sight of a cowboy hat. *Mine?*

He got up slowly, crossed the room and lifted the hat off the bookcase and inspected it. *So, this is where my gray hat went. And I wasn't wearing it when I left today. What's she doing with it? And she let another man wear it!*

Carefully he went back to the couch and sank onto it while heat flushed through his body and his heart pounded. He ground his teeth, hoping he could hold onto his sanity until Cab arrived.

Rand's gaze followed Netty when she returned with two cups of coffee. "Who were you talking to?" She gave him one and sat in the chair.

He took a casual sip from his cup. "Cab. I asked him to bring me a shirt. He should be here soon."

As if on cue, they heard footsteps on the fire escape and a short rap on the door.

Netty moved the chair back from the couch and opened the door. "Hi." She greeted Cab.

He stepped inside and his attention immediately landed on Rand. "What happened to you?" He stopped abruptly as he eyed the bandage on Rand's arm.

Netty peered at Cab. "Want some coffee?"

He forced out a breath. "Yeah—hey! What happened to your face? You guys didn't have a fight, did—?"

"No." They both responded.

As soon as Netty left, Rand whispered frantically. "Help me change my shirt."

Cab pulled the torn one off and quickly, while trying to be careful with his injury, tugged the fresh one over Rand's injured arm first and then the other and over his head.

Cab frowned. "What happened, man?"

"I had an uninvited visitor." Netty huffed as she joined them. "A nightmare from my past and he was armed. If it wasn't for this cowboy," she winked at Rand. "I might not be here."

Cab's eyes opened wide. "Really! Is that a bullet wound?"

Rand half shrugged. "Just a scratch."

Netty shook her head. "More than a scratch, I'm afraid, but the doctor said he'll be okay. Gus brought him here because he was supposed to rest."

Cab pressed his lips together. "I'll come back later and take you home."

"Cab, he showed up at just the right time." She began with Jacque knocking her down and told him the entire story. "And Rand's lucky Jacque isn't a great shot. It could have been a whole lot worse."

Luck had nothing to do with it. This time Rand kept the comment to himself.

Cab glanced from Rand to Netty. "So, you're both okay?" He asked as he scanned her face and then his.

She gave him a quick smile as she stared at Rand. "Like I said, he showed up just in time."

Rand stood. "It's late and I'm tired. I think I'll leave with you, Cab. You need to get some sleep too." Determined to act like everything was normal, he brushed Netty's cheek with his forefinger as a corner of his lips lifted. "Thanks, for everything." He whispered in her ear and then turned from her to grasp Cab's arm and head for the door.

Forty-One

The next morning Rand was using a T-square to measure an end of a board for a corner piece when the phone rang. He picked it up on the second ring. "Hello?"

"Hey, Cowboy, have you had breakfast?"

He frowned, as he laid the pencil and T-square on a work bench. Netty's sultry voice warmed his insides until he remembered his hat sitting on her bookshelf as if it belonged there. He rubbed the back of his neck. "I am kind of hungry."

"Good, how soon can you get here?"

"Twenty minutes."

"Great." She laughed. "The gumbo we didn't eat yesterday will be nice and hot." She hung up.

He frowned, staring at the receiver before putting it down. Was she kidding? He closed his shop, took a quick shower, put on clean clothes and knocked on her door in less than fifteen minutes.

"Come in." Her voice welcomed him from inside.

He opened the door and savored the aroma of bacon and something sweet, which made his mouth water. His jaw clenched when he noticed his hat was missing. *Easy pal, give her a chance to explain.* He sighed. "Something smells good." Sitting at her dining table, he hoped he sounded cheerful when she set scrambled eggs, bacon and cinnamon rolls on the table and then brought cups of coffee.

She sat across from him. "Would you like to pray?"

He raised his eyebrows, but closed his eyes to offer a quick prayer. "I could eat gumbo like this for breakfast every day."

She grinned. "I wondered if you'd even come. You didn't seem too thrilled about it yesterday."

He took a bite of cinnamon roll, chewed and swallowed. "Not sure I've ever had it before, but I'm mostly a meat and potatoes man."

She chuckled. "I pretty much figured that out long ago." When they finished eating, she stood. "We can have more coffee in the living room. I have something I want to tell you."

He took his dishes to the sink, strolled to the couch, and settled on one end of it. *You have something to talk to her about too, pal.*

She brought their cups and set them on the coffee table.

He smiled to himself when she settled next to him on the couch, which suggested whatever she wanted to say was more than casual conversation.

She eyed him coyly. "I heard what you called me last night."

He picked up his cup and took a drink to hide his grin. "What?"

She scooted a little closer. "You called me, sugar."

One eyebrow rose. "Must have imagined it."

She stared at him. "I know what I heard."

Once side of his mouth hitched as he took another drink from his cup.

She chewed on her bottom lip. "Your hat was laying on my shelf, but you didn't say anything about it."

He sighed and crossed his arms. "Where is it?"

"It would be better if I show you."

He frowned. "Show me what?"

She tried rather unsuccessfully to keep a straight face. "I'll be right back." She hurried into her bedroom and was gone several minutes.

He continued to drink his coffee but the longer she kept him waiting, the more agitated he became over another man wearing his hat.

Finally, she returned, holding a giant teddy bear. It was wearing his cowboy hat and his shirt.

His mouth dropped open and he sat completely still.

She set the bear on the couch between them. "Rod gave me a key to the mansion and asked me to keep an eye on it because he and Cab were spending a lot of time with you while you were in the hospital. Neither one gave me much hope, more because of how upset they appeared than what they actually said. I had to wait until you were out of intensive care before I could even try to see you. So, I went to the mansion and cleaned it for you. It was the only thing I could think of to do. While hanging your clothes in your closet, I saw your hats on the top shelf." Her eyes filled with tears and she placed her hands in prayer like fashion in front of her mouth until she regained composure.

"I didn't know if I'd ever see you again." She swallowed a couple of times. "So, I took a hat and a shirt, thinking at least I'd have something to remember you by. Oh, and I took the bottle of your aftershave that was almost gone. The whole time we were separated I danced with this bear that I'd put your hat and shirt on." Tears streamed down her face as she finished. "I intended to return them, but I'm having trouble parting with them." She smiled around her hands, which partially covered her mouth.

Warmth engulfed him from within. All the disappointment he'd endured while gazing at the silhouettes on her shades evaporated. *Thank You, Jesus, that I kept my mouth shut. I can't begin to explain to her what she did means to me.* The broken pieces of his heart began to mend while she shared and her tears chipped away at his determination to guard against ever trusting another woman with his heart. He set the bear on the floor, sat next to her, pulled her into his arms and held her close. "Sugar, that was a real sweet thing you did." He whispered hoarsely.

Time past in silence as they sat wrapped in each other's arms, until finally he released her. "I need to pick up a few things at the hardware in Montecito." He kissed her cheek and then stood.

"You're not upset with me, are you?" She searched his eyes.

He shook his head as his Adam's apple bobbed. "No."

"Don't you want to take your hat and shirt with you?"

"Not now. See you later." He let himself out, made his way down the stairs, climbed in his truck and drove out of the village. He needed time alone to absorb all she'd told him.

———⟩⟨⊃⟨⊃⟩⟨———

Late the next afternoon Rand stepped into the post office and Willis came running from the back room with an envelope in his hand. "Hey, Rand, you got a strange letter!" He said, sliding it across the counter.

Rand's jaw dropped open at his name and Fire River printed in capital letters on a plain white envelope. The only other information on it was the postmark. He snatched it off the counter and spun around to leave.

"Hey!" Willis called after him. "Heard you got shot the other day. You doing alright?"

Rand gave him a backhanded wave, stepped out the door and crossed the street. As he strode toward his truck, his mouth was dry. He got in and sat fixated on the bold lettering on the envelope. *Someone's idea of a joke?* He tapped a fist against his lips before tearing the envelope open. He read. **YOU CAN RUN BUT YOU CAN'T HIDE!**

The scrap of paper fluttered to the floor. Who sent this? He wasn't running and definitely not trying to hide. He snatched the paper, stuffed it back in the envelope and stared at the postmark, Omaha, Nebraska. He frowned. First the delayed letter from Jess, the fiasco at Netty's and now this. Could they be related? Planning to keep it quiet until he was able to figure out what it meant, he stuffed it in his glovebox. *Is it a practical joke?* Just in case, he strolled back into the post office as Willis was closing for the day.

"Hey, Rand!" He rushed toward him. "Figure out who sent the letter?"

He shrugged. "Let's keep it between you and me, okay?"

Willis grinned. "I get it, somebody's playing a trick on you and you want to figure out who did it so you can get them back."

Rand pulled his hat lower on his forehead. "Right."

"Sure thing, my lips are sealed." He drew two fingers across his mouth.

He nodded and left the building. Willis had difficulty keeping secrets, but he hoped he could count on the postal worker this time.

———⋅⟨⟩⋅———*

He drove out of the village, parked his pickup off the road, snatched his jean jacket from the seat, where he'd left it earlier and hiked up a rocky ridge. The wind whistled along the slopes and rustled the fir trees. A condor screeched from high above and a nearby branch on the underbrush snapped as an animal skittered out of his path. Pebbles shifted under his feet as he climbed and he stepped carefully over loose shale as small rocks clattered down the mountainside.

When he reached a plateau, he stopped, leaned against the worn rock face and crossed his arms. He drew in a deep, appreciative breath and expelled it slowly. The air was crisp and scented with pine, decayed leaves and bark. It was cooler up here and he was thankful for his jacket.

His thoughts returned to the mysterious note along with the delayed letter from Jess. He scowled as the fiasco at Netty's shop played on his mind along with the remembrance of the bruise on her cheek. He would have liked to pound that scrawny man senseless. He picked up a rock and hurled it as hard as he could, but drew in a sharp breath when pain shot through his injured arm. The rock continued to echo within the canyon as it struck the wall on its descent.

He mulled over the words on the scrap of paper, *you can run, but you can't hide.* Chills raced up his arms and down his spine. He'd never been to

Nebraska. He drew a deep unsteady breath. A harmless prank or something more sinister? The hair on the back of his neck tingled and he rubbed his arms. *What if . . . don't go there, pal.*

He clenched his fists. *Thanks to You, Lord, with Clayton's help I'm beginning to feel good about myself.* He slid down the rock behind him and sat with his knees pulled up to his chest. But his past was never far from his mind. *What if that note's from him?* He shuddered and shoved that thought into the recesses of his mind.

Raising his head, he stared at the clouds which lazily floated across the sky. *I will never leave you nor forsake you.* He started at the voice and hastily glanced in every direction. Once he comprehended it wasn't audible, but came from within him, the tension in his muscles eased. He breathed normally again and gazed into the distance as he marveled at God's care for him. Still, he was more than a little anxious about the strange message. His heart beat a steady rhythm as he slowly stood and carefully wound his way back down to his truck. He still needed time to think rather than be bombarded by questions for which he had no answers.

Nearly an hour later, he drove onto his property and parked near the beach. He strolled to an old dead tree, leaned against it, and reflected on the day's events while a breathtaking panorama spread out before him with the sun setting over the craggy shore. Foamy waves rolled slowly over rocks and lapped at the narrow beach. The sky held bright clouds surrounded by navy blue. As the sun reached the horizon, a brilliant ball of fire perched briefly on the edge of his world. Crimson fingers stretched outward until they faded away. Before long, darkness descended and a damp breeze chilled him. He ran his tongue over his lips, tasting salt. Shivering, he plodded back to his truck and climbed inside. Far enough away from the village, he felt safe within the boundary of his own property. He gave in to mental exhaustion and drifted into a restless sleep.

It was after ten thirty when he awoke with a stiff neck and aching shoulder. He put his hat on, left his property and drove back to Candlewood. Light shone through the library windows and since he wasn't confident Willis could keep quiet about the note, he decided to take a walk to avoid being confronted by Cab. A light was also on in Netty's apartment, but neither was he ready to answer her questions. He was still sorting through recent events besides what she told him after their breakfast yesterday.

He could take Angel with him, but she was likely inside so he concluded, walking alone was his best choice. He strolled west on Chino Avenue, hoping to avoid arousing Netty's curiosity and turned north on Fountain Street. He passed the bakery, inhaling the aroma of freshly baked bread which made his mouth water and his stomach rumble, reminding him he hadn't eaten since a quick breakfast alone before leaving Candlewood. He strode past the firehouse and a glass factory. Next the courthouse and police department, which were located in a group of buildings separated by walkways.

Near the northern end of the square was the library. Its dark interior held only shadows from the dimly lit lobby. W. T.'s gas station and garage were located on the northwest corner of the square. The school, playground and parking lot were next on the north and were cloaked in darkness except for an occasional street light. There was also a meat market, a deli and several small shops.

He stayed on the south side of Cambria Avenue and walked along the park. By the time he reached the corner of Cambria Avenue and La Mirada Streets, he was thoroughly chilled. He crossed diagonally through Riverdale Park, which occupied more than two thirds of the inside of the square while the mansion and its garden dominated the remainder of the property.

A dark cat ran across his path as he stepped onto the grass. An owl's eerie hoot pierced the silence of the night from a tree somewhere deep within the mature black oak and big leaf maple trees. His ears picked up the swish-swish of the grass against his boots as he walked. Another owl screeched nearby and his muscles tensed. He quickened his steps, hoping the extra exertion would chase away a sudden prickly sensation that someone was following him.

A crescent moon was partially obscured by clouds and periodically disappeared altogether. Fallen leaves carpeted the grass in between the trees and crunched beneath his feet. Bushes and shrubs loomed in the darkness in macabre shapes. Park benches emerged from the shadows as he approached them.

He flinched when another chilling screech from an owl in a nearby tree penetrated the stillness. He shrugged deeper into his jacket, pulling the collar up around his neck. Water gurgled from the fountain in the pond on the east side of the park and blended with the ghost like whisper of the breeze as it rustled through the tree tops.

As he headed for a path enclosed by bushes on the south side of the park, metallic squeaking alerted him to the sudden movement of a swing on the empty playground as if suddenly vacated. His brow furrowed. *Not windy enough to move that swing, pal.* Soon, the shrubbery secluding Candlewood's Garden became sparce and he knew the hidden gate was only a short distance away. The hairs on the back of his neck stood up. He spun around and jabbed with his right fist at a man's head and immediately followed it with his left to the man's solar plexus. Before the man hit the ground, Rand was hit from behind and shoved forward.

Forty-Two

A wet tongue swiped across the side of Rand's face and dog-breath assaulted his nostrils. He groaned. He was lying in the grass and his head was throbbing. He raised up, pushed the furry head away and stared at the man lying on the ground nearby.

Angel whimpered and pressed her nose against his hand.

Sitting up slowly, he tentatively examined the back of his head and winced. He raised his arm to check his watch, but it was gone. He shivered as the world spun around him, making his stomach queasy. He scratched Angel behind her ears and waited for the dizziness to pass. "Guess I should have taken you with me, girl." She licked his face again and he snatched his hat from the ground, scrambled to his feet, and staggered toward Candlewood's closed gate.

He peered at Angel. "You jumped the fence?" She barked softly. "Good girl." His head was throbbing so he carried his hat. They entered the garden and he made it as far as the bench, sank onto it, and waited for his queasiness to settle enough to walk. Angel gave two sharp barks and Rand groaned. She licked his hands. "Okay, okay." he complained.

When they reached the veranda, he almost fell before opening the kitchen door. He stumbled inside too dizzy to remain on his feet, pulled out a chair, and sank onto it. He laid his hat on the table as Angel's toenails against the floor penetrated the silence.

Cab was reading his Bible when Angel entered the library whining. Cab laid the Book on a table nearby. "Did Rand let you in, girl?" She barked, grabbed his sleeve, and pulled him out of the chair. "What's wrong, girl?" He followed her to the kitchen.

Rand sat at the table holding his head in his hands.

Cab took in his dirt-streaked clothes and hair standing on end as if he'd been jamming his fingers in it. "What's going on, man?"

"Got surprised from behind." He groaned.

Cab stood next to Rand peering anxiously at his pale face. "Want me to take you to the hospital?"

"Need to call Gus. Left a man on the ground in the park.'" He wobbled on his feet when he stood.

"Whoa there, buddy." Cab shot an arm around Rand's waist to steady him. "I'll call him."

"I can do it." He took off his dirty jean jacket and absently tossed it at one of the chairs. It fell on the floor as he picked up the phone and dialed. "Hey Manny. Gus there? Two men attacked me in the park. Just a few minutes ago, I think. One of them should still be there. No, I'll be—" He started to lose his balance and grabbed the table for support.

Cab's arm shot out quickly to steady him while he took the phone. "Manny, it's Cab. I'm taking Rand to the hospital. He may have a concussion. I'll call from there and let you know. Thanks." He hung up the phone. "Come on, buddy, we need to make sure there's no serious damage."

———⸙———*

Once they returned to Candlewood, Cab waited at his passenger door for Rand to climb out. "Are you still dizzy?"

"Nah. Guess I won't be going to bed anytime soon, but no sense you staying up too."

"Hey, what's going on?" Netty asked, running up to them.

Rand scrunched his brows. "Where'd you come from?"

"Saw you from my window." She replied as she inspected him. "What's going on?"

"Someone assaulted him in the park." Cab offered. "We just got back from the emergency room. He has a mild concussion and they said he should only sleep a few hours at a time for at least the next twenty-four."

"I'll be glad to keep him company. There's no need for you to stay up." She told Cab as she moved to Rand's other side.

Cab chuckled. "Seems I've heard that before." He and Netty helped Rand up the steps.

Once Rand settled on a couch in the library, Netty stared at Cab with arms crossed. "What did they tell you at the hospital?"

"Not much more than I already said." He's been a little dizzy and unsteady on his feet."

She crossed her arms. "Did you call Gus?"

Rand groaned.

"We spoke to Manny before we left, so Gus should know by now."

Netty smirked. "Did they give him any medicine?"

Cab raised an eyebrow at Rand. "The doctor said to wait a couple hours and he can have aspirin as needed."

Netty waved an arm at Cab. "Go on to bed. I'll make sure our patient is taken care of." She winked at Rand.

Cab shook his head and started out of the room. "You should call Gus." He directed to Rand.

"I have nothing more to tell him." He growled.

"You need to change your clothes." Netty said when Cab left.

Rand's cheeks puffed out and he slowly expelled a breath.

Netty shook her head. "I promise I won't look unless you need help." She tugged on his arm. "Come on, cowboy, your clothes are too dirty to be sitting on that couch."

He managed to get up and started walking toward his room. "I can do it."

She followed him and watched him sit on the bed. "I'll wait for you in the kitchen." Fifteen minutes later he still hadn't come out and she knocked on his door and then entered.

He was still where she left him and struggled with the buttons on his clean shirt.

She stopped in front of him. "Let me help." She finished with the buttons, and winked at him. "Come on, cowboy, I'll fix you something to eat."

He padded bare-footed into the kitchen behind her "Coffee's fine." He suggested as he brushed past her.

She followed him into the library, watched him sit on the couch, and covered him with an afghan from a nearby chair.

"Netty." He huffed and tossed the afghan aside. "I'm okay."

She crossed her arms. "Are you missing anything? Were you robbed?"

His brow wrinkled. "My wallet, keys, and watch."

She smoothed his unruly hair out of his face. "I'm sorry. I'll make coffee. Do you want anything else?"

"No thanks." He closed his eyes and leaned against the back of the couch.

Later that morning, Rand opened his eyes as Netty rushed from the room when someone pounded on the front door. Her voice and the sheriff's reverberated in the hall. "So much for rest." Rand grumbled.

Gus strolled into the room with Netty on his heels. "What happened this time?" The lawman fired the question at Rand.

A wry grin tugged at Rand's lips. "Nothing serious."

Gus shot an irritated glance at Netty. "Glad to hear it. So, answer my question."

"Somebody attacked him and stole his wallet, keys, and watch." Netty responded.

Gus glanced at her and back to Rand. "Where?"

He tilted his head back and stared at the ceiling. "The park. I told Manny."

Gus fastened a questioning look on him. "When?"

Rand sat up and firmly planted his bare feet on the floor. "Didn't he tell you I called?"

Gus sighed. "I'm asking you. What time?"

"Around midnight, I think."

"What were you doing there at that hour?"

"Walking."

"Is that a habit?"

Rand's eyebrows drew together and he rubbed his forehead, which was pounding with the ferocity of a thundering herd of cattle. "Could be."

Gus crossed his arms. "Why last night?"

Rand squinted. "Felt like it."

"Why so late?"

He stared at Gus, blinking. "Just got back."

"From where?"

He huffed. "My property."

"What were you doing there?"

His nostrils flared. "Nothing!"

"Last I checked there's not even a shed on that property."

Rand rolled his eyes. "It's my property."

Gus glared at him. "Okay, smart mouth, just answer the question."

Heat spread up his neck and onto his cheeks. "What are you getting at?"

"What are you hiding?"

A vein pulsed in Rand's forehead. "Nothing. It was late. One man tried to jump me, but I took him down and his partner surprised me, that's all." He answered in a quietly, controlled voice.

Gus frowned. "I repeat, what were you doing there at that hour?"

Rand rubbed his throbbing temples. "Are you serious?"

"How long were you there?"

He lifted an eyebrow. "You're kidding."

"So how long did you do nothing on your property?"

"I. don't. know." He drew a slow steady breath after each word.

Gus's brow wrinkled. "Confound it, Rand, just answer the question."

"A long time." He forced the words through clenched teeth.

"Gus, take it easy, he has a concussion." Netty interrupted as she massaged Rand's shoulder from where she stood behind the couch.

Gus threw a quick glare at her before he continued. "Where were you before that?"

Rand tugged on his shirt collar, which was suddenly too tight. "What does that have to do with—?"

"Just answer th—" Gus uttered an impatient oath.

"Yeah, yeah. Spent some time in the mountains." His voice was flat.

"Who was with you?"

"No one."

Gus crossed his arms. "What were you doing there?"

"Thinking." Rand muttered, leaned forward and rested his head in his hands. "Something you should try doing."

Gus snorted. "How long were you there?"

Rand closed his eyes and shrugged.

"Were you thinking about something specific?"

"I told you already. I. don't. remember." He raised his head to squint at the clock on the fireplace mantle: 8:15. *Will he ever give up?*

Gus scrutinized him. "Where did you go before the mountains?"

A nerve in Rand's jaw twitched. "Montecito."

Gus took off his hat, scratched his head and set it back on. "Before or after you went to the post office?"

"How did you—?"

"How long were you there?" Gus grinned.

Rand stared at the floor. "Where?"

Gus tugged on his hat. "I heard you were pale as a ghost after reading your mail. What did it say?"

Rand rubbed the back of his neck. *Willis, you'll be hearing from me.* "Someone's idea of a joke."

Gus stood. "So, you walked half way around the square around midnight, before that spent an unbelievable amount of time doing nothing on your property, and an unspecified time in the mountains, thinking." He paused before continuing. "Somewhere in between there and Montecito you stopped at the post office, which I might add you neglected to mention. Did I forget anything?"

Rand's face heated and he bared his teeth. "You calling me a liar?"

Gus tugged on his hat. "Your story is questionable. The man you met turned on you. Sounds to me like someone's trying to blackmail you. If that's the case, you won't be able to handle this alone, Gray." He started for the door. "If you think of anything else, no matter how small, call me."

"Sheriff," Rand waited until he had Gus's attention, "don't give up your day job."

Gus put his hands on his hips and fired visual daggers at Rand. "What's that supposed to mean?"

Rand's nostrils flared. "You'd never make a comedian."

Gus scowled at him. "You're not a good liar either. So, where's the letter?"

"In my glove—" He started to yell.

Gus grinned. "I'll let myself out and stop at your truck on my way."

Rand's shoulders stiffened as he leaned back against the couch cushions and scowled at the cold hearth. *Guess he got what he wanted, pal.*

Rand glanced at Netty, still frowning at Gus's parting remark. "You don't have to stay."

She maintained eye contact with him. "If you want me to leave, I will, but I'd like to stay a while longer."

He sighed. "How about some coffee then and maybe breakfast?"

"Coming right up, darlin'."

A little later she rejoined him, carrying a tray filled with scrambled eggs, ham, potatoes and coffee. "I'm hungry and thought you might be too." She eyed him while, setting the tray on the coffee table beside his legs, which he rested there. "Scoot over and I'll sit beside you."

He removed his legs from the table and made room for her on the couch. "Smells good." He took a bite of eggs and a few potatoes.

"Since you're supposed to stay awake for a while, I thought it might be easier if you had company."

He took a sip from his cup and pondered her comment. "You're probably right."

"Tell me something about your life as a boy." She sat with one knee bent as she faced him, giving him her complete attention.

He stared blankly at the coffee table, reminiscing. "Spent a lot of time on a ranch from an early age. Won a gold buckle in a mutton-busting event when I was six."

"What's mutton busting?"

He grinned at her. "Riding bucking sheep instead of ponies. It's not that far to fall to the ground. Still takes skill and grit to stay on though. Carried that buckle around in my pocket for years." The corners of his mouth drooped briefly at the memory. "I enjoyed being around animals, especially horses. They were actually my best friends." His lips hitched. "A friend of mine gave me my first hat and boots when I was five and I've been wearing them ever since." His eyes grew heavy while he replayed the memories in his mind and soon after eating, his head rested against the back of the couch and he drifted off to sleep.

A few hours later, she stroked the back of his hand to awaken him. "You were dreaming and it didn't seem good. Do you want to talk about it?"

He yawned, enjoying the gentle sensation of her fingers on his skin. *That threatening note is now public knowledge, thanks to Willis.* "Things from the past I don't want to think about."

"Rand, look at me." She whispered softly.

He peered at her and his Adam's apple bobbed at the tenderness he found on her expressive face. It was as if she sensed the depth of his anxiety. If he admitted it, that note nearly caused him to panic.

She placed a hand on either side of his face. "Will you tell me what that letter said?"

He blinked rapidly several times. "No, I—"

"Friends are supposed to trust each other, remember?" She licked her lips as she searched his face.

He gazed longingly at her lips, wishing he dared kiss her, but afraid of what would happen if he did. He focused on her lips to ground him as he spoke. "It said, you can run but you can't hide."

She licked her lips again. "What does it mean? Who sent it?"

He stared at the ceiling to avoid her concerned gaze. It was several moments before he spoke. "I'm not sure what it means, unless—"

"Unless what?"

He shrugged. "Don't even want to guess."

"But you have an idea?" She insisted.

He exhaled slowly. "Not now."

She considered him briefly before getting up and picking up the tray with the plates and cups. "I'll wait until you're ready to tell me." She quietly turned toward the rear hall door.

"Netty?" He glanced at the clock on the mantle: 4:35. Cab would be home soon.

She pivoted toward him from the doorway with raised eyebrows.

"Thanks for staying."

Her eyes twinkled mischievously. "You have my number. See you later, cowboy."

"Yeah, later." He was tempted to reach for her, but he didn't and the room seemed cold after she left. He expelled a heavy sigh and rubbed the base of his neck as his shoulders sagged against the couch. There was an ache deep in his chest, but he refused to admit that it had anything to do with Netty. *Better be careful, pal.*

Forty-Three

The following morning, Angel was eating while Rand stood on the veranda, watching her. The kitchen phone rang, he stepped inside, and lifted the receiver from the wall. "Candlewo—"

Laughter erupted on the other end of the line. "If that monstrosity starts answering, I'm leaving on the next train."

Rand's lips pulled to one side. "Who kicked you out of bed so early?"

"For your information, smart mouth, I found your keys and wallet. If your highness will exercise your feet instead of your mouth, you can run over here and pick them up. No surprise, your wallet was empty."

Rand hung up, frowning.

"Who was that?" Cab asked as he entered the kitchen.

Rand glanced at him. "Gus, he found my keys and wallet."

Cab smiled. "Are you going to get them?"

Rand crossed his arms. "Yeah, see you later."

"Later, man."

He snatched his jacket and cowboy hat from his room before going out the door. "Come on Angel. This time you're going with me." He marched down the path with Angel trotting beside him. After leaving the garden, they turned west through the park until they crossed Fountain Street.

Outside the courthouse building, which also housed the jail and police station, Rand paused a moment before opening the door for Angel and following her inside.

"Hey Rand." Sam McCalister, one of the deputies, called to him. "You get yourself a guard dog?" He laughed.

Rand sneered. "Careful, Sam, she's well trained."

He doubled over laughing until Angel bared her teeth and growled. "Oh, man," he sputtered, still chuckling. "I'm real scared." He was a relatively short man, but had a muscular build. Unlike Manny who was noted for his jovial personality, Sam was a no-nonsense type.

"Come on, girl." Rand headed toward the sheriff's office, stepped inside and closed the door.

Gus raised an eyebrow. "Since when did you start using a guard dog?"

Rand shrugged. "Where's my wallet?"

"Right here." Gus picked it up and started to give it to Rand, but Angel lunged at his hand, teeth bared and snarling.

"Hey!" Gus yelled. "What's up with that dog?"

Rand paused to consider Angel's reaction. "She's never acted like that before." He knelt beside her. "What's wrong, girl?" She was staring at Gus with her ears laid back and teeth bared. "Easy, girl." Rand scratched behind her ears. "Lay it on your desk."

Gus frowned, as he set it on the desk.

Rand picked it up and Angel raised her head and stared at him with her ears laid back. He dropped it on the floor, she grabbed and shook it as she snarled and growled. His brow furrowed as he exchanged a glance with Gus.

"I'm keeping it. Meet me in the hall and I'll give you the contents." He tossed Rand his keys.

Catching them he pivoted toward the door. "Come on Angel." She growled at the wallet one more time before following him out the door.

Gus joined him and gave him his personal items. "Where're you headed?"

Rand's lips tilted upward, as he observed Gus's waistline, which bulged over his belt. "How about some exercise in the park?"

"Sure, got to help you help keep your girly figure since you're no longer working on the docks." Gus snorted.

They crossed the street and Rand strolled toward the swings, glad there was no one in the immediate area. As they drew near the playground, Angel began to growl. Rand peered at Gus from under the brim of his hat. "I heard one of the swings squeaking that night and thought someone must have been sitting there."

Gus put his hands on his hips. "Where'd you get this dog?"

"She found me the night I was run off the road. Did you find my watch too?"

"No. Still no clue who caused your wreck?" Gus squinted into the distance.

"It wasn't a wreck." To avoid a further argument, Rand coughed to disguise his huffed response while he observed Angel sniffing the ground.

The dog's actions captured Gus's attention also. "I'd better do some checking with the local K-nine patrol. I'll post her description. Maybe they're missing a dog."

Rand mulled over the sheriff's comment while he admired Angel. "Their loss is my gain."

Gus rubbed his chin. "Near the swings is where we found your keys and wallet, laying in plain sight. Appears the second man was in a hurry to leave the scene. Manny found the one you left behind. We're holding him, but so far, he isn't talking." Gus stopped, removed his hat and scratched his head. "How about taking a late-night stroll through the park once a week for a spell? See if we can catch him that way."

Rand adjusted his hat. "Why would I wanna do that?"

Gus eyed him with a grin. "You scared?"

"No." He drew out the word, frowning.

"You're safe, Sam volunteered." Gus chuckled.

Rand nodded and they walked over to the place Gus pointed out. When they reached it, he subconsciously touched the back of his head.

Angel began growling as she sniffed around the immediate area and suddenly stopped.

Gus grabbed Rand's arm to prevent him from taking another step. "Let's see what she found." He pulled a plastic bag and gloves out of his jacket pockets, picked up a cigarette butt and dropped it in the bag. "Might be nothing, but right now it's the only clue we have besides your wallet."

Rand knelt and rubbed Angel's neck. "Good girl."

"Do you remember anything else, anything at all no matter how insignificant?" Gus adjusted his hat and stuffed the bag and gloves back in his pocket.

Rand shook his head. "I had a feeling I was being watched, especially when the swing started moving."

"Swing, did you say swing?"

Rand stood and stared in the direction of the playground, which was no longer visible. "The squeaking caught my attention." He shoved his hands in the pockets of his jean jacket.

Gus raised his hat and scratched his head. "There've been too many muggings around here recently. Most of the victims left Donavon's Bar shortly before the occurrence and were parked around the square because the bar's lot was full." The bar was located two blocks down the alley between city hall and the newspaper's offices. "Some of them also mentioned a squeaking swing. Everyone was attacked from behind, but so far there've been no serious injuries. You're the only one who mentioned a second man so the muggings could be a cover up. Just a hunch. If you think of anything else, let me know."

"Sure thing." He whistled for his dog. "Come on, Angel, let's go home."

After leaving Gus in the park and Angel at Candlewood, Rand crossed Chino Avenue and ambled to the café. It was between breakfast and lunch for most people so he was surprised to find it crowded. Cab waved to him from a corner table. Rand smiled as he sat with his back to the wall, facing Cab.

"Did Gus have any idea who stole your wallet?"

He shrugged. "There've been some others mugged around the park." He lowered the brim of his hat as a waitress approached their table.

"Hi, Cab, good to see you again. Hi Rand."

His eyebrow hitched. "Hi." *She knows me?*

Cab poked him in the ribs with his elbow and asked the waitress. "Did you end up visiting your aunt over New Years, Rosey?"

She smiled at Cab, but focused on Rand as she nodded her head. "I just got back yesterday."

Cab threw a glance at Rand.

She studied him. "I'm sorry I couldn't make it New Years Eve, Rand."

He tipped his hat. "No problem."

"What can I get you guys?" She kept staring at Rand.

He studied the table top. "I'll have coffee, a cheeseburger and fries."

"How about you, Cab?" She asked without removing her gaze from Rand.

He smiled. "I'll have the same."

"Coming right up." She paused and then headed for the kitchen.

Cab waited until she left. "She decided to visit her aunt instead of going with us on New Year's. You two know each other?"

Rand glanced at the door and tugged on his hat. "Any news about Cory's dad?"

Cab's eyebrow lifted as he eyed him. "No, but Cory's doing good. He's smart and catches on to things quickly. I spend as much time with him as I can. Right now, I'm helping him plan for college. He wants to be an engineer of some kind. I've been talking to the school principal, trying to get a scholarship program started for kids without working parents. His mom is apparently disabled."

Rand focused on switching places with the salt and pepper shakers. "If you need support, I'm more than willing to help. Seems like a good kid."

Cab grinned. "I'll take all the support I can get."

"Have you mentioned it to Rod?"

"Who do you think suggested it?" Cab winked at him.

Rand chuckled as he leaned his chair back on two legs. "Figures."

Rosey came just then with their food, placed it and their coffee cups on the table and stood gazing at Rand with her hands on her hips. "Can I get you guys anything else?"

He shook his head and she walked away with a puzzled expression on her face.

The door opened, letting in a draft. "Wal, lookey here! If'n it ain't Cab and Rand." W. T. pulled out a chair and sat down. "I been lookin' fer ya. That shelf you made me is mighty popular with my customers. 'Spose you could make something for others sides me and the missus? Since I put it in my shop to display my wares on, everybody wants one a thar own. 'Specially with yer initials carved on it." He pushed his chair away from the table. "I gotta git afore the missus eats lunch by herself. Be seein' ya all." He laid an envelope on the table beside Rand's cup and made his way out the door.

Rand stared at Cab and his mouth dropped open as he counted five one-hundred-dollar bills tucked inside the envelope.

Cab grinned. "Appears you'll be busy for some time if W. T.'s bragging about your work." His plate was empty and he finished his coffee. "I've got an appointment at the school." He stood, tossed a tip on the table and strolled to the register to pay his bill.

Rand pushed his empty plate aside, and proceeded to finish his coffee.

As Cab left, he clapped Rand's shoulder in passing. "Later, man."

Rand raised his cup in acknowledgement, then set it down and tossed his tip on the table.

Rosey approached their table and began clearing off the dishes. "Couldn't help overhearing. Would you be willing to make a table for me? It doesn't have to be very big, just enough for two."

He peered up at her from under the brim of his hat. "Might be able to, but don't know how soon."

Her eyes opened wide as she ogled him. "Perfect. I'm in no hurry."

He touched the brim of his hat with a forefinger. "I'll see what I can do."

Her cheeks turned pink. "Thank you, Rand."

Forty-Four

Rand got up at five as was his habit, fed Angel and fixed some bacon and eggs for himself while the coffee brewed. When he finished eating, he took another cupful to his workshop and continued with his current project, a small dresser he'd been making for one of his mother's suites. After a couple of hours, the poignant aroma of varnish filled the room. He removed sawdust from a second workbench and swept it up along with the wood shavings on the floor. Daylight began to filter into the room through the windows when Cab called to him from the hall.

"Morning." Rand greeted him as he crossed the room and headed for his bedroom.

"You leaving this early?" Cab asked when Rand stopped in the kitchen to shrug into his leather jacket.

"Need to get in a few hours of riding." He had an appointment with Dr. Mills later, which he'd keep between himself and the doctor.

"You've been spending some serious time riding." Cab commented.

"Practicing for a race on May eighth. It isn't far from here and I'll be gone for a couple days."

"Great! Let me know when and where and I'll come cheer you on."

Rand smiled, gave him a two-finger salute and left.

Rand focused on perfecting his skill, riding trails in the mountains and practicing for the upcoming race, hoping to push back his anxiety over the threatening note and following attack in the park, He swerved around tight bends in the path, outcroppings of rock and unexpected boulders or fallen trees, which he jumped the bike over. He used every available hour to practice maneuvers, which had won him trophies in smaller competitions.

He loved the sport and enjoyed honing his skill, but participation in a race could lead to more exposure. Rosey's recognition of him stunned him like it was a warning. After receiving the note followed by the park incident, nightmares from his past began reoccurring. He startled awake, breathing hard as his heart palpitated furiously. Afterward sleep was near impossible as it was all those years ago.

Almost daily he was anxious over when the next surprise attack might occur. He was edgy, flinched at the smallest unexpected things, and was obsessed with being followed. He barely managed his nervousness by concentrating on whatever job at hand. It didn't help that Gus hadn't said a word about the threatening note, which still rankled Rand.

He'd survived the first attempt on his life because his boss, Frank Sims, stopped the attacker with a rifle. The memory of the breath-stealing strikes of the belt as the buckle bit into his flesh gripped him even now. Sweat beaded on his forehead at the remembrance and humiliation of having his hands and feet tied while enduring his enemy's insane laughter. He tried to suppress the thoughts while he practiced his riding skills on little used mountain paths.

Later that day after his counseling session with Dr. Mills, he parked his truck in front of Chino Café and as he got out, Rosey exited the building and began walking toward him.

He blinked twice. She was wearing cowgirl boots, jeans and a short-sleeve western shirt.

"Hi Rand." Winking at him, she appraised his hat and boots. "You here for a late lunch?"

He tipped his hat. "Yes, ma'am." He perused her from the corner of his eye. "Did you live on a ranch before coming here?"

She stared straight ahead while she answered him. "Yes, my daddy was a ranch foreman for years before he died."

"I'm sorry to hear about your dad."

She tilted her head and observed him. "I started barrel racing when I was in my teens so I'm more comfortable dressed this way, but I doubt the café manager would approve of me dressing this way for work. I just came to pick up my check. Don't forget about my table. Okay?" She grinned at him as she walked toward a pickup parked across the street.

Wings of Steel

Could she be Nick Jackson's little girl? Not so little now. He eyed her curiously while she climbed in her truck and drove away.

"Hey cowboy." Netty greeted him as she approached.

He turned his head to lock gazes with Netty's wide eyed one. "Hey red, want to join me for lunch?"

She indicated the bag in her hand. "For a few minutes, but I need to get back to the shop for an appointment soon."

He winked at her. "I have things I need to do too." He opened the café door for her.

"You know that waitress?" She grinned as she strolled past him and stepped inside.

"Could be." He headed for a corner table.

Netty sat across from him and scrutinized him. "She hasn't been here long. In fact, I heard she just started right after Christmas."

He studied the menu even though he had it memorized. "That so?"

Meg, one of the owners of the establishment approached their table. "What'll it be guys?"

They placed their orders and drank coffee while they waited for their food.

"Seemed like you two knew each other." Netty remarked as she glanced at him over the edge of her cup.

He frowned. "Might have worked with her dad a long time ago. If so, she was quite a bit younger than me so I didn't pay much attention to her. If she's even the same girl, she had freckles and a pony tail back then."

Netty's eyebrows rose. "You remember her hairstyle and her freckles? Sounds serious to me."

"Nah, she was just a kid." Rand tugged on his hat as Meg set their lunches on the table. The woman reminded him of Alice Ferris, who he hadn't seen since he left Arizona the first time. He frowned as he quickly ate his lunch.

Netty was quiet while she ate hers, but continued to observe him.

When he finished eating, he stood. "I have to run so I'll pay for this." He indicated both their plates. "See you later, red." He made a hasty exit before she could ask any more questions to cause him to go any further down memory lane.

———)◯◯(———*

When Rand got back to Candlewood, it was after dark. He parked in his usual place and flinched when Netty suddenly appeared beside him. "Where'd you come from?" He snapped at her.

She moved over as he climbed off his bike. From the corner of his eye, he saw her scan him from his head, which was hatless, to his boots and back up again to focus on his face.

She smiled. "I made jambalaya just the way you like it, nice and spicy."

He concentrated on checking his bike to make sure it was ready for the next time he practiced his skills. If she noticed his edginess, she chose to ignore it. "I appreciate the invite, but—"

"All I have to do is dish it up. I almost bought a bottle of wine, but since you don't drink, I made iced coffee. Hope you like hazelnut."

He was suddenly more interested in the hand brake on his bike. "I'm sorry, Netty, but I'm trying to avoid the whole Valentine thing. Mother has been on me about dinner and flowers and getting a date for the—"

"But we're not going out, just to my apartment." She protested. "And it isn't even Valentine's Day."

He opened his mouth to spout off another lame excuse, but instead swallowed it.

"Come on, cowboy, I promise I won't bite. I don't have candles and won't turn down the lights. It's a simple dinner between friends, with an emphasis on friends, okay?"

He forked his fingers through his hair. *Friends, she said. Is that what we are? Do you want more, pal?* "Been riding. I'm all sweaty."

She hooked her arm in his. "You're fine, besides if you go inside, I doubt you'll come back out." She tugged on his leather jacket. "Come on, I'm sure you're hungry. I doubt you stop much when you ride."

He raised an eyebrow as he threw her a worried smirk. *If she's aware of your riding habits, who else is, pal?* "You don't give up easily, do you?"

She peered up at him with a teasing quirk on her lips. "Depends."

He regarded her, trying to stifle a grin. "On what?"

She winked at him. "Not what, who." She tugged on his arm until he was forced to take two steps just to keep his balance. "There, you moved forward. That wasn't so hard, was it?" She lowered her hand from his arm and grasped his hand. "Come on, cowboy, stop being so stubborn."

"Look who's talking." He chuckled as he let her take him across the street, around her building, up the fire escape and into her apartment. *Maybe this is just the sort of distraction you need, pal.*

She didn't let go of his hand until he closed the door behind them.

He dropped his jacket on the nearest chair and sat down at her table, noticing it was set for two. There was nothing fancy, no candles or flowers and she left the overhead light on over the table just like she promised. He drew in a deep breath and tried to relax. At least there were no romantic overtures, not even soft background music. Then why did he have a sudden desire to wrap his arms around her? *Don't go there, pal.*

She dished up the food, set a casserole in the middle of the table and sat across from him. "Do you mind, praying?"

He raised both eyebrows before slowly closing his eyes. "Thank You, Lord, for this food and for the one who prepared it." He sat in silence, thankful too for being kept safe as he rode today even though he sensed someone was watching. When he raised his head, Netty was smiling at him.

She filled his plate from the casserole dish. "I like listening to you pray. It's like you're talking to someone you know." She passed him a basket of bread.

He took a roll and offered her one before setting them on the table. "I think I'm only beginning to know Him." He took a bite of the jambalaya and savored the varied flavors exploding in his mouth. "This is better than usual."

After they finished eating, she grasped his hand and led him to the couch. "I'll get our coffee." She paused to peruse his mint-green, black and white chambray shirt, faded Levi's and scuffed almond-brown cowboy boots. As she pivoted to leave the room, she spied his jacket, which he'd dropped on the chair next to the door. It lay in a heap on the floor and she frowned as she picked it up. He'd been mentally distracted when he entered her apartment.

She reentered her living room carrying their coffee and found him leaning against the couch cushions.

He peered at her from under his long eyelashes and met her perusal with an unfocused gaze. When she handed him a tall chilled glass, he sampled the drink and raised an eyebrow. "Not bad." He took another drink and set the glass on the stand beside him.

She eyed him closely as she sat next to him, tempted to run her fingers through his thick wind-tossed hair. His eyes were dark as charcoal just then and the ever present five o'clock shadow made her fingers itch to stroke his angular jaw. Briefly her attention lingered on his mouth and a memory of his warm lips played upon her mind. Mentally she shook herself. Now wasn't a good time to dwell on such things. He appeared anxious about something. He flinched earlier when she walked up behind him. Normally, he didn't startle so easily. "You seemed tense earlier. Would it help to talk about it?"

He picked up the glass again and took a long drink before setting it back down. "Was it that obvious?" His voice held no emotion.

She studied his curled knuckles as he bounced them against his mouth. Something was deeply troubling him. She longed to put her arms around him or stroke the bristly skin on his chin and upper lip, but refrained from touching him. "You didn't eat much even through you apparently enjoyed it."

There was a grim twist to his mouth as he focused on the floor for so long that she wondered if he was going to respond at all. "I've tried to, convince myself there's nothing to worry about, but . . . I have a gut feeling." He crossed his arms over his chest and shrugged.

Instinctively she rested a hand on his arm. She told herself to wait for him to say more. When he remained silent, she lightly grasped his hand. "What are you worried about?"

"Nothing." He whispered. "It's nothing."

"Nothing?" She drew a quick breath at the dismal expression on his face when he glanced sharply at her.

He heaved a deep sigh and shook his head. "Probably just my imagination."

Sensing he needed encouragement to continue, she clasped his hand gently with both of hers. "I think it's more than that."

He didn't even blink. "Things from my past keep resurfacing."

Netty's mouth flew open. "Like the cowgirl, waitress?"

He stared at the floor. "Three weeks ago, I got a letter from my friend, Jess, postmarked October thirtieth, but he died on December eighth. Last week I got that note that seemed to be a threat, but there wasn't a return address or a signature. It was postmarked, Omaha, Nebraska. I've never been there and don't know anyone who has." He swallowed hard.

Netty sat dumbfounded for a few minutes, trying to understand his anxiety. "Do you think the note was really a threat?"

He shrugged.

She smoothed his hair with her fingers, enjoying the soft, thick waves. "Have you prayed about it?" The question even surprised her.

He shot her a quick look before closing his eyes. His features held a pensive expression. "I hoped I was through dealing with that stuff."

She frowned. "How can I help you?"

His hands slid to his lap where he loosely clasped them and then glanced at the clock on the wall: 10:45. "You already have." He stood. "Thanks for dinner. It was really good, but I need to go."

"What about the waitress?"

He crossed his arms. "What about her?"

"She was all dressed up like a cowgirl. Was that meant to impress you?"

He shrugged. "No idea."

Netty tilted her head. "She appeared to be interested in you."

He spread his hands wide and outward with palms up. "No clue." He raised an eyebrow. "Any other questions?"

"Nope." She made the end of the word pop, stood next to him and squeezed his hand. "I'm here, whenever you want to talk and I'll help you any way I can."

He gave her a weak smile. "Thanks." He opened the door and left, leaving it open behind him.

When he crossed the street to start up the steps to Candlewood, the back of his neck prickled. He paused for a second and then went casually up the steps, entered, and closed the door. He moved away from it and leaned against the wall. *Was someone following me or is it only my imagination brought on by recent nightmares along with the memories Rosey stirred up and then Netty's questions?*

Angel came around a corner of the hall and padded toward him. She stopped in front of him, tilted her head and emitted a low growl.

He stooped to her level. "Someone out there, girl?"

She bared her teeth and growled louder.

He hesitated. *Should you let her chase whoever is out there? Do you want them to know you're aware of them?* He began petting Angel. "Do you want to go out?"

Her tail began to wag and she spun in a circle and padded toward the opposite end of the hall.

He straightened and rolled his shoulders. *Maybe it was nothing, pal. Who are you kidding?*

Cab stepped into the hall. "Why are you standing out here, man?"

Rand frowned. "Just," he drew a breath, "thinking." He strolled down the hall, went around the corner, headed for the kitchen, and stopped to let Angel out.

Cab followed him. "Are you okay?"

"I need some air." He tossed over his shoulder as he stepped outside, glanced right and then left before making his way to the fountain. He appreciated that Cab hadn't questioned him further.

He reached the bench, sank onto it and leaned forward with his elbows on his knees and hands clasped in front of him. *Has someone been tailing me or is it only my imagination?* He whistled for Angel and sat there petting her, alert to her every move.

Cab waited for over an hour for Rand to come back inside. When he didn't return, Cab followed his instincts, believing Rand would remain within the borders of the property. He stepped onto the veranda and began following the path. The garden bench was a popular place for all of them when they wanted to be alone. It had been for Rod when he lived here and Cab also found it to be a place of refuge at times.

He approached quietly not wanting to agitate Rand more than he already was. Cab suspected Rand was troubled about something and recognized all the signs; nervous energy, edginess and curt responses that were even more so than usual. As he approached, the moonlight afforded him enough light to make out Rand's tense posture even from a distance.

He was sitting on the edge of the bench as if ready to spring into immediate action. His posture was rigid even though his hands hung limply over his knees. His head was bent forward, which caused his hat to hide his face completely.

Cab's eyebrows pinched as he observed Rand. He breathed a silent prayer, asking the Lord to help him because he had no idea what troubled Rand. Cab closed the distance between them quietly and stood in front of him. When Rand didn't acknowledge his presence, he took it as an invitation to join him so he sat and waited for Rand to respond. The silence between them stretched out so long that Cab began to wonder if he'd made a mistake in coming.

Wings of Steel

Suddenly, Rand exhaled a sigh as if he'd been holding it in for a long time and not just the few minutes that Cab was present.

He took his hat off and set it on the bench on the opposite side of him from where Cab sat. "Have you ever been scared? I mean really scared?"

Cab remained silent, knowing Rand's question was more or less a hypothetical one, which required no response. He reached across the space between them, placed a hand on Rand's shoulder, and felt him shudder.

"I keep telling myself it's just my imagination, but I can't seem to shake the feeling that someone's following me. I showed you the letter I got from Jess." Beginning with that for the next several minutes he told Cab all about his suspicions and nightmares.

"Tonight, when I left Netty, I thought someone was either watching or following me. When I came inside, Angel joined me and began growling so I knew someone was out there." He swallowed his frustration as he lowered his head into his hands and covered his face. "I want to win that race so much I can taste it." He drew in a shaky breath. "But the threat of someone following me will always be a reality as long as I live." He raised his head and gave Cab a direct look. "I don't know what to do."

Cab folded his hands in his lap. "Maybe it's someone who's afraid you will win that race. We all face fears at times. Some are real and some not so much, but isolation is no way to deal with it. If the threat is as real as you believe, Gus is at least partially aware of it, perhaps you should tell him what you just told me. Let him know it could be someone participating in the race. Sometimes we are forced to swallow our pride and ask for help."

Rand scrubbed a hand through his hair. "Maybe you're right, but I've always taken care of my own problems."

Cab cuffed his shoulder. "Let me pray with you. Father God, You know Rand's concerns and whether or not they're real. Help him to trust You instead of letting fear hold him captive. Help him be alert to any real danger while keeping him in Your perfect peace. I ask it in Your Name, Jesus. Amen."

"Thanks." Rand sighed.

Cab stood then. "Anytime. Tell Gus your concerns. It couldn't hurt, especially since you've already been attacked."

Rand crossed his arms and rubbed them, suddenly chilled after Cab left. *There's no way I'd admit any of this to Gus. He'd laugh in my face. Besides that, even Cab doesn't believe they're real, pal.*

Forty-Five

Monday morning Rand stepped into the main hall, heading for his workshop and found Cab and Gus standing at the front door.

"Just the person I came to see." Gus said as he strode toward Rand. "Got a job for you and your dog."

Rand crossed his arms. "What kind of job?"

"There was another incident in the park last night only this time the victim ended up in the hospital."

Rand cocked his head. "Who is it?"

"A teenage boy whose says his name is Cory.""

"Cory?" Rand and Cab responded together. Rand's posture stiffened. "Is he okay?"

"He can't remember his last name or where he lives." Gus adjusted his hat. "A reporter from the Gazette found him early this morning in the park beside the pond. I went to the hospital to talk to him, but all I could get out of him was his first name."

"I know—" Rand started.

"We both know him." Cab interrupted.

Rand eyed him. "We want to see him."

Gus shook his head. "First things first. We're taking your dog to the park, hoping she'll find a clue for us."

Rand's eyes narrowed. "Let's go."

"I'm going to see Cory." Cab told them as he went out the front door.

Rand cut through the library and kitchen, snatched his hat off his dresser and went out the veranda door, uttering a shrill whistle as he stepped outside with Gus right behind him.

Angel came running and Rand stooped to pet her. "Let's go out the back gate." He started jogging in that direction, Angel loped ahead of him and

Gus. Once in the park, Rand sprinted to the pond and stopped. "What are we looking for?"

"Anything that will give us a clue." Gus growled.

Rand scanned the area.

"I brought your wallet." He gave Rand a plastic bag. "Maybe your dog can get a sent from it."

Rand took the bag and opened it. "Here girl."

She sniffed at it and snarled.

"Find him, girl." He started walking around the pond's edge.

Angel ran back and forth beside the water until she stopped and began pawing at a nearby bush. Rand and Gus reached it at the same time and both began searching the shrubbery.

"Hold your dog." Gus yelled as he reached under a low-hanging branch.

Angel wined when Rand held her back.

Gus pulled a bag from his pocket and slid the object inside.

"What is it?" Rand peered over Gus's shoulder.

He raised the plastic bag.

"A knife." Rand's eyebrows furrowed. Angel was snarling and trying to snatch the bag from Gus.

"Might be just what we need." Gus inspected the knife through the bag.

Rand studied the knife, which had a fancy H on the handle. "This looks like the one Hollis had that day on the docks."

Gus frowned. "You sure?"

Rand took a closer look at it. "Positive. How bad is Cory hurt?"

"I didn't get to talk to the doctor. Want to come to the hospital with me?"

"Sure. I know where he lives. I got the impression his mother has a drinking problem and his dad left them."

"Where did you get that information?"

"Met Cory and his parents when I gave his dad a ride home one night awhile back."

The two men got off the elevator at the hospital in Montecito and strolled to the nurse's station. Gus showed them his badge. "I need to visit the patient in room 230. Is his doctor here?"

"I'll page him for you sheriff and have him meet you in the boy's room."

"Thanks." Gus nodded and started down the hall. When they entered the room, a nurse was checking the boy's vitals. "I'll be finished in a minute, sheriff." She acknowledged Rand. "Are you, his father?"

Rand tipped his hat. "No ma'am, a friend." He walked to the other side of the bed.

"His youth leader was here. He said he'd be back later." She told Gus. "I've made Cory as comfortable as possible. His doctor will be in shortly. Excuse me, sheriff." She went around Gus and left the room.

Rand clasped Cory's hand. "How're you doing?"

He stared at Rand without responding.

He smiled, hoping to reassure Cory. "I'm here, pal." Rand withdrew his hand and eyed Gus.

He moved to stand on the opposite side of the bed. "We're here to help you, son. There's nothing to be afraid of." Gus assured him.

A doctor came into the room just then. "Sheriff Palmer." He greeted Gus, but turned to Rand. "I'm Doctor Quale. Are you, his father?"

Rand stretched out his hand. "A friend, Rand Gray."

"We need to contact his parents. Do you know them"

Rand crossed his arms. "I can tell you where he and his mom live."

Gus frowned. "What's wrong with him?"

The doctor pushed his glasses up on his nose. "He's suffering from some trauma although we've been unable to detect anything physically wrong. He's scheduled for tests this afternoon. We'll be able to give you a diagnosis afterward."

"Is he not able to talk or just refusing to?"

Rand rounded the bed and put his hand on the sheriff's shoulder. "Easy Gus."

"If there's nothing physically wrong with him—"

"Sheriff," the doctor interrupted, "I cannot allow you to badger the patient."

"Excuse me, doctor, but I'm here to help him. He needs to answer a few questions."

"I strongly suggest you come back when he's in a better state of mind, Sheriff."

"Fine, when he's able to talk, call me." Gus pivoted on his heel and marched out of the room.

Rand glanced at the doctor and shrugged.

Gus stuck his head in the door. "Are you coming?"

"I'll wait for Cab." Rand said as he pulled a chair close to the bed.
"Suit yourself." Gus huffed and left.

---*

Rand eyed the doctor. "Cory's youth pastor is also a friend of mine. I'd like to stay until he comes back."

The doctor nodded. "Press the buzzer if the boy needs anything."

Rand gave him a half smile and reached for Cory's hand again.

The doctor appraised them a moment before leaving the room.

Rand continued to watch Cory's face for any sign of recognition. "Do you remember me?" He focused his gaze on Cory, hoping he responded.

His eyes closed and a tear wound along his cheek toward his ear. After a few moments, he fell asleep.

A short time later, Rand was staring out the window and spun around when he heard footsteps behind him.

Cab entered the room and indicated the hall with a jerk of his head.

Rand followed him into the hall, but Cab kept walking.

"Where're you going?" Rand jangled his keys in his pocket.

"To my car." Cab took quick strides, descended a set of steps, exited a side door and crossed the parking lot. When he reached his car, he jumped in and shut the door behind him.

As Rand climbed in the passenger seat, his brow knitted at his friend's odd behavior.

Cab faced him. "Cory's in trouble, man."

He tilted his head. "What kind of trouble?"

"Gus went to his house and found his mom, lying on the floor. According to him, she'd been dead for several hours. He told me about the knife you guys found in the park near where Cory was found."

Rand's jaw dropped. "You don't think Cory did it, do you?"

Cab shook his head. "No, but Gus didn't offer any opinion."

"Don't tell me he's going to arrest him."

Cab frowned. "He was still at their house when he called me."

Rand scowled. "He's innocent. I'm sure of it."

"Do you have any idea why he went to the park?"

He shrugged. "No, but I don't believe he—"

"Listen, buddy." Cab grasped his shoulders. "You need to leave your past out of this. Okay?"

Rand sank against the seat. "I know that. But I can't believe he did anything to her either. I'd bet my life on it."

"I don't believe it either, but let's let Gus handle this."

"His mom was the only family he had. He told me just last month that his dad left because of her drinking."

Cab blinked. "He still has us, buddy. Gus said their house was a mess like someone was definitely looking for something. We need to stay calm in order to help him."

Rand stared at him as his lips pressed into a thin line. "Where do you suggest we start?"

"Let's go see if he'll talk to us."

They returned to Cory's floor, and when they stepped off the elevator, Cab nodded toward the boy's room. "You go on, Gus told me to leave all the information I have about Cory at the nurse's station."

Rand consented with a jerk of his chin and continued to Cory's room and found the teen awake. He pulled a chair close to the bed and sat on it. "Hey, how're you doing, pal?"

"Did they find my mom?"

He swallowed before responding quietly. "I'm sorry, Cory."

"I didn't kill her. I swear." Tears streaked his face.

Rand placed his hand on the teen's shoulder. "Take it easy. We believe you. No one's accusing you."

"I saw the way the sheriff looked at me, like I did something wrong."

"He's concerned because you were found unconscious in the park and you couldn't tell him what happened."

"But he thinks I did it. That's how it always is. I never have anybody on my side when bad stuff happens. I always get blamed for it." He spoke through his tears.

He blinked at Cory's words, feeling like he'd been punched in the gut. *You know how that feels, pal.* "I don't believe you did it and neither does Cab. We're with you, pal. You won't have to deal with this alone, I promise you."

"Even you can't protect me from the law." He sniffed.

Rand frowned. "Hopefully it won't come to that." *You know you can't stand by and let him be blamed for something he didn't do, pal.*

"But you're friends with the sheriff."

Rand's mouth quirked with annoyance. "Doesn't matter. God's bigger and I guarantee He's on your side."

The sides of Cory's mouth drooped. "You sound like Pastor Cab and Tommy."

Rand raised his hat and peered steadily at Cory. "He may not prevent you from going through stuff, but He'll go through it with you."

"You had your say so you can leave now." He turned his back to Rand.

Rand grasped his arm. "I'm going to help you no matter what it takes." He jerked his hand away.

Gus walked into the room with his arms crossed and glared at Rand. "I heard that and I'm warning you, Gray. Don't get in the way of this investigation or I'll press charges against you."

Rand stood, meeting Gus's eye without wavering. "Is that a threat?"

"It's an order. Don't interfere."

"You asked for my help."

"And only when I ask for it." He emphasized the first two words.

Rand growled and spun around to stare out the window.

Gus approached Cory. "I heard you talking to him so I expect you to answer me. If you don't cooperate, I will have to lock you up."

Rand grumbled unintelligibly.

Gus turned to scowl at Rand before addressing Cory again. "What time did you get home yesterday?"

"I, I'm not sure, late." Cory's voice was a mere whisper.

"How late?"

"After six, I, I th-think." He sniffed.

"Why so late?" Gus pressed him.

"Because, I was, I didn't wanna go home."

Rand sighed. Cory wasn't helping himself. His hesitation made it sound like he had something to hide and Rand hoped that wasn't the case.

"Why?"

"Cause I, I knew she'd be drunk again?" He almost whimpered.

"She, your mother?"

Cory nodded.

"Did you see or talk to anyone?"

"Not after school." His voice fell even lower on the last word.

"Where did you go that no one saw you after school?"

"No, no place in particular."

"You aren't helping yourself here, son. I repeat, where did you go?"

"Just walked around." His response was almost a whisper.
"Why?"
"I, I wanted to be, be alone."
Rand pivoted to observe them.
"Why did you want to be alone?" Gus asked the boy.
"I needed to, to think about stuff."
"Did you go back home later?"
"Yeah, I, I got hungry." Tears began spilling from Cory's eyes again.
Gus crossed his arms. "What happened when you got there?"
"She was laying on the floor an, and there were empty bottles around her."
"What did you do then?"
"I, I heard a, a noise."
"Then what did you do?"
"I ran outside."
"Why?"
"There, there was a, a man." His lower lip trembled.
"Did he see you?"
He nodded. "He chased me to the park."
"Then what happened?"
"I hid in the bushes."
"Did he find you?"
"No, it was dark."
"Did you go back home?"
"No, I was too, too scared."
"When you went home after school, did you try to wake your mother?"
"No, she was—"
She was what, drunk, not breathing?" Gus pressed him.
Rand huffed. "Stop."
Gus glared at him. "I warned you. Stay out of this or get out of the room."
"Don't put words in his mouth." Rand growled.
Cab entered the room. "What's going on?"
Gus scowled at him. "I'm trying to talk to Cory, but your friend insists on interrupting. Get him out of here before I arrest him and have him hauled off to jail for interfering with a police investigation!"
Cab scrunched his nose as he walked toward Rand and laid a hand on his arm. "Careful," he whispered, "this isn't your fight."
Rand clenched his fists. "I'll. make. it. my. fight, if I have to."

Gus fastened a piercing glare on Rand. "I'll give you three seconds to get out of this room!"

Cab nearly dragged Rand out of there.

On his way out, Rand threw a glance at Cory. "I'll be back."

Gus shoved the door closed behind them.

Cab put his hand on Rand's shoulder. "Let Gus ask his questions, buddy. You aren't helping by riling him."

Rand crossed his arms. "He's trying to get Cory to admit to doing something wrong."

"Unfortunately, you have to let him do his job his way."

"He asked me to help." *As long as it served his purpose.*

"Gus will figure it out in his own way. I don't think he wants to believe Cory's guilty any more than we do. You can help him more by trying to work with Gus instead of against him, buddy."

"I don't want Cory to think nobody cares what he's going through. No wonder he was in a state of shock if there was a strange man in his house. And he obviously didn't know what happened to his mom." Rand hissed.

"You're right." Gus said as he came up behind them. "He just admitted he found her on the floor, got scared and ran when he realized a stranger was present."

Rand jerked his head toward Gus. "You believe him?"

"Contrary to what you think, I want to believe him. I've got to figure a way to place him under protection because the man who chased him through the park was apparently looking for something he hoped to find in their house. He seems desperate and that could mean he may think the boy has some idea where it is. Not to mention giving me a brief description of the man's appearance."

Rand drew in a deep breath, mustering up a calm he didn't feel. "He's welcome to stay at Candlewood."

Gus's smile was forced. "I appreciate what you're trying to do, but it's too risky. You've been attacked also and it appears, if we can trust the description of a frightened boy, the same person who ransacked the Yarrow's place may have attacked you. I have no choice, but to place him under house arrest."

Rand met Gus's direct eye contact with a furrowed brow. "He's only fourteen, Gus."

Wings of Steel

He glared at Rand with pursed lips and hands doubled in fists. "I know how old he is. Do you think I like the idea of putting him in jail? We don't have a juvenile facility and I certainly don't want to send him to another city where he could be locked up and forgotten."

"Then let him stay with us."

"Doggone it, Rand. I can't do that. So, get off my back." He swung around and marched half-way down the hall before turning back and pointing at Rand. "And stay out of it, that's an order." He punched the elevator button and got on.

The doctor stopped beside Rand and Cab. "I'm holding Cory here as long as I can." He left them to enter Cory's room.

Cab shook his head. "Are you ready to go?"

"I want to tell Cory I'm leaving."

"Okay, buddy, I'll wait in my car."

Rand waved at Cab and walked into Cory's room.

An orderly was leaving after bringing Cory's lunch. "Hi," she addressed Rand. "Are you, his father?"

He shot her a glance and emitted a strangled laugh.

The orderly gave him a perplexed look.

Rand tugged on his hat, looking at Cory. "Why do they keep asking me that?"

The orderly shook her head and left.

Rand sighed. "I need to go home, but I'll be back. Here's my phone number if you need anything, call me, even if it's just to talk, okay?"

"Okay." The boy's lower lip quivered. "Thanks for trying to stick up for me."

Rand's gaze riveted to Cory's face and his heart ached for him. "Call me anytime, day or night. I'm a light sleeper and there's a phone in my room."

"Can I ask you a question?"

"Sure." Rand studied him.

"Why do you care?"

He blinked. "Let's just say, I know how you feel."

"Have you ever been in jail?"

Rand swallowed hard. "Yes."

Cory gaped at him as understanding dawned on his face. "How long?"

Rand cuffed his shoulder. "Get some sleep. I'll be back tomorrow." He started for the door.

"Rand," he called quietly. "Can I give you my house key?"

He studied the boy's face. "Why?"

"There's a little book in my room on the bedside table. I'd like to have it, if it's still there. The key's in my jeans pocket."

He pulled Cory's dirty jeans out of the closet and found a small ring with three keys on it. He also grabbed the rest of his soiled clothes. "I'll take these, get them washed for you and try to get your book."

"Thanks for believing me." He chewed on his lower lip.

Rand tugged his hat lower on his forehead and proceeded out the door. In the hall, he swallowed around the lump in his throat.

Forty-Six

Rand awoke with a start and glanced at the clock on the fireplace mantle: 2:13 A.M. He stretched, got up from the chair and made his way outside through the library door and headed for his truck. Angel licked his hand in greeting. "This time you're going with me, girl." He opened his truck door and Angel jumped up on the passenger seat. He drove quietly around the square and turned onto the street where the Yarrow house was located. "Maybe I'll find something Gus missed, but mainly I want to get Cory's book." He told Angel and she yipped as if to agree.

The street was dark and he parked a few houses away from the Yarrow's. Police tape was all around the property and he was thankful he'd remembered his gloves. He jumped from the truck and waited for Angel before quietly closing the door.

He took the keys Cory gave him from his pocket, unlocked the side door, and followed Angel inside. *I'll find Cory's book and have a look around.*

He surveyed the sparsely furnished living room, which was a mess. He took note of the markings made by Gus and his deputies, which indicated the position of Mrs. Yarrow's body. Rand's throat constricted. He continued his search for the teen's room. It was the smaller of the two bedrooms with a twin bed, dresser and a small table with a lamp, but no book.

He left that room and crossed the hall to step into an office and found that room in the same disarray as the living room except for the carpet. A tingling sensation traveled up the back of his neck.

Angel sniffed briefly as a low growl rumbled in her throat. She barked and started running around the room sniffing and growling.

"Get 'em, girl." Rand's foot caught on something and he leaned over to grasp it. Before he could straighten up a hard object slammed into his side. He stumbled as a fist connected hard with his jaw. He threw an upper cut, which hit his attacker's throat.

The man hit the floor and kicked Rand's feet out from under him. Before he recovered, Angel was on top of the man, pinning him to the floor with her teeth bared.

Rand switched on a lamp and his eyebrows rose. "Sloan."

"Get this mutt off me!" He growled.

"Don't think so." Rand picked up the phone and dialed. "Gus, I'm at Yarrow's house. Think I found your man. I'll wait." He hung up.

Sloan threw a menacing scowl at Rand. "Should have killed you when I—"

"Assaulted me in the park?" Rand finished for him.

"I ain't sayin' nothin'." He grumbled.

Angel bared her teeth at Sloan when he sat up.

"Better chill." Rand warned. "She hasn't had breakfast yet."

"I'll kill you, Gray." He snarled.

Suddenly out of nowhere there were two loud blasts.

Rand hit the floor and lay completely still afraid to breathe. "Angel?" He whispered.

She whimpered and crawled over to him.

"You're hurt!" He raised his head slowly and peered over her to find Sloan's shirt covered with blood. The scuffle of running feet outside seized Rand's attention. A few minutes later, sirens filled the night along with voices outside. "Gus, in here!"

The door burst open and several pairs of feet stomped into the house.

Gus was the first one in the room. "What the—Rand, you alright?"

"Angel's been hit."

Gus stalked over to where Rand's attacker lay in his own blood. Gus rolled him over and stared at him in disbelief. "He's one of the men from the docks."

"Sloan." Rand mumbled.

Gus stooped and pressed a hand to his neck. "He's gone."

Rand inspected Angel's wound. "She needs a vet." He managed to say around the huge lump in his throat.

"I'll take you. Manny, you boys finish up here and bring me the report."

"Got it, boss."

Rand took off his jean jacket and carefully wrapped it around Angel. He picked her up and followed Gus to his car where she laid limply in his arms.

"What were you thinking? You could have been killed. I could arrest you for trespassing, obstructing justice, and interfering with a crime scene investigation. Do you realize how much trouble you could be in for this?"

Rand focused his attention on Angel, avoiding Gus's glare. He knew he'd overstepped the bounds of their friendship.

Gus took a deep breath and expelled it in a woosh. "Sloan was shot from behind. Did you know he had a gun?"

Rand shook his head.

Gus frowned. "Do you have a weapon?"

"A rifle locked in the gun cabinet at Candlewood." He responded while holding Angel. "Hollis pulled that knife on me when he and Sloan jumped me on the docks. You can verify that with Gage Fuller. Just before the shots, I think Sloan started to admit he attacked me in the park." He swallowed dryly. "The bullet that hit Angel was likely meant for me."

Gus shook his head. "I ought to arrest you for your own good."

Rand peered at the time on Gus's dash clock: 5:03 A.M. and then carefully lifted Angel from the car. They walked into the veterinary clinic in Montecito. He was thankful it was open at such an early hour. Angel had lost a lot of blood and Rand bit his lip as he laid her on the examining table. She fastened a sad expression on him. He patted her head. "You'll be alright, girl."

"Mister?"

Rand glanced at the man who wore a white coat.

"Please wait in the outer room."

He gave Angel one last pat and left the room.

Gus was standing, staring out the window when Rand joined him.

"She's going to make it, Gus. She has to."

He slowly faced Rand. "Sit down. I have something to tell you." They sat and Gus cleared his throat. "I just spoke with a special agent who happened to be here. He thinks Angel's the German shepherd they lost several months ago."

Rand swallowed hard. "What?"

"Agent Crawford thinks Angel's their dog. Think about it. She's been trained. We've both witnessed her in action."

"She's my dog now." He spoke with jaw clenched.

"I know how you feel. I've gotten kind of attached myself. But if they prove she belongs to them, you'll have to let her go."

Rand got up and began to pace. "She saved my life, twice. She even took a bullet for me."

"I wish there was something I could do, but—"

"There's got to be a mistake. You need to convince them—"

Gus stood and put his hand on Rand's shoulder. "Let's be honest, how many dogs have been trained the way she has?"

He shook off Gus's hand. "You don't understand."

A man in uniform interrupted them as he approached. "Special agent Larson." He showed them his badge. "I understand my dog got shot while protecting you, Mr. Gray. She's been missing since September. Surely you realized she's had special training."

"Just a minute." Gus interrupted. "I posted a notice that a dog, which apparently had some kind of training, was found in our area. No one responded even though I included a detailed description." He stressed the last two words.

The man's mouth stretched tight. "She has a lightning bolt tattooed in her left ear. That's how I identified her. You've taken good care of her. I appreciate it and I'm prepared to give you a thousand dollars."

Rand gave him a blank stare. "I don't want your money." He ground his teeth so hard it made his jaw ache. "I'd like to say good bye to her."

"I'm sorry. I can't allow that. She needs retrained to respond to her original name. No one but me will be speaking to her anytime soon. I already made out the check. Please, take it." He offered it to Rand.

He snatched it, tore it up and dropped it at the man's feet. Without a word he spun around and strode from the building without a backward glance. He flung himself onto the passenger seat of Gus's car as heat flushed through his body and his nostrils flared.

"Thanks, Larson!" Gus's retort was loud enough to reach Rand's ears from inside the police car.

Wings of Steel

Rand appreciated Gus's silence on the way back to Fire River. His posture was stiff and muscles rigid as he clenched and unclenched his fists. When Gus parked in front of Candlewood, Rand got out and shut the door harder than he intended. To avoid further conversation with Gus, he quickly marched across the stone pavement, up the steps, opened the door, entered and closed it behind him with a bang.

Cab came out of the library and stopped abruptly before he took a small step toward Rand. "What happened to—?"

He shook his head and indicated his blood-stained clothes with a wave of his arm. "An-gel's." His voice broke.

"Where is she?" Cab grasped Rand's shoulder.

His jaw clenched. "Gone."

"Gone?"

"Not now." Rand's words were a mere whisper. He shuffled through the library and out the side door. For a moment he half-expected Angel to lick his fingers in greeting. He tried to swallow the dryness in his throat and plodded down the path to sink onto the bench. He tried to imagine life without her and focused on the ground near his feet. *I'll never even know if she makes it.*

Netty watched from her shop window as Rand practically lunged from the patrol car. He stormed up the steps appearing as if he were ready for a fight. She chewed on her bottom lip, wondering what happened with Gus to make Rand so angry. Waiting only long enough for the sheriff's car to leave, she crossed the street, ran up the steps and let herself inside. "Rand?"

Cab came out of the library.

She took note of the grimace on his face and paused from her pursuit. "What's wrong with Rand?"

Cab shook his head sadly. "I got the impression something bad happened to Angel."

"I'd like to talk to him." She eyed him warily.

He sighed. "I'd give him some time—"

"I'll be careful." She responded quickly.

Cab shook his head and gestured toward the garden door.

She pondered his reaction for a moment and then hurried through the library and stepped outside. She scurried along the path toward the fountain. The closer she got to it the faster she walked.

Rounding the last curve, she spotted Rand. He was hurling stones at the fountain in rapid succession.

She jogged the rest of the way and stopped a few feet from him. She took note of his fisted hand, the swift motion of his arm as he drew back to fire off another stone. His legs were planted wide and everything about his stance screamed, approach with caution. He'd only invoked fear in her one other time. She discovered he was capable of withholding physical violence even when pushed to that point. She moved to stand at a safe distance from his side. "Rand," she spoke quietly, "what happened?"

He turned toward her, lowered his arms to his sides and released the remaining stones through his fingers. They hit the fountain's foundation. Clunk, clunk, clunk.

She gasped at his blood-stained clothes. "You're hurt!"

He was sweating profusely. His eyes were black as coal and his lips had a hard edge. His face was void of expression and his features pale and drawn.

She hesitated before lightly touching his shoulder. "What happened, cowboy?"

He drew his lips between his teeth to stop their quivering. and lowered his head to avoid her scrutiny.

"You're bleeding." She stepped close to his side.

He slowly shook his head.

She wrapped her arm around his waist. "Tell me what happened." She ran her hand across his back.

He swallowed hard without responding.

"Let's get you cleaned up a bit. Hopefully it'll make you feel better, okay?"

He squinted at the bloody streaks on his clothes and barely whispered. "Angel's."

She sighed with relief and smoothed his cheek with the palm of her hand. "Are you up to going back inside?"

He began walking so she caught his hand and stayed close to his side. When they stepped into the kitchen, he headed for his room, and shut the door behind him.

She stood by his door with arms crossed until she heard his bathroom door close.

Cab entered the room behind her. "Did he tell you what happened?"

She glanced at him. "Not exactly. Do you want to eat breakfast with us?"

Cab studied her a moment. "No, thanks. I'll check on him later."

She shrugged. "Suit yourself." She proceeded to fix bacon, eggs, toast and a pot of coffee.

When Rand came out of his room, breakfast was nearly ready and the coffee was brewing. She scrutinized him with her hands on her hips. "You look a lot better. Are you hungry?"

He shrugged and sat at the table. "Not really." His voice was a rough whisper.

"Maybe you'll feel more like eating later."

He gazed at her with a hollow expression. "Angel's gone." He drew circles on the tabletop with an index finger.

Her eyebrows arched. She decided she wasn't very hungry either. "What do you mean, gone?"

He shook his head. "She was . . . is a police dog."

Netty pulled a chair next to his, sat down and grasped his hand. "It was her blood on your—?"

"She saved, my life, again, and they kept her." He blinked rapidly several times then raised his head to peer at her with a perplexed expression. "I didn't even get to say, good-bye." His lips pulled into a wry smile.

"Let's go in the library where it's more comfortable." She suggested as she moved her chair away from the table. She could always reheat their breakfast later.

———

Once there, he sank onto one end of a couch, rested his head against the back and stared at the ceiling. "I don't even know if she's still—" He swallowed hard as he scanned the room and kept watching the door, as if he could by sheer effort cause Angel to materialize, push it open and bound into the room. He glanced at Netty as she sat beside him, but when she rested her hand on his chest and slipped her fingertips between the buttons of his shirt, he flinched and then frowned as he stared at her hand.

"Sorry!" She jumped up and smoothed her hands down the sides of her slacks. "How about some coffee? We can eat later if you get hungry."

His lips pulled into a thin line. "Okay."

She left and came back with a tray that held two cups and a carafe. After an uncomfortably long silence while they drank their coffee, she began asking questions. "Can you tell me now?"

Rand finished his coffee. "I was trying to help Cory."

She refilled their cups. "Who's Cory?" She took a sip and considered him with her head tilted slightly.

He twisted his cup in his hands. "A friend of Tommy's." *You can identify with him more than anyone you've ever met, pal.* He snatched a glimpse at Netty. *With one possible exception.*

"A teenager then?" She shook her head.

"Yeah." He sighed sadly.

Her brow creased with concern. "Where are his parents?"

He forked his fingers through his hair. "Gone."

She grasped his arm. "Don't make me pull it out of you, just tell me. It's plain it's upsetting you. I care about you and when you're hurt, it concerns me."

He flashed an apologetic smirk at her. "He found his mother on the floor, of their living room. Gus said he doesn't think Cory killed her, but he acts like Cory's guilty of something, but I believe there's more to it than any of us know." He bounced a fist against his mouth.

She put down her cup and drew him into her arms. "Why is he your problem?"

"I want Cory to stay with me."

"You're willing to take on responsibility for a teenage boy you barely know? At least you've never mentioned him to me."

"I'll get a lawyer and get custody if necessary."

She backed away and regarded him with wide-open eyes. "You're serious."

"I've never been more serious about anything."

She hugged him. "But you have your own worries. How can you take on any more?"

He raised an eyebrow as his heartrate quickened. "You object?"

She kissed his cheek. "You have a tender heart, Rand. I can hardly believe how much you've changed since I first met you."

He held his breath when she paused. *I haven't changed that much. Maybe she's beginning to see the real me.*

She winked at him. "I think maybe I'm only starting to find out what really makes you tick, cowboy."

He shrugged. *Does that mean she likes what she's discovered, pal?* He pulled her into the circle of his arms and as she rested her head against his chest, he told her every detail of the entire episode, beginning with accompanying Gus to the park and finding the knife. When he stopped talking, she gazed at him with what he hoped was admiration if not understanding. He lowered his head until her breath caressed his mouth, but pulled back just in time. He didn't want to give her the wrong impression again. They were still just friends and for now, he wanted to keep it that way.

Forty-Seven

Two days later Rand left the village square, turned onto East Twelfth Street and headed for the Yarrow house. He planned to run in, grab Cory's book and then take it to him. Not wanting to draw attention to his presence, he parked his truck behind the house in the alley. As before, he entered through the side door. In the daylight, he found Cory's room easily. The book was on the floor near the bed. He snatched it and tucked it in an inside pocket of his leather jacket.

"Hold it right there, Gray!" A deep voice ordered from behind him. "Put your hands up where I can see them."

Rand did as he was instructed and slowly spun around to confront the steely glare of the local deputy. He frowned. "Manny, I was just—"

"Deputy Perez to you, Gray. You're under arrest for trespassing and interfering with a crime scene."

Rand expelled a breath. "I can explain, I came to—"

"Save it. Turn around, put your hands behind you and no funny business." The deputy smirked.

Rand's chest constricted as he obliged and winced when a pair of handcuffs were clamped onto his wrists.

Afterward, Officer Perez grasped Rand's arm, ushered him out of the house and into the back of a patrol car. Once they reached the station, the deputy got out of the car and grabbed Rand's arm. "Let's go. Being a friend of the sheriff doesn't earn you the right to interfere with the law!"

A little while later in Montecito, Rod shook his client's hand. "It's been a pleasure doing business with you, Mr. Montrose. I'll have these blueprints ready by the first of next week. Once you have approved them, we'll visit the site together."

The slightly balding man smiled. "Thank you, Rod. I'm looking forward—"

The phone rang. "Monday morning at eight? Excuse me." Rod observed his client bob his head in agreement as he picked up the phone. "Coolidge and—what?" He waved at Mr. Miller and swung his back toward the door. "When did that happen? I'm on my way." He hung up, locked his desk and left his office. Outside he climbed in his car and quickly drove to Fire River.

Nearly an hour later, Rod parked behind the municipal buildings and entered the police station through the parking lot exit.

Gus met him in the hall. "Come in my office."

Moments later Rod stood next to Gus's desk. "Why is he here?"

"Why don't we sit down?"

Rod listened intently as Gus started from when he asked Rand along with Angel for help and finished with the second time Rand entered a house which was under police investigation.

Rod expelled a long-held breath and steepled his fingers while his elbows rested on the arms of his chair. "How long are you planning to keep him?"

"Doggone it, Rod, I warned him, several times to keep out of it, but he's dad burned bull-headed when it comes to that Yarrow kid."

Rod considered Gus's words. "I heard that both Cory's parents are gone."

Gus acknowledged his statement with his arms crossed. "Rand went to their house after I ordered him to stay away from that house. Twice!"

Speechless, Rod raised an eyebrow.

"My deputy arrested him and locked him up. And if that wasn't enough, his watch was found near the dead woman's body."

"What? You're not suggesting he's invol—" Rod crossed his arms. "Did he resist arrest?"

"That's not the point. I can't have him ignoring my orders without suffering the consequences." Gus took off his hat, swiped his brow with a handkerchief and put it back in his pocket. "I'm convinced he's in this only because of Cory, but there are those who aren't so sure. Rand better be careful. If he gets in any deeper, I may not be able to convince them of his innocence of anything other than interfering with our investigation."

Rod was aware that his brother often acted without considering the consequences, but he also believed he usually had good reason for his actions. "Does he know about his watch? You can't think Rand had anything to do with her death."

"At this point, it doesn't matter what I think or believe. You do remember the previous sheriff was relieved of duty when he was found to be incompetent." Gus held up his hands. "I don't believe Rand is responsible for what happened to her, but he hasn't listened to my orders to stay out of this either."

"Is there some other way we can work this out?"

"Will you guarantee he'll stop interfering in this case?"

Rod stroked his upper lip with his index finger. "I'd like to talk to him."

"Cab's already tried, but go ahead. Just so you know I'm not making any promises concerning his release." Gus growled. "He's in the back."

Rod reflected on Gus's comments for a moment before heading for the jail cells. He stopped in the doorway and regarded Rand, who was sitting on a cot with his arms resting on his legs and his head bowed, staring at the floor.

Rand raised his head when Rod stepped through the doorway.

Rod took note of the wary expression in his brother's eyes and heard him expel a low groan. He grabbed a chair and placed it in front of the bars. "Do you want to tell me what this is all about?" He asked as he sat down.

Rand scowled. "Figure Gus already did."

Rod crossed his arms. "He told me his version. I want to hear yours."

Rand matched his gaze without wavering. "Gus said he doesn't think Cory killed his mother, but that's not how he's acting. Like I already told you, I know what it's like to be accused of something I didn't do. I want Cory to know I believe he's innocent and want to help him."

Rod's brow wrinkled. "And how is getting put behind bars helping him? Be careful that you don't allow your past to determine your thinking about Cory's situation."

Rand gave him a wry grin.

Rod pressed his lips into a fine line. "Did Gus ask you to stay away from the crime scene?"

"More like he ordered." Rand grumbled.

Rod's steadfast look held Rand's attention. "But you haven't done as he asked."

Rand gave his head a curt shake while holding Rod's attention.

Rod sighed. "Why?"

"Cory asked me to get a notebook from his room. It seemed important to him."

Rod continued to maintain direct eye contact with Rand. "Did you get it?"

Rand's head bobbed affirmatively.

Rod slid his arm between the bars. "May I see it?"

Rand pulled the notebook from an inside pocket of his jacket, which was on the cot beside him. Tentatively, he gave it to Rod.

He took it and began leafing through it. "Have you looked at this?"

"Yes." His brow wrinkled as he bounced his fist against his mouth.

"It appears to be a collection of drawings." Rod contemplated them. "Except for the numbers on the inside of the back cover."

Rand leaped to his feet. "Let me see that."

Rod gave it back to him.

Rand mulled over the numbers and then reached in his jacket pocket and pulled out a ring of keys. "Look at this." He held one key separate from the rest and compared it with one of the numbers in the book. "This number matches the one on this key. My post office box key looked just like this. Will you show these to Gus?"

Rod pulled his keys from his suit pocket to study them.

Gus stepped into the room just then. "Show me what?"

Rod gave the notebook and keys to Gus. "Compare the number in the book to the number on the little key. Then look at my key to the post office."

Gus studied them with arched brows. "So, they're the same. What am I missing?"

Rand gazed steadily at the sheriff. "The sketches in that book were made by Cory's dad. One of those numbers, which appears to be a random figure in the list, matches the number on the little key on the other ring, which also belonged to Cory's dad. The little key's exactly like Rod's post office box key."

Gus stared at the number in the notebook and then at the one on the small key on the ring. "Where did you get these?"

Rand tilted his head. "Cory's dad gave his keys to him along with the book before he left. He told Cory not to tell his mother he had them."

Gus raised an eyebrow. "Cory gave these to you?"

Rand chewed on the inside of his jaw before responding. "Just before I left the hospital. I found the notebook in Cory's room on the floor."

Gus's brow furrowed. "I'm going to pay Willis a visit. Will you be here when I get back?" He asked Rod.

He nodded, and watched Gus leave before continuing his conversation with Rand. "Cab told me you want Cory to stay with you."

Rand concentrated on his hands before responding. "Did he say whether he approved or not?"

Rod crossed his arms. "He isn't totally against it."

Rand's mouth drew a straight line. "So, he's hoping you'll change my mind, is that it?"

Rod shook his head. "There's something I want to discuss with you."

Rand mumbled something unintelligible under his breath. "Okay, shoot."

Gus returned to interrupt them and unlocked Rand's door and opened it. "You're free to go, for now, but stay out of this. Next time I'll lose the cell key on purpose."

Rand grabbed his jacket and hat and quickly stepped past Gus.

Rod crossed his arms and appraised Gus's face, waiting for an explanation. "Hopefully there won't be a next time."

Gus took off his hat, ran his fingers through his hair and turned his hat in his hands. "I will be very interested to hear what happens because of the contents of that box. It could be what they were looking for."

"What about Willis?" Rand asked.

A smirk appeared on Gus's face. "I sent him on an errand while I confiscated the contents of that box."

Rand set his hat on his head and shot a grin at Rod. "Let's get out of here."

Rod put a hand on Rand's shoulder as they left the station. "Where's your truck?"

Rand fired a sheepish glance at him. "I left it behind Yarrow's house. But—it's parked out here."

Rod frowned. "I'll bring you back here then, but first let's grab a cup of coffee."

Rand climbed inside Rod's car without a comment.

A short time later, Rod parked next to a coffee shop in Montecito. "After I drop you off, I need to pick up some paperwork from my office." He explained as they stepped inside.

Rand chose a secluded corner table and Rod sat across from him.

A waitress took their order and returned with two coffees.

After several minutes, Rand peered at Rod with uplifted brows. "You said you wanted to talk to me about something?"

Rod nodded and took another sip from his cup. "Saun and I have been praying for Cory since Tommy told us his dad left and his mother was an alcoholic. I spoke with Mrs. Yarrow a few weeks ago after Cory told Tommy she was talking about sending him away. Saun and I would like to help him, but didn't want to pursue it any further without talking with you first."

"She was talking about sending him away? Where to? What do you have in mind?"

Rod regarded him closely. "We were considering the same type of action you were until Cab told me this morning what you said about Cory."

Rand twisted his coffee cup back and forth on the table.

"If you're serious about Cory staying with you—"

"You're thinking of taking on another teen?" Rand stared at Rod with his mouth open. "Don't you and Saun want kids of your own?"

Rod lowered his gaze to the tabletop. "We aren't able to have biological children, but we both feel very strongly about helping those who need responsible parents."

Rand's face flushed. "Are you saying I'm not responsible?"

Rod grasped Rand's balled-up fist. "Of course not. I was referring to Cory's parents. You'd make a wonderful father, but do you really want to tie yourself down with that kind of responsibility. I get the impression that you aren't happy here in Fire River and it's only your newly-found family that's keeping you here."

The fire in Rand's face cooled somewhat at Rod's comment. "You really want to take on raising him?"

Rod took note that Rand didn't refute either comment about his happiness or intent on staying. "We could give him a good home. He and Tommy are friends and we would be able to provide for Cory's college education."

Rand crossed his arms. "I've given serious thought to applying for guardianship of him."

Rod rested his elbows on the table and steepled his fingers. "You can still do that if it's what you want. We will defer to your plans for the boy."

Rand's jaw clenched as he focused on the table in silence for several breaths. Finally, after composing himself, he raised his focus to lock on Rod. "I didn't know you were that concerned about Cory, but you have better resources, a home and ready-made family. I think he would be better off with you in the long run. He needs stability. I don't even have a permanent job." His lips tipped in a wry grin. "At least I'd get to be his uncle."

Rod's eyebrow raised. "One more thing."

One corner of his lips tipped upward. "What's that?"

He steepled his fingers and peered at Rand over the top of them. "I promised Gus you'd leave police business to him."

Rand flashed him a wide grin. "You shouldn't make promises you can't keep."

Forty-Eight

Rand entered Clayton's office and was ushered into a private room. "The doctor will be with you shortly." The receptionist told him before closing the door.

Unable to sit still, Rand paced the small space in front of the desk. Dr. Mills told him this would be his final session, if everything went well today. Weary of going over his past, he tugged at his collar and then the brim of his hat. He stopped abruptly when the door swung open and Clayton entered.

"Good morning, Rand." He greeted him with a handshake and closed the door behind him. "I'm going to ask you to do something that you may be uncomfortable with. Will you trust me?"

Rand rubbed the back of his neck and gazed at the floor while he pondered Clayton's question. After several moments, he responded with a hesitant bob of his head.

"I want you to go in that room." The doctor pointed to a closed door. "Once you shut the door behind you, take off your shirt and then turn on the light. Please do it in that exact order."

Rand's eyes narrowed. "What's in there?" He cocked his head to the side. "Will I be alone?"

"Completely. You can leave your jacket and hat out here."

Sweat beaded on Rand's forehead as he angled away from Clayton to squint at him for several heartbeats. Finally, deciding the good doctor had proved to be trustworthy, he removed his jean jacket and hat. He dropped the jacket on the chair in front of the desk and set his hat on top of it.

"I'm setting a timer. I want you to remain in there without your shirt for at least ten minutes."

He stared at the door the doctor indicated. "I don't understand, why do I—?"

"Relax. You will be able to hear the timer with the door closed. When it goes off, you can open the door as soon as you choose." He set the alarm.

Rand shuddered involuntarily at the ticking of the timer. What could it hurt to step into an unfamiliar room?

"It's completely empty." The doctor encouraged him.

His jaw clenched as he stared suspiciously at Clayton. "I'm not sure—"

"I know this seems strange, so you'll have to trust me."

He fastened a probing gaze on Clayton's face, trying to remember every encounter he'd ever had with the doctor.

"I can't force you to do it, Rand."

With his hand on the doorknob, he rubbed the back of his neck as he eyed Clayton. "This seems like—"

"I'll stay right here." He sat down at his desk.

With trembling fingers, Rand opened the door, but before stepping inside made sure it wouldn't lock on the outside. He stole a quick glance at Clayton, who gave him an encouraging smile.

When Rand shut the door, he was enveloped in utter darkness, except for a small swish. Something moved in front of him and the hairs on the back of his neck tingled. His heartrate escalated rapidly and he extended his hands in front of his face. He came in contact with cool drapery-like material. *The soft swish I heard.* His chest was tight. It was difficult to breathe. He rubbed sweaty palms against his jean-clad legs.

He ground his teeth and pressed his lips tightly together when the timer on Clayton's desk sounded. *I've been in here for the whole time and all I've done is close the door.* He took a deep breath. With trembling fingers, he slowly unbuttoned his shirt, let it slide off his shoulders, and down his arms. He grasped it in one fist in case he needed to pull it back on quickly.

Frantically, he inspected the smooth walls, searching for the light switch. Finally, he took a step to the side as a string hanging beside his head startled him. He snatched it and gave it a quick yank. A bright overhead light came on and he blinked at his reflection in the mirror in front of him. His mouth dropped open and his shirt slipped from his fingers.

He stared speechless at the reflection of his face in the mirror. He perused his image, beginning with his head. He didn't consider himself a knockout, but some women found him attractive. His mother, in fact, recently referred to him as 'a charmer'. He shrugged as a small smile tugged at one side of his lips. He did appreciate when a particularly good-looking woman noticed him, but he'd also been burned by that kind of attraction so he learned to let those go by without much thought.

His face heated as he recalled how Claire's scathing insults devastated him emotionally while he was still vulnerable from the physical abuse he'd suffered at Monza's hands. Rand believed she loved him and when he had recovered sufficiently enough to return to work, he proposed to her, but instead of saying no, she degraded and ridiculed him. His jaw clenched.

Reluctantly, he let his gaze travel slowly down to his neck and then his shoulders. He inhaled sharply. There were no welts or ugly red marks. All at once he discovered he was surrounded by mirrors. His mouth dropped open and he began to gingerly examine what he could reach of his skin. He fixated his attention on his back, which had received the most damage. There were scars, but after fourteen years the tiny thread-like marks were almost invisible.

Lord, I forgive her and myself for allowing her cruel, degrading words to torment me for so long. He raised his head as a slow smile hitched a corner of his mouth. The tension left his body and he began to laugh. In a dimly lit room, the scars would be totally invisible. He ran his hands through his hair as his eyebrows squished together for a few moments until a sort of giddiness bubbled up within him. His head reared back and his deep belly-laughter filled the small room.

After a time, he spun around, opened the door and stepped out of the closet with a slow, disbelieving shake of his head. Unable to express what he experienced, he stopped to stare at Clayton before he strode across the room and grasped the knob on the office door. A wide smile stretched his lips upward. "Thanks, Doc."

Clayton stifled a grin. "Hold up there, Rand. You're forgetting something."

He froze, his hand immediately going to his bare chest as his face heated like it was on fire. He ran back to the room and snatched his shirt from the floor. Hastily he slipped it on, rushed to grab his hat and jacket and sank breathless onto the chair in front of Clayton's desk. "I don't know what to say except I feel kind of stupid, right now." His skin was tingling and he could hardly sit still long enough to button his shirt.

Clayton chuckled as he appraised Rand's face. "I'm glad the experiment worked."

Rand grinned as his body temperature rose with restrained laughter and appreciation for the good doctor's unconventional method. He set his hat on his head and touched the brim as he stood. "Guess I won't need to come back."

The corners of Clayton's eyes crinkled. "I'm always available if you need me."

He slung his jacket over his shoulder. "Yee ha!" He yelled before jerking open the office door and striding out the exit.

---***---

Rand's shoulders relaxed and a slow smile played on his lips as he drove back to Candlewood. He parked in his usual place, scrambled up the steps and burst into the hall. "Cab?" After a quick search of the library from the hall doorway, he spun around to peer out the door. His car wasn't out there. He paused. *She'll understand, pal.*

He rushed into his bedroom, tossed his jacket at a chair and set his hat on his dresser. He discarded his shirt and snatched a black T shirt from his closet and set his matching hat on his head. Before rushing out the door, he paused. *Lord, I need Your help with what I'm about to do.* His steps slowed. *If this is a big mistake...* He took a deep breath to curb his adrenaline rush so he wouldn't arrive at her shop sweaty and breathless.

---***---

A few moments later, he bolted into her shop and tossed his hat in the air. "Yee ha!" He watched her hands fly to her chest.

"You startled me." She laughed. "What's going on?"

He grabbed her around the waist and twirled her in circles, causing them both to laugh.

"What're we celebrating, cowboy?" She managed in between spurts of laughter.

"Freedom!" He tried to slow his breathing so he could talk.

She raised her eyebrows and her gaze appraised him from head to toe and back again. "I don't think I've ever seen you so, excited, or happy. Your face is flushed and your smile is stretching off your face!" She laughed.

He peered at her beneath his dark eyelashes while his heart drummed in his ears and warmth radiated through his body. *Please help her understand, Lord.* "Don't jump to any conclusions, but I want to show you something. And then I'll try to explain."

He grasped her hand, pulled her into her stock room, closed the door and turned on the light. Slowly he swung his back toward her and then pulled his shirt off, but held onto it with one hand. "This happened a long time ago." He paused when she drew in a deep breath and the back of his throat began to ache. He forced himself to remain still even though he was tempted to pull his shirt back on and run out the door.

"Oh." She whispered.

He flinched at her tentative touches on his back and shoulders. Every contact sent prickles of electricity skittering along his skin. As he started to pull his shirt back on, she sucked in air that was more like a sniff. He froze as his stomach churned and dizziness struck him. *She's shocked, disgusted, or worse. Pities me.*

"What caused these marks, Rand?" She whispered, caressing his back with exploring fingers that were both curious and soothing.

"I told you about Al, my best friend. His brother—" His voice was husky and he found it difficult to breathe. He stood trembling as her fingers trailed gently back and forth across his back, and he imagined she was tracing the lines, which were all that remained of his scars.

She continued stroking his skin several times before, resting her head against the back of his shoulder so that her mouth was close to his ear. "What happened to you?" She whispered.

He leaned his head against hers, enjoying their closeness. Netty's tender acceptance soothed his shattered self-esteem and belief that no woman would ever want to be with him for long.

Netty wrapped her arms around his waist from behind him and held him tight.

Desire permeated his core like hot lava at the brush of her warm breath on his neck and he was tempted to throw away all restraint. He spun around and held her close to his chest and allowed himself to thoroughly enjoy her acceptance for a moment. Quickly, before he could no longer suppress his longing, he backed out of her embrace and pulled on his shirt. "I could use some coffee." His voice was a hoarse whisper as he leaned against a supply shelf. He peered at her and winced at the mixture of puzzlement and desire on her face. "I'm sorry, Netty. I didn't mean to start something, I—" He blinked and lowered his head to stare to the floor.

"No offence taken, Rand. I get this is monumental for you." She raised his head, cupped his chin in her hands, and kissed his cheek. After gazing at him for a moment, she slid her arms around his waist and held him tight. "I'm going to close. No more appointments today. Let's go up to my apartment." She stepped away from him and went to lock the front door.

As soon as she left him, he missed the warmth of her presence. *Help me explain this to her, Lord.*

He settled back against the couch cushions in her small apartment as his muscles lost their tension. He closed his eyes and inhaled the spicy scent of Netty's perfume, which permeated the couch and pillows.

She entered the room, carrying two cups. She gave one to him and then sat next to him. "I'm all ears, darlin', if you want to tell me about it."

He smiled at her over the edge of his cup and released a breath he didn't realize he'd been holding. He allowed himself to unwind as he drank his coffee and scanned the room. He peered at a picture of her and her dad on the bookshelf. With cup in hand, he leaned his head against the couch. *I could get use to this.* Mentally, he shook his head. *Where did that thought come from, pal?*

Netty touched his hand. "Your cup is empty. Do you want more?"

He turned his head without lifting it from the cushion and gave her the cup. "Maybe, in a little while." His eyes were half closed. *How can I even begin to tell her?*

She set her cup next to his on the coffee table and grasped the hand he rested on the couch between them. Holding it with both of hers, she stared at him. "What caused those marks, Rand?" She asked softly.

He drew a deep breath, exhaled and slowly began telling her the story of his life. "I told you I spent time in jail—"

"Yes, and the way you were treated wasn't fair. It wasn't like you meant to hurt your friend." She grumbled.

He gave her a wry grin and sighed. "Yeah, and they also gave me five years on probation."

"Rand, I'm so sorry." She hugged his side. "Is that when you got hurt while you were in jail?"

He stared at her for several moments. "I worked on Frank Sim's ranch during probation. One day when I was mucking out the stalls while Frank went to pick up feed for the horses, someone knocked me out from behind."

Netty waited a few seconds and when he didn't continue, she crossed her arms. "I can't imagine you not putting up a fight."

He hung his head as his cheeks began to heat. "I woke up when a wave of cold water hit my face. My hands and feet were tied. Monza kicked me several times with the toe of his boot and laughed when I had trouble breathing." Rand slumped against the cushions as the memory assaulted him. "After that he hit me with his belt. Every time I passed out, he threw a bucket of water in my face."

She sniffed. "How old were you?"

He blinked. "Seventeen."

Her jaw dropped. "What stopped him?"

"Frank told me later that he came back and ran Monza off with a shotgun."

"Was the monster punished for what he did?" She growled.

"He was the judge's son and apparently ran, but no one bothered to go after him."

"How badly were you hurt?"

"I had several cracked ribs and had to have skin grafts on my back and shoulders."

Netty's eyebrows rose. "Was that him at the restaurant up in the mountains where we went last year."

Rand clenched his teeth and stared at the floor. "Yeah."

"But we managed to get away. Do you think he found you?"

"I'm not sure. I think he might be responsible for my wreck, but Gus thinks it was locals."

She took a drink from her cup and sputtered. "This is cold. I'll make a fresh pot."

"Wait." He threaded his fingers through hers, thankful she didn't seem bothered either by his appearance or worse for being a coward. "If I don't finish now, I may never find the courage again."

She set her cup back down. "Sorry, I didn't mean to interrupt." She slid her arm around behind him and held him close. "You must have been badly hurt if you were hospitalized. How long were there?"

He shrugged. "Too long." He glanced at her tear-streaked face. "Please don't, don't pity me, Netty." There was a hitch in his voice. "I couldn't stand—"

She kissed his cheek. "I don't, pity you, Rand. You're the bravest man I've ever known and I'm not just talking physically."

"Frank's daughter returned shortly after I went back to work for him. We'd been going together before I was hospitalized." His brows drew together and his Adam's apple bobbed. "I asked her to marry me. Instead of telling me no, she—"

"You deserve someone better than her, darlin'." Netty pulled him close and slipped her arms around him. Softly she stroked his back and shoulders and kissed his cheek, his hair and his forehead.

He whispered quietly "She got all hysterical when she saw—"

"She left because you'd been hurt?" Netty's voice arose several decibels.

He raised an eyebrow at her enraged tone. "That's what I thought, at the time. Now I think it was just an excuse."

"Whatever her thinking was, Rand, you are better off without her." Netty's gaze captured his.

He found only honest compassion in her warm expression. He brushed a tear from her cheek with his thumb. "I hoped you'd understand." He whispered hoarsely. "I wanted you to know why—"

"Shh, it's okay." She placed a finger against his lips.

One side of his mouth lifted when she removed her finger. Unable to say more he dared to entertain the thought that they might eventually be more than friends.

She slowly searched his face. "I'm proud of the man you've become, Rand. I want to kiss you, but it doesn't feel right at the moment."

Agreeing, he swallowed hard. "How'd you get so smart, red?" He wanted to kiss her too, wrap his arms around her and hold her close, but not after talking about his past. His emotions were too close to the surface. His desire for complete acceptance too strong and he was more vulnerable at that moment than he'd ever been with anyone since Claire. He stared into her soft blue-green eyes, which always reminded him of the Eastern white pines in Arizona. He breathed deeply and heaved a sigh of relief. "I think I'd like that coffee now."

Forty-Nine

Monza left a diner and strolled down the street. He'd passed a church on the way and the singing from within reminded him of the few times he and his brother went with their mother on Sundays. They'd endured it mostly to please her, but neither of them paid attention and often made fun of the people who attended, except for her. He paused almost a block away near some bushes to listen to the music, which was so familiar that it brought tears to his eyes.

Drawn by an unexplainable emotion, he stood still on the sidewalk, observing as people began spilling out of the doors. He watched an old woman make her way slowly down the steps and head in his direction. Even as he took off his leather jacket and tossed it into the bushes, he found his actions curious even to himself. He paid special attention to the familiar person who began to descend the steps and turned to say something to the man who was behind him with a woman and two young boys.

He zeroed in on the people on the steps at the same time keeping an eye on the old woman navigating toward him. He put on his friendliest face and summoned up his best manners. "Excuse me, madam, I got here too late for church, but I want to surprise Rand Gray. We went to school together and I was passing through the area and hoped to see him."

The woman gave him a toothless grin as she pointed at the church. "That's him there on the sidewalk with his brother, Rod, and his family. They're lovely people, active in the church too. Rod is an architect in fact his office is right here in Montecito over on Rosewood Boulevard. Hope you have a nice visit, sonny." She meandered on down the walk leaning heavily on her cane.

Monza kept his gaze fastened on Rand during his encounter with the woman. He noted the truck Rand drove and the car his brother and his family climbed into. He chuckled to himself as he kept the bushes between him and the church goers until all the cars left the church's parking lot.

Once he was sure everyone was gone, he extricated himself from the bushes, retrieved his jacket, and strolled toward his bike.

Fifty

Rand parked his truck in front of Chino Café, climbed out and crossed the patio to enter the front door and walked up to the counter.

"Hello, Rand." Silas Jones, the small owner with thinning hair, greeted him. "Rosey's in the back checking out. Can I get you something while you wait?"

"Coffee, thanks." He reached in his pocket for his wallet.

"It's on the house." Silas waved away Rand's hand as he set a cup on the counter.

Rand grinned. "Thanks, Si."

"Hey, I was wondering if you could make me a China cabinet or something similar. My wife's been collecting tea cups and I'd like to get her something real nice to display them in."

Rand shrugged. "Sure. Do you have any specific ideas?"

"As a matter of fact, I do." He pulled a small notebook out from under the counter. "Here's some pictures I found in a magazine. I took the liberty of estimating the size and even wrote down some measurements." He passed the notebook across the counter.

Rand opened it and scanned the pictures as he drank his coffee. "Do you have a favorite or two out of these?"

"Not really. I was thinking more like a one-of-a-kind. The pictures are just to give you some idea what I have in mind. I'd prefer you use your own creative imagination. I was getting a haircut at Netty's shop last week and saw the shelf you made for her. You're a real craftsman, Rand. I'd be willing to pay you more than what they're asking for those machine-made cabinets."

Rand raised an eyebrow. "I prefer to have some idea what you'd like."

"Okay then, light colored wood, maybe maple with glass doors and wood shelves with lighting inside. Other than the dimensions, that's the only real requirement I can think of. I'll leave the rest up to you. I saw the treasure chest you helped Tommy make for his girlfriend and the shelf you made for W. T. The carving on that little box is beautiful. My wife would be thrilled with a well-crafted cabinet with fancy carving like that on it."

Rand thumbed through the notebook. "Okay if I take this with me?"

"I was hoping you would."

Rand closed the book and smiled. "I'll take these and sketch some ideas. Are you wanting it anytime soon?"

"No hurry, thanks."

"Hey Rand." Rosey greeted him.

He tipped his hat. "I have your table in my truck. I can follow you to your place if you're ready to go."

"I'm ready. Thanks for letting me leave early, Si. I'll make up my time tomorrow." She pivoted to follow Rand out of the café.

He followed Rosey's blue Ford pickup until she pulled into an alley along the side of a three-story brick building.

She parked behind it and got out of her truck.

Rand pulled into the spot beside her. As he strolled around to the back of his truck, the hairs on his neck began to tingle and he scanned the entire area.

The asphalt parking lot was bordered by alleys on both sides of the building with two large pockmarked dumpsters along the back. Take out wrappers and cups, beer bottles and cigarette butts were scattered around the perimeter. A scroungy dog rooted through a bag of garbage on the ground beside a dumpster. The air behind the apartment building reeked with motor oil, animal waste and the odor of burnt food, which drifted out from one of the tenant's windows.

Rand lifted the table from his truck bed while a stiff breeze threatened to snatch away his hat. He set one end of the table down and tugged on his hat to set it more firmly on his head. As he followed Rosey to the side where the entrance was located, yeast from the bakery on the other side of the alley began to mingle with the stench made by the rest.

Inside the building, they climbed three flights of stairs. He waited for her to unlock the door and then entered the apartment after her. "Where do you want this?"

"Under the hanging light in the dining area, please."

He set the table where she indicated.

Since she only got a glimpse of it from the back of his truck, she walked all around it and admired his craftsmanship. "It's beautiful! I love the designs you carved on the legs and around the sides. I'll have to leave it uncovered to enjoy when I'm not using it." She stepped into his personal space. "Thanks, Rand. Here's the money we agreed on, and I'd like to fix you dinner sometime. I have a feeling it's worth a lot more than you charged me."

He backed up a step, smiling, arms uplifted with palms out. "I'm glad you're happy with it." He tipped his hat. "I have things I need to do so—"

"Okay, thanks again. Next time you come in the café, I'll fix you something special."

He shrugged and went down the stairs.

Since he was in Montecito and in no particular hurry to return to Candlewood, and parking places around Rod's office were usually filled, he chose to walk the few blocks. He strode up to the office, but it was dark inside and the door was locked.

Stuffing his hands in his jean jacket pockets, he chose to walk back the way he came and stop at a little coffeehouse. He passed storefronts, having windows with colorful displays. Some were adorned with striped awnings over their entrance. The sidewalks were tree-lined with wooden boxes overflowing with bright flowers or potted plants on either side. The light posts also held hanging flower baskets. Pedestrians passed him going the opposite direction and some stopped to talk to their acquaintances.

The streets were single lane traffic each way and he only crossed one, having a traffic light. He also passed a post office, a bank, a pawn shop and a deli before reaching his destination. Loud music from a bar, which opened into the alley behind the coffeehouse, accosted his ears before he stepped inside.

He breathed deeply, appreciating the aroma of freshly brewed coffee mixed with fresh-baked cookies and muffins, which tempted his taste buds. He stood in line at the counter while customers who called out their orders tried to be heard over coffee grinders, the murmur of voices, laughter, spoons clinking against the sides of mugs and the ding of the cash register.

After paying for his coffee, he chose a small corner table and sat with his back to the wall. Once seated, he lowered the brim of his hat and observed the patrons. His drink was strong and hot, just the way he liked it. There was a table of four young women, all of them trying to talk at once. At another table two men dressed in suits were having what appeared to be a serious discussion when one of them suddenly leaned back in his chair, and laughed heartily. Rand smiled to himself, finished his coffee and left.

He walked a little faster on the way back, hoping Rod had returned, but his office was still dark with the door locked. Rand sighed and proceeded to the parking lot where he'd left his truck. Large oak, maple and palm trees lined the back of the lot behind the dumpsters. Rand guessed they were intended to create privacy for the residents on the other side since the spaces between the trees were filled with shrubbery.

The back of his neck prickled. There was no one else in the lot and even the birds that were chattering when he got out of his truck earlier were silent or gone. He quickly scanned the immediate area as he reached in his pocket for his keys.

"What's your hurry, Gray?" An all-too-familiar voice accosted him from behind.

He swiftly pivoted to face the one person he dreaded most and freed his hand from his pocket.

The man reeked of alcohol and wore a smirk.

Rand immediately assumed a stance and raised his fists in self-defense.

"Surprise." Monza scoffed and threw a punch at Rand's head.

He ducked.

Monza aimed another at Rand's belt.

He dodged that strike also.

Monza swung again and his fist made a dent in the door of Rand's truck when he side-stepped it. Monza growled and swung again.

Rand took the hit on his shoulder and countered with a left hook.

Monza avoided it, grabbed Rand's wrist and twisted it behind him.

He clenched his teeth to keep from yelling.

Monza's foot connected with the back of Rand's knee and shoved him forward.

He dropped to the ground, rolled out of Monza's reach, and quickly sprang to his feet.

Monza's body slammed into his side with full force.

The impact stole Rand's breath, making him stumble, but determination kept him on his feet.

Monza grabbed him and began squeezing Rand's neck.

He pivoted his hips and jabbed his elbow into Monza' torso with full of force.

"Oof!" Monza doubled over, wheezing and glared at Rand with glassy eyes. "I'll kill you, Gray!" He gasped barely speaking above a whisper. He leaned with his hands on his knees while his features contorted grotesquely.

Rand breathed in small gulps. His side throbbed as he stared at Monza with wide open eyes. Resuming his stance, he poised to throw another punch. Sweat beaded on his forehead and his shirt stuck to his skin.

"Police, put your hands up!" A deep voice penetrated the silence.

With a quick jerk upward, Monza bolted for the bushes and disappeared through the trees.

Rand's entire body pulsated from the unexpected exertion. Physically drained he gaped at the bushes where Monza escaped seconds earlier. His side throbbed, where Monza rammed into him. He stood panting.

"You okay, son?" A hand rested on his shoulder.

Rand flinched and attempted to shake his head, but could only manage a short bob.

"That your truck?" The older man, holding a bullhorn, pointed at Rand's pickup.

"Yeah." Rand whispered hoarsely.

"Name's Jasper. I own Beck's hardware." The man was muscular, but a few inches shorter than Rand. "My neighbor ran into my store and said there was trouble out here. Figured the police wouldn't get here in time so thought I'd help out."

Rand leaned against his truck. "Thanks."

Jasper scrunched his nose as he gave Rand the once-over. "Do I know you?"

Rand paused. "I've, been in your store several times."

Jasper scratched his chin. "I recon that's why you seem familiar. You going to be alright?"

Rosey came running around the corner and joined the two men. "Are you okay, Rand?"

"Yeah." He unlocked his door and sank onto the seat.

She held a paper cup filled with water. "Drink this"

Rand swung his feet under the steering wheel, received the cup, and then leaned his head against the back of his seat. After drinking the water, he closed his eyes.

Jasper walked up to the driver's side of Rand's truck. "Might want to get yourself checked out at the hospital. You look kind of peaked." He closed Rand's door.

Rosey slid into the passenger seat. "Do you need to go to the hospital?"

Jasper turned from the truck. "You best let him catch his breath first."

Rand's lips stretched into a thin line as his mind replayed the entire scuffle. *Faced Monza, still alive.* Mentally he shook his head. *My defense stunned him. Was that fear in his eyes along with anger? What if he hadn't surprised me the first time? Could I have defended myself back then?*

"Rand."

He flinched and peered at Rosey.

"Jasper said he'd call the police if you want him to and tell them you went to the hospital."

Rand thought about the ramifications of involving the police. They would ask questions, which he wasn't prepared to answer and would likely detain him possibly for hours. Meanwhile Monza would have opportunity to stage another surprise attack. "I don't think it's necessary to involve the police. Did he see you?"

She studied him momentarily and then shrugged. "Maybe, before I went to get Jasper. Why?"

Rand clasped her hand. "Go throw a few things in a suitcase and come right back."

"Rand, what in the wor—"

"Just do it, fast!" He gently, but firmly squeezed her hand.

"But I—?"

"Hurry!" He raised his voice more than he intended. "You won't be safe here."

She jumped out of the truck and ran back into her apartment building.

Sitting alone in his truck, Rand kept sweeping the area with his gaze, quickly focusing on anything and everything that moved. A stray tiger-striped cat, a squirrel, a sack that tumbled across the lot with the light breeze. A woman parked her car and eyed him warily when she got out and scurried across the lot and up the steps. A few seconds later a door slammed.

Rand scrubbed his hand through his hair. Climbed out of his truck, and walked across the lot to retrieve his hat. He picked it up and slapped it against his leg to get the dust off and set it on his head. As he started back to his truck, Rosey came out of the building, carrying a suitcase and an overnight bag. He took them from her and winced as he placed them behind the seat.

Rosey frowned when he headed out of Montecito. "Don't you need to stop at the hospital?"

He shrugged. "Why'd you move here?"

"My horse fell during a race six months ago and I hurt my back. I've been told I can't race anymore." She was silent for several moments. "I saw you ride out the other day on a motorcycle. Wouldn't you rather be riding horses?"

Rand chuckled at the disbelief in her voice. "Never owned a horse. Biking is more fun because all the skill depends on me."

She licked her lips. "Do you ever ride with anyone?"

"I'm pretty much a loner."

She stared at him. "My doctor told me before I came to spend time with Katie that I'd never be able to race again and I was pretty bummed about it. Still am, I guess."

He snatched a glimpse at her face. "I'm sorry, especially since it's something you really enjoyed."

"I was well on my way to win a championship." She raised and lowered her shoulders. "So now I have to figure out the rest of my life, you know?"

"I understand." He observed her chestnut hair, which cascaded over her shoulders in deep waves and her dark blue eyes. He found her personality pleasant and she obviously enjoyed ranch life, but he wasn't interested in anything other than casual female acquaintances. She caught him perusing her from the corner of his eye and he tugged the brim of his hat a little lower.

Rosey smiled. "Have you lived in Fire River very long?"

"Two years." He focused on the road.

"Where are you from?" Her gaze was penetrating. "I mean where were you born?"

"Arizona."

"Katie and I were best friends in school. She came here after college, but we've always kept in touch."

Rand took note of the looks Rosey tried to sneak at him and a wry grin tugged at his mouth. "What?"

Her face heated to a bright shade of pink. "I don't mean to stare, but you seem familiar. Did you ever go to the local rodeos?"

He raised one brow. "A few."

"Did you ride broncs?"

Took her long enough to make the connection. He swallowed before responding. "Might have."

She scrunched her nose as she stared at him. "Did you go by Smokey Roe?" She relaxed as if relieved for having solved her puzzle.

He rolled his neck and pointed to the Inn. "We're here."

They exited his truck at the same time and walked into Seabreeze together. After he introduced Rosey to his mother, he carried her luggage to her room and set it down outside her door.

"Are you doing all of this just to protect me from Monza?" She asked as she opened her door.

He tipped his hat. "Just a precaution. I don't want him coming after you because he saw you with me."

"What about the table you made for me? I don't want anything to happen to it."

He frowned. "Do you have any other furniture?"

"No, the apartment was furnished." She grasped his arm. "Won't you at least let me pay for my room here?"

"You'll be able to walk to work from here and I'll get your truck and the rest of your things to you as soon as possible. If you need anything before then, have mother call me. She usually knows how to find me." He tipped his hat and turned to walk back down the hall.

"Rand?"

He stopped without turning to face her.

"I guess you'll need these."

He turned to see her keys dangling from her fingers. A smile quirked his lips. "Might come in handy at that."

"Thank you for being so—oh, just thank you."

He gave her a backhanded wave and left.

———◦◦◦———

That night Rand awoke with a start and glanced around the room in a state of temporary confusion. He was lying on a couch in the library. Alone in the room, he'd been dreaming, again. After running into Monza, trying to sleep in his room made him feel trapped so he moved into the library where there was more than one exit. His heart pounded and his body was drenched with sweat.

Cab entered the room. "Are you alright, man? I was in the kitchen and heard you talking."

Rand blinked, not completely awake. "I'm fine." He mumbled. "Sorry if I woke you."

Cab stood next to the couch. "Sounded like a nightmare. You okay?"

Rand gave him a half-smile. "Yeah."

Cab cuffed his shoulder. "I'm here, man, anytime."

Rand's head bobbed. "I know, thanks."

"See you in the morning." Cab left the room. A few seconds later the stairs creaked as he proceeded to his room.

Rand sat up slowly, rubbed his aching side, rested his elbows on his knees and covered his face with his hands. He took some aspirin for pain so he could breathe more comfortably, but other than rest and an ice pack on his side, there was nothing else to be done.

A few hours later, Rand was still awake when Cab's head appeared around the doorway. "You want breakfast?"

Rand blinked. "Think I could eat a whole cow."

Cab chuckled. "If you'll settle for pig, it'll be ready in a couple minutes."

Rand smirked. Feeling a chill, he pulled the afghan up to his chin and raised his feet to the coffee table. He peered blankly at the cold hearth and evaluated his encounter with Monza. He still found it curious that he didn't receive any serious injuries, but was thankful for Jasper Beck's quick action. He closed his eyes. Just thinking about it made his shoulder hurt along with his side.

Cab called from the kitchen. "Breakfast's ready."

Rand put his reflections out of his mind and shuffled into the kitchen. He stifled a groan as he sat in a chair, said a quick silent prayer and began eating, eggs, bacon, fried potatoes and toast.

"Coffee is almost ready." Cab said as he filled his own plate.

Rand peered up at him. "Thanks." He managed around a mouthful. A few minutes later, he finished eating, got up from the table, and filled a cup. "Think I'll take this to the library."

"I'll join you shortly." Cab responded.

Rand took his cup, went back to the library, sat down and leaned back against the couch.

A short time later, he took two aspirin with some water and winced when he heard Cab talking to someone at the front door. He leaned back against the couch, closed his eyes, rested one hand on the cushion beside him and the other on the arm of the couch. When something wet swiped across the back of his hand he flinched, his eyes flew open and his jaw dropped. "How'd you get in here?"

Angel wagged her tail, licked his cheek and jumped up on the couch.

"Ow. Easy girl." He put his arms around her and hugged her.

She sat next to him, pressed her nose against his arm, whined softly, and then proceeded to lick his hand.

Cab entered the room with a quizzical expression on his face. "Agent Larson's here to see you."

Rand expelled a breath. "Okay."

Rand regarded Larson as he entered the room. He was the man who claimed Angel was his dog. *Lord, she just got here. Do I have to give her up again?*

The agent stood on the opposite side of the coffee table from Rand and Angel. At that moment he wished she'd waited a little longer to come back to him.

"Mr. Gray, I believe we've met before."

Rand frowned. He well remembered the man's abruptness at the veterinarian's when Angel was hurt. "What do you want?"

Larson squared his shoulders. "Lightening's handler was killed shortly before she found you. I tried to retrain her, but she isn't responding. We assume she inadvertently transferred her loyalty to you because of similar circumstances in which she found you. Since you have obviously bonded with her, I've been ordered to give you the opportunity to accept legal ownership of her."

Rand sighed as a slow smile played on his lips. "How much do you want for her? I know she's had extensive training."

"She's no longer of any value to us. We'd appreciate it if you'd be willing to keep her. If you will sign this form, I'll give you a copy stating she's had all the appropriate shots and is legally yours."

Rand signed the paper. "I appreciate this." After the man left, he hugged Angel's neck. "Now you really are mine." He buried his face in her fur and held her close.

Fifty-One

The following Tuesday Rand's head snapped upward from the Newsweek Magazine he was reading when he heard Cab and Gus in the hall.

Rand eyed Gus warily as the two of them entered the room. "Is this a friendly visit?"

Gus met his gaze with a frown. "Cab just told me you got Angel back. How did that happen?"

Rand crossed his arms. "She didn't work out for the feds so they gave her back to me."

Gus opened his mouth and then shook his head in disbelief. "I'll be a—" he cut himself short. "Thought you might like to know Cory's dad apparently was involved with the good ole boys who gave you trouble on the docks. Found some interesting things in his box, which I'm not at liberty to disclose. Appears he may have double crossed them so, that's why he left." Gus rubbed his chin and eyed Cab. "I need to get back to the station, but let's finish this discussion outside."

Rand followed him out the front door. "What will happen to Cory now?"

"I'm checking into that as well, but that isn't why—"

"Rod and Saun want him or—" Rand interrupted.

"I'm here to thank you for inadvertently stopping our park mugger, Winter's nephew, Mortimer. He'd been living in their garage and stashed most of the loot he'd stolen in an empty tool box. Manny discovered it and we locked him up. He also told us he saw Sloan in the park the night you were mugged, but he didn't admit that until he found out Sloan was dead. Now all we have to worry about is Kane, but I'm confident he won't be difficult to catch."

Rand rubbed the back of his neck. "The one who ran me off the road is sharper than either of those two."

Gus crossed his arms. "It was them all right and we'll get the other one soon. By the way, I have some information on Virgil Monza."

Rand drew in a breath as if he'd been punched in the gut. "What about him?"

Gus's brow furrowed. "Police up in Santa Clara County found the remains of a motorcycle in a ravine, which appears to belong to him. So far there's no trace of a body, but he's believed to be dead or seriously injured. They're combing the area."

Rand leaned against a porch pillar and stared at his truck. "When did they find the bike?"

Gus gave him a once over. "Early yesterday morning. By the way, what happened to your truck door?"

Rand's gaze snapped to Gus's face. "Is there any way you can verify it was his bike?"

Gus placed his hands on his hips. "You have a reason for asking aside from thinking he might be connected with your wreck?" He smirked.

Rand grimaced. "If he's behind it, it was personal and intentional." He swallowed the bitterness that threatened to choke him.

Gus took off his hat, scratched his head and reseated it. "Sounds like a lot of history there."

"Let's just say it cost me several years." Rand growled.

Gus whistled. "You have a record?"

"It was conveniently erased or as the LA cop friend of Rod's put it, expunged." His lip curled, showing his teeth as he spoke.

Gus pinned him with an intense look. "Tell me about it."

Rand gave him a brief account, ending with his probation.

Gus studied something at their feet, frowning. "Good to know."

"Only those closest to me know about it." Rand shifted his position as his hands balled into fists and then loosened.

"Understood." Gus tipped his hat back and scrutinized Rand's face. "You holding out on me, Gray? Still haven't told me how your door got dented."

He kicked a stone and sent it bouncing down the steps. "Ran into him in Montecito."

Gus's eyebrows rose. "Monza? When?"

Rand nodded. "Last Thursday."

Gus crossed his arms. "What happened?"

"We sort of fought." He kicked another stone, but it only toppled onto the first step.

Gus grasped Rand's arm. "How the heck do you, sort of fight?"

Rand scrubbed his fingers through his hair. "He'd been drinking so it was more of a standoff. We both threw a couple punches and he ran when the hardware store owner used a bullhorn, pretending to be police." Rand's lips drew into a wry grin at the remembrance of Monza's hasty retreat.

"Did he say anything to you?"

"Not much."

Gus's cheeks puffed out. "What exactly did he say?"

Rand focused on Gus's boots as heat climbed up his neck and his jaw clenched. "Said he'd kill me."

Gus placed his hand on Rand's shoulder. "I want you to stay in Fire River until he's apprehended."

Rand shook his head. "Can't promise that."

Gus frowned. "Don't make me put you under house arrest. Let the law handle him, Gray. And get your door fixed."

A wry grin tugged at his lips. "Have to leave the village for that."

Gus pointed at him. "I mean it. You. Stay. Put!"

Later that afternoon, Rand raised his head as Rod stepped into his shop.

"Who ordered the chair? It's fancier than your usual work."

"It's for mother. Her birthday's May first so I'm making her a new set for her kitchen. This is the last one. The rest are over there," he pointed to a back corner of the room, "under that tarp." He wiped his hands on a cloth that was laying on his work bench. "I started a fresh pot of coffee a few minutes ago." He headed for the kitchen with Rod on his heels.

Once in there, Rand filled two cups and set one on the table while he leaned against the sink, holding his cup. "I'm glad you stopped."

Rod peered at him over the rim of his cup. "I wanted to come by yesterday, but didn't have time. You left church in a hurry."

"Had to get back and feed Angel. She didn't work out for the feds so they returned her."

Rod nodded. "I'm happy for you, but you used to feed her before you left."

Rand heard, but ignored the question in his voice. "Gus stopped by a while ago."

Rod sat at the table. "What did he have to say?"

"Police in Santa Clara County found a wrecked motorcycle believed to belong to Monza. You and your family should consider staying here for a while."

Rod steepled his fingers and regarded Rand. "Why? You just said they found his cycle in another county."

Rand observed Cab as he entered the kitchen, poured himself a cup and then sat across from Rod. "I think it's a trick to make it appear that he's gone."

Rod got to his feet and began pacing in front of the veranda door. "Let's not jump to conclusions. There is still no proof that he's involved with running you off the road." He forked his fingers through his hair.

Rand glared at him. "Sloan is dead and maybe Cory's dad too. He was tangled up with Sloan and Hollis. In any case, according to Gus, at least one of them is dead, Rod."

He sighed. "I sent Saun and Tommy to her brother's last year. If I do that again, her family will conclude that I'm not capable of taking care of them."

Cab raised his head. "Bringing your family here might be a good option, man." He glanced at Rod and then gave Rand a sad smile. "Why don't you tell Rod why you aren't sleeping in your room, man, or why you try hiding the pain in your side when you move too quickly."

Rand grit his teeth. "You still—" he hurled his cup at the sink, "don't believe me!" It missed, hit the floor and shattered, splattering coffee in every direction as he stormed out the door, letting it slam behind him.

Rod appraised Cab's wrinkled brow. "You can't pressure him like that, especially when he's already upset."

"I know, man, but he needs to spill it to someone. Keeping it to himself is tearing him up inside. I'll pray hard that he talks to you." He got up and left the kitchen.

Rod continued pacing for a few moments before he picked up the phone and called Clayton. "May I speak to Dr. Mills?" He leaned against the wall and waited. "This is Rod. Is there anything you can tell me about Rand that could help me understand why he's been so upset? I'm not asking for specifics. Yes, I do know a little about his past. Okay, thanks." He hung up and rubbed his chin and prayed that God would show him how to help Rand. Quietly, he opened the door, stepped off the veranda and walked to the fountain, praying each step of the way.

Rand was sitting in the middle of the bench bent over, petting Angel.

Rod approached quietly and sat in one of the chairs, giving Rand the extra space, he seemed to need.

He kept petting the dog without raising his head.

"I'll discuss your suggestion with Saun. If she's agreeable, we'll come and stay for a while. Is there anything else I can do to help you?"

Rand raised his head and met Rod's direct gaze. "Monza surprised me in a parking lot not far from your building Thursday. We threw a few punches. I held my own, but he'd been drinking so that might have slowed him down a bit, especially after he dented my truck door with his fist."

Rod crossed his arms. "Don't underestimate yourself."

"I got some bruised ribs and I'm a little sore, but I threw a couple good punches too. So, he's angry, and dangerous. That's only one of many reasons why you should stay here." He regarded Rod's face steadily.

He steepled his fingers while his elbows rested on the chair arms. "I believe you and hope you aren't considering leaving."

Rand shook his head. "Too late for that."

Rod stood. "I'm on my way home so I'll talk to Saun. If you need anything, call me." He started toward the path.

"Rod."

He stopped.

Rand expelled a long breath. "Thanks for listening."

He nodded and began walking back the way he'd come.

As Rod drove home, he went over his conversation with Rand and questioned whether his brother was overreacting. Clayton told him Rand was dealing with some delayed stress responses and still had some unresolved issues. He warned Rod to expect short, angry and unrelated answers from his brother. Rod sighed. He didn't want to stay at Candlewood, but couldn't come up with any other suggestion to put Rand's mind at ease.

His musing began to focus on the love of his life as he left Fire River and turned onto Cochella Road, which crossed the lane to his house. He pictured Saun with her luscious raven hair that cascaded to her waist and her deep brown eyes filled with love for him. The memory of the graceful movements of her slender body caused a sigh to slip from his lips. She'd be waiting for the sound of his tires crunching on their gravel driveway. Her soft lavender scent still lingered in his car from Sunday and reminded him of her loving caresses on his face when they shared their usual kiss or two before going inside to have dinner with Tommy.

He was only a few miles from home when the steering wheel jerked out of his hand and his side window shattered. He raised his hand to his head, found it was streaked with blood, and passed out.

Fifty-Two

Saun opened the door to find the sheriff standing on their front porch. Her face paled as she fixed her eyes on Gus. "Has something happened to Rod?"

He took his hat off. "He had an accident, Mrs. Gray. I was in the area so I've come to take you to the hospital. I'll call Rand once we're there."

She took a deep breath and her smile wavered. "One moment, I'll get Tommy." She spun away from the door. She knew something was wrong when Rod didn't come home before dinner and hadn't called either. She hurried to Tommy's room and leaned in the open doorway. "Tommy, quick, the sheriff is waiting for us." By the time she snatched her purse from the master bedroom, Tommy was standing by the front door.

"Where's Dad? Why's the sheriff here?" He asked with scrunched brows.

She put her hand on his shoulder and ushered him out the door and locked it. "Rod had an accident. Before you start asking questions, just please listen to the sheriff explain, okay, honey?"

His eyes opened wide while he nodded and followed in silence.

She took note of the moisture on his cheeks even before they got in the police car. "What happened?" She asked Gus as he sped up their lane to the road.

"I was in the area, got a call and came to get you. Apparently, a tire blew out and Rod lost control of his car. A volunteer fireman found him, called an ambulance and me. I'm sorry, but that's all I know. We'll find out the details once we get to the hospital." From the back seat, sniffing filled the silence that settled over the adults.

When they arrived at the emergency entrance at Lakeside Hospital, Saun got out with Tommy on her heels as Gus followed them. She approached the reception desk. "Can you tell me where Rod Gray is? He was brought here in an ambulance not long ago."

"Are you related?"

"I'm his wife."

"Allie will show you where he is. Is the boy with you?"

Saun threw a glance at Tommy. "Yes."

"He'll have to wait out here."

Saun turned to Gus who placed a hand on Tommy's shoulder.

"I'll stay with him." He offered.

She followed the nurse down a long hall and stepped into a small curtained room. Rod was lying on his back on a narrow bed and was clothed with a hospital gown and covered with a blanket. She gasped and shoved her fist against her mouth to stifle a sob.

Rod's face had several cuts and bruises, a bandage covered most of his head, and both eyes were turning dark. Gently, she took one of his hands and held it between hers as she sank onto a bedside chair. She stared unblinking at the man she'd loved from the first day they met. Her heart broke with each labored breath he took. Gingerly she touched his battered face and found his skin abnormally cool. The pallor of his skin made her nauseous. The vertical lines on his forehead suggested he was in pain even though unconscious. She pressed her lips against the back of his hand.

A nurse entered. "Your husband will be transported for x-rays in a few minutes. Is there someone with you, Mrs. Gray?"

Unable to speak, Saun nodded.

The nurse smiled. "We'll take good care of him."

Two men in scrubs wheeled in a cart and Saun moved out of their way while they lifted Rod from the bed onto a gurney and rolled him from the room.

"I'll escort you to your friends in the waiting area and make sure you're told where your husband will be after the x-rays." The nurse walked with Saun to the admittance desk. "When you're finished here, whoever came with you will be waiting on the other side of that door." She pointed to it. "Will you be okay or would you like me to stay with you?"

Sanu responded with a shake of her head and a small smile as she occupied the chair next to the desk. She gave the attendant there all the necessary information for Rod's admittance. With that accomplished, she joined Gus and Tommy.

Wings of Steel

Cab picked up the phone in the kitchen. "Hello—Gus, what's go—? Okay, thanks." He rushed out of the kitchen and sped through the short hallway. As he stepped into the library, he silently prayed while he tried to hold on to positive and optimistic thoughts about Rod.

Rand peered up at him from a book he was reading and offered Cab a smile that didn't quite reach his eyes. "What's wrong?" He asked in a strained voice.

Cab's gaze fastened on Rand's face as he inhaled and attempted to speak calmly. "Rod's in the hospital." He spoke quietly and observed the immediate disappearance of all color from Rand's face.

The book he'd been reading slid from his hands to the floor as he lunged to his feet. "No!"

Cab grasped Rand's shoulder. "Gus is there with Saun and Tommy. They're waiting for the result of Rod's x-rays."

"Should have told him to come here sooner." Rand growled, heading out the front door with doubled fists.

Cab caught Rand's muttered words while he ran to catch up with him.

Rand opened the door of his truck, but Cab closed it. "I'll drive, buddy." He offered with a side-glance as he opened his passenger door.

Rand's brows furrowed but he settled into Cab's car and they sped out of Fire River.

All the way to the hospital, the ache in the back of Rand's throat increased. *Should've insisted they stay with us weeks ago.*

When Cab pulled into the hospital parking lot, Rand leaped out, ran inside, and rushed to the emergency desk. "Where's Rod Gray?"

A nurse checked. "He was just sent upstairs so you should check with the main desk in the lobby. It's down that hall and around the corner to the left."

He frowned, pivoted on his heels and nearly knocked Cab off his feet. "Follow me." Rand huffed as he took off running with Cab following close behind.

They arrived at the main desk. "What room is Rod Gray in?" Rand glanced from one nurse to another, tapping his fingers on the desk as he waited for a response.

"He was admitted a few minutes ago, third floor, room 305." The nurse directly in front of him answered. "The elevators are down the hall on the right and please walk."

Rand shoved away from the desk, nearly at a fast walk and together with Cab arrived at the elevators.

When the doors opened, Rand spotted Gus and Tommy standing in the hall and quickly approached them. "What happened?"

"We'll have to wait until he's conscious. Pax Warner found his car not far from his house. He radioed for an ambulance and a dispatcher called me. At this point, all I can say is, it appears Rod lost control when a tire blew out. I'm having it towed to the station. I'll get in touch with you later. Rod's wife called Netty and asked if Tommy could stay there temporarily."

"Uncle Rand?" The boy fastened him with pleading eyes.

Rand sighed. "Stay with Netty. We'll all be at Candlewood soon." He started down the hall.

Gus grabbed his arm and stopped him. "I'll have to release Cory. Are you still willing for him to stay with you?"

Rand's nod was slight before he pulled away and quickly strolled down the hall. He entered Rod's room and peered at Saun who sat in a chair beside the bed. Rand stood silently beside her while he scrutinized Rod's cut and bruised face and bandaged head. "What have they told you?" He asked in a deep tone of voice after several moments passed.

She blinked and restrained the tears, which filled her eyes, and rested her hand on Rod's arm. "He has fractured ribs, a concussion and stitches in his head."

Rand lips curled as he ground his teeth.

Cab lightly placed a hand on his shoulder. "Easy, buddy." He whispered.

Rand's nostrils flared as he doubled his fists. "Has he responded at all?"

Saun nodded her head slowly and avoided looking at him as she smoothed Rod's matted hair away from his forehead. "A little."

Rand observed the way Saun's fingers caressed Rod's hands. The gesture reminded him of Netty's soothing fingers on his skin. He shivered, quickly discarded the image and redirected his focus to Rod. Rand's Adam's apple bobbed as he crossed his arms and stepped back away from the bed. *Does she blame me?*

Cab moved to take the place Rand vacated and drew Saun to her feet. He wrapped his arms around her and whispered to her while her shoulders shook with silent sobs.

Rand moved to stand near the door and swallowed against the sudden surge of desire to be included in the familiarity the three of them shared. His chest tightened and he stealthily exited the room. In the hall, his nostrils flared as he cracked his knuckles. *Rod was targeted because of me.* His shoulders curled forward as he leaned against the wall.

"Hey, buddy, why're you out here?" Cab spoke next to him, causing Rand to flinch. "Rod's made of tough stuff. He's been through worse things than this. And stop blaming yourself."

"You take up mind-reading?" Rand scoffed.

Cab rested a hand on his shoulder. "Your face says it all, man. That's the last thing Rod would want."

Rand concentrated on the floor. "I'll try to keep that in mind." There was a hard edge to his words.

They both raised their heads as a doctor walked into Rod's room. Rand swung around to follow the doctor's footsteps and caught his response.

"I see you're awake, Mr. Gray?"

Rand stepped into the room, but Cab pulled him back into the hall. "Let's wait out here." He whispered. "We can talk to the doctor when he's finished."

Rand leaned against the wall beside the door of the room. With ears tuned in to the conversation inside, he fisted and released his hands several times.

"Do you know where you are?" The doctor asked and after a short pause he posed another question. "How old are you? How many fingers am I holding up?"

Rand cocked his head toward the open door, but still couldn't catch Rod's responses.

After another pause, the doctor asked. "Can you tell me our President's name?" This time his pause was much longer. "You rest now and when you're feeling better, we'll release you to go home. Are you staying for the night, Mrs. Gray?"

Rand didn't hear her answer, but knew she would stay. *I'm not leaving either.*

The doctor exited the room and Rand blocked his path. "I'm Rod's brother. How is he?"

"He's suffering from a concussion and some fractured ribs. His memory is somewhat foggy, but that should clear up eventually."

"What are you doing for him?"

"We're keeping him as comfortable as possible. We'll know more what we're up against in a day or two. If you'll excuse me, I have other patients to check on."

Rand frowned, but stepped out of his way. He had more questions, but they'd have to wait. He caught Cab's drawn eyebrows and followed him back into the room. Rand stood on the opposite side of the bed from Saun and Cab. He regarded his brother with a frown. "How're you doing?" His voice was quiet and without expression.

Rod's smile was weak. "Go home and get some rest. Looks like you need it."

Rand smirked. "I'm staying here."

Rod's expression sobered. "Where's Tommy?"

Saun interrupted quietly. "I called Netty and asked if he could stay with her. She said she still has a key to Candlewood. Gus took him there."

Rod frowned and stared at her for a few moments and then squinted at Rand. "Saun said Tommy cried all the way here. He needs you, Rand."

Rand breathed a low growl and then cleared his throat. "You don't make it easy to refuse. I'll go, but only if you promise someone will—"

"Cab, please take him home so I can get some rest." Rod squeezed his eyes closed.

"You got it." Cab chuckled. "I'll be back later. Come on, buddy." He clapped Rand's shoulder. "Both of you try to get some rest." Cab gently ordered them as he ushered Rand out the door.

Rand peered over his shoulder. "I probably won't sleep. If you need anything."

Rod managed a half wave.

Rand hesitated before getting out of Cab's car at the mansion. "Aren't you coming in?"

Cab shook his head. "I told them I'd be back. Saun is barely holding on and I need to be there to support them both. I'll stay with them at least for tonight."

Rand clenched his teeth, but withheld further comment. He got out of the car and started up the steps.

"I'll keep you updated." Cab called after him.

Rand raised his hand and continued up the steps. Once inside, he expelled a deep breath.

Tommy came running to him with Angel on his heels. "Uncle Rand, is dad—?"

"He's resting. He'll be fine." Rand clasped his shoulder, swallowed hard, and hoped it was the truth. "It'll just take some time." *Are you trying to convince him or yourself, pal?*

Netty stepped into the hall. "I saved you some dinner."

He gave her forced smile. "Maybe later." He glanced at his watch. 10:45. "It's past your bedtime, Tommy, and you have school tomorrow."

Tears pooled in his eyes. "Dad's hurt. Do I have to go to school?"

Rand raised an eyebrow and glanced at Netty.

She placed her hands on her hips. "Can you help him get better by skipping school?"

"No, but can't I go see—?"

"No!" Rand responded sharply. "He's in intensive care." He answered in a softer tone at the presence of tears streaming down Tommy's face.

"But you got to see him." He pouted.

"And he told me to leave!" Rand growled.

Tommy stared at him.

Rand took two steps and grabbed the boy in a bear hug. "Sorry, pal. I'd like to be there too, but sometimes we don't get what we want."

Tommy hugged him back. "I'm glad you're here, Uncle Rand."

Rand tousled the boy's hair. "Me too, pal. Now go on up to bed. It's late."

Tommy glanced at Netty. "Take care of Uncle Rand, okay?"

She winked at him. "You bet. Good night, Tommy."

"Night." He stared at Rand for a moment and then hugged him again. "Good night, Uncle Rand. I love you."

Moisture burned Rand's eyes, but he gave the boy a two-finger salute. "Love you too, pal. Get some sleep."

Netty caught Rand's hand and led him into the library. "How about a cup of coffee?"

He sank heavily onto one of the couches. "Sounds good."

She studied him for a moment. He was trying to hide his feelings about being sent home, but she knew he wanted to stay with Rod. Her first clue was his deflated posture. The clincher was the way he snapped at Tommy, which was totally out of character, especially with the boy. Fortunately for them both, he recovered quickly enough to minimize any damage. Her heart hurt for Rand as she sensed he somehow felt left out of the friendship between Rod, Saun and Cab. She'd often felt it too. It was special and something they'd developed before either Rand or her was present. She left the room determined to show Rand how much he was needed and appreciated, at least by her, if it took all night.

She returned to the library a few moments later with a tray that held two cups of coffee, some crackers, and cheese squares. She set the tray on a low table on one end of the couch. Sitting next to him, she felt his body heat radiating off him. Quietly, she perused him.

His posture was rigid, there was a scowl on his face and his arms were crossed.

She sighed quietly. This might not go as well as she'd hoped. "Would you like that coffee now?"

He flinched. "Hmm? I guess." His tone was even deeper than usual.

She passed him a cup.

"Thanks." The word was clipped.

She took a sip from her own cup. "How's Rod doing?"

His jaw clenched and the cords in his neck stood out. "He's in pain, barely coherent."

"What happened to him?"

"Something happened with his car. He has a concussion and some fractured ribs." His response was toneless as he stared at his cup.

"Saun told me Gus took her and Tommy to the hospital. Didn't he know what happened?"

He set his cup on an end table. "He said was he was having Rod's car towed to the station." He rested his elbows on his knees, leaned forward, and covered his face with his hands.

She set her cup down and began to rub circles on his back. He was tense and his muscles were hard and tight. She began to massage his neck and shoulders.

After several moments passed in heavy silence, he leaned back against the couch and closed his eyes. "I tried to warn them, but not one of them believed me." He muttered in a thick, emotion-choked voice.

She grasped his hand and slid her fingers between his. "This isn't your fault, cowboy." Her voice was nearly a whisper.

He turned his head toward her without raising from his slouched position. "I should have insisted they stay here sooner." His voice was quiet, but the words were clipped.

"You couldn't force them to stay. Your brother is more stubborn than you are. So, stop blaming yourself. It won't help anyone."

The pain in his eyes was instantaneous and he quickly lowered his gaze.

She was tempted to throw her arms around his neck and kiss him soundly on the mouth and then lightly brush his cheeks, his chin and his hair with her lips. Instead, she clasped his hand with both of hers. "I know you care deeply for Rod, but you can't blame yourself when he doesn't listen to you."

He glanced at their joined hands. "He isn't the only one." He grumbled.

"I know, darlin', and I'm sorry. I wish I had answers for you or knew what would make you feel better." She brushed his hair back from his forehead.

He drew her into his arms and held her close. "Do you believe me that Monza is behind all of this?"

She leaned away from him to gaze deeply into his eyes. "Of course, I believe you. Unfortunately, you have a history with him that no one seems to understand. Unlike the others, I've seen the man and believe everything you've said about him and then some."

He pulled her close again. "Stay here for a while?" He whispered next to her ear.

Her insides tingled at the rumble of his voice, which she felt clear to her toes. "I'll stay as long as you want me to, cowboy." She whispered.

Fifty-Three

The next morning Tommy went to school, but not without protest. Rand took advantage, while he was alone to make his small room as comfortable as possible for Rod and Saun. He removed the twin bed and desk and set them in the dining room close to the door, which lead into the kitchen through a passage under the stairs.

When he finished emptying the room, he drove his truck to W. T.'s gas station. As he entered the station's convenient store, the slight man, wearing a straw hat greeted him from behind the counter. "Wal, glo-ry be! Ain't you a sight fer sore eyes? What kin I do for ya, friend?"

He heaved a deep sigh. "Filled-up my truck and wanted to tell you Rod's in the hospital."

"Tarnation! Will he be alright?"

Rand's jaw clenched. "Eventually, has a concussion and some fractured ribs."

W. T. removed his hat. "I'll call Sadie and tell her to inform the prayer partners."

"Thanks." He paid for his gas and proceeded to leave.

"If'n ya all need anythang, give us a call. I'll tell the missus ta call the ladies so's they kin bring you folks some vittles."

"Appreciate it, but not sure how soon we'll need it."

"Sadie'll see to it. Give me a ring if'n ya need anythang else afore then."

Rand gave him a back-handed wave as he stepped outside. Yesterday's date, March sixteenth, struck him with such force that he stumbled and nearly fell into the seat in his truck. Once behind the steering wheel, he grasped it so tight his knuckles turned white. An intense ache filled his core. *Monza did it. The message couldn't be clearer if it was written in the sky. Need to convince Gus.* He froze. *Al died the next day. What more would Monza do?*

He made a few stops in Montecito to purchase the supplies needed to refurnish the small room, stopped and enlisted Cab's help, and then returned to Candlewood to finish setting up the room for Rod and Saun.

While Netty was trimming her customer's hair, she caught glimpses out her shop window of Rand and Cab as they carried some furniture around the side of the old mansion. She paused before she finished Mrs. Albert's haircut to observe them. Once she completed the task, she rushed the Albert woman out the door, discovered Cab's car was gone, and closed her shop.

She hustled across the street and stepped inside the mansion. "Hey, cowboy, where are you?" Receiving no answer, she began searching for him. *His truck and bike are out front.* She stopped when hammering from one of the back rooms reached her ears.

Angel greeted her as she stepped into the main hall. *How did she get back here?* "Where's Rand, girl?" The dog bounded off toward the dining room, but skidded around the corner toward the kitchen. Netty shook her head. *Angel acts like she's part human.* She found him in his room setting up a double bed. As she strolled up to him, she observed how his shirt stuck to his skin as if he'd been working hard for hours. "What's going on, cowboy? Did you get tired of trying to fit your six-foot plus body into that tiny single bed?" She chuckled.

He hung his head, staring at the floor. "We're putting Rod and Saun in here when he gets out of the hospital."

She appraised the lack of color in his cheeks and his wrinkled brow and wished she could take back her teasing. "Have you seen him today?"

"No." His hoarse response was curt.

She gently took hold of his chin, raising it until his gaze locked with hers. "What aren't you saying, Rand? I know that look. It's more than just worry." She peered at him as he exhaled like he'd been holding his breath.

He gave her a brief glance. "You take the same mind reading class as Cab?"

"In case you didn't know, cowboy, you have the most expressive face of anyone I've ever met."

"So I've heard." He responded avoiding her scrutiny.

Netty took note of the sudden moisture in his eyes, which he was trying to hide, and hugged his waist.

He winced and barely stifled a groan.

"You're hurt!" She appraised him carefully. She'd surprised him.

He drew a long breath and expelled it slowly. "What are you doing here? Aren't you supposed to be working?"

She squinted at him. "Nice try, cowboy. Tell me or I'll squeeze you again."

He quickly removed her arms from around him. "Some bruised ribs, no big deal."

"Uh-oh. Who'd you tangle with this time?"

He arched one eyebrow. "Wouldn't believe me if I told you."

"Try me." She perched her hands on her hips, knowing he was purposely trying to avoid the subject because he hated fighting.

He dropped his focus to the floor. "Monza."

"The Monza?"

He expelled a short huff. "Yeah."

She took his face in her hands. "Bruised ribs, are you kidding me?"

He smirked, but his eyes twinkled with mischief.

"Did you hit him back?"

He quickly sobered. "Mr. Beck from the hardware store shouted through a bullhorn that he was the police." A restrained grin appeared on his lips accompanied by a faraway look.

She kissed his cheek. "I sense there's more to that story. I didn't think you'd be afraid if you ever saw that creep again. He's just a big bully."

"Yeah." He choked on the half-truth.

"Rod will be okay." She offered to change the subject.

"I hope so." He picked up the last piece of the bedframe and pounded it into place with a mallet.

She winked at him and ran a finger along the lines on his forehead. "What's going on in there, cowboy?"

He shrugged. "Thinking about yesterday's date. I—"

"What about it?" She appraised him.

"I told you about the accident with my friend, Al." He swallowed and kicked at a leg of the bed.

She grasped his hand with both of hers. "I thought that was a long ti—"

"Fifteen years ago, yesterday." He lowered his head and focused on their clasped hands.

She gently ran her fingers through his hair and stroked his cheek. "I wish I could erase those memories, darlin'. It was an accident. You need to let it go."

"Can't, with all that's happened." His Adam's apple bobbed.

She tugged on his hand. "Let's take a walk, cowboy."

"Where to?"

She winked at him. "How about to the kitchen. I could use some coffee and maybe some lunch."

One corner of his mouth lifted slightly. "Do you have a suitcase?"

Her eyes opened wide. "You're not leaving?"

His eyes twinkled. "I need to get some of Rod and Tommy's clothes and figured maybe you'd help with some of Saun's things."

"Oh, you did, did you." She teased.

"Mm-hmm." He winked at her while he slipped his arms around her waist and pulled her close. "If I ask real nice?"

She leaned into him and peered into his eyes. "How nice?"

A grin tugged at a corner of his lips. "Please. I'm thinking enough clothes and stuff for at least a couple weeks."

She shook her head, staring at his lips. "Not nice enough."

He lowered his head and placed a quick gentle kiss on her mouth and then pulled back to observe her response.

She stared at him as her heartrate quickened. "I could maybe be persuaded."

"Oh yeah, what do you say now?" He began tickling her.

She pulled away from him, laughing. "I give up, for now, but I think we need to discuss this more later. I'll fix us some lunch."

On Friday after Tommy left for school, Rand stepped onto the veranda. He stood with arms crossed observing Angel as she wandered about in the yard. He'd surrendered to Cab's insistence on using his church's van to bring Rod and Saun to Candlewood because the ride would be more comfortable for his brother. He hoped Rod would be able to settle into his temporary home with minimal stress.

It was a breezy morning and Rand shivered as he stood gazing up at the cloudy sky before retreating inside. He filled a cup with coffee and carried it to the library where he could peer out the windows to the street. He took a sip from his cup, set it on a side table and snapped his fingers as he paced back and forth in front of the hearth, which still held ashes from the previous night. The scent of charred wood filled the room.

He stopped pacing to stare outside and rubbed the back of his neck. He was aware that his brother valued his privacy and might not be happy with this living arrangement, no matter how temporary. He'd discussed the situation with Cab and they'd agreed the downstairs room, which had access to a private bathroom, was the best option for Rod and Saun. Also, it was located next to the kitchen and veranda doors.

Rand was concerned for the safety of his family and hoped Rod didn't object too much to staying at Candlewood. He'd tried to convince Rod it was the best place for all of them until the threat to their safety was gone. Rand's insides quivered as he considered the possibility that Monza intended to include them all in his pursuit of revenge. He tried to shake off the dark imaginings as he entered the hall and stood staring through the glass in the front doors.

When the van parked at the curb, he raced down the steps to assist Cab as he helped Rod. He seemed unsteady and Rand was tempted to pick him up and carry him to his room.

"We have a room all set up for you." Rand told Saun as she held open the front door for them to enter. "If you need anything else, just ask."

She flashed him a brief smile. "Thank you."

Rand and Cab stood on either side of Rod while she got the bed ready for him. When she helped Rod lie down, Rand moved to the door into the kitchen. He leaned against the doorframe and watched while she covered Rod with a blanket. Rand crossed his arms and observed Cab who stood beside the bed with his attention riveted on Rod.

A few moments later Cab joined Rand and whispered. "Even the van was a rough ride for him."

He acknowledged Cab's remark and abruptly left the room.

Cab quietly closed the door behind them. "How're you doing, buddy?" He asked as they walked through the kitchen toward the hall.

He rolled his shoulders. "Concerned about him."

Cab raised his head to meet Rand's gaze. "Giving up your room was a good idea."

He shrugged. "The rest of us can eat in the dining room and use the veranda door as little as possible."

Cab smiled. "Good idea. I have obligations. Gus stopped by the hospital before we left. Rod's lawyer is proceeding with their adoption of Cory, so Gus said Cory will be coming here after school."

Rand nodded and leaned against the wall as his shoulders curled forward. "I'm sleeping in the dining room and Angel will guard the veranda door. Would you mind sleeping in the library to listen for the front door. I stashed my rifle on the far side of the fireplace in the corner and while I was in Montecito today, I bought a pistol."

Cab's mouth dropped open. "Do you think that's necessary?"

Rand crossed his arms. "I'm positive Monza caused Rod to lose control. Any of us could be targeted next. I can't be everywhere. I'd rest a whole lot easier, knowing I'm not the only one alert at night." *Is Netty even safe?* His heart twisted in anguish at the thought.

Cab frowned. "Do you really think he'd come into the village?"

"Anything's possible with him."

Cab crossed his arms. "Have you talked to Gus about this?"

"He knows." Rand huffed. "But keep what I just said between us."

Cab crossed his arms. "I'll stop by his office on my way back. Can't hurt to let him know. See you later, man."

Rand watched Cab head out the door. "Hope he listens to you." He grumbled to himself as he strode into the kitchen. The engine of the church's van stuttered, whined and then vibrated the walls of the mansion as Cab drove away. Rand refilled his cup and sat in a chair. With elbows on the table, he plunged his fingers through his unruly hair and bowed his head in prayer.

Later that afternoon, unable to endure the silence any longer, Rand escaped to the veranda. He closed the door quietly behind him, walked to the edge of the tiled floor, leaned against the lone supporting center pillar and crossed his arms. Angel wagged her tail. He stooped down and scratched behind her ears.

Afterward he moved further away from the mansion to lean against an outside corner wall and gaze at nothing in particular. *No one believed me even when I told them Monza could be a real threat to all of us. He's responsible for what happened to Rod's car and won't stop until. . .* "This is all about him and me." He slammed his fist into the wall, winced and drew in a sharp breath.

"How's come you're standing out here?" Tommy called as he came up behind Rand on the path.

Rand pivoted quickly as his cheeks heated. "Needed some fresh air." He growled.

"Oh." The teen briefly studied him. "Is Cory here yet?"

He flinched. "No."

Tommy scrunched his nose before starting inside.

"Wait." Rand's hand shot out to snag his arm. "Use the plaza door so you don't disturb Rod."

Tommy whirled around and ran in the opposite direction.

Rand slumped forward and leaned against the outside wall with downcast eyes. *If you expect to keep them safe, you'd better be more alert. Can't let your guard down even for a second.*

A little later, Cory came bounding up the path and skidded to a stop in front of him. "Is Rod here yet?"

Rand acknowledged him with a quick bob of his head and started walking in the opposite direction, but the boy leaped in front of him.

"Will he be okay" He blinked.

Rand's lips stretched into a thin line. "Eventually. Use the plaza door, okay?"

Cory's brow wrinkled. "Okay." He stooped to pet Angel and then ran back down the path and around the corner.

Cory kept the conversation moving during dinner. He was excited about a project he was working on at school and described it in great detail to Cab and Rand while Tommy focused on his plate and ate in silence.

After dinner, Rand went upstairs to the bedroom he would only use for taking showers and changing clothes. He stood staring out the windows at Fountain Street, one of the main entrances to the village. *Can't help questioning whether Rod and his family are even safe here.* The fact that the police station was located a few blocks north of the mansion on the same street was small comfort to him. Restless, he paced the room until he felt the need for fresh air.

Leaving the room, he descended the stairs quietly, passed the library where Cab was watching TV at a low volume. Rand strolled through the kitchen and stepped outside.

Angel was nowhere in sight, but he filled her dishes with food and water. She'd eat when she was hungry. Sighing, he leaned against a pillar and stared off into the distance with unfocused gaze. After a while he stepped off the veranda to wander along the garden path in the direction of the fountain. Angel was standing at the back gate intent on something on the other side. Her tail was wagging.

Rand walked up to her. "What's out there, girl?"

"Uncle Rand?"

He froze and held his breath. *Second time you were surprised, today. Not good.*

Tommy came up beside him. "Are you okay?"

He attempted to keep his tone light-hearted. "How was school today?"

"Okay." Tommy squinted up at him with a curious expression on his face. "I heard what you said earlier after you hit the wall."

"You did, huh." He blew out a breath, walked over to the bench and sank onto it.

The teen nodded and sat next to him. "How come you think it's your fault dad got hurt?"

The teen's nod was so much like Rod's response that Rand's stomach tightened.

"I know you love dad as much as I do."

Rand hung his head.

"Know what else?"

He stole a quick side-glance at Tommy.

"Dad would really be sad if he knew you felt like that."

Rand clasped his hands between his knees. "You're pretty smart, pal."

He grinned. "Sometimes, I guess."

Cory came running down the path. "Is this a private party?" He plopped down on the bench on the other side of Rand.

He threw his head back and laughed at the boy's exuberance. "Nope, it's just starting." He peered at them until they stared at him with raised eyebrows. Rand pulled off his boots. "Let's have some fun!"

They both gazed at him with wrinkled brows.

He leaned over, pulled a shoe off each of them, and then removed his own socks.

Cory and then Tommy followed Rand's example.

Rand stood and pulled them both to their feet and then ran toward the fountain. "Last one in's a rotten egg!" Rand stopped short of the fountain wall as the two boys leaped in, splashing water over the side in a wave that drenched Rand.

"No fair!" They called laughing as they continued throwing water at him.

He sputtered as he removed his belt, wallet and keys, tossed them at his boots, and then vaulted over the wall followed by Angel as she leaped in to join the fun.

Both boys began shoving waves of water at Rand.

He lunged at Cory who was closest to him, grabbed him and dunked him.

Cory came up spewing water and shaking his head.

Tommy clung to Rand's back and tried to push his head beneath the water, but Rand tossed him over his head and dunked him instead.

Cory jumped on Rand's back while Tommy knocked his feet out from under him and Rand went under.

It was long after dark when they finally climbed out of the pond. Their clothes clung to them and made them shiver as a slight breeze teased their wet hair and clothes. They slogged back to the mansion, alternately laughing and shivering. The boys carried their shoes and Rand his belt and boots as Angel happily padded along with them. Once inside, they all tiptoed upstairs and each escaped into his own room.

Fifty-Four

The next morning Rand got up from the couch in the library. He was the only one there, except for Rod and Saun, who tended to stay in their room. He glanced at the clock on one of the bookshelves: 9:15am. The last time he checked the time before finally being able to lie down and rest it was after four that morning. He ambled into the kitchen and picked up a note from the table. Cab wrote. You were asleep when the boys and I ate breakfast so, we decided not to wake you. Be back ASAP.

Rand spun in a full circle blinking and shook his head. *Fine bodyguard you make, pal.* He raked his fingers through his hair, started a pot of coffee and headed upstairs to shower while it was brewing.

A short time later, he poured his coffee as Angel wined quietly at the veranda door. He took his cup and stepped outside, shaking his head at the dog. "I'll bet you ate earlier with the rest of them." Her nearly empty bowl confirmed it. "Nice try." He sat on the veranda step and Angel sat down by his feet. He enjoyed the cool morning breeze and the solitude, no matter how brief, while sipping his coffee.

The door opened behind him, he shifted his position, and eyed Netty who was standing there staring at him with her arms crossed. One corner of his mouth lifted as he waggled his eyebrows. "Enjoying the view?" He imagined his hair stuck up in all directions, since he hadn't combed it, didn't shave and was wearing only a faded pair of jeans. He remembered there was a varnish-smeared T-shirt on the workbench in his shop, which he figured he'd put on once he went back inside.

She grinned. "I'd enjoy it more from a different angle. Aren't you chilly?"

"Umm, got any suggestions?" He responded with his back to her as he took another drink from his cup.

"I might have, but I'd like some coffee first."

"Help yourself."

She chuckled. "Thanks, cowboy." She went back inside and soon returned to sit next to him. "How are things going with everyone here?" She asked as she stared at him and sipped her coffee.

He was silent as an image of Netty's fingers caressing the scars on his back and shoulders filled his mind and a shiver of pleasure ran up his spine.

"You are cold!" She pulled him close and wrapped an arm around his waist.

His skin tingled beneath her fingers, but other than a jolting sensation at her touch on his skin, his breath came easy and his muscles relaxed.

She ran her hand back and forth across his back as she stared directly at him.

He caught a glimpse of her longing before she quickly hid it while she drank from her cup. It was all he could do to keep from pulling her against his chest. He continued to stare at her as a slow smile tugged on his lips.

She peered at him over the rim of her cup, her eyes twinkling. "This is a much better view, cowboy. Are you going to make me guess or answer my question?" She began finger-combing his hair.

He nearly spewed coffee on his bare feet and quickly stood. "Coffee's cold." He started to step around her.

She reached for his hand to pull him back down. "I'll gladly get more for you." She offered with a wink.

He pulled her to her feet, she leaned into him, and he caught her waist to steady her. Warmth immediately ignited his desire at their contact, but he made sure she retained her balance before he quickly released her. "Let's go inside. You refill our cups and I'll finish getting dressed."

She pretended to pout. "If you insist, but I have to admit, this is a view I'd enjoy seeing more of."

He chuckled with an attempt to check the way her words intensified his longing. "I bet." He opened the door and followed her inside with a wink. Then quietly, but quickly escaped upstairs to grab a clean shirt from his room.

When he returned, she was sitting on a couch in the library with their cups placed side by side on the coffee table. He raised an eyebrow.

"Nothing says we can't sit next to each other in here." She whispered.

"Guess not." He stood near her as he buttoned a long-sleeved navy shirt.

She wrinkled her brow, avidly intent on his fingers. As they moved down his shirt, she chewed on her bottom lip.

He tilted his head. "What?"

She took a sip from her cup while peering up at him.

He left the top two buttons undone with his shirt-tail hanging loose and sat next to her. His brow furrowed as he refused to let the sultry gleam in her gaze side-track him.

She grasped his hand. "What's wrong, cowboy?"

He shrugged off his wayward thoughts. "I hope Rod's comfortable. I know he likes his privacy." He answered quietly, staring at the table as he made small circles on his knee with his coffee cup.

"Does Gus know about any of this?"

"He took Saun and Tommy to the hospital." His voice rose on the last word.

"Has he done anything about it?"

His insides quivered. "Haven't seen him since the night at the hospital."

From the veranda, Angel gave a warning bark and Rand put his cup down and jumped to his feet.

Gus walked into the library. "Is this a private party?"

"Coffee?" Netty asked.

"Yes, thanks." He answered as he sat in a chair. "Sit down, Gray. You aren't going anywhere."

Rand fixed his eyes on Gus and resumed his position on the couch.

"We found bullets in Rod's front and rear tires. I'm guessing that's what caused him to lose control. Pax gave me this." He handed Rand a crumpled piece of paper. "He told me it was under one of the wipers on Rod's windshield. Care to guess what it means?"

Rand spread the scrap of paper on his knee and read. *Your son's next.* He broke out in a cold sweat as the coffee he just drank burned his throat. His heartrate increased and his chest hurt. He gulped a breath and tried to stay quiet. "Tommy?" He whispered. *The threat wasn't meant for Rod, but for him but he didn't have a son. Cory?*

"Is this gang related?" Gus interrupted his thoughts. "Rod didn't remember much of anything when I saw him last."

Rand's chest tightened and it was suddenly difficult to breathe. "You talked to Rod?" His voice was a harsh whisper.

Gus raised his hat higher on his forehead. "While he was in the hospital."

"What did he say?"

"He was confused so nothing he said made much sense. What bothers me most is this note." Gus observed Rand closely.

Rand was suddenly dizzy and had difficulty breathing. He stared at the floor as cold fingers squeezed his heart.

Gus frowned. "You know who attacked Rod?"

Rand focused on breathing. "Told you already. It's Monza. The date confirmed it!" He whispered hoarsely.

Gus's brow wrinkled. "What date?"

"He attacked Rod on the say day his brother was injured fourteen years ago." Rand growled, trying hard to fight against the nausea rising in his throat.

"I put out an APB on him, maybe I'll even contact the feds. Can you give me a full description?"

"I can." Netty placed her hand on Rand's shoulder.

He flinched as she sat beside him.

"No need to badger Rand. He's had enough!" She grasped Rand's hand. "The man's a beast. Every bit of six four and over two hundred pounds of solid rock. He has cold dark eyes, oily black hair worn in a stringy ponytail half-way down his back. That's how he looked when I saw him over a year ago. He was dressed all in black, leather jacket, pants, shirt, and motorcycle boots and he was wearing a studded belt. He has a scar from the edge of his left eye to his ear. Besides that, he definitely needed a bath. He's the most repugnant excuse for a human being I've ever met!"

Gus studied Netty and then switched his attention back to Rand. "Anything you care to add?"

Rand's head drooped. "Heard he's expert with martial arts and he's got a snake tattoo the entire length of his arm." He swallowed hard and had difficulty keeping bile from spewing from his mouth.

"Why would he go after Rod?" Gus demanded.

"Re-venge." His voice broke on the last syllable as he leaped to his feet, quickly exited, and let the library door slam behind him.

———◦◦◦———

He strode toward the fountain, leaned against the stone wall, and slid to the ground. With knees drawn to his chest, he felt his heartbeat in his throat. His head was pounding and his heart ached. He shivered and couldn't remember when he'd ever felt so cold. *Should have left when you had the chance. Monza would've followed you like he always did. This is all your fault, pal.* If he gave in to the moisture burning his throat, he was afraid he would never be able to regain control.

Angel pressed her nose against his hands, which drooped over his knees. Even she was unable to comfort him. He sat with his arms resting on his knees and supported his throbbing head with his hands. He willed the paralyzing memories to fade into oblivion. He jammed his fingers in his hair and pulled at it while his nerves quivered and he breathed in deep gulps. *Monza's threat was meant for me, not Rod. But what did your son's next mean? Did Monza even know about Cory?*

He flinched when Netty sat beside him. His face and neck heated and sweat beaded on his forehead. He hated that she was witnessing one of his worst moments. He tried to take some comfort from her hand, which caressed his back in gentle circular motions. His body trembled involuntarily, but he remained the way he was with his head in his hands and his eyes squeezed shut.

After several moments, she tugged on him until he sat upright and then she wrapped her arms around him and held him tight. She began praying quietly, caressing his back and shoulders. "God, touch the shattered places in Rand's heart and mind. Help him stop blaming himself for things that madman does." She kissed his hair and rested her head against his as she continued gently caressing his back.

After a while, his trembling stopped and he slipped his arms around her and held her close, receiving the strength she offered. Finally, he stretched his legs out in front of him and tentatively scrutinized her. He found comfort in her moist blue-green gaze and was stunned by the depth of her understanding. *When did she start praying?* He traced her cheek with his forefinger and then her jaw until it rested against her lips. Slowly he leaned toward her until he could feel her breath on his mouth.

She drew back. "Don't, Rand. When you kiss me, I want it to be because of your desire, not gratitude for my support, okay?"

His vision blurred as he too pulled back. "Thanks for giving me something else to think about." He whispered hoarsely, shaking his head. He marveled at the serious tone of her prayer and felt the sincerity of it all the way to the core of his being.

"You're okay now so I'm going back to my shop. When you're ready, I'd like to hear the rest of the story." She kissed his forehead. "You rest now, okay?"

He stared after her disappearing form unable to gather his thoughts into anything coherent much less find words for his jumbled thoughts. There was a weight in his chest as he watched her until she was out of sight. *Were you dreaming that God sent her to draw you out of that dark place, pal?*

Rod's attention focused on Saun's face as she helped him lay down after he finished his lunch. "Saun, will you ask Rand to come see me?"

Saun smiled and ran her fingers through his hair. "I'll see if I can find him, my love."

Rod frowned. "I'm worried about him. I think Cab is too."

"I hope he talks to you." She kissed his forehead and left the room.

Rod closed his eyes against the pounding in his head. Before long, the door opened and Rand entered the room.

Rod stretched his hand toward Rand, who stood and silently studied him.

He strode across the room and grasped Rod's hand.

Rod contemplated his abnormally pale face. "I'm worried about you."

Rand's Adam's apple bobbed. "I'm fine. Concentrate on getting well, will you?" His voice was husky.

"Saun told me Gus was here a while ago."

"If you're thinking I'm in trouble with the law, the answer's no." He whispered harshly.

Rod withdrew his hand.

Rand sucked in a breath as he sat in Saun's chair. "I didn't mean to growl at you. But let's wait until you're on your feet again before we talk about this."

"Tell me now!" Rod nearly shouted and wrinkled his brow as the throbbing in his head grew stronger.

"Take it easy. Let it rest, for now."

In spite of his own pain, he could sense Rand's inner turmoil. "At least stop blaming yourself."

Rand's jaw muscles tensed as he nodded. "You need to rest." He stood and went to the door. "Get some sleep. I'll check on you later."

Rod's pulse picked up. "Sometimes, keeping things to yourself is worse than talking." He responded to Rand's back.

Rand paused, his hand on the doorknob. "I'm sorry, Rod." His voice was barely audible. He opened the door and closed it quietly behind him.

He headed for the drawing room. Slowly he moved to one of the bay-window seats where he stared outside at nothing in particular with arms crossed tight against his chest. His stomach felt like it was filled with lead.

He wanted to tell Rod, but didn't know where or how to begin. *How did one put a lifetime of anger, pain and humiliation into words? And what did Monza's note really mean?*

A door squeaked on its hinges behind him and he pivoted toward the intruder. Door needs oiled. "Saun?" *She's never talked to me without Rod being present?*

"Rand, I'd like a word with you." She crossed the room slowly.

He offered her a flash of a smile, but there was a sudden tightness in his chest at the sight of her sullen expression. "I'm listening."

She stepped into his personal space and pinned him with an unflinching gaze. "Rod is extremely worried about you and all you've given him are vague answers, which only serve to worry him more and that makes his head hurt even worse. I don't know how much more he can take. Don't make me ask Clayton to ban your visits by posting a sign on our door, no visitors allowed, doctor's orders. Or perhaps Rod would be safer and more comfortable at the hospital. Don't tempt me, because I will enforce it." She stood so close he could feel her breath on his face and her words were spoken in a steady, low-pitched tone.

"But—"

"I mean it, Rand!" She jabbed his chest with her forefinger. "One more visit like this last one and you will no longer be permitted to see him under any circumstance." She gave him a curt nod and spun around on one heel.

He leaped to his feet, grasped her shoulders, and turned her toward him. "You want to know why I'm not telling him?" He snarled at her. "I'll tell you. There's a madman out there who's intent on killing not just him, but all of you. Why? Because that's the only way he can hurt me." His voice broke. "Now, you go tell Rod that if you think it will make him feel better!" He dropped his arms to his sides as if they were too heavy to keep raised.

Saun stood staring at him with her mouth hanging open as tears filled her eyes. "Then, why don't you just leave?" She lowered her head and slowly walked from the room.

"If it would do any good, I'd already be gone." He whispered into the empty room. His heart hurt from the pressure building in his chest and he crumpled onto the window seat like a deflated balloon. Grasping his hair in his fists, he let silent tears cool his burning skin.

Fifty-Five

An unfamiliar man barreled into the dock door of the post office on Thursday morning when Willis opened it, nearly knocking him to the floor. The man grabbed Willis's shirt in his fist and shoved a note in his face. "Give this to Rand Gray. If you value your life, you won't tell anyone else. Got it!"

"Ya, yes, sir, I, I'll do it ri, right a, way sir!"

The man shoved Willis toward the front room. "Go!"

Willis stumbled into the counter and managed to maneuver around it to unlock the front door with shaky hands. Without so much as a backward glance, he ran across the street, up the steps to Candlewood and pounded on the door. As he waited, he read the note.

Cab opened the door and glanced at Willis's stricken face. "Hey, what's the—?"

"What's going on?" Rand asked, stepping into the hall from the drawing room.

Willis pushed past Cab. "This is for you!" He jammed the note in Rand's hand, spun around, fled out the door, and down the steps.

Rand unfolded the scrap of paper and silently read it. *Meet me on Old Canyon Road or else.* Sweat broke out on Rand's forehead and he could hardly breathe. *Same road I was run off of before.*

"What is it, man?" Cab asked as he approached him.

"Nothing." Rand hurled himself out the door and down the steps.

Cab stepped onto the porch and yelled. "Where're you going?"

Rand threw a glance at Cab and shook his head as he grabbed his gloves and helmet from his truck. Pulling them on, his nostrils flared as he bared his teeth and leaped onto his bike. His front wheel rose off the ground momentarily as he took off and rounded the square at full speed while his heart pounded wildly in his throat. *Help me, Lord!*

---------)⟨⌘⟩(---------*

Monza had sent his bike off a cliff to make it appear he had an accident. Afterward he stole another bike, hoping to throw the police off his trail. Cops thought they were smart, but he was smarter. They'd be searching for his injured or dead body. He roared with laughter at the image of them trying to find it. He'd gotten lucky by finding those two dock-workers. The balding man made the mistake of thinking he was smarter than the smaller one so the weasel took care of him. He promised the little man a fat reward for helping with his plan. What the stupid weasel didn't realize was he was expendable too. Monza never left any witnesses to identify him. He'd take care of the postal worker later.

He had no trouble getting to the appointed rendezvous ahead of Gray. He laughed gleefully, watching from a cliff above the road as Gray appeared around a bend on his bike. He rubbed his hands together in anticipation of victory. This time, he'd make sure Gray didn't get away. The weasel was waiting up ahead to force Gray into taking the fork in the road that led to a dead end.

He was going to suffer excruciating pain while unable to resist the punishment he deserved. Monza anticipated describing in graphic detail what he was going to do to each member of Gray's family while his life oozed from him a little at a time. Poor boy, he wouldn't even be strong enough to get to a phone to warn them. Shaking with laughter, he tore off after the weasel and Gray, staying just far enough behind to keep Gray guessing when he'd be attacked.

---------)⟨⌘⟩(---------

Thirty miles outside the village, Rand turned onto Old Canyon Road and spied a motorcyclist, obviously waiting for him. He frowned. *That's not Monza.* The bike now following him was larger and more powerful, while his was only a street-ready trail bike made for power as well as durability.

Hope the extra weight of his bike works to my advantage. Where's Monza? Are they planning to box me in somewhere up ahead and force me off my bike?

He knew he'd have little chance if any to stay ahead of their bikes so, he veered off the road onto a steep and narrow mountain trail.

He checked his mirrors. Two riders now followed him. The second rider kept a distance between himself and the first rider. *Monza's, letting his buddy wear me down.* Sweat oozed down his spine. He increased speed. The other biker did too.

The trail ahead narrowed. Rand was confident he could navigate it. He'd ridden this trail, which ascended the side of the mountain, many times. His bike was made for this kind of terrain. He hoped it gave him the edge he needed.

The other bike was gaining on him. Around the next curve the trail would split in two. He'd opt for the unfamiliar right fork. The other biker blocked him. He was forced to go left. Rand sped onward. With sweaty palms he gripped the handlebars, thankful he wore gloves. He focused on staying ahead of his pursuers. He knew the trail ended at a cliff that plunged downward for hundreds of feet. His heartrate increased. *Jesus, help me!*

Monza laughed when Gray was forced to take the fork he tried to avoid. He increased his speed. He'd catch up with the weasel. They'd overtake Gray and have some fun. When he finished him off, Monza planned to toss him off the mountain along with his bike. They'd never prove it wasn't another accident. They wouldn't be able to determine the cause of death. He grinned. Gray didn't have a chance. He'd either ride off the cliff or get off his bike and take his chances at hand-to-hand combat. Either way Gray was going to die and he knew it. Monza tilted his head back and laughed. He'd let the weasel wear Gray down and then move in for the kill. He smacked his lips, tasting sweet revenge.

There were all shapes and sizes of rocks and brush on the trail. Rand rode cautiously through loose pebbles caused by recent rock slides. He swerved around a sharp curve, throwing dirt in the air.

The engine on his pursuer's bike sputtered.

Rand sped up. His front tire slid around the next curve. He maintained his balance and slightly decreased speed.

Wings of Steel

His pursuer closed the distance between them.

Yelling assaulted Rand's ears. His blood ran cold. *Hollis. He's the other biker.* He struggled to keep his bike upright. He sped around another curve. The dirt was dryer, but there were more rocks littering the trail. It became more and more narrow. He rounded another curve. He was forced to ride at a slope to stay upright and staying on the trail became exceedingly difficult.

Hollis yelled again as they rounded another curve.

Rand leaned forward, coaxing his bike to go faster. The roar from his bike was overwhelmed by the engines of the other two.

Monza's accomplice was gaining on Rand, fast.

He swerved to keep the biker from coming alongside him. He glanced at his gas gage, nearly empty. He gripped the handlebars until his hands ached. His forehead beaded with sweat. *Jesus, help me!*

The trail veered upward. Rand gained a marginal lead. The trail suddenly dipped and so did his stomach.

Hollis closed the distance between them.

Rand was aware of the two bikes closing in on him, but focused on the trail ahead. His grip was even tighter as his bike hopped over stones and rock. Another boulder jutted onto the trail and he barely avoided it. The front wheel of Hollis's bike contacted with Rand's rear one. He swerved and clenched his teeth hard when the man screamed. He snatched a glimpse in his mirror and saw Hollis and his bike flip backward over the side of the cliff.

Momentarily distracted, Rand drove too close to the side of the mountain. His leg was pinned between it and his bike. His engine stalled. Pain seared his leg. Sweat dripped off his nose. He re-started the engine and lunged forward.

Monza's bike came roaring, closing in on him.

Rand gasped as he raced along the narrow ledge. *Gotta get through this pass.* He sped into semi-darkness. Towering cliffs blocked out the sun. A large boulder loomed in the trail ahead. Rand was forced to stop, get off and walk his bike around it.

Monza stopped behind him. "I got you now, Gray. Get away from your bike!"

That voice struck sudden, intense fear in his core. Rand leaped onto his bike and rounded the next curve. His breath caught in his throat. The dead end loomed formidably ahead. Sweat trickled down his back. Stopping would mean slow death at Monza's hands. He focused on his bike and the jump ahead. He had no options. The incline rose sharply upward and then dropped off.

He took a deep breath. *Jesus, help!* He kept his focus on the other side as his bike left the brink of the cliff. Time froze. *I am with you.* Rand heard the Voice while suspended in air. Then suddenly his back wheel and then the front hit the ground, hard. The impact jolted his entire body, but he managed to slow his bike down and stop. He turned to look behind him, but there was no sign of Monza. The silence was deafening. Rand managed to get off his bike and set the kickstand before his trembling legs buckled and he crumpled to the ground.

A loud whirring filled his ears and he raised his arm to shield his eyes from dust and dirt, which swirled all around him. A helicopter set down several yards ahead of him. Dazed he blinked to clear his vision. *Am I dead? Dreaming? Where's Monza?* Someone was shaking him.

"Rand, are you okay?"

He shook his head, trying to clear the fog from his brain. "Gus?"

"Can you get up?" He grabbed Rand's shoulders and helped him stand.

Rand held onto Gus as his head spun. "Where'd you come from?" He forced his words between clenched teeth.

"Saw the whole thing from above. Let's get you to a doctor. Looks like you hurt your leg when you hit the side of the mountain."

Rand pivoted his head to search the area. "What happened to Monza?"

Gus shook his head. "Must've thought he could follow you." He shoved his hat back off his forehead and pointed to the ravine.

Rand's heart froze and then began pounding furiously as his gaze followed Gus's finger. "He always thought he was better than me at everything even if he had to cheat to prove it."

"You related to Evel Knievel?" Gus asked with eyebrows raised.

Rand's eyes opened wide as he stared at the canyon, took a step and stumbled. "He needs help." He recalled his own situation when he awoke in that gulley months ago.

Gus grabbed his arm. "There's no helping him."

Rand's stomach quivered and he staggered. "Are you sure?"

"I'm sure. Let's get you to a doctor and then home. Your family's worried about you. Cab called me right after Willis. I took a guess and had the chopper head in this direction." Gus informed him. "You ever done that before?"

"No and never will again!" Rand gaped at his bike and then the gulch and shook his head.

Gus put his arm around Rand's shoulders as they headed for the helicopter. "I told the pilot to radio the station and tell your folks you're okay."

Rand breathed a deep sigh as he sagged against his friend. "It's really over. Thank You, Jesus."

"Yeah." Gus chuckled. "Wish I got a picture of you flying over that canyon. You've been holding out on me, Gray." He chuckled. "It was like that bike had 'Wings of Steel.'"

Rand sat in the helicopter trying to comprehend the events of what seemed like hours, but was actually only minutes. He groaned, clutching his injured leg, but his shoulders relaxed and he breathed deeply. *It was Your voice I heard, Jesus. Thank You for saving me, again!*

Fifty-Six

A slow smile stole across Rand's lips as Gus parked next to his truck. He gazed heavenward when Gus exited his car. *Thank You, Jesus, it's finally over.*

Gus opened the passenger door. "Come on, Evel. You going to sit there staring into space or do you need me to haul you out of there?" He sneered as he reached for Rand's arm.

Rand blinked. "No thanks." He struggled to his feet and tried not to limp as he made his way toward the steps.

Netty came running and threw her arms around him nearly knocking him off balance.

"Whoa there, give the man some room." Gus chided her with a grin.

Rand held Netty in a tight embrace while he struggled to keep his composure. "I'm okay."

"You're hurt!" She chided him.

"Nah," he shook his head, "just a scratch. Come in with me. I have something to tell all of you." He put an arm around her waist and together they went up the steps with Gus following.

Cab held the door open for them.

Rand smiled at him. "Meet us in Rod's room."

Cab raised his eyebrows. "He and Saun are in the library. He got up right after you left."

Rand entered the room and his gaze landed on Rod. He appeared pale and Saun was sitting next to him. Rand swallowed and tightened his arm around Netty, thankful for her physical support because he was a little light-headed. He guided her to a love seat across from Rod and Saun. "I wanted to tell all of you at once so I don't have to repeat it. Virgil Monza followed me for fourteen years because I accidently caused his brother's death." He took a deep breath and Netty squeezed his hand. He smiled at her. "I thought I lost him when I came here, but somehow, he found me. I knew sooner or later I'd have to face him or none of you would be safe." He paused as his Adam's apple bobbed.

Gus placed his hand on Rand's shoulder. "He outsmarted his enemy today. Rand was chased by Monza and another guy, who we'll identify soon. I'll just say neither of them will ever bother him or anyone else again." Gus tipped his hat. "I'll talk to you later, Rand. I'm sure you want to spend some time with your family. I'll see myself out." He pivoted and exited the room.

There was a collective sigh before they all began to talk at once.

Rand's shrill whistle pierced the air. "I only want to say this once so, please listen up. I'll answer your questions after I'm done." Once all eyes were directed on him, Rand told the whole story as briefly as possible. When he finished, he studied his brother and took note that his color was returning and the frown between his brows was receding. Angel appeared to sit at Rand's knee. After a short while, Saun and Rod stood as if to leave the room, but Saun grasped Cab's arm and headed for the kitchen.

Rand stood and faced Rod. "Are you okay?"

"I am now that we can all breathe easier. I sensed there was more that Gus wanted to say, but I'd rather hear it from you."

Rand reached for Netty's hand and drew her to his side. "I'm free, Rod. Free of my past and the threat of it ruining my future. Monza drove his bike off the cliff."

Netty drew in a sharp breath.

"Gus doesn't want that part to be common knowledge and I agree with him."

Rod nodded. "You're right about that. I was informed Gus ordered Willis to be locked in a cell until he returned because he didn't want anyone else following you."

Netty's brow puckered and she put her hand on Rand's arm. "Monza followed you, didn't he? If he went off that cliff, then what did you—?"

Rand placed a finger against her lips. "Just between the three of us, I jumped over the canyon. Gus said the bike looked like it had 'Wings of Steel', but I prefer to think of them as angel's wings and I don't mean my dog." He chuckled.

Long after everyone else retired to their rooms and Netty went home, Rand paced the floor in the drawing room. He was free at last but the events of the day kept replaying in his mind. The determination to survive and the adrenaline rush from all that was at stake, not only his own life but also the lives of everyone he cared about. A door squeaked and he raised his head to peer at Saun. *Now what?*

She entered quietly as before and walked toward him, holding his attention with each step she took. She stopped directly in front of him and tilted her head to gaze directly into his eyes. "I'm sorry. I was wrong to tell you to stay away from Rod. He—"

"I knew I couldn't tell him what I was facing, even if I could've found the words to explain it. I know he thought I didn't want to tell him but I—"

"Rand." She placed her hand on his arm, still staring into his eyes. "I had no idea what you were going through. None of us did. Will you forgive me for being so hard on you?"

"You were looking out for Rod. How could I be upset about that?" He swallowed hard.

Tears filled her eyes. "I didn't think anyone could ever love him as much as Cab and I, but I was wrong. May I give you a hug?"

He opened his arms and she stepped into his embrace.

"Welcome to the family, Rand."

His Adam's apple bobbed. "You'll never know how much that means to me." He whispered.

She stepped away from him. "I think I do. Now that it's all over, I hope you sleep well. Good night, Rand." She squeezed his hand and left the room.

He sank onto a window seat and stared at a lone star he found in the sky. *Thank You, Jesus.*

Epilogue

Rand Gray awoke to birds chirping and a heaviness in his chest, which if physical would have crushed him. It was Friday, March 26, the day after his fateful jump across the gulch. He sat on the side of his bed, lowered his head into his hands and plunged his fingers deep into his hair. *Lord, what's going on? Why don't I feel relieved that Monza is gone?* He waited several heartbeats, but the weight didn't lift. Mentally he agonized over the events of Al's accidental death and everything leading up to the anniversary of it. Finally, he sighed and raised his head, knowing what he needed to do.

A short time later, he entered the police department and proceeded to the sheriff's office. He knocked, let himself inside and closed the door.

Gus raised his head and grinned as he ended his call. "I'm honored. Our hero came to visit."

Rand frowned. "I want to ship Monza's remains back to his home town. Can you help me or tell me who can?"

Gus pushed his hat back off his forehead and stared at Rand like he'd lost his mind. "Care to run that by me again, Gray?"

Rand crossed his arms. "Monza's brother was my best friend. Virgil has no other family and I doubt he has many, if any, friends. I want him buried in the same place as his brother."

Gus set his hat on his desk as his brow furrowed. "Are you serious? That perp nearly killed your brother after making several attempts on your life. You want to send his remains home for burial?"

Rand met Gus's steely gaze. "Never been more serious about anything. Can you help me or not?"

Gus scratched his head. "I'll contact a friend of mine and see if we can make arrangements for your request, but you will be responsible for freight and burial expenses. They aren't exactly—"

"Send him to Cove Creek, Arizona. They only have one small cemetery, at least it was a few years ago."

Gus shook his head. "You really are serious about this?"

Rand stood and gave Gus a two-finger salute and left.

On May eighth Rand won his hoped-for racing trophy. Cab brought Netty, Tommy and Cory with him to watch and then celebrate Rand's victory with a shared meal. Afterward in the parking lot of the restaurant, Rand jingled his keys in his pocket while they all stood in a circle talking about the race. "Thanks, Cab, Netty," he nodded to each of them, "for sticking with me through the past few months and you guys too." He included the boys. "I appreciate all of you for being here. I wish Rod and Saun could have come too."

Tommy and Cory each gave him a side hug and congratulatory slap on the back. Cab shook his hand and Netty planted a lingering kiss on his mouth.

Rand reached to tip his absent hat and forked his fingers through his hair instead. "I hate to run, but I still have to check-out of my hotel and the officials told me to come back to collect my winnings and trophy. I'll catch up with all of you later."

It was late when he drove his pickup back to Candlewood. He grabbed a small suitcase from his room, which he'd previously packed, stopped in the kitchen to leave Cab a note and collected Angel, her food and bowls.

As he left Fire River with Angel on the seat beside him, a slow smile tugged at his lips. Suddenly he slapped the steering wheel. "Yee-ha!"

Angel barked and licked his cheek.

"I'm free, girl. After all these years, I'm really free!" He laughed and scratched behind her ears as he drove. *Now, you can pay your last respects to Jess and put the past behind you for good, pal.* He planned to secure the trophy on Jess's grave marker, and maybe visit Frank Sims for a few hours before returning home to Fire River." He grinned at Angel and laughed again. "Yee-ha!"

www.ingramcontent.com/pod-product-compliance
Ingram Content Group UK Ltd.
Pitfield, Milton Keynes, MK11 3LW, UK
UKHW040000311224
452994UK00001B/104